WHITE PO

The Smuggler and the Whore

Paul Whiteside

Kindle Edition

The Opium Poppy (*Papaver somniferum*), White Poppy of the Chinese opium trade.

Prologue

A flower and not a flower; of mist yet not of mist; at midnight she was there; she was as daylight shone. She came and for a little while was like a dream of spring, and then, as morning clouds that vanish traceless, she was gone.

Across the rippled sand to the far edge of the East Kent coast sea, the tide having long since gone out; the water calm spills out across the beach. It is already getting dark, the sky clear with the first sprinkle of stars: the answer has to be 'yes', we are ready, although I do not want to be. The many tens of folded red paper lotus flowers, squares of red paper soaked in pine oil to make them waterproof, the water-lily lamps. One by one I light the vegetable-oil-soaked wicks, let them float away, watch them scattering in the breeze, the swift current carrying them bobbing out to sea. The lights glow softly in my tears, a miniature streaming fairy sea, and I strain my eyes to see them until the last winks out and is gone.

For Eliza, White Poppy, Yin Hsueh-yen (Yin Shooeh-yen): for that, which is forbidden, taboo. My sweet one, my dearest, one day you will read these words in English and understand exactly what they mean. How much I wanted to tell you then! How I longed to know you, to really know where and why you were, and why and who you were, White Poppy. I read your every emotion, every blink of your gorgeous almond eyes, every movement of your nimble-fingered hands, your bittersweet lips. In the vast army of the anonymous, some few of us manage to make a name for ourselves. A lot is confused now, but I will do my best to remember alongside these words of Life tiptoeing quietly over Death.

These are my writings, my journal, my own understanding of things as they were; the waking moments of my brief China dream. I love you. Quite simply I have loved you more than I have ever loved another, and my life would have been incomplete without you. White Poppy, Eliza, Yin Hsueh-yen, subject of the most impossible dream, these words immemorial are dedicated to you.

Charles Paul Sansovino, 17 September 1857, Birchington, Kent.

BOOK I MIRROR OF PERFECTION

Gwong-Jau (Canton), China
July 1834

1

Use words sparingly then all will fall into place. The smell of opium wafting on the breeze, teenage boat-girl standing out above me, conical straw hat, wide-brimmed around her shaded Chinese face, head dropping, poppy bud drooping, long black hair strained back high behind her head, drop-pearl gold earrings, and finest threads of gold around her slender neck. Drab grey smock dress, sleeves bound with grey silk to just below her elbows, forearms naked, soft, energy bound, repressed, yet flowing deep like the deepest currents of the River Pearl. Fifteen, sixteen, maybe seventeen years, gorgeous, glistening, black-bronzed almond eyes, blinking slowly, sadly, polished ebony reflecting all around; long lashes flicking, eyelids closing over beautiful polished stones. The cruel penetration of her gaze, solid, strong, unnatural, sad, a look so sharp, so severe for one so young: a look at the same time powerful, but tinged with fear. Luscious, crimson, open mouth, entrance of the most erotic lips, wisps of raven hair blowing about their silent moistness, a sad smile hiding tears, White Poppy.

Beyond the scattered anchorage of multiple offshore islands, the rocky coast of the *Wah Naam* or South China Sea opens into a jagged maze of creeks and channels. It runs past Lintin Island into the broad tidal river basin that leads along the *Kin-kiang* or Pearl River to Canton itself. Canton, City of Willows, busiest trading port in China, home of the best China whores. Gwong-Jau (Canton), where East meets West by the South China Sea. In that year, my twenty-eighth, the year following the abolition of slavery throughout the British Empire, there was still much about China that a Sicilian-English sailor like me would never understand; where pretty girls, young women, led the confined life as slaves.

My name is Charles Paul Sansovino, opium smuggler, sailor, adventurer: 51 years, six feet tall, black leather patch over my blinded right eye, black hair like my Sicilian father, and my London mother's ice blue eyes; brought up at the edge of the London docks where one ship arrived as another left. This is my journal; these are the gathered memories of my long-parted China dream.

Dusk falling, we sailed in past a string of the brothel-junks that form one small part of the fascinating jewelled necklace around Canton's throat. The long and slender 'flower boats' or *hoa thing*; all-seeing eyes that stretch back far along the chattering river, chimneys smoking, scented wood-smoke wafting, blue-smoke-burning opium, in the evening breeze.

Lifting her head slightly, tilting her shining face away from the sun, hat rising slowly, the poppy flowered. The sun was hot, very hot, but although the sun was bright, the brightest light, darkness was hidden behind. The white water lily floating beautiful above the leaf-muddied pool: within those eyes, within that head, deep within that perfect Chinese body, were the secrets of the universe, the secrets of all time, access to that which would last eternal. I saw her only the once but I 'felt' her; 'felt' her inside me, took her deep into my dreams – red lips that moved, a spider's thread of saliva hanging in-between.

It had started when I lay in the corner of my squalid London room, when I shut my eyes and saw the sea-girl I'd read about in my books, the girl of my dreams. She never left my side, never let me down, was more real to me than any woman I had ever seen. She grew from my sadness and my fear, from the lust and love that fought for a position in my tortured soul. And that mixed with details gleaned from what I read set against what I experienced daily in real life, for I had an education that I earned, nothing ever just given to me. Most of all I saw her eyes, that sea-girl, her intense black shining eyes. And I knew that one day I should find her would recognise her for who she was - the details of that dream. I had travelled the oceans of the world in search of someone special, in search of my deepest desire. Then there she was before me! I was not prepared for the strength of it, the power of that 'passion' laced with pain. Her Chinese name was Yin Hsueh-yen (Yin Shooeh-yen), but for me she was White Poppy, and liaison with her was forbidden, taboo!

2

Will you walk into my parlour? Said a spider to a fly, 'tis the prettiest little parlour that ever you did spy.

The Painted Lady fluttered out in jewelled elegance from the houseboat stern, alit along the wall. Young Chinese eyes bright like shining polished stones; sleek, shoulder-length black hair cut across in a thick fringe combed down to her brows; high-collared lemon silk gown with a soft pink sash around an hourglass waist, her feet bound, small. She clasped her small hands around her marble neck, pressed her elbows to her breasts, pursed her blood-red lips (pushed forwards already by protruding top teeth); tiny teenage face powdered and rouged; legs closed, embroidered slippers on her naked feet, Yu Chi (pronounced, Yu Ji). Inside, the main boat saloon, entrance torches blazing, couches jade green along the walls, rich emerald carpets, cabin-window curtains green, enshrined in vermilion and gold. Innermost ornamentation immense centred on a large oval ebony table surrounded by rosewood furniture, gilded and inlaid, black lacquer ware carved in deep relief. But there was darkness behind that light.

She made reverence to me, this young girl – 14, maybe 15 years – and sinking to her knees she offered me a cup of tea, Chinese chubby thighs glowing in the lamplight. I watched her mouth, her slightly parted lips. She aroused my interest, Yu Ji, starting the burning fire; her intimate female smell; heat of her hot flesh, perspiring body wet, round breasts firm against my chest, thighs full in my hands. This was forbidden, punishable by death – were we really alone?

She stripped herself slowly, Yu Ji, stepped out of her clothes, made her breasts bare, Chinese body shown off in the bright cabin mirrors reflecting flickering European lamps; crystal pendants showering light over a row of Chinese dolls. She danced in front of the houseboat's innermost looking-glass walls, stood up high on her foot bound, lotus toes, turning slowly with sweeping movements of her arms, twisting like a naked ballerina.

Coming forwards, drawing me backwards to where wooden steps rose up to the cabin-loft: encouraging me up, pushing through a curtain into a tiny attic room with papered wooden partitions, Yu Ji led me across to the narrow bed and simple table. The small space lit by the full moon, fractured light from the neighbouring boats coming in through a small, square glass window, set with a leaping white tiger. I could hear her breathing in the silence, watched the movements of her blood-red lips. Legs together, she knelt before me, carefully filling a cup with warmed wine, passing it to me, filled another for herself, drank it in one swift movement, followed by a second and a third to match my own. She drank first; I followed her. She fed me plump Canton oysters and mussels from the coast.

In the floating bedroom was a single ink-brush painting of a gateway before a rounded hill with a small white temple on the top, glazed green tiles shining brilliantly in the sun overhung by the dull green of a solitary pine. It was quiet, still, birds circling overhead, red lanterns all around, two lovers sitting in close embrace.

The sound of her voice, Yu Ji, her laughter, soft touch of her lips on my body. The wine made me sleepy, relaxed, as she massaged my tired back, the muscles of my arms and legs, singing to me softly in Cantonese, as she pressed on top of the bed beside me, took me in her arms, closed her cold wet lips over my lips. But in that lust there was the dripping kiss of death.

However, she was not White Poppy. She was not the girl whose memory meant so much to me. She was not what I had been promised: this substitute, replica whore!

I heard screaming, beyond the boat, heard young shrill screams. I saw the quick movement of her almond eyes, but her face remained calm as she continued with me. I listened – total silence now, only the fast beating of her Chinese heart – outside the terrors of the night – threatening – fear. That silence – death?

I felt sudden fear of the power that might be released through Yu Ji, the evil that might be unleashed because of this boat-girl, whore. If anyone should find out, I was dead. And yet my eyes were really only for that other, White Poppy. Who was I, though, to think I could compete for this other as the prize? Who was *she* really I was searching for, and why?

Pulling aside the silk coverlet, she lay down beside me naked on the divan stroked my face with chubby fingers, turning her agile body slowly, legs now wide apart, plump bottom to the air. I listened to the rustling of her fabric, the movements of her skin, the tinkling of suspended mirrored glass. It was too quiet otherwise, the sound of the wind blowing chill outside. It always sounds different when it is most cold, drawing in the potential terrors of the South China Sea.

Twining her legs round my shoulders, she pushed down on to my lips; cool lips opened wide, her mouth burning like green ginger, below. Grey-brown spider spinning her web – fragile sticky net: legs moving, vibrating new-spun silver. The spider shifted in her web, legs moving, vibrating the silver threads, checking its trapped perfection, waiting, tucking her in for the night.

3

Summer shadows deepening, the 'Sing-Song' girls get custom for the floating village, skim the water-trafficked surface of the Pearl like lazy insects shrilling to the descending cloak of night. A Christmas tree of paper lanterns around the lolling flower-boats, air heavy with jasmine and musk, their chattering giggles carry far on the breeze, beyond which red paper lanterns of the public brothels dot the suburbs where the sky burns crimson.

I had travelled the oceans of the world in search of something special, in search of a dream that I thought I might find along the contested territory of the waterfront with its opium-dens in whose refuge girls provided the bloody sacrifice of corruption. The waterfront where men became poisoned by bitter, brittle lips, in the winding *Hoa-Giai* or Street of Flowers, at the two-storey *dsing-loo* or blue houses (the colour of their lowered daytime blinds); girls selling flesh to all tastes in the upstairs cubicles, trapping men for their basest desires, the life-blood of disease. But lowest of all in the hierarchy were employees of the brothels called flower smoke rooms, *huayan jian,* places where Chinese smoked opium in the company of prostitutes, 'flowers'. Distinguished from surrounding buildings by a ladder leaning in the doorway, they were small, filthy, barely furnished, and layered with smelly quilts. The 'flowers' stood or sat in the doorway singing lascivious songs like Ten Cups of Wine, ready to hijack men and pull then upstairs. Ships' crews drank behind the warehouses in Hog Lane, a strong stench of sewage hanging heavy in the dark lanes, where the whores wallowed like pigs in a privy. Nail sheds, *ding-peng,* were brothels housed in shacks where labourers went with none of the courtesan-house obligations or social rules.

Appropriately decorated, dressed, and named, the courtesans of the special courtesan houses elsewhere, were showcased in exquisitely appointed establishments several storeys high, with a foyer and banquet spaces downstairs, and small rooms with curtained doorways on the lower and upper floors, intoxicated whole in the light of red lamps. Each house hung a lamp from a window above the front door, taking it down when the house was full. The Interpreter told him of the pleasures for customers of spending time with virgin prostitutes.

'A daughter was groomed carefully for her first night,' he said, 'usually sometime after she turned fourteen. The occasion was known variously as lighting the big candles, *dian da lazhu;* comb cage, *shulong,* after her hairstyle change once she began sleeping with customers; defloration, *kaibao,* opening the calyx; or more brutally,' he added, breaking the melon, *pogua.* The lives of these prostitutes,' he continued, 'generally speaking are leisurely, unburdened, and spoiled. They eat rich foods and wear rich silks, doing nothing in the daytime, living a quiet and leisurely life in their dove-cage-like rooms. At night they rush about the streets like a school of silver carp moving downstream, each powdered and rouged, wearing red and green, seductive, lascivious beauties, making a speciality of hooking youth.'

The Sing-Song women were brought to Canton from afar, chosen with discrimination, each in imitation of the Chinese lady. Flat, oriental faces; large volumes of black hair, gummed, built up into huge edifices adorned with combs, and jewels, and feathers and flowers, above. China's greatest commercial city, Canton, floating homes stretching as far as we can see – anything up to 400,000 lives daily rising and falling with the tide, sometimes without ever having set foot on land, other boats carrying passengers and transporting merchandise: some 40,000 floating homes.

It was the evening I saw the boat-girl, White Poppy, the wolf in the wood, the shipwreck at sea; her perfect heart-shaped face, chin like a pointed lemon. It was the day that would change the course of my life; such that what had been in my past was never more to be.

The boat people thronged noisily in the safety of their floating homes crammed together like sardines; met us with blank stares. They showed outwardly the signs of every kind of religion – Confucian, Buddhist, Taoist (Dowist), a belief in Nature, in the spirits of the river, the rank growth beneath the waterside trees. They adorned their boats and their bodies with devices and charms that took them on the journey from their birth to their death: these floating families of several thousand sons.

Many of the boats are surprisingly luxurious, according to the Tankias' (boat-dwellers) order of life. Though the majority of boats are quite small, a thatch of palm leaves or a cover of matting protecting the boat-family from sun and rain, being the place where they eat and sleep – conceive the next generation. On the larger boats considerable space in the bow is set apart for gardening with flowerpots and boxes. Pigs and chickens are reared, sometimes in a box or cage suspended from the stern.

Down river, looking east, there are ranges of larger boats, brilliant frontages like floating guesthouses or small hotels, pleasure palaces, river dwellings of more beautiful construction, the flower-boats of debauchery and sin. Stretching back to the ancient walled city these are the floating summer-gardens of Canton, gorgeously furnished within, gaudy inside: the woodwork is carved, walls hung with pictures and embroideries, mirrors duplicating everything within, growing with garish flowers, both natural and artificial. They are unsafe places to visit unless accompanied by a guide.

At night these boats are illuminated brilliantly with lamps and lanterns, and patrons come and go by boats along their projecting bows. Each night many Chinese float their way along these avenues of popular resort – opium smokers, gamblers, seekers of women, idlers and professionals, who come to win at cards, at dominoes or dice; who come to win Chinese women in vice, and on occasion lose a life. The China 'poppies' have painted faces – high-arched, pencilled eyebrows, small, round mouth, full and slightly sensual deep vermilion lips, and long slit-shaped, half-closed eyes. They are intense patches of beauty at the edge of the widespread dark. But there is something in the shadows, movement in the dark. Dressed in embroidered blue silk tunics and bright trousers threaded with gold or silver thread, they wear thin white stockings, and abnormally tiny feet enclosed in rich slippers, with white soles shaped like an inverted pyramid. The higher class women's feet are crippled; bound tight to dance on the image of a large lotus flower. Before the girl's fifth birthday, the mother has bent back the toes under the sole of the foot, and the broken foot is bound with bandages. This is done for 10 to 15 years, with more suffering than I can imagine, to achieve the 'golden lily', the staggering, tip-toeing proof of her capacity to suffer and obey. Undamaged feet are required of those who have to work.

What words are spoken of in silence? What is of greatest value? The effect of crimson lipstick on an otherwise white naked whore; the effect of one white wisp of cloud in a clear blue sky; of red on white - fresh blood on white snow? Perversion or preservation – what choice is there for these Chinese poppy whores?

'We have no rights,' the boat-girl had shouted out in Cantonese (her words interpreted into English by the Interpreter for me). She'd stared at my black leather eye-patch, at my left eye, blue. 'We have nothing but our bodies and even they do not belong to us.'

She cleared her throat, coughing deeply, and spat into the grey water of the Pearl River, before the lemon trees. The Interpreter translated with no sign of emotion. We had first met at 'The Factories', a trade meeting to discuss

China tea. He was not pureblood Chinese. In his early thirties, he translated the transactions, looked after the 'chops' or permits that allowed us British to trade there. He knew every side of Canton, had influence in many things, looked after me for my initial two-week stay, showed me the sights, the girls. He had access to all things, except one, White Poppy.

'There are two rules,' the boat-girl muttered, 'you would do well to remember them.' She opened her slit eyes wide, black orbs staring with the full sadness of her position. 'One, Chinese women are sold into perversion by those who love them most. Two, Chinese women have no power against the men who have the right to rule over them.'

The China whores with their sensuous, sexual scent. *But elsewhere was young female death; the stench of putrefaction was nauseatingly intense.*

4

That those eat now who never ate before; And those who always ate, eat more. Thomas De Quincey, *Confessions of an English Opium-eater*, 1821.

Blue smoke burning, ashes rising, floating, flying heavenwards, free. Valley bottom rippling through the wood smoke haze above the gentle wooded slopes of the Assam Indian hills. Snow melting high on the ridges; water dripping from the hanging mountains. Up the slope from the viridian lake, scented white begonias, camellias burst in flower, rhododendrons smothering the trunks of fallen trees, as spring advanced along forest slopes daubed from a palette of intoxicating colour. Fields of conspicuous nodding poppies, waxy grey leaves, large paper thin flowers in floppy violet, purple-blue and white, purple patch at the base of the petals – the Opium Poppy (*Papaver somniferum*), White Poppy of the Chinese opium trade.

For ten days of its annual life cycle the seed capsule of the poppy exudes a milky juice from which is derived a bitter, brown and granular powder – opium. When the seed capsule is scratched with a blade or fingernail, a milky latex-like substance soon accumulates. As it hardens, the raw opium turns dark brown.

Into the immature green poppy capsules Indian women cut quickly with sharpened bamboo, wiping off the milky juice on bits of cloth; coagulated bitter brown latex mixed with water, boiled until thick, rolled into balls of crude opium which might be kept for years. Chests of Patna opium: each containing 40 dumpling-sized balls of crude opium, thick treacle juice enclosed in a shell of dried poppy petals, sold by auction in Calcutta, shipped to China in swift-keeled clippers, smuggled under racing canvas to Canton which seethes with prostitution.

She dipped a needle into the prepared extract, dried it over the flame, the thin girl, put the bead of the flame-dried opium into a tiny pipe-bowl of tobacco, lit it with a wood-splint-taper and inhaled the noxious fumes. A few grains of opium gave the young prostitute a feeling of euphoria. Xiang had a body as pale and thin as lotus roots hidden in the mud. She had painted kohl around her almond eyes. They looked huge in her tiny triangular face: wise and worldly well beyond her years. She smoothed a thin cream all over her face and applied pale pancake makeup.

Pipe burned out, she lay down listless, white smoke dissipating all about her: became loquacious, muttering, laughing to herself, giggling like a child, drifting slowly into fitful sleep, twitching with its dreams. Afterwards she felt weary, tired.

One pipe smoked daily became three. One day without opium made her feel dizzy, her eyes watered, until exhausted, lethargic, weak, she was unable to move. More than one day without opium, she would feel the shivering chills of Hell, an ache in every bone, would have diarrhoea, mental pain, bound now to Morpheus Greek god of dreams.

Elsewhere, in the China hills, the poppy flowers take on their own most perfect disguise, the dispersed white and purple: not solid fields of Opium Poppies, like in India, but scattered, individual plants camouflaged amongst fields of tendril-climbing white and mauve peas, hidden deliberately from the mandarins as financial security for the future that frequently never arrived for those who were not truly ever free.

After drugging her, the China prostitute, the craftsman etched a huge spider on the whole of her beautiful pale back. Spider Woman, Black Widow, straddling her guest, she spider devouring the male. Earth mother, whore, who spreads her thighs wide, squats inches above his open mouth, takes him to oblivion.

5

I took great pleasure in watching British and American clippers – sharp bowed for fast sailing, ship-rigged vessels slicing through the waves. There had been a change in the character of Chinese piracy thanks to the growth of the opium trade, and there were women to be explored and large sums of opium money to be made. Although forbidden by the Emperor, that trade then had our British Government's support because of the revenue, it brought

India. The 'patriotic' China pirates had started to raid our opium clippers with their valuable cargo, scourge of the South China Sea.

In February 1834, we rounded the southern cape of Formosa, heading westwards across the China Sea, soon among the Ten Thousand Islands on course for Canton. We made our way through the Portuguese Pescadores, visited by the myriad junks of the fishing Chinese. Skirting these islands, sighting hundreds of junks, we were in fear of being attacked by the devil's work pirates who were ferocious Chinese. Carrying all sail we could set in a fair north-easterly breeze, we stood away from the islands and the fishing-fleet, parading all hands on deck, muskets at the ready whenever we passed near the larger junks.

Approaching Lin Tin Island, 45 miles from Whampoa Reach in the Canton River we were hailed by a Chinese junk-master that could speak English well. We hove-to in sight of the small, lone junk, which had made its way towards us, met the 'family' crew of father, mother and numerous children. It came as a pleasant surprise that the junk-master could speak some brief broken English. He said he had been a steward in a British East India merchantman on a voyage to London, and was now acting as a Canton River pilot.

The junk-master stripped off his jacket to show off the fantastic tattooing from his days at sea as a cabin boy. Every inch of skin on his arms was marked with some blue or red design. On his right arm was an anchor, a crucifix, the Royal Coat of Arms, a sailor dancing the hornpipe, and the verse - *From rocks and shoals and every hill, May god protect the sailor still.* His left arm was even more brilliant, with Britannia, the sun, moon and seven stars, the Union Jack, a Masonic emblem, a mermaid, a barometer, another anchor, and a sailor embracing a half-naked woman and a bottle of rum.

We shared a pipe of tobacco and he gave me a present of several cigars, which he said were from South America: wild tobacco cured and rolled into cigars, which were a strong smoke, and induced a trancelike state. He told us he was from Whampoa where English and all other foreign ships anchor near the mouth of the Canton River. We steered there by compass westwards. We ranged alongside the East India merchantman, *Elsinore*, beautifully built vessel, aristocrat of the sea – well found and famous for her speed. The *Elsinore*, loading tea, silk, and dried rhubarb; cargo brought down-river from the Canton warehouses to Whampoa. She carried passengers, mails, and cargo, and was well armed with guns for defence against pirates or privateers.

6

As Confucius says, we do not know life, how then can we know death? At the new or full moon certain Chinese parishes celebrate the Union of Breaths (Ho Ch'i), a collective sexual orgy. Men and women have intercourse like animals without regard to family ties or social status. I have read about this. After joining in a square dance called the coiling of the Dragon *(yang)* and playing the Tiger *(yin)*, the participants retire to have intercourse in adjoining cubicles, with frequent changes of partners. Semen is the essence of *yang*; the Chinese say that the man who nourishes his *yang* will live long and have male children; *yang* is most effectively nourished by the female orgasm *(yin)*.

There is male lust for the virgin, for the letting of the first blood, essential essence of all human life. In Canton hundreds of Chinese dens held ten to fifteen girls of every nationality: brothels for native Chinese, brothels for foreigners, and brothels for those of mixed race. Sexual need, desire – the male element is controlled by the female, cup overflowing from which male lips drink eternal, and the female world is controlled by the prostitutes, those who hold true power (but who are controlled by the men, the brotherhood of Chinese).

I had known the comforts of prostitutes since my birth. My Mother was one: she who drew men with her cherry lips, her ice-blue eyes, her heavy breasts and pungent thighs. She who did her business in the London night before the oak doors of a great church; she who died crying, dying, legs broken wide, fucking the mud of the Thames as she rolled gently by.

There will always be born *girls* surplus to requirements; baby girls murdered at birth – drowned in warm water, throat pinched, wet cloth over the mouth. In Canton, in China, there was no open sale of girls, but it went on all the same, and families came first with no such thing as individual dignity or responsibility. Each year, whole families lost everything to the China river floods, made a market of their own flesh and blood – a pretty girl sold could restore their few 'riches': rare beauty attracting its own price, its own special pain. *But there is a girl beyond every woman, a woman beyond the whore: the girl that is in every woman, the girl that remains eternally pure inside.*

Young girls walking alone were kidnapped, stolen, sold into perversion: young girls who provided common pleasure for money, for sex without love, for protective male power: heavily perfumed flowers attracting bees to sip their sweet nectar; corruption everywhere, and the corrupt used to keep it so. So the Interpreter told me, but warned me to be careful about what I asked to know.

Girls were bought up to the age of 20 years: there was always a ready market for those above the age of puberty. But there were too many girls and in some places baby girls were exposed, eaten by dogs and carrion birds, or were drowned and left floating down river: *a life of prostitution was a life at least*! On the common ground among the Canton grave-mounds, I saw a carrion dog gnawing the leg of a dying child. Beyond the thick covering of graves, a trodden path led to a rough conical stone tower, a baby tower – the strength of female putrefaction was intense.

7

The place of execution was at the opening of the vegetable market, the broad street filled with soldiers and officials. All around, the flat, low roofs of the closed shops were crowded with male spectators. Amongst the group of thirteen prisoners, including two women, a murderer was to be decapitated.

A little further down the street, high officials sat in a semicircle, with a red-button mandarin at their head. To one side a bloody altar displayed the tools of execution – the five short-bladed, chopper-like swords (the Lords of Execution) and bloodied string, and the tourniquet and strings for strangling. Before the altar, a cauldron of water boiled over a wood-block stove, for warming the swords.

Extreme terror and fear: the women were strangled – two pieces of cord passed around the neck with a loop, each prisoner facing down to the ground, pleased nevertheless, for their release. As we defile, as we destroy with one hand, yet we reinforce and build with the other: we cannot give up such precious things, such shatteringly beautiful forbidden delights – we can only replace them, substitute them with more!

Opium dealing was a British-Chinese affair, the rules of which were well known to both sides, but China had been in conflict with us since 1757 when our trading ships were confined to Canton. Although the Chinese strictly prohibited the importation and sale of opium in 1729, opium and tobacco had been smoked routinely together throughout China since 1793. There was a huge demand for opium in China from Calcutta, its sale financing the East India Company (the 'John Company'), who monopolised its production, the Indian Government collecting revenue from its sale, and Britain swelling her balance of payments to China. British opium was sold at auction in Calcutta, after this the Company abjured any responsibility for the poppy drug; the opium in some way providing the wealth of all the major trading houses at Canton; bought by Chinese dealers eager for the huge profits to be had from its resale, from the means to misery and death.

The biggest trade in opium never reached Canton itself. Traders set up a depot on the island of Lintin in the mouth of the Canton River, from which we smugglers took supplies at out own risk into China, and north along the coast. Ships arriving from India unloaded their opium chests into the vast hulks moored in the Lintin roadstead, before sailing up river to Canton. The way to evade Chinese control was to have this convenient depot far out in Canton bay: the small, mountainous island of Lintin, 20 miles north-east of Macao, where the opium boats were considered safe under their own guns, as they were also at the six islands near Amoy. And there were British and American vessels stationed at Foochow, Woosung and Chinchew, and in the Cap-Sing Moon passage, near Hong Kong.

Moored at Whampoa Island some 13 miles from Canton (and limit for the largest sailing ships) were the black and white chequered sides of graceful double-decked East Indiamen. With tall masts that punctured the sky, gilded figureheads thrusting seawards, Canton's opium factories, gun-ships, surrounded by floating sampans like greedy piglets around a sow.

Despite the Imperial Chinese opium-smoking ban of 1799, the East India Company maintained friendly terms with Chinese merchants. The Company's tea business and all foreign trade was carried on outside Canton, in The Factories in the south-west suburbs outside the massive city walls, in the stone block of offices and warehouses beside the River Pearl (merchants were not allowed to enter the walled city itself). 'The Factories', where American, British, Dutch, French and Spanish flags were hoisted daily, to salute the rising sun.

Canton, on the far side of the Pearl River, branch of the Hsi-chiang (Si-kiang) or West River, has the very strongest walls, well made of good height: twenty-five feet high, twenty feet wide, 12,350 paces in compass, eighty three bulwarks, seven gates with breast-works, entries sumptuous and high, battlements above like steps; the gates themselves plated with iron, strong portcullises in front, always up.

I could trust no one, yet no one betrayed themselves to me, every one of them as honest or as dishonest as the rest: agent and spies, and spies' agents and agents' spies. I thought more about *the* boat-girl, I saw her lifting her head slightly, turning her face away from the sun, woven hat rising slowly: a movement in all that was still, a flash of colour in all that was dark.

8

I could not sleep at night, struggled with dark phantoms, fearless angels of death, ghosts of my past; saw the twinkle in the beautiful boat girl's Chinese eyes that looked back across the great divide, the point at which two civilisations were bound to collide. I saw the territory overlooked, and that one great face at the centre. And I resolved that one day I would know her would make love to her, this Chinese whore (for that was what she was).

It was opium that had led me to this boat-girl of boat-girls, the boats about her ready for the sale, the silver that I kept safe, saved in 'The Factories'. I wasn't sure what it was about her that stayed with me that took over my thoughts, but there was something left inside. White Poppy – I saw her in all the female faces that passed before me, was becoming obsessed with a vision remembered of something that had long since passed and gone by with the days.

Passing her left hand up to her pretty face, I had seen the tattoo of the snake on her upper arm, intense vermilion and blue, the *ourobouros,* or snake swallowing its own tail. I felt concerned – had seen the same symbol on the flag flying high over the Grand Junk that lorded it in the Canton harbour. A circle is a symbol of satisfaction, the Interpreter informed me; said it with a strange smile.

I watched a grey-brown spider spinning her web – fragile sticky net: legs moving, vibrating new-spun silver. I closed my eyes. There lay the boat-girl, naked beneath gossamer gauze, opium-drugged, unconscious, wet, opium pipe hanging from her slender fingers, viscid residues of sex at the parting of her thighs. The enticing sharp fragrance of the black mess of her unwashed hair, stuck to her head in its oily human essence. I had seen it, yet had also not seen it: memories, bits and pieces gathered from the past – images that were now coming together to create the horrible whole.

Opium, as a cure for pain, as euphoriant and supposed aphrodisiac. Opium, which brings sleep and relief from pain, a cure for headache and sleeplessness. For most of its history not smoked, but rather the black sticky resin was dissolved in wine and drunk, or rolled into a pellet and swallowed. Opium for crying children - Victorian nannies dose infants with opiate-laced Godfrey's Cordial to keep them quiet. Laudanum, a tincture of opium in alcohol, is used as a cure for colic in infants, a women's tonic, cure for dysentery. Opium, the intoxicating delight that led me to the boat-girl.

I could not bring myself to ask the Interpreter about *her* tattoo, was not certain of his position in the affair, or how far I could trust him with the details of this one woman so lovely she had the power to destroy Canton, to bring China to her knees: I knew it, I felt it, the narcotic power of the White Poppy!

There was no door that opium would not open, nothing that silver could not buy: if you had enough of either, then you were rich, the richest man on earth – powerful, yet without power: for every one who gave you what you wanted in reward, there were ten more waiting to take it back from you, to steal from you, hurt you, kill you.

Tears... trickling sands... That teenage boat-girl standing out above me, conical straw hat, wide-brimmed around her shaded Chinese face, head dropping, poppy bud drooping, long black hair up high, strained back behind her head, drop-pearl and gold ear-rings, finest threads of gold around her slender neck: this Eve, this shocking image of seduction.

'The snake is a ghost,' the Interpreter told me later, 'which may mimic human shape and seduce men in the guise of a beautiful girl.'

He laughed at me, what interest could I have in snakes? But his dark eyes held a hidden message of terror and fear. What right had I to keep asking him questions? Did it inconvenience him having me there? How much trust can there be with a stranger? His slant eyes were friendly enough, but I felt the pull of fear.

9

July, fifth Chinese month. Spring over, the China summer began in earnest: heavy, wet, tormenting heat agitated by torrential rain, white mould growing on damp leather, grey spots of moisture staining the walls. The China sun beats down on female peasants working the fertile soil, broad bamboo hats shading their sharp faces, cheekbones high, calm eyes piercing. The wet river dirt from which grows the lily. Clutches of women baiting their lines, mending their nets, where the floating craft had good fung shui – evil-preventing mountains and trees to the North, floating river village fronts facing the warm South, water down the river extending for miles, the Interpreter told me, kept me informed about such things each time we sailed down the Pearl.

Adjusting the black leather patch over my right eye, the drizzle of morning rain having stopped, I watched a string of ducks passing high over the noisy clutter of sampans and junks. They flew across the Canton harbour, running clear of a massive gilded junk (surrounded, protected by three war-junks), burnished gold blazing deep-water bright in contrast to the forest lanes of gaudy red and green. I watched them fly beyond the huddle of house-boats, continuing along the perspiring river above banks lined with dripping orange and lemon trees, lychee and peach, disappearing over the giant twin pagodas of the Sea Pearl temple that stand erect mid-river, vast defended citadel with gun-ports against coastal pirates.

I had decided to stay longer in Canton, spent some time at the home of the Chinese Interpreter, a modest house near the produce-market area, where I was given a cool reception by his wife and family – she interfered, got in my way.

Through a merchant at the Creek Factory I found alternative accommodation in one of the 'bungalows' near the waterfront, the end furthest from the erotic, floating village. The small, sparsely furnished room gave a pleasant enough view across the river and with little else to do I sat and watched the many boats moving about their business, the disappearance of the evening sun that turned the water to liquid gold.

To the locals I was a curiosity, a sailor, a traveller, and I entertained them with my leather eye-patch and a sight of my only book, gold edged, black, leather-bound Holy Bible. I read frequently to pass the hours, sitting in a chair, the only chair, riddled with woodworm, a crimson cushion, faded red – like an aged velvet-covered whore ravaged by disease.

I watched the Chinese junks sailing in and out of the Canton harbour, the fishermen unloading their catch before the forest lanes of gaudy red and green. The Chinese junk, one of the strongest and most seaworthy vessels in the world, is a large flat-bottomed box. Solid bulkheads running lengthways partition off its hull and crosswise, dividing it into watertight compartments. It is structurally rigid and does not easily sink. It has a heavy steering oar or rudder to compensate for the lack of a keel. The rudder can be raised or lowered. The sails are made up of narrow horizontal linen or matting panels, each secured by its own line, or sheet, so that each sail can be quickly spread or closed.

I watched chests of tea being loaded on to melon-shaped barges, towed away from the waterfront, ten miles downstream to deep water at Whampoa (with its famous nine-storey pagoda and groves of China oranges – 'mandarins'), and final transfer to ocean-going sailing ships (my route home).

Most numerous near the shore, most active all around, passenger-carrying 'egg-boats' (crude hand-painted signs, covered above in rough roof matting like half an eggshell), ferried Chinese male clients to the whores. Each rowed by a slant-eyed girl in blue trousers and smock, crimson lips, black hair plaited with ribbons and flowers.

I saw the half-closed, slanted eyes, those silent vermilion lips; saw the distance of a thousand years, the China mountains, silent peaks, silent rocks, silent trees, gateway of jade that led through to a certain heaven. White Poppy.

Listening to the vibrating grumble of the softly-beaten kettle-drum of the heavens, the dying heartbeat of God's orchestra, I remembered wrecking waves mounting jagged, ripping rocks; two ships held inshore by the gale, first ship striking, foundering as she came in, sails blown out in tatters... splintered back broken, sprawled across the rocks like a dying whore... bleeding wounds that could never heal.

I saw the brilliant human fair, tall boards on which were painted life-size replica whores, standing legs opened wide, against which men stood in line with their backs to me.

Behind each painted hole where the vagina should have been was the wet sucking mouth of a female Chinese. Suck and spit, suck and spit. Eyes closed, I saw the Chinese noble lapping at his lady's fount, moment of transformation, her vital fluid dripping into the flask beneath her parted thighs.

10

The growing boy stands in the centre of the low church close by the London docklands. The growing boy, black-haired, anxious, frightened, sharp eyes blue.

I had an appointment with God, wandered ragged through the shadows of that church, petrified beside the marble font, looking towards the altar with all its finery, its silver shinning, walking down between the dark wood pews, stopping before the steps, my eyes drawn to the red lamp burning in the sanctuary. I wanted to run away, but I had been asked there. Overawed, frightened of confinement, of being trapped inside, I kept my young eyes on the door, waiting, found myself kneeling on the chequer-tiled floor.

I recall the fervour with which the devoted Catholic father revealed the secrets of his Church, the unravelling of his religion, his life. He provided me with a life where there had not been one before: the first person who cared for me.

Our opinions disturb us. If there are briars in the road turn away from them, leave them behind. Don't question why they are there. Building castles in the air, that was what I was accused of as a child. But I went further, created vast bastions in the clouds that trundled over London in competition with the belching soot and smoke of forested chimneys. Lying on my back in the cemetery, amongst pyramids of black marble, panels of rose-pink quartz, where white marble angels kept one eye on heaven, I watched ships sailing through the clouds.

I saw great fortresses in the sky, walls that towered upwards towards the sun. And I watched oriental princesses walk along those walls, long hair flowing, soft bodies enclosed in figure-hugging silk; wide walkways, crenellated walls lit by the stars, princesses with lips as cold as ice and breasts as hot as coals.

The labyrinth of London's dockside slums, boarding houses kept by 'crimps'. I was determined not to be crimped in this way, pressed into naval service, and found work as a rigger, and subsisted, half-starved, overhauling the running and standing rigging, replacing worn cordage and bending new sails on the yards of ships in harbour. But later, in my own way, I was drawn to a life at sea.

Twelve years old, I paced the deck for the rest of the day, without being noticed by any one, and started ready for the sea life that every sea-boy has to endure - physical hardships, pain, the privation of every comfort, even of sleep, miserably torn to pieces by as hard service as any ship's crew ever performed.

I was baptised a Christian, purified in water, in the name of Jesus, taken *into Christ*, in order to be saved from all that was evil. And my later proof of education? I could say the Lord's Prayer.

Living at the edge of a bright world of colour and lights, a street urchin, nothing more, I watched elegantly dressed couples descending the steps from their homes, to enter a waiting carriage that would hurry them away to another world in the parts of London that I never saw, only imagined beyond the grime that was all mine.

London in winter, floating in the quiet fog, veiled wonders along the Great River Thames over which hung bridges with coronets of lit gas, where smoking chimney buildings sailed like tall ships. On the fifth of November giant effigies were carried around the cobbled streets arranged in spangles and paper, paraded by men and boys dressed up as clowns, brave men who wore happiness on their faces that hid the misery of their squalid dockside lives. Fireworks lit up the ink black sky, rockets chased the wind, blew great holes through the clouds, scorched the sky.

The chill winds blew down the empty red-brick house-lined streets, late afternoon in December, the sun pale yellow in a slate-grey sky: the children *going snowing* (going out to steal linen drying in the yards), in the bitter wind that accentuated the security and comfort to be found within the tall houses on each side, the warming red glow from curtained windows, extinguished at last by closed shutters or drawn blinds, where men used the women for the satisfaction of their own sordid lives.

I got to know that Father Patrick, Catholic priest, a tiny man with a powerful spirited nature – he found me sitting huddled in the dock land porch, crying, shivering with cold. He took me in, gave me Christmas food, a home, let me sleep by the warmth of his coal fire, let me look at his picture books, started teaching me to read, told me about India and China.

'Act to give your friends no occasion for regret,' he told me as we parted, 'your foes no cause for joy.'

Set dreaming by the passing clouds, we looked out to sea together on a day trip to the coast. We watched a grand sailing ship back from the Orient, pinpoint pricking the horizon, wind blowing fresh in her sails, blue sea running with whitecap waves, growing in size, becoming a vast pyramid of billowing virgin white, sails catching the winter sun as she made her way along the coast.

'Take care, Charles, me boy... look out for yourself now!'

There was a tear in his eye when he left, for a mission school in Africa. The following year it was my turn, leaving the shores and whores of London for the shores and whores of San Francisco...

So it was that at 13 years I found myself on my first sailing ship, the *Morning Glory*, bound for America. A massive square-rigger: complicated, graceful lady, clothed in profuse rigging that grew from the long sweep of her decks, tall masts scraping the sky, fine-spun tracery above. From San Francisco there were tall-masted sailing ships to New York and Europe, sailing past Tahiti, round the Horn, back to England, and ships on from Europe to India and China. There is security in ships, within the hustle and bustle of the harbour, where nothing is ever still.

'Make yourself happy where you are,' Father Patrick had said, 'and not where you wish to be.'

To desire what you do not have, what you cannot have takes your mind away from your job, from the ship; makes you dissatisfied and dull.

Sailing on tall-masted ships, I experienced my own darkness, my own inner pain. Coming out at night, wind screaming in the mast-stretched shrouds, blasting whipped up spume, crested waves crashing over the rail, white foaming, salt spray stinging. No stars shining, no moon to break the shattered, screaming heavens, showering sleet and snow, freezing fingers to the bone. Six of us sent up to pull the damaged tops'l down, balancing on the foot-ropes, canvas flapping; hanging on for life. Slipping, falling, rag-doll-like to the deck' sharp iron piercing, blinding pain, blood, the sight of my right eye (ice blue, like my Mother's) gone.

11

The conjuror showed the audience the magic box containing the living head of an ancient Sphinx. 'Sphinx awake!' Slowly the head opened its eyes and surveyed the audience as if gaining consciousness. He closed the box then opened it again. Gone was the head and in its place was a little pile of dust.

Nightfall. Fifth Day of the Fifth Month: battle with the dark, folk hired boats for pleasure; music spilling out across the mouth of the West River; breathless breeze keeping the boats in constant agitated movement, floating aimlessly like lily pads broken off in a storm. The Parade of Dragon Boats: craft, long and narrow, prows thrusting high, decorated with fierce, fanged mouths, red-painted, gilded sides; raucous rowers, men waving flags to the crash of cymbals and gongs – throbbing heartbeat for that sex. Sharks tearing, feeding round the flesh of the freshly bloodied corpse.

The boat-girl? The beating of her heart, pumping of her blood, gentle movements of every muscle twitch of her forbidden female flesh. Hot breath – full heat of her Chinese passion. What was there written in her horoscope, in the movements of the stars? What was there to be spoken of in her silence, written there in sisterhood, written there in blood? Who was she – foetal dribble fond or forbidden, at the parting of whose legs?

And I desired her. Oh how much I desired her, a longing that made me go hot to the knees. It was all about a face, the most beautiful oriental face, and its large almond eyes and the position in relation to the nose and the most adorable vermilion lips. It was the face of all faces; once seen, one could never forget. But that wasn't all of it, there was something more, and the strength of feeling for the unseen, was out of all proportion to what was seen. Within those eyes, within that head, deep within that perfect Chinese body, were the secrets of the universe, the secrets of all time and I vowed to unlock them, to gain access to that which would last eternal.

There is much pain within the tears of whores, within that sex without love: there is a world within each water-drop, another person in every tear. And there are the 'tears' of horror that are cried dry, 'tears' with no moisture in that death state seized with fear: those of such pain, dried up like ice, water locked away. I heard shrill screaming; watched a small girl twisting, turning in the arms of a well-dressed Chinese merchant; trying to escape from his powerful hands. I watched as he lost his hold on her, as she tore away from him, running off beyond the street traders with their stalls: yellow silk soon lost behind the cluttered Chinese wares in the streets leading back to the waterfront. Her short, straight black hair gone, he stood there scowling, banged himself on the head with his fist, and made his way towards the walled city that stretched before him to the sky.

I saw children wandering the waterfront daily, but I didn't see the same children long. Every few days a familiar face had gone. I saw two girls floating face-downwards in the river, dead. In a man's world the birth of a boy is most important, is celebrated with unending joy, while the birth of a girl is a potential financial proposition, gives one more for them to whore. The Interpreter told me of a man, who desperate for working sons, hacked off his daughters' hair, shaved their heads like Buddhist monks, but because of what they had hidden between their pretty legs, were they ever really free?

We pick those flowers that catch our eye, take them home, put them into water, feel pleased that they live on, their beauty fully in our power, under our control. Until they start to fade. In picking them we break a thread, destroy their direct contact with nature, and ensure that they will die before their time.

A pot full of agar-agar jelly used as vaginal lubricant: prostitutes lowering their under trousers, raising their skirts, jamming fingersful of it up between their thighs before and after sex.

'Every man,' the Interpreter had said, 'has his own taste in women.' He laughed. 'Some of us like our girls to be little, plump and lively. Others,' he smiled, 'prefer them to be slender, elegant and tall.'

The whores sat in rows like communicant virgins, fresh faces stern above their soft white frills: so different when quickly see out of the corner of the eye, rather than seen full on. There was a job to be done for money, a valet service for the body. The men had sex with them although their bodies never touched. It was like going to the toilet, instant release, from fingers and diseased lips; that was all.

The poppy season is a short one. On rough roadside mounds at the edge of English wheat fields turning gold, I had watched the nodding heads of solitary red – watched them in their black-centred, blood-red splendour (prostitutes standing naked, red-bending, raw); watched them nodding heavy, waiting for the first petal to drop (silken clothes shed to reveal soft flesh), falling, floating to the ground.

But I knew also that the first quiver, first movement of any petal, would signal the doomed future of the rest.

12

We went to war with China, a game of hide and seek between the islands in the typhoon sea. After dark, it again began to blow strong, when suddenly a cry was heard on the deck that the ship next to us was on fire and the flames soon mastered the ship. By the prodigious light of this conflagration, the situation of the Chinese and the British fleets could now be perceived, the colours of both being clearly distinguishable.

About ten o'clock the ship blew up, with a shock which was felt to the bottom of every vessel. Many of her officers and men jumped overboard, some clinging to the spars and pieces of wreck with which the sea was strewn, others swimming to escape from the destruction. This tremendous explosion was followed by silence. The firing ceased immediately on both sides.

The first sound that broke the silence was the dash of her shattered masts and yards, falling into the water from the vast height to which they had been exploded.

A dry mud ring, a pair of brightly coloured cock-birds fought each other: feathers ruffled – brilliant yellow, scarlet, and peacock blue: heightened sexual activity, in contest over the selected hen. Desire. The biggest cockerel strutted ahead, bright eyed, proud movements of his scarlet head, pecked his prize-won hen. That was how I won my first girl, Daisy, with a wager, breast-feeling bet.

I amused myself with the sports and occupations of Canton. Peering through latticed screens, the silvery sound of female voices, soft laughter like feathers in the wind;

glimpsing the brilliant pink and purple silk, the gloss of long hair in the shadows within; elegant strains of a lute plucked by dainty feminine fingers, of a very different kind of flute played by practised swollen lips. Taboo. China is a land of great mystery, of timeless beauty.

Dancing, 'Shallow River – deep River', the Chinese girls in flower, like flowering rushes that swayed and bent, raised the hems of their silken garments, crossing a river of silk, a teasing genital display, hidden intermittently by spreading fans, the naked women dropping their clothes to fan bared flesh.

Crouching, legs held open with their hands, inner right and left sides of the parted vulvas, the young men admire the 'Examination halls' of the women before them, moving up and down like wild horses bucking through a stream. Swiftly alternating deep and shallow strokes, like sparrows picking rice grains from a jar; deep and shallow strokes, like large stones sinking deep into the sea; deep and shallow strokes until each experience the final flare of the oil lamp before it goes out.

I was curious to find out more about the Canton flower-boats, their buds of beauty and in particular their prettiest human flower. The meeting was arranged through the Interpreter who seemed to know more than he would admit, but there was no one else I could trust: his friendship had come on the highest personal recommendation.

There were some ten thousand prostitutes in and around Canton and I had to find just one of them once more. The boat-girl, White Poppy, where was she, who exactly was she, that blooming Chinese flower? To find her would be taboo, the greatest taboo, but her presence and her purpose had now become the only China focus for me!

I had it in my mind to buy her, to take her home with me to England. I had it in my mind to barter for her, to pay those in silver that could engineer her release for me. I had it in my mind to do many things, but where to start?

Dressed in merchant's clothing (as disguise), short serge jacket, long close-fitting trousers, tall and cylindrical hat, short black leather boots, I spent the afternoon in the company of Chuan-chuan (Juan-juan) a delicate girl from the eastern provinces.

Arousing flirtatious, wearing a *ch'i-p'ao* (Ji-bou) of thin white, gold-threaded gauze, like the wings of a cicada, her lips pomegranate red, she sang to me in Cantonese, a high pitched wailing song of love and death; showed me the 'Instruments of Love' – 'Case for Mutual Enjoyment', 'Trembling Voice and Lovely Eyes', 'Bell of Excitement', 'Silver Clasp'; showed me the geography of her Chinese body with no mystery at all. I paid her in silver: for her inadequate open slit. Taboo!

'Make yourself happy where you are,' Father Patrick had said, 'and not where you wish to be.'

13

White smoke floating away around her, she giggles like a child, drifting slowly with the vapours, the fume of opium. Inhaling in one breath, tasting the dry pleasure she was transformed, head lolling, slant-eyes unfocussed, lost. Her body moved slowly, audibly, bones shifting, cracking. Sitting there with her pretty legs wide apart, laughing tears.

The Chinese girl became unconscious from drink. Carried upstairs, the little whore, she was thrown face downwards on the bed, lips apart, head lolling, legs open wet and wide, enjoyed by the men who mounted her from behind: great Chinese whore, unwanted daughter of Hell.

She received no male respect, this common prostitute, this disposable sexual toy, choking on her own vomit. Discarded, free.

In the middle of her web the spider waited, silent, still, waiting for the first pull of the thread that would mean death to the victim who cannot pull free. I was the fly drawn into the Chinese web, blown there by the sea-winds, drawn in, trapped by the very threads of China. I knew I was being watched, but I was not sure who was watching me.

The Chinese believe themselves to be the superior race, insist on trying all foreigners under Chinese law. There is much official pomp and circumstance, and we bow down before them (but thumb our noses at their backs), offering a token respect to their faces: kow-towing, making the series of expected triple-kneelings, bowing our heads three times to the ground, making the nine-fold prostration, in the name of Victoria, our Queen.

Official trade payments were made to the Superintendent of Customs at Canton, the *Hai Kwan-pu* or Hoppo, civil mandarin of the first rank, who wore a bright ruby in his cap, purple robes, and a girdle fastened with a clasp of jade set with rubies. I didn't like him. Under his power were the Tide-Waiters, who handed out the official *chops* or permits to foreign traders, who gave the permission for our ships to enter the Canton River, and the Association of Chinese merchants, the *Kuang Huang* or Cohong, appointed by the Manchurian Hoppo himself.

The Cantonese were shrewd businessmen. They spoke 'Pidgin' ('Business') English for trade – several hundred words adapted to Chinese pronunciation. They offered their best *European* women in the way they offered their best opium.

'He number one chop.' ('It's first class quality').

Of course Chinese women were taboo, *the* taboo of all taboo. But there were corruptions in all articles of trade: the Chinese Tide-waiter in front of the Creek factory, soliciting foreigners to land goods at his Chop House, gaining his silence and assistance in return for money; the Chinese Guild-Merchants who certified foreign ships as being contraband free as they entered the mouth of the Pearl, having (as the Guild-Merchants were perfectly aware) sold their opium already at sea; and the swarming *yen-fei*, the Chinese opium-smuggling bandits themselves.

We brush past death every day, move through its shadow, and uncaught, pass out the other side for more life. White Poppy had become my obsession, that first image of her had burned itself into my soul. I went to sleep each night thinking of her, I woke each morning thinking of her, and how with opium I could buy access to her soul.

Many of the Hong merchants lived in the grand style, entertaining us generously in their splendid houses set in vast flowering gardens (houses furnished through drug money). Chinese courtesy, pride and keeping 'face'. The Cantonese took care about who sat in the place of honour, who picked the chopsticks first.

'Never lift the main dish. Don't reach over another's chopsticks. Do not stick chopsticks into the rice bowl.'

The Interpreter, tapped my fingers, pushed away my arms, showed me the right behaviour so as not to offend my Chinese hosts. Customs, rituals and routines - a matter of the correct bowing and scraping, the Canton Factors played a game of manners, 'Chinese Chequers', with the Hung Men.

Through the merchants at 'The Factories' I became friendly with more of these wealthy Chinese, most particularly the respected syndics of the *Foo-j'ow* Junk merchants, made some profit myself, asked basic questions, kept them to the topic of European women at first. We laughed about those colonial women who insisted on the European fashion in spite of the suffocating heat. But the Brotherhood (*di-hoo*) of the Canton triads was another matter: the Brotherhood who made their money from gambling, prostitution and the bitter poppy-drug, opium. The secret society of the Triad (Heaven - Earth – Man) or Three in Accord; the Hung Society had an origin common with the White Lotus of north, central and western China, but developed characteristics of its own in non-Mandarin-speaking Kwangtung. I was right to fear them – the 'three million who were one'.

The Canton chapters of the Brotherhood, the Hung men, included those amongst the shroff merchants, compradors, dock hands, yamen clerks and small shopkeepers; corrupt mandarins, corrupt river-police, professional criminals and pirates; there were also the gentry, the clan elders, the village heads, all part of a threaded net of secret sects spread across China.

When the Manchus assumed power in 1644, they took action against the secret societies: their leaders were strangled and their accomplices sentenced to 100 blows with the long stick followed by lifelong exile more than 300 miles from home.

But secretly, silently, the triad network grew anew. It was my belief that under their Chinese leadership, or *ling-shih*, the boat-girl, White Poppy, was kept hidden; a rare treasure possessed – a ransom fit for the Emperor himself.

Luscious, crimson, open mouth, entrance of the most erotic lips, wisps of raven hair blowing about their silent moistness, a sad smile hiding tears, taboo. The spider shifted in her web, legs moving, vibrating the silver threads, checking its trapped perfection, tucking her self in for the night, waiting.

14

On the third day of the wedding, a grand dinner, musicians and singing-girls to perform the plays and music, she dressed in pearls, Yu Ji, put on a scarlet cloak, an embroidered skirt, a girdle with a gold buckle. She went concealed in a large sedan chair to the Canton Town Hall. A pair of little silver globes pushed into her vagina, one containing a drop of quicksilver, the other a tiny copper tongue, provided an erotic quiver at the slightest movement of her hips.

Entertained with the ladies in the Great Hall, the Mandarin's wife was there to receive them. Young girls, faces painted like blossom, full sensual deep-vermilion lips, faces lit by suspended paper lanterns. She made her way with the others to the back rooms, made ready for the men. They blindfolded her, hid her eyes.

The 'birdman' with his tiny bamboo cages, walking, whistling round the park: pretty songbirds, thrushes, larks, trapped inside the bamboo cages of the gentleman bird fanciers who strutted around the Canton parks ahead of him, whispering to their captive prey.

The place of execution was at the opening of the vegetable market, the broad street filled with soldiers and officials. All around, the flat, low roofs of the closed shops were crowded with male spectators. Amongst the group of thirteen prisoners, including two women, a murderer was to be decapitated.

A little further down the street, high officials sat in a semicircle, with a red-button mandarin at their head. To one side a bloody altar displayed the tools of execution – the five short-bladed, chopper-like swords (the Lords of Execution) and bloodied string, and the tourniquet and strings for strangling. Before the altar, a cauldron of water boiled over a wood-block stove, for the warming of the swords.

Extreme terror and fear: the women were strangled – two pieces of cord passed around the neck with a loop, each prisoner facing down to the ground, pleased nevertheless, for their release. As we defile, as we destroy with one hand, yet we reinforce and build with the other: we cannot give up such precious things, such shatteringly beautiful forbidden delights – we can only replace them, substitute them with more!

Beneath the bluest blue sky we made our way up river to Honan temple, the largest and wealthiest of the Buddhist sanctuaries, standing on the south bank of the River Pearl. Passing beneath the ornamental gateway, we walked together slowly along the tree-lined way with its bold hydrangeas, dodging the sunlight through neat compass-point gardens with potted trees flanking the covered trellised walkways, sunlight reflected in lily-pools with golden-orange fish, chattering birds above us. We walked to the temple itself where the Interpreter left me.

Beyond the grounds of Honan, is very ordinary open cultivated countryside with rice paddy fields intersected by winding banks, mounds scattered with graves, narrow dirt roads leading to the outlying villages and deepest China. I stared out there, lost in my thoughts, watched a heron lifting its wings. It smelt sour, the air no longer fresh around me.

'Good morning... lovely day isn't it?'

The pressure on my arm was firm, demanding, and very English. Turning towards the voice, an extended hand came forward in greeting. We shook hands briefly. It was sticky, sweating, hot.

'Good morning,' I replied. 'Yes, it is. Very bright.'

His blue eyes were calculating, clear and cruel.

'You must be Charles?' The clipped speech, English precise. 'Charles Sansovino? Pleased to meet you.'

I took an instant dislike to the small man before me: round, balding, face like a walrus, bright beady eyes peering through steel-rimmed spectacles. This was the Factor? This was the source of the foul smell.

Coming out from the temple shadows, he glistened in the sun, wiped away the sweat gathering heavily on his forehead with a white silk handkerchief. I listened to the whoop and chatter of the birds, the pulsating buzz of grasshoppers in the long grass.

'It's going to be a scorcher,' he continued, beckoning me towards a bench in the shade.

'Do have a seat dear chap!'

Silver pool sparkling in liquid golden sunlight. The fish swam strongly, so many of them, turning, heads and tails breaking the surface of the water in an orgy of delight: frenzied copulation in that confusing, fusing mass, seething spawn of the wet Canton womb. White Poppy.

I thanked him. Sitting down he clapped his hands for tea, 'Ching-Chah!' (A young monk came running), gazing beyond me, out across the shimmering River Pearl busy with its traders, small boats moving slowly in both directions.

From behind the distant waterfront, bungalows floated serene on beds of flowering pink and red and blue; houses stretching to the wide steps that led up from the boat-cluttered Pearl to the enclosing white-iced compound of the Thirteen Foreign Firms (The Factories). Multinational flags fluttered high in the breeze, above where American and European merchants lived separated from old Canton by a shanty town of dwellings in the shadow of the city wall against the lush green of rocky hills. Ancient wall guarded with gates and watchtowers, mysterious with its temples and pagodas, the occasional tall, square pawnshop tower, and milk-white Chinese houses with tiled roofs that turned up at the corners. There were also the tall poles with cross trees like those on the mast of a ship – each marking the residence of a mandarin.

'Charles,' he said suddenly, firmly, 'I hear you have some opium to sell.'

Out of the corner of my eye I saw a mirror light flashing from the Grand Junk out across the harbour, flag flying high – richly displayed vermilion and blue serpent swallowing its own tail; watched the raising of her flat mast sails, as she turned and sailed out with the wind, sea-serpent making her way to the mouth of the Pearl.

'Oh, and Charles?' he grabbed my arm, pungent, acrid. 'A word of advice. You will not go back to Yu Ji!'

He caught a grasshopper in his cupped hands, pulled off its wings.

My drug-won silver, he had been given a fair reward: I was not in the business of handing out bribes. Another would have stabbed him, would have cut him in the back while his defences were down. It is the easiest thing in the world to inflict pain, fighting for one's own power – money, women, protection: these are the motives for much human suffering, for much human gain.

I let him go back, marked the details of his face, watched the exit of the Grand Junk down the Pearl.

15

Up beyond the temple landmark, across the broadest granite steps were the sumptuous houses of the mandarins (magistrates, *yamens*): high stone entrance portals, gates with two giants painted with clubs in their hands; a reception court beyond a protective wall of good height, built along the street right against the gate. Outside the houses, hanging from the green, carved, eaves, tiny bamboo cages held an army of buzzing cicadas.

We walked beyond them, the Interpreter and me, through a tiled entry into a court with solaces of small trees and bowers within and a fair little fountain. Inside was as white as milk, paved with square stones, banded at ground level, dyed with vermilion, almost black. The teahouse had long tables, displayed seasonal flowers, lavish paintings; sold different teas according to the season, like *Lung ching*, Dragon's well tea – young, unfermented green tea from Hangchow, served before and during meals, or Cantonese *Bo lai.* Tea brewed in an earthenware pot served in small china teacups on lacquer ware trays.

They were places where government officials and educated men met their friends, where one saw even officials of the third and fourth ranks, their long-sleeved gowns, caged birds before them, sitting among the poorer folk who brought their own tea-pot and tea, and paid for the hot water only. *The Bird of Happiness having once taken flight, seldom perches twice on the same branch.*

'Flower teahouses' were similar, but more glamorous, had prostitutes on the upper floor. Both haunts offered me refreshment, potential information about the boat-girl whose image had never left me. But I was careful, talked carefully while I watched and I listened. I did not speak much Cantonese but I spoke the visual language of women and men, of prostitutes and those who paid them the fee. I kept my face turned forwards and never let my back feel the wall.

The court-official took great care to conceal his identity; he was a procurer, dealing in girls for prostitution, living off the large profits to be made. I knew him only by name.

I was introduced to Chiao-Yun (Ji-ou Yoon, Elevated Clouds), large breasts hanging low, who said she had seen the girl I mentioned (the Interpreter described her as best he could), but that had been some time ago. She knew nothing.

'Dui m jue!' (I'm sorry!')

'M gan yiu!' ('Never mind; it doesn't matter!')

I was enticed further from the familiar friendly ways, drawn deeper into the maze of streets, down narrowing alleys, through enclosed squares, and each time I arrived where I thought I should be I met objection, refusal, no help at all. The Interpreter raised his eyebrows, opened his slit eyes wide at me. I spoke to Fu Hsi (Foo Shi), who suggested Kuan Yü (Guan Yoo), who told me about Lu Pi (Loo Bi) and the women of Lu T'ang (Loo D'ang). Snarling vicious tigers sat taut in the candle-smoking darkness; lips, legs opened wide, lolling vacant like dolls. The fantastic Hsiao Chung-hung (Shi-ou Choong-hoong, Laughing Peach Blossom), showed me what lay beneath her gown, but I was not impressed, had seen it all before: the two-edged sword between her legs, by which destruction came to foolish men.

At the front door they let in the father, while by the back door they welcome the son: they soon forget their old clients, with their brief affections for the new. I left the Interpreter back at The Factories, and went back alone to

Yu Ji. She excited me. To feel her naked breasts pressed close against my chest. Chinese mouth open, lips apart, swelling, glowing; lips taut for a kiss, she excited me. Peaceful lips, prominent teeth, I remembered the erotic saliva salt-sweetness of her pretty mouth, thinking of her daily as a thirsty man thinks of water. Almond eyes burning bright, she swallowed although there was nothing to swallow, and yet, even she, was not White Poppy.

She sat still, watching me, knees up to her chin, Yu Ji: the flicker of her eyelids, clumsy repositioning of her mouth - to put a finger between those fine legs. Her mouth open slightly, hot lips apart - to feel the warmth of her mouth on my face, her gentle breathing, and to close my mouth over hers. To explore her silent other lips, with my tongue. To feel the full pressure of her thighs, hips pressed tight against me. Her slitted eyes: looking beyond her, past the wisps of her fragrant hair. Soft hair hanging loose; watching the pressing of her immature thighs, the flexing of her childlike knees, the positioning of her ankles as she touched the floor with her feet. Chinese lips forward, she lowered her head slightly, mouth open, lips full towards the floor - to feel her black hair, to let it flow through my fingers. She nibbled her lip. Her eyes were large, bright, manic, mad. To lift her transparent shift and to pull it over her head; her head thrown back, neck arched and exposed. She lay there beside me; almond eyes opened wide, legs opened wide, eyelashes flicking - the soft tiny slit between her legs. Parting her swollen lips, running my fingers over them, she nibbled them then pulled away: white semen pearly in her outstretched right hand.

16

Luscious crimson, open mouth, entrance of the most erotic lips, red lips, wisps of raven hair blowing about their silent moistness, a sad smile hiding tears. Gorgeous, glistening, black-bronzed almond eyes, White Poppy blinking slowly, sadly, reflecting all around; long lashes flicking, eyelids closing over those beautiful polished stones - those eyes, those beautiful staring brown eyes, penetrating, deep.

There were war-junks again down in the Canton harbour, dominating the other craft. I saw them every day, guardians of the sea, the ragged China coast; they stood out large, heavy guns ready for attack. I watched small boats moving towards the waterfront; rowed away swiftly from the evening shore, making their way into the flat-masted China Dragon fold, where imperial flags fluttered in the breeze. They manoeuvred into position, lantern lights reflected orange in the creeping evening indigo darkness above the wind-churned sea: guardians of the illuminated fairy-garden whole, beyond the waterfront before the great walled city where flares smoked red on the walls.

Sitting one afternoon down by the waterfront, watching the crowds flowing all around, I caught sight of a train of girls clambering ashore from a small covered boat that had wound its way slowly into the floating village: seven girls on their way to some secret hideaway in the walled city? Heads covered, chaperoned by an old woman, they walked briskly in single file. The little group walked close below me, turning into a closed alley, the old woman stopping to talk to a mandarin of the ninth and lowest rank, his cap button of worked silver, long-tailed jay embroidered front and back on his robes, a girdle fastened with a clasp of buffalo horn. The old woman laughed loud, and the group moved on.

My heart stopped - the girl at the back? I recognised the well-defined cheekbones, the 'eager' face, the set of her lips, pomegranate red (the plump pod full of seeds, symbol of love and fertility), the flash of her bronzed-ebony eyes, as she turned, and the full memory of her, returned. Hat rising, lifting her head slightly, tilting her shining face away from the scorching sun, shading her eyes with her right hand, the poppy flowered, the White Poppy. On her left wrist she wore a bangle of serpentine green jade, celestial semen turned to stone.

What is peace but an interval between wars? The boat-girl was all right, the Interpreter later informed me quickly. The information would cost me dear. I was to meet her at the deserted pagoda; he would take me there. Perhaps, at last, this was the unravelling of the intricate Chinese knot?

The morning sun was warm but not yet baking hot. Riding through Canton on horses borrowed from the Factors, leaving behind the festering hovels that slouched across the rough land between The Factories and the towering city-wall, we cantered past groups of barefoot coolies. Wearing caps, rough calico tops and short trousers to just below the knee, they carried buckets or bundles of cloth, suspended on wooden poles across the back of their shoulders.

Overtaking the carried private sedan chairs of civil mandarins, of wealthy individuals of rank, we rode by a pair of military mandarins of the fourth rank, wild tigers embroidered on their flowing robes. We moved slowly through the crowded back streets, picking up speed as we left them behind, passing numberless temples, Buddhist pagodas, gardens; galloping across the dusty fields with skylarks singing, and along dirt roads that give rise to clouds of dust on windy days, on towards the outskirts of the city where the air was fresher.

Twin dragon kites rising, soaring, flying; twin dragon kites falling, sweeping, lying, heads touching, diving to the ground. *The mysterious passions that lead us to break the rules; what are they, where are they from?*

We made our final approach to the pagoda, grand but dilapidated tomb on rising ground, seven-storeyed tower tapering up to the cloudless sky, each storey with an outside balconied terrace and a decorated, narrow, projecting ornamental roof, painted dark vermilion; the tower now decaying, the remnants of its once fine decoration, peeling red and gold above its buff sandstone base. We tied the horses to an iron loop by a water trough, the merest trickle running through it from the nearby spring. I'd been told to meet the merchant there, to arrange for White Poppy's release. But my mood was uneasy, pessimistic, grey.

Leaving my Chinese friend outside, I entered alone, the silence of the cool darkness disturbed only by the sound of a cricket, a vibrant quivering in the air. Walking up the first flight of winding stone steps my footsteps echoed back at me, the light increasing above as I ascended, slowly, turning the last corner, sunshine streaming across the large and empty room, battered, vandalised, graffiti on the walls. Up another flight of steps, another floor, more emptiness and so on up to the seventh and final floor where the wind moaned through the rafters.

No one in sight, I strode out on to the terrace, walking towards the mighty stone balustrade and a superb view across Canton. Flat, rolling fields beyond, where thousand upon thousand widespread graves dotted the landscape between the massive city wall and the distant mountains, the towering White Cloud Mountain to the Northeast. The boat-girl had been hidden somewhere down amongst the stinking hovels in that overcrowded stain, claustrophobic enclave like a parasite on the Pearl. It smelt sour; there was an odour on the breeze.

I felt a firm pressure on my shoulder, heard the familiar English voice welcoming me. Turning round, I recognised the bespectacled face of the well-groomed opium merchant from The Factories that matched exactly the clipped, perfect speech of the English gentleman.

'You have a message for me?' I asked, shaking the outstretched hand. 'I was told to come here for information about White... about the Chinese girl.'

He nodded, looking past me towards the distant, ragged sprawl beyond the patchwork of dry fields; dusty trails winding back to the dark stain of Canton's tight packed waterfront. And on to the more spacious, rich parts, fine buildings radiant in the sunshine, The Factories of the European merchants standing icing-sugar proud.

'She is all right. She is being looked after.' He paused. 'But it is impossible for you to see her.'

'I thought, I was told that...'

'Yes, my dear chap, I am perfectly well aware of the situation. But you must realise that things have changed.'

I felt hot and angry, had made the gravest mistake of all, had been lured there as a foil, while the White Poppy was elsewhere, taken even further away from me? As for the silver I had paid for this meeting, well I might just have well thrown it into deep water out at sea!

'Look,' I shouted, 'I demand to see her, I was told...'

'You were told, you were told?' he glared at me angrily, his face now very red, small eyes penetrating me with their pain. 'What does she matter to you, she is just a boat-girl? There are hundreds of girls like her: they have no real lives. Why worry; leave them to the river! What is it to you whether she lives or she dies a worthless whore? She will become an opium addict...' he smiled a shallow smile, 'will die from the drug, or rot from disease, end her days a mindless ghost!'

I wanted to hit him, this *siu min foo* or smiling tiger, this fierce person disguised as a friend, to strangle him then and there. But I swallowed hard, repressing my rage for another time. I walked away, felt hands suddenly round my neck from behind, pressing tight against my throat. He pushed me forward over the balustrade ledge, pushed my face against the peeling paint of the stone tower, the ground a dizzy height below.

He pressed hard into my neck; his breath was warm in my ear. He spoke quietly, calmly, reserved.

'Leave her alone!'

17

Rain pelting down, sky heavy with cloud, no moon, not a star in sight, the wind blew a gale, rocking the water, churning the boats, jarring my bungalow down by the water, screaming through the shutters of my room.

I sat wide awake in the darkness, thinking of the boat girl, peering out at the foaming harbour-waters; thought I saw a figure in the garden moving away from the house, but straining my eyes, the shape became indistinct, disappeared into the distant shrubbery.

The morning light crept into my room, the sun shining in a clear, bright sky, the storm having blown out in the early hours. There was wreckage in the garden, a few shacks had lost their roofs and there was some damage to the trees, but the air was fresh, and it felt good to be alive.

I stepped out on to the veranda: beheaded cockerel at the door, legs tied together above the feet, blood spatters over the wood where it died, a sticky clotted redness washed out at the edges by the rain; the sign smeared in blood on the wall, the 'men' (gate) of the Triad lodge of Canton, the Brotherhood of the ancient Chinese city.

The sea is large, the sharks are few, yet they exert a perfect reign of terror. They continued to watch me, the Brotherhood, tailing me, waiting for me to do something, for something to happen, but I initiated no action myself, went along with them as I thought they expected me to. I saw them staring at me, looking sideways, backwards, a quick glance over the shoulder, their slant eyes like dying stars; waiting for something to happen, for something to betray me.

Canton seethed multicoloured Chinese milling about like garments boiling in hot dye. It became unbearably close and humid. Late afternoon, the heated sky grew dark, thunderclouds brewing overhead. I witnessed the violent mating of the two China Dragons: the Celestial Horned Male of Heaven, and the Female Dragon of Earth; their intercourse manifest in the soaking rain, juice of life dripping from the burst-open clouds, quenching the parched earth. And with the breaking of the Monsoon came insects and snakes into the houses, plagues of biting mosquitoes along the humid coast.

Water washes away dirt and cleanses that which is impure, while that which is within, remains dirty, defiled. The water purifies, makes the woman clean, but it cannot wash away new life. The water bathes the new born baby tainted with her mother's blood, but can only make her disappear by drowning.

It seemed that the Brotherhood was now after me because of the boat-girl, *that she somehow was involved with the opium trade herself.* Starting my search for White Poppy I had released the genie from the lamp. 'Knowing her' had opened a door that refused to shut. Try as hard as I could to walk off, they would not let me go: closing doors to hinder my movement forward, opening others to lure me further in.

I saw her everywhere in those Chinese faces saw her when I knew it wasn't her; I smelled her in the fragrance on the breeze, odours wafting stirring female scents; I tasted her in the seafood meals served with rice, in the storm-emptied rain water as it ran down my face, across my lips, over my tongue; I spoke to her as if she was there with me, talked to her of the things we might do together, of the things that (in my sleep) we had already done; I heard her in the voices of the women along the waterfront, heard her in the sighing wind, the rustling of the leaves on the trees; and I felt that I knew her, that she was somehow of my distant London past, and that together we should be free.

Night falling beyond the Jinghai Gate, the silver coin of the moon rippled in the water in competition with the clear-sky stars, the wind blowing cool across the river, fragrant, spicy, sour.

In spring the plum blossom falls there, blows all around, showering the ground like snow, like wind-scattered poppy petals blowing in the fields of India. In the distance was the 'sacred city', old Canton, the City of Willows furthest from the river, strong walls keeping foreigners out from that which was hidden, deep within.

I moved in under the cover of darkness, the streets lit dimly with oil lamps, the night watchman making his rounds, calling time, beating his gong. I saw the Canton butcher hacking at his meat, cutting roughly, cutting deep, beside a ragged boy scraping the last flesh from the ribcage of a drying carcass, amidst innards hung up for sale, steaming, stinking offal, executioner most glad.

Two young boys fought, hitting each other with their bare fists, knuckles punching, faces twisted with pure hate: fighting over the girl who watched them, egging them on.

An old man squatted nearby, dreamed about sex – in his half-closed eyes you could see he remembered the girls of his youth.

I went to those who would know, in the shanty town beneath the walls (where the water enters the city through strong portals, strong iron gates that are closed at night): the solitary crimson lamp, basic curtained cubicles, closed the stained rag that passed as a curtain, saw her lying there beyond a bowl of water, filthy towel, grubby mattress on the floor, dried fungi hanging above her, snakeskins, powdered teeth, aphrodisiac drugs all around, gave her my silver. Sold into perversion, she was one of the many, and the many might lead to the one. I handed her a silver coin and she smiled an expectant smile. Taking a stick I traced out a crude diagram of the snake tattoo I had seen on the flag on the Grand Junk out in the Canton harbour, and on the boat-girl's arm.

The whore's smile changed to an expression of anger, disgust. She threw down the silver coin.

'Snake girl bad... snake-girl no good... bad!'

18

Will you walk into my parlour?

'Come in here'. He beckoned to me with stringy hands, the pawnshop owner Lo Ta Kang (Lo Da Gang); hard-faced, grey-bearded old man, he spoke some little English. He said he knew where White Poppy was, or at least his wife did.

Walking in front he pushed through a screening curtain, calling out in a refined tone.

'Ah Zi, where are you, there is a gentleman here to see you? Ah Zi?'

I had been taken in secret (sedan-chair enclosed) to the Cantonese pawn-shop, its characteristic square tower rising tall above the surrounding roofs, iron railing and a narrow walkway around the top; ground floor office inside with free-standing wooden scaffolding running right up to the roof, divided into rising floors with ladders – bulky furniture at the bottom, jewellery at the top.

A chubby woman appeared carrying a baby; she had black hair cut with a fringe, slit eyes as big as saucers.

'Hello, please to meet you Mr.? I am Ah Zi'.

Crying, the baby pushed itself against her breasts and opening her clothing she offered a full nipple to its lips: a handsome black-eyed boy, not more than three months old. She was joined by several other slit-eyed children, dressed brightly in reds and yellows, two boys and a toddling girl. They came round me and stared, looked hard at my leather-patched eye. I handed her the package, and she gave me the address.

19

Twelfth Day of the Ninth Month, the moon was bright. Entering the star-lit grounds passing between two stone lions in front, like those at Trafalgar Square, I walked below a cover of bushy trees along the lamp-lit road to the Palace of a Thousand Dreams, fireflies hovering golden above pools of liquid silver. The full moon appeared quite large; I had watched her silver rising, her white light rippling across the water down in the bay.

I felt excited, saw the boat-girl in my thoughts, aware of her fragrance – in the warm river-breeze she had smelled hotly of jasmine, or opium, of the odours of her sex. Had I any doubts about what I was doing, it was too late to turn back; my arrival had been watched from the lions.

The spacious bungalow ('green bower' – woodwork lacquered green), protected with awnings at the windows and a screen of bamboo on the veranda, had intricately carved eaves and exquisite painted columns, light shining out from behind paper-screen blinds, from whence came sweet music. Walking up the low stone steps, I rang the bell, and announced myself at the paper-screen door: heard soft feet shuffling within. This was it, fulfilment of the greatest Taboo! I watched the old woman sitting by the door, who pretended not to watch me.

An attractive young girl, face painted white like blossom, full sensual deep vermilion lips, cheeks like the coloured clouds that precede the dawn, gold-embroidered red silk from her ankles to her chin, bowed gently before me, waving me inside, took me through the front entrance into a courtyard lit by glowing paper lanterns, rooms leading off from it on three sides.

Given warm tea, given warm wine, I remembered what I had been told: I was not to interrupt this in any way, was to let my host do everything. I looked around the spacious room, walls of harmonising brown and green, hung with bright paintings, filled with polished black wood and ebony furniture, ivory figurines, delicate carvings, an inlaid lacquered screen, bamboo lamps of red silk; a set of twenty four framed prints showing the pleasures of love.

Listening to a two-stringed lute of catalpa wood in the sisterhood of singing-girls, dancing-girls, high-class whores in that Brotherhood harem, I glimpsed the quick, hot, laughing glances, the clever furtive smiles of girls enshrined in sweet scent, voices vibrating, soft.

Deep within, beyond beaded golden-spangled curtains, a large room was set for evening dinner: Chinese girls wearing trouser-suits of duck-egg blue, hair plaited neatly on top, stood waiting to serve, below ink-brushed paintings on the walls. Chinese paper lanterns hanging from the ceiling diffused their mellow light over islands of tables decorated with a mass of silver plate, silver-mirrored globes multiplying, reflecting the brilliant scene around them.

I sat down to eat, kept my eyes on the table as I had been told. We began by wiping our hands and face with hot moistened towels. When a new dish came in the host made a gesture towards it with his chopsticks. The Chinese eat anything that is edible: some of them have in times of famine been forced to eat babies. The Chinese will not starve.

The meal proceeded at a sedate pace, dish following dish, meat, fish, vegetable – in no particular order, the table swimming with hot sauces, with steaming spiced odours, strong scents, accompanied by the noisy slurping and shovelling in of food, the spitting out and sucking in, the clatter of chopsticks from many mouths dipping into each dish placed before them: sesame-baked king prawn, followed spicy barbecued ribs, spiced rice, sweet and sour fish.

The whole pleasure of the banquet comes down to texture and mixture: how cabbage tastes when it is cooked with chicken, when the flavour of each has gone into the other. How women taste so different, too. There was once one who said she loved me: I suppose she loves me still. I never had time for her then, preferred my time away at sea, while she waited for my return. I remember well her cinnabar mouth, her honey-fluid lips, the clever actions of her tongue. Her hair was honey-blonde and she had brilliant bright blue eyes. Her name was Hermione. Her father was a merchant, a well-to-do man who owned a string of shops near Covent Garden including a grocer's and a flower shop. Hermione was proud of my adventures, took me home to meet her parents, treated me to the greatest range of expressions across her face as her family quizzed me through afternoon tea. Her father's conclusion – she later told me – was that his daughter was far too good for me. I left her behind one summer afternoon, didn't tell her I was going. I suppose I was in love with her, although I never told her – never realised it then.

20

Lying still in bed, sophisticated, seductive, surrounded by the most exquisite Chinese drapes, I waited for the black-arched painted eyebrows; the long, slit-shaped, half-closed eyes, staring, unmoving, watching me like an owl. I watched the grand scene before me painted with the Taoist (Dowist) Paradise of P'êng Lai Shan, situated in the Eastern Sea, home of the Eight Immortals and those who win the blessings of eternal life. I looked at the gold and silver houses, trees of coral and pearl, flowers and seeds of sweet flavour – those who eat of them do not grow old; those who drink from the female fount of yin, taking it straight from the source.

Hair swept up off her face, piled high in elaborate coiffure threaded with beads and pearls, above heavy gold earrings, she came towards me in the darkness, stepping across the single shaft of entering moonlight, preceded by the most exquisite scent. She bowed low; walking forwards slowly, her silhouette erotic in her gorgeous flowing silk embroidered with sparkling thread of silver and gold.

She let down her hair, took out the pins, unfolded its silken mass, letting it cascade free, running down across her shoulders, flowing over her soft-arched back. Removing her white stockings, jewelled girdle, sash untied, her dress falling open, the moonlight revealed the soft curves of her small but full figure, her breasts hanging full, exposed, large oval nipples, erect; naked thighs delightfully pudgy, soft black hair where they parted.

Mouth round, her lips English holly berry red, she knelt over me, undressing me, kissing me, her breath as sweet as jasmine, her mouth as cool as ice; holding my hand in hers, plump fingers, the warmth of her Chinese skin. Turning, I saw a familiar tattoo on her upper arm, the snake vermilion and blue, but she was not White Poppy.

She laughed at me: the young Chinese prostitute flicked back her hair and laughed at me. I felt blood in my mouth, had a strange taste on my tongue, saw the room shaking before me, felt myself falling asleep – I had been drugged. The spider waiting patiently in her web now rolling her victim in silk. I prayed to God for forgiveness.

It was only after I left the house that I knew the old woman I had seen sitting by the door, was she who had led the single line of seven girls from the boat: led them to some secret hideaway within the walled city. The spider moved, pulled the silk threads tight.

Sun shining orange, cyclopean eye opened wide at me, closing as it sets, sinking into shredded crimson fire. A red kite distant, floating, lifting, rising, soaring heavenwards, free above the distant walled city. Shadows shifting, disappearing into descending darkness, floating boat village stretched far before me, myriad lights twinkled like stars burning in the water, hissing, steaming; mirror-images of the stars above them, armies of the night, blazing bright.

21

On September 25th 1835, the paddle-steamer *Jardine* (58 tons) arrived at Macao under sail, steaming into the mouth of the River Pearl on January 1st 1836. It was just one more new beginning as we moved closer to the end.

Sunrise – I resorted to the Official Chinese, made representations to the mandarins of Canton, they who had the keys to open doors (but who also supplied the locks to keep them shut). We rode before the riverfront Gaol. The prison walls were high and very strong with a watchtower above the main gateway. By mid-autumn, the Morning Glory had grown all over the artificial mountain, covering the rock face in the deepest blooming red.

We rode past a stand of ancient zigzag cypress trees on the crown of the hill, winding our way down through the vast canopy of trees, descending alongside shallow terraces with summer-blooming rockeries and ornamental towers surrounding a lake on three sides. At the entrance to the garden, the gatehouse had an arched roof of semi-circular tiles; lintels and lattices, carved with intricate designs both painted and gilded; walls of polished bricks; white marble steps carved with strings of passion-flowers. The whitewashed wall of the garden stretched each side of the gateway, with a splendid mosaic base of striped 'tiger-skin' stones.

The house we required came slowly into view, its oriental grandeur protected by the green shade of trees that hid it from the upper road, trees that kept it cool in summer.

Leaving my horse with the Interpreter, I walked across to the entrance steps, began my way into the enchanting Chinese house with its grand redwood and rosewood pillars, eager but apprehensive to ask about White Poppy inside.

The anteroom was dark but brightened by its white-paper walls. The yamen-clerk slid out through the partition opening.

'Jing yap lai la!' ('Please come in!'). He looked at the pile of papers in front of him. 'Sin saang, nei gwai sing a?' ('Sir, what's your name please?).

'Siu Sing... ('My humble name is...') Charles Sansovino.' I knew little Cantonese, nothing but the merest formality.

'Yam ja la,' he offered ('Have some tea, please.').

And I had tea while I waited, watching the secretary at his table, busy with his papers, working with his round-tipped writing brush, ink and stone; his hand held flexibly, brush turning quickly, fluid, free.

In the room, partially lined with carved ebony, there were glazed earthenware dishes with mountains miniaturised as rocks – small basins holding a single rock and a single tree (p'en-ching). The miniature garden, like the brush-painted handscroll containing mountain scenes, led the eye on a winding path through a landscape with solitary pine trees, up rock-cut steps, cliff-walks to the mountain summit shrine. There were huge mirrors of all kinds, musical boxes with mannequins on them, magnificent china of every description, heaps and heaps of silk of all colours and embroidery.

The shout made me jump – the Mandarin's voice was cold like the watered-green of his flowing robes. Preceded by his footman he came forward slowly from a dark wood screen. I bowed several times as he expected me to. I was introduced first to the son of the Canton civil officer - a handsome little fellow; soft, shining hazel eyes, gleeful, kind. What contrast to those of the elderly Ou Ch'i (Oo Ji) with his cold, apathetic indifference, the veiled contempt of the polished Confucianist gentleman, head shaved at the front, braided in a single plait behind, with his Aladdin hat and silk robes, his fancy brocade footwear – the oh-so-proud magistrate or mandarin.

Sending the boy out of the large room, he gestured to me to sit down on a straight-backed bamboo chair, and talked to me quickly through his Interpreter. I watched the water-clock to his side, the series of water containers descending, water dripping from one into the next below it, the time measured on a stick of bamboo in the lowest; water rising by the second.

It took less than three minutes, and his final remark was 'No', nothing could be done for the girl. He closed his file.

'Joi gin.' ('Goodbye.')

22

So much for recourse to the law. I felt fearful – another enemy had been made? I was on my own with the memory of the snake swallowing its own tail that I had seen engraved on the Mandarin's thick gold ring, the outline that matched exactly the flag flying high on the junk, rich vermilion and blue: like the tattoo of the bungalow whore, and that of the boat-girl, before, White Poppy.

Who is it that can eat himself whole? Only death can consume life. The snake in the grass, double-tongued, hidden, poisonous, deadly to those who step upon his head. The closed circle of eternity, of fraternal friendship, with no beginning, no middle and no end: the wheel comes full circle in male-controlled perversity. Terror and fear. I knew it had everything to do with the snake. The snake was the key to the whole puzzle and it linked all of my interest in Canton: the snake, White Poppy, my Canton dream?

It was life that took me there through no purposeful planning of my own. We had opium to sell, silver to take back in return, and anyway, Canton was the best place to be, at the centre of all things that meant so much to British trade. I had it in my mind to make something of my life, to be something that my Mother and my Father could never have been. And it was White Poppy that was to be my route to my dream, to be the king to my very own queen. I was to be shown what had been kept hidden, discarded, thrown away, entering the forbidden city (for what purpose I did not know). I knew that this could be the end of my life.

Leaving behind the imprisoning human sea, the red lights and the lanterns, we slipped into a narrow side street, buildings tall above us, lamplight flickering as we passed; taken semi-conscious into the great walled city, through a studded wooden gate in the shadow of the rocky hills, into the Canton I had not expected to see. No way out, no way through. This was it, the moment of truth, every fear conquered by sweet desire, the prospect of love, of death.

My body shuddered, blind in both eyes now with a tight band of cloth wound round my head; led down winding stairs, along an alleyway, through doors, turning right then left then right again, the air colder as we descended below.

Blindfold removed, head dizzy, the room stretched black before me, velvet darkness pierced by a thousand glowing lights, a ceiling dotted with sparkling silver stars.

My escort disappeared into the glare of many tapers and the sound of golden chimes.

Taken before the Goddess, the mirrored shrine, incense burning, my head forced down low in supplication, hooded figures turned inwards to the centre of a crescent moon, faceless, silent, still. There sat the girl, the boat-girl, White Poppy, ornate before the stellate mirrors, multiple reflected loveliness in purple, silver and gold; a garment covered in little bells and chains of gold, shimmering, shining, melting at the edges where the flaming air burned crimson above her fertile throne, decorated with the *withered vine for thousands of years*. Was it truly her? Had she ever been forgotten, this renewed memory of her image that brought her back to life. The glistening flesh, the soft lips, the almond eyes of the boat-girl who had enchanted me; the painted mask, white powder tinted with carmine, cheekbones polished, high, chin inclined upwards, cinnabar mouth opening with silent words; full breasts, heavy, feet quite broad and soft. Moon orbs dangling from her ears. Her feet were normal – the boat-girl had escaped the binding of the feet, had not been enough of a Chinese lady!

In the darkness her white face shone in the candlelight, glowed with power, emphasised the redness of her lips, the blackness of her eyebrows, her gorgeous, glistening half-closed eyes. No smile. Unholy light. Smell the jasmine, taste the sickly perfumed air.

I heard her breathing, listened to the salivation of her lips, the paper rustle of her clothes, that flash of colour in all that was dark, bright butterfly with her iridescent wings, prostitute on high - priestess: White Poppy Goddess, Whore. Were they women's faces inside the hoods?

White smoke floating away around her, she giggled like a child, drifting slowly with the vapours, the fume of opium. Inhaling in one breath, tasting the dry pleasure she was transformed, head lolling, slant eyes unfocussed, lost. Her body moved slowly, audibly, bones shifting, cracking. Sitting there with her pretty legs wide apart, laughing tears, her head thrown back in ecstasy, black hair hanging, red lips opened wide in the most glorious ' O': the circle, symbol of satisfaction.

Written there in blood? Who was she – foetal dribble fond, at the parting of whose legs? Love. The moment: the critical moment when the lover meets his soul-mate, the one person in the whole wide world who was made for him or her, made to be loved forever, here and hereafter. But that wasn't all of it, there was something more, and the strength of feeling for the unseen, was out of all proportion to what was seen. Within those eyes, within that head, deep within that perfect Chinese body, were the secrets of the universe, the secrets of all time and I vowed to unlock them, to gain access to that which would last eternal.

I watched in horror as a girl came towards her, slant-eyed, hard, olive-skinned, dressed in white chintz, the white of death, pushing out her fat tongue, ruby-dribbled lips sucking vigorously at the quivering mouth, the glistening wet cushion of her lips, to taste that which made her young flesh woman. Sitting cross-legged on the floor, knees opened wide above the pungent purple. *Red lips that move; a spider's thread of saliva in-between.*

The ringing of bells, jangling of chimes, sweet music of pipes, resonant bell-like tones, monotonous beat of a gong in that closed circle of hooded heads, 'talking' in signs: Chinese whispers from their lips, syrupy sugar sweetness reflected all around them in the mirrors. She ran a finger along her lips, glistening wet lips, but her lips were cold, her whole being cold.

Drawing up her knees (sobbing, crying), they tortured the girl with her own sex, took her to the very edge and left her there, dying, destroyed. Head forced down between my knees, arms bound tightly behind my back, I wanted to look once more, felt compelled to force my head back upwards to look further inside her, when out of the corner of my eye I saw a shape that made my blood run cold: the purple robes, the embroidered crane, the bright ruby on the cap of the Manchurian Hoppo himself, Head of Chinese Customs and the second most important man in Canton. I knew him from the procession at The Factories; remembered the cold eyes.

23

The Grand Junk sailed from the Canton harbour – burnished gold blazing deep-water bright, its flag flying high, rich symbol of a vermilion and blue serpent swallowing its own tail: protected by three war-junks, I watched it leave.

Beyond the huddle of houseboats the Junk had stood for all my time in Canton, before the gaudy red and green, where the fragrance of smoking jasmine and opium cut through the stink of the brackish, steaming river. Where a mirror had flashed its message, winking eye from one giant of the twin pagodas of the Sea Pearl Temple that stood erect mid-river, and the Grand Junk had flashed back its reply.

BOOK II CHAIN ROUND MY NECK

Canton City Gaol
1836

1

Bronzed ebony eyes... blood red lips: the boat girl, Whore? We despair with what we have until it's gone; that fruit taken away just as it's almost in our grasp. Misfortune and unhappiness follow those who make their fortunes in opium, I had been warned.

Pushed as I was into the dark stone cell, patches black with dampness on the walls and floor, the heat pressed down heavily on Canton. At night, worse, no breeze through the high window, my face and arms running with sweat, my mind running with thoughts that I would rather forget; when would the rats start nibbling at my rag-covered toes? On one side of prison cell, running the whole length, a wooden bench of rough boards extended a little distance from the stone block wall. My hands were handcuffed, the short chain which connected them being connected to the chain that descended from my neck to my feet. I was then laid on the bench with my feet towards the wall, directly under one of the chains hanging from the beam; to this the chain round my neck was attached and I was thus able to lie only flat on my back. Even that was painful with my elbows pinioned by my sides. I was kept like that until they took it upon themselves to enable me to move on and off the bench with a lessened degree of discomfort.

Helpless in prison, powerless, I plotted in darkness while the world shone around me outside, while the flower girls budded, blossomed, faded and died, my thoughts on the one particular blooming Chinese flower. Many times the prospect of death became welcome to me imprisoned in that stale room locked with heavy iron bolts, helpless, God my only companion (and the boat-girl in my dreams).

In prison I saw death around me every day, heard girls screaming for life in the midst of death and decay, saw the foul tortures of their bodies on the one day of each month that I was taken outside of my cell, shown the enclosed foetid air of the salt-blood-scented inner chamber beyond which dripped hell.

The casualty rate among the prisoners was high, half-naked demons, savages: the Chinese prisons infected by small maggots, which if they got into wounds caused by the rubbing of fetters caused inflammation, fever, delirium and death.

2

Gentle fall of tiny droplets, water vapour linking my lungs to nature, fog penetrating the narrow opening into the cell: the South China coast has its fogs in spring. I felt its dampness, water droplets in the suffocating air, saw a thick North Sea fog, isolated at the mouth of the Thames: chill coldness, sunlight breaking through, warming, burning the moisture from the air, fog disappearing slowly over the steaming Kent coast sea.

The more forbidden the love, the greater is the passion: I craved her, the boat-girl – her mystery, her body, her own special magic, they were the only thoughts crashing round in my mind. I felt repulsion for what she had done, at where those soft lips had been (remembered the wet running sores on the lips of the other whores), I craved her – desired to close my mouth tight over hers.

I couldn't find her now, had lost all hope of escape from China. Because of my interest in White Poppy I would lose everything. I knew my rented home would be searched, I knew my personal possessions would be destroyed. I knew the Chinese authorities would search for information but there was nothing to find. I had only two possessions – my Holy Bible and my silver cross and chain – the rest was inside my head.

What was the role of the Canton Brotherhood in all this? I was a British name entered in a British book at one of The Factories. I was accounted for in one way, and could not just disappear. But kept imprisoned under Chinese law, I wondered what the true reason was for which they kept me confined. Was it because of my *liaison* with a Chinese prostitute – several? Surely not: that was punishable by death. I was still alive and had long hours between the rise and fall of the China sun to think about the folly of my days. Transporting the poppy drug was a dangerous business, but it was not the real reason I was in China, more because of my love of sailing the high seas. I did it for adventure; I did it because it was all I knew.

The opium issue had become so severe with the Imperial appointment of Lin as Commissioner in Canton, given the task of stopping the forbidden opium trade. The dealers got themselves in such a panic that it was impossible to sell a single chest of opium on any terms, nothing but to run it to the Namo a and Chincheau bays. Before the sale of opium, Chinese rhubarb (a valuable laxative), tea and silk had been worth more than the bales of longcloth and Bombay cotton which we British traded with China; silver was sent into China to make up the difference. But with imported opium from India, this state of affairs was reversed and silver now came out of China to restore their trade gap. The Emperor, his senior officials and Commissioner Lin were determined to end the opium trade on humanitarian grounds as well as for its economic disadvantage to China.

The prison walls were high and very strong with a watchtower above the main gateway, within which three low iron-barred gates blocked the way in succession, leading to an enclosed paved courtyard, vaulted overhead, serving as an exercise area for the warren of cells: in each, a commodious gallery wherein every night the prisoners lay at length, their feet in stocks, their heads in wooden grates (hefty wooden collars over the shoulders) that stopped them sitting, making it impossible to lift their hands to their mouths to eat; night silence pierced by the lanterns of the watch, the question-and-answer of clanging bells.

3

New flesh comes from the aborted foetus eaten by sharks in the sea.

Chiao-Yun (Ji-ou Yoon, Elevated Clouds) was taken to the prison courtyard where she was stripped naked by two Chinese guards, made to kneel down in anger, large breasts hanging low, her face slapped hard across each side, beaten with bamboo rods on her red mouth. She had been hung up the night before by her long black hair. I had been introduced to her, she who said she had seen the boat-girl, but that had been some time ago.

Head pushed down between her knees you could hear the cracking of her bones. Given 30 strokes with the bamboo cane, young informant that she was, but not yet killed: that is how they treat their women. They pinned down the naked whore by her arms and her legs, dangling a living rat by its tail over the parting of her legs, and she screamed in terror, writhing, thrusting, wetting herself in panic as the rat was lowered over her: disgusted, as they shot it, the animal rupturing over her, spattering her with its warm blood.

A rope tied round the wrists, hung up, bare feet only inches from the floor, lashed with the whip, she was left there unconscious, hanging limply like meat, dying, dead: Chiao Yun (Ji-ou Yoon, Elevated Clouds).

4

The blood of our Lord Jesus Christ, which was shed for thee, preserve thy body and soul unto everlasting life. Through the inadequate open slit, high up with its red-rusted bars, I saw the remains of daylight, imagined I could smell the sea in the bittersweet odour of magnolia, listening to the river-water lapping free, waiting for the night. I gauged everything by the light or dark that entered through it, the roar of thunder and the wet rushing of rain, the howling of the wind, bird-song from the trees I pictured all around me. Or deathly silence broken only by the occasional shout of the Chinese who guarded me: I had no faces to put to those harsh voices.

Looking at the opening, I became transfixed by that narrow slit of sky, moved closer to the wall to receive more of the life-sustaining air, the bright light that shafted into the prison cell, as late afternoon turned to evening and then to darkest night. Mosquitoes entered through it, I was bitten severely, listened to their whine in the dark. Bitten, itching, bleeding, I watched the shifting shadows of the bars as the morning sunlight penetrated the cell, the shaft of light as it moved daily across the floor, along the prison walls, tracing its regular path through my little world where time stood still, where seconds lingered long, yet whole weeks disappeared with no memory of their passing. I kept my mind busy with thoughts of White Poppy, sleeping in the intervals, too tired, too hungry, too miserable, to think any more, drifting into fitful nightmare dreams.

Time changes our perception of things, distorts the small details, blends together the separate parts. And so the days became weeks and the weeks became months and time ran together and ceased to exist. All I possessed was a vision, a fantastic vision that grew fainter by the day: the image of the boat-girl that had burned itself into my soul; craving the separate bits of the perfect moving whole – the black hair, the brown eyes, the nose, the lips, the hands. The parts were themselves so beautiful, so erotic, so perfect and pure. I desired each and every one of them. My life depended on a vision, a collection of dreams that disappeared by the day.

5

One heavy, wet, grey Monsoon morning, well away from land, when the South China Sea stretched heavily ahead of us, my dark mood had been disturbed by familiar singing in the skylight, a cheerful warbling song from the lemon-yellow canary in its cylindrical bamboo cage: how happy he sang from his swinging prison, alone. I talked to him.

'Look at you, not a blade of grass or a tree within a hundred miles, and yet you trill for a hen bird, sing your little heart out.'

I felt ashamed, that he could be so happy with so little, with nothing more than seed and water. It was a lesson that I never forgot watching white sails lost in white clouds. A silent act needs no translation.

As a boy I had sat in the front of the balcony, near the stage of the large City of London hall, and waited for the delights of 'A Night in the Palace of Pekin' including The Famous Goldfish Bowl Production and Metempsychosis:

advertised on the large posters outside the Theatre. At length, after some music the curtains were drawn back, and there appeared on the stage hundreds of lights from gas jets, electric currents and spirit-soaked candle wicks. The silver and gilded paraphernalia of the Wizard came into view, as he walked between two wonderfully clothed footmen, who bowed low at his entrance. He had on a handsome robe decorated with serpents, stars and mystic signs, with pepper-palaces and thorn-tree halls, and a very tall conical hat surmounted by a crescent moon. He proceeded to fill hundreds of glasses of wine from an 'inexhaustible bottle'. Then he mounted a sort of low table that isolated him from the stage. After a few manoeuvres to prove he had nothing about him, he threw a shawl at his feet. On lifting it up he displayed a glass bowl filled with water, in which goldfish swam about. He did this three times with the same result, until there were three bowls of swimming goldfish at his feet. In a separate inner compartment about twelve feet square, hung on three sides with blue curtains, a basket of oranges became pots of marmalade, and a chest of tea became a large tray bearing a steaming teapot and a row of cups.

Fog and mist at the mouth of the Thames – ships' masts and rigging like offshore church-spires. My London remembered: the rookeries - maze of courts and narrow dark streets, sickly light glimmering through the thick black, fires blazing deep inside, strange figures moving about; black pools of water with playing children black like coal. From the windows of three-storied houses stuck out rude wooden rods with drying clothes - cotton gowns, sheets, trousers, drawers, and vests, old and faded, ragged and patched. Holes in the Wall – near the level of the Thames; the warren of caves and hiding places, beyond gloomy warehouse alleys, stretching shabby to a confusion of jumbled spires at the top of the smoke-brick hills.

At the age of seven years I was convinced the Devil lived in the shadows outside my father's door, I thought I saw movement in those shadows, the flicking of a swiftly whirling tail; convinced that my father had brought into the world all the children of Hell.

In my youth I had read of a mysterious Chinese garden where grew the apple-bearing Tree of Immortality. The Tree guarded by a Dragon, winged Serpent (national emblem also of the Celestial Chinese Empire), the symbol of Infinite Intelligence keeping ward over the Tree of Knowledge. There are two antagonistic Dragons, the one crooked, crawling, and slimy, the emblem of everything that is obstructive, loathsome, and disgusting; the other winged, radiant, and beneficent, The Reconciler, the Deliverer, the Spirit of All Knowledge.

I had vowed then in my young London to travel the seas to China, to search for that mystic walled garden and to eat of that fruit. It was a dream of boyhood, but the opium ships took me ever nearer to that Paradise dream.

How to survive death, the only time we are truly on our own, the only journey from which we do not come back? How do you accept it? The answer is you don't. Like the sea bird soaring high you go where the wind takes you, feel it in your hair, your eyes, your nose: feel it caress your bound nakedness. In time, I would freeze up completely, would be wrapped in white and buried beneath the ice-hard ground. I wanted to die. I wanted to get beyond the pains of life and hell.

I lay down in the corner like a wounded ferret and waited to die, feeling the creeping cold, the chilling numbness that entered my feet, freezing my toes, working its way up my legs, chilling my bottom, paralysing my spine, ice in my veins, constricting the slow beating of my heart.

6

My hands had been tied behind my back for a long time and all feeling had gone from them. Thinking of the White Poppy, the sunshine in her eyes, I tried hard to recall vivid scenes from the past, bright images of days gone by, but the pain in my hands reminded me where I was. Pressing each finger in turn, eyes watering, so painful. Lying on my side was uncomfortable, as it was also on my back: lying on my stomach gave momentary relief, though much of the time I slept sitting up, dozing, squatting in the corner nearest to the window.

I felt very cold, held my ragged blanket tight around me. Outside it was snowing, and I watched the balls of white cotton fluff descending slowly, free. My nose poured mucus, my throat was raw, my head pounding, my body hot, burning up inside. The winter light was dim, barely penetrating my unheated cell and I sat in gloom, banging my puffy hands together, stamping my feet to keep them warm in their rags. The wind blew snow flurries through the barred opening, there was no way of closing out the weather, and even if there had been, I would not have shut out that tiny passage to the world outside. My teeth chattering, spasms of shivering jolting my aching bones, taking all of my energy to breathe.

'She's a whore, a worthless whore!'

I woke stiffly, my Mother's words loud in my ears, but opening my tired eyes there was no-one there, no warm female face bending down through the blackness to comfort me. Do not spare the rod or spoil the child whose will needs to be brought into subjection. My body burned with pain, my back scorched by the lash of the whip, feeling it slowly, carefully, running my bruised and bleeding fingers along the stinging weals.

My mother hit me as a child, thought it necessary discipline when I irritated her, got in the way as she had her 'fun', earning her living down in the Docks, when she ran home trailing clouds of glory, bringing me presents, telling me that I was her 'best boy', otherwise hitting me for getting in the way, for being 'a bleedin' nuisance'. She who never showed me true love, I wanted to hit her back, I wanted to kill her but dreaded being alone.

I threw driftwood from high into the escaping Thames, tried sinking it with rocks as it floated away, to send it down where I wished my Mother. Narrow alleys running down by the Thames at Charing Cross, smoking chimneys silhouetted against the smoke-filled sky, in tunnels where the air was sharp and dark, where girls let you feel them for a fee. Nearby were the local 'cock and hen clubs', places of disrepute, playground of common prostitutes as much as for cock fighting and ratting: the *London Cyder Cellars*, the *Coal Hole*, *Shades* – underworld vice: not too dissimilar to Canton after all!

Walking by moonlight beyond the London Docks towards a tiny back-street City churchyard, peering through its ferocious iron-spiked gate, I saw the dark church-gaol ornamented with the skull and crossbones, the spectral child at its window, listened to her cry within, the unborn child, heard the activities of the whores on the church steps, watched them fucking like dogs, and inside, the Christmas scene, the baby Jesus tucked up in his manger.

I watched the blizzard beyond the red-rusted prison bars, overjoyed at the power of the whirling snow falling thickly from the grey, building up in layers on the ledge, blowing into the cell where the flakes formed a little pile of iciness, a stalagmite of snow, remaining there unmelted in the chill. Scooping them up, I touched them to my bleeding lips, pressed them against my tongue, tasting freedom in their frozen wetness.

The *Medusa* had drawn out of the Thames, penetrating fog, chill coldness, sunlight breaking through, warming, burning the moisture from the air; fog disappearing slowly over the steaming Kent coast sea. She rounded the North Foreland before nightfall, and headed southwards, close inshore. As was usual with a foreign-going ship under government charter, she anchored in the Downs, the stretch of water between the Kentish shore and the treacherous Goodwin Sands. She lay there awaiting naval clearance.

Rocks to be avoided; shifting sands; risks of grounding and of being wrecked: the Goodwin Sands, a constant danger to shipping, the shifting sands of the Shoals do not support lighthouses; lightships and numerous buoys and fog sirens mark their position. Final dispatches obtained - sent overland by stagecoach post from London, driving out through the Dover Straits into the fast open Channel of the great and dangerous North Sea, we set sail for China.

7

Look at 'er lamps (eyes), she's been drinkin' heavy, full up to the knocker she 'is with wet!

MOTHER: little girl lost in an adult body. When I was very young I watched *her*, only woman in my life: moving deliciously, unbleached linen stirring about her, striding forwards in glee, sitting herself down beside me, touching her loose hair against my face. Eyes ice-blue, peering through the shadows, young skin soft as it brushed against me, deep carnation of her cheeks, her lips cold, her whole face cold, pressing my hand against her naked stomach, letting me feel its pressure, the place where there grew new life. Life gave her so little, and she wanted so much.

Shut your head woman! Give me that sticker (knife). I'll put its lights out.

FATHER: he killed that new life, killed the girl, my sister that she aborted from her smashed-in womb. Bleeding she had lain there, dabbing between her legs with her skirt, mopping up the thickening blood with the tatters of her rags – the curse of women, lasting stain.

And all for a dry crust of bread, an onion, food. Crammed into one room in the maze of courts and narrow alleys; brothers and sisters sleeping together like little animals – dirty, verminous, itching, restless; where pregnancy results in the immature child who knows too well the mysteries of life and death firsthand; who sees the mother die in the same room in which her brothers and sisters were born. Mother dead, the oldest girl takes her place. Is it any surprise that girls are attracted to the slum alley streets for a way through poverty – some brief few coppers - as the flame attracts the moth, crackles up its powdered wings?

Thinking of my Mother, I was the part of her that had never died. My Mother at the Docks where the dockside girls played their skipping games, I heard their very distant voices echoing then around the prison walls, saw them dancing before me.

Poor Lizzie lies a-weeping, a-weeping, a-weeping, Poor Lizzie lies a-weeping on a bright summer's day.

Pray tell me why you're weeping, a-weeping, a-weeping, Pray tell me why you're weeping on a bright summer's day.

I'm weeping for a sweetheart, a sweetheart, a sweetheart, I'm weeping for a sweetheart on a bright summer's day.

Oh, pray get up and choose one, and choose one, and choose one, Oh, pray get up and choose one on a bright summer's day.

I heard male voices outside my door every day, got ready for the spring, went through certain familiar sequences in my mind, patterns set up to stop myself going insane. Then one morning the door of my cell opened and I was led outside; led out to the central exercise area where a document was read out to me in Chinese. Ahead of me, beyond a thin eyebrow of evergreen trees, stood the rough wooden crosses of the Execution Ground.

The rough wooden crosses in the Potter's Yard; wooden crosses standing firm against the *nose* of the far wall. I had seen them in use by those guilty of killing their parents, strung up high to receive death by Ling Chi, death by ten thousand cuts, and common burial before the other *eyebrow*. Further still were the narrow roads, tracks that led out into China, beyond the down turned *mouth*, of the scarred depression in the rocky hills.

I was weak and ill, could hardly walk, but was free to go. For the lack of anywhere else to send me, I was handed over to the English merchants, the 'Factors' along the waterfront, not so distant neighbours to the foul markets of frenzied female flesh.

For the first time in many months, I saw the Canton harbour, dominated by its shipping, long strings of brothel-junks, the 'egg-boats', where the Grand Junk still sat so proudly on the Pearl: burnished gold blazing deep-water bright, its flag flying high – rich symbol of the vermilion and blue serpent swallowing its own tail. Great ship protected by three war-junks (each with its own protective general); it dominated the waterfront before the great walled city, watching over the harbour-fringes of the boat-cluttered river.

8

Red kite flying at low tide, dipping over ochre sand running down to the retreated sea. Cold unwinding, uncoiling: red kite rising slowly, lifting, soaring; tilting her face to the late afternoon sun; climbing, gliding, rising, hovering bird-like still.

With the short winter-shipping trading season over in March, and the important tea crop shipped down the Pearl, the foreign merchants left Canton to return to their villas, their Chinese girls at Macao (the merchants, tolerated at Canton during the trading season only): Poppy-less I went with them, taken to the harbour under armed guard – a group of Chinese watching my every move.

The energetic boats set sail to the beating of gongs, firecrackers exploding, the religious burning of hundreds of strips of red paper.

It was a three-day journey, past the gilded flower-boats – the floating brothels with their painted female flesh, through the anchorage at Whampoa; past the clumps of acacia and bamboo marking the first bar; past the Bogue Forts forty miles downstream, guarding the mouth of the river; then the final forty miles along the shores of Canton Bay until Macao's skyline came into sight, the towers and spires of its twelve churches and monasteries, a crescent of white houses fringing the bay, where sea breezes cooled the humid summer air. I was out of gaol, but could I ever be really free of the imprisoning Canton life outside?

BOOK III THE UNCARVED BLOCK

Macao, China
1838

1

Walk along this sea; walk along this shore; in the spring sunshine, who could ask for more? What is well kept will not escape. Lao Tzu, *Dao De Jing, 54, (Arkana).*

The Vanishing Lady: The magician spread a newspaper on the floor, placed a chair upon it and asked a young lady to sit down. He threw over her a piece of silk, which barely covered her from head to foot. He then rapidly removed the drapery, and the chair was empty. The trick was done in a strong light, the audience sitting on the edge of their seats in amazement, and the hall was filled with the loudest applause as the young lady walked on from the side and bowed her acknowledgements.

Crimes are committed which remain forever hidden, while innocent people are arrested, imprisoned and tortured to shield those who commit them; charges invented because of spite, for the gratification of revenge. For one man's folly, whole families are cut off, male relatives 'of age' are put to death: while each foolish whore simply dies within.

I had found out that the snake symbol belonged to the Syndicate, the controlling Brotherhood of the drug barons of Canton: that perverse and vicious sect of outlaws and profiteers. The Brotherhood – behind their cryptogram, secret hand-signs, closed initiation ceremonies, mystic blood-rites and traditions, they operated within, through and around Cantonese society, working at every level from street beggars to the law-enforcing mandarins.

My White Poppy, the boat-girl Yin Shooeh-yen, Eliza as I called her, was associated with the high-class Whoredom of the Snake.

I heard the evening gun, fierce report echoing across Macao Bay, saw the ship standing still in the silence that followed: triple masts rising high into the sunset, apricot sky, clouds lined in red above the burning horizon, sizzling orange water rippled with her reflected masts. I saw the pirate boats running; saw the smoke rings from their guns. It was time to sail: time for bloody war.

By July 1838, *HMS Wellesley* and the brig *HMS Algerine* arrived from India. Viceroy Teng controlled the waterways leading to Canton with war junks, and reinforced the Bogue forts. He struck at the fast-armed galleys, owned by Chinese profiteers. Operating from the shore, all were destroyed, while Lintin Island and its receiving ships remained safe beyond Chinese control.

I watched a white-sailed ship making its way out to sea: grand sailing-ship, pulling away from me, wind blowing fresh in her sails, blue sea running with whitecap waves, watching her diminish in size, the pyramid of canvas, sails catching the late-summer sun, shining purest virgin white, shrinking to a pin-point pricking the horizon, tiniest dot that disappeared suddenly in the South China Sea.

Hui-neng tamed a dragon by catching it in his begging bowl after challenging it to reduce its size: could I tame one, too?

By lying still the muddy water becomes clear. This time I knew my enemy, knew the advantages of lying low. There is wisdom in appearing foolish, strength to be gained from appearing weak! My accommodation was part of an extensive crumbling ruin, former slave barracoon, rat-infested home of an ancient merchant-adventurer, a *marinheiro* from Lisbon, whose loves were *vinho* and *tabaco*, the occasional romp with a *prostituta*.

Separated from Chinese territory by a long neck of grave-covered sand, a wall with a guard-house, Portuguese Macao boasts two ranges of hill standing at right-angles to each other, rocky prominences with forts; and the lighthouse, barracks and assorted churches stand openly visible above walled gardens, the fine white houses of the well-to-do, the rich merchants who profit from the local opium trade. Like many Victorians, these colonials, their lives were defined by the great distances between them and their loved ones; long degrees of separation from home, many children being sent home to be educated at boarding school. For a colonial girl there (or in Calcutta), the separation from her parents was merely the first in a lifetime of separations due to her future husband's need to work.

A hot summer night, sitting on an upturned boat looking out across the dark water towards Hong Kong, myriad scattered stars broke up the night-sky spangled with the silver lights of Heaven, full Moon bright - awakener and assembler of the stars, glorified souls of saints and heroes. Gazing up at the navigational stars, I knew I had to go back to Canton: White Poppy's was the brightest, winking back at me with its white light, single silver eye into my soul. I could not leave China without her. Indeed it would be *impossible* to leave China on my own!

All eyes blink, no-one's attention is one-hundred-percent concentrated fully on anything they do. My new friends in Macao were vintage sailors like myself: together we formulated the plan for the Prostitute's release. *I would be the drug-baron, the spider, and the flies would come to me.* Every man has his price, a value for re-sale. I let word get round that a large quantity of purest Indian opium was available at a good price – that price being negotiable in conjunction with a proposed long liaison with one of the prettiest whores in Canton. We had access to a lot of opium from the wreck of a pirate junk along the coast: the old sailor engineered that wrecking, the salvation of the sickly cargo, he would get back White Poppy. Initial brief enquiries informed me that she was alive.

2

The *marinheiro* did his business for me, saw it as a way of getting back some of the old glory of his past: a way of getting revenge on those Cantonese who had put an end to his life when his wife and three daughters were taken away from him, tortured and killed, their dismembered bodies thrown into the sea. I told him:

'You will know her because of her unique beauty, her sparkling almond eyes, her vermilion lips...the snake tattoo.'

What was I saying, it was not enough, no matter how full the description, her beauty was inside my head, only I could recognise the living physical manifestation of the desire that had torn me apart.

I wanted to go to Canton myself but it was too risky: she had been seen last in the company of the Manchurian Hoppo, bright ruby on his cap, embroidered cranes on his purple robes. I remembered something else, it was only a little clue but surely there would be no other like her, no other with the exact same features. The tip of the little finger of her left hand was missing. I had seen it as she turned away from me, as she lifted her hand to her eyes. There was eye contact – fully for ninety-nine hundredths of a second, there had been eye contact between us, the transference of something invisible, an exchange of souls. Who knows what it is that happens when male and female recognise the reflection of the missing part that will make them complete in the eyes of that other?

Would she recognise the leather eye-patch, would it jar a nerve, bring back a memory of the man who had fallen at her feet? Only the one time had I come into the White Poppy's presence, only the once had I seen her close up, from the position of intense humiliation, laughed at?

I felt excited. The opium was left in the trap, the flies were attracted to the web, and access was given to girls who gave information about other girls, and over the weeks we began to penetrate the female ring, began to narrow down the choice. The old sailor told me later of the agonies of that choice, the panic that went through his heart as he looked into the slant-eyes of the final two: satisfied in every respect except one as to the genuiness of the girls, including the missing finger-tip, the tattoo of the snake, he made the final choice; although the eyes were those of my White Poppy, her pretty Chinese face was disfigured by twin scars above her right cheek. *Shown the leather eye patch, only this one girl had looked away, only she showed its recognition.*

I weighed up the chances. What was a dream and what was for real? What had I achieved so far in pursuit of my deepest dreams? I didn't know, but I had belief, belief that things would work out all right in the end. We were right for each other; I believed it, a human belief that goes right back to the beginning of time. White Poppy – there was no one else for me, but White Poppy.

I had survived, surely White Poppy would survive. But where was the logic in that, except that it was in my mind, what I wanted her to do? And yet if I was never ever to see that dear face again, she was still a part of me, could never go away. We brush past death every day, move through its shadow, and uncaught, pass out the other side for more life. White Poppy had become my obsession, that first image of her had burned itself into my soul. I went to sleep each night thinking of her, I woke each morning thinking of her, Jade Fairy Maid.

It may sound stupid, and there are those who will criticise me for being weak, for being sentimental over a China whore. But I don't care, that is the way I am, and that is why I believe to this very day that White Poppy was always right for me. Would it work, or not: each new plan is exciting, but its execution can bring its own pain.

Can you grasp the wind? Blue smoke burning, ashes rising, floating, flying heavenwards, free: in the China hills, the poppy flowers take on their own most perfect disguise. Eyes closed I saw the White Poppy, Yin Shooeh-yen.

3

The Chinese basket was packed with lotus leaves above the horrible surprise inside – the hacked-up torso, butchered arms and legs of the prostitute complete with tattoo, the intense vermilion and blue of a snake swallowing its own tail, the gold jewellery of this high-class whore, sent back by boat from Hong-Kong to those in authority in Canton.

The serpent coiled upon the cross was a symbol of regeneration or salvation – the (reptile) periodically sloughs its skin and is born anew (spiritual re-birth) – also close analogy between the serpent's crawling in the dust and the earth-creeping attitude of material wealth.

The *marinheiro* had obtained the dismembered arms and legs cut fresh from the body of a condemned woman, the tattoo done as a brilliant fake by a master tattooist who copied White Poppy's: sent back as evidence of the White Poppy's death. It was, as he put it, 'One person's useless death for the salvation of another'.

The bargain struck, the old sailor received bribe-won custody of the grand whore, taking her down-river to Hong Kong as planned, from where she would travel to India. He stroked his heavy grey beard.

'You said nothing about scars,' he pleaded, 'you told me nothing about any disfigurement to her face, but those gorgeous eyes made me certain she was the one!'

With the substitute 'White Poppy' dead, the real White Poppy would be free, but I had not bargained for her opium addiction, the terrible mental state she was in. The clear night, glitter-spangled sky, drawing us out into its enormous immensity. In my mind I watched her, saw her turning her eyes skywards, viewing the heavens which contain the very source and secret of life. Slipping up the Pearl River under cover of darkness, taking White Poppy to the Interpreter's house (my last hope, my only friend in Canton), I began what seemed would be the longest struggle of all my life, for which the boat-girl was the treasure, precious cargo, prize.

Deep love is the most painful yet the most glad, for without it we might as well be stones at the edge of the sea, rolled helplessly backwards and forwards with each tide.

4

The savage tiger trusts its own strength. Her pretty eyes that held so much dark power; incredible warmth that shone like polished stones. Her hair was matted, flat, but I refused to let the tangled hair to be cut off by the Interpreter's wife, and myself spent hours over several days, brushing it, teasing out the separate strands, getting it clean.

Water for washing was brought to the house; washing in a bowl that stood on a plank, half a coconut shell containing a bit of strong, yellow soap, as hard as flint, and a square of old shirt tail for the face of the defeated woman, who lay before me like a corpse. For many awful moments, it was my own Mother lying there, drunk and dying. Her scars, her broken fingers – who had done that to her? Who had filled her with Death's disease?

It was getting light in the east, the egg-white mist dispersing in the breeze blowing in from the sea, the sky tinged with red, the golden bowl of the sun casting new rays over the ashen grey. The Interpreter's house was cool inside its mud-brick walls, milk-white on the outside like burnished paper, a pointed clay-tiled roof. We slept on woven mats with coarse blue cotton-wadded bedclothes.

Lying still on her own rush mat I saw White Poppy for who she really was, quiet, vulnerable, scarred, soft sallow skin holding the marks of the opium years that had passed since I first saw her, the passage of the years, her body wasted, lifeless, gaunt. Her disfigurement and her scars – missing little finger tip of her left hand, crooked fingers, contours of her scars – twin outlines bitten deep above her right cheek. Who had done that to her?

Alone together in the small room, I watched her carefully, listening to her gentle sighing breathing, buried in her mass of hair that flowed down wild across her shoulders; dawn sounds of the produce market beyond the shutters, traders getting ready for another day.

She woke early, opening her black eyes wide in restless agitation, long lashes flicking, eyelids closing over those beautiful polished stones; gathering the bed-clothes about the beautiful curve of her young body, shivering, teeth chattering: she who had let men lie over her – she who had served men's base desires.

The first hour she began to sweat, talked fast, restless with a nervous irritability, her eyes afire, could not sit or lie still, paced around like a caged tiger, picking at her cracked fingers, smoothing out the rough folds of her dress.

The second hour she pleaded with me, held both my hands, rolling her eyes, nostrils flared, gabbled on in Cantonese, imploring me to give her some opium to release her to sleep.

The third hour, she lay still on the mat, mouth open, staring up at the ceiling, shaking, teeth chattering, her arms stiff, her legs knotted together, knees up, writhing, pushing backward with her heels. I tried lifting her, but she struggled against me, stiffening, arched her back like a cat as the Chinese devils threw themselves around inside her, bruising her within. Memories of that luscious crimson, open mouth, entrance of the most erotic lips, red lips, wisps of raven hair blowing about their silent moistness, a sad smile hiding tears.

I sponged her face with water, ran my fingers down the double scars on her right cheek, holding her hands tightly behind her back as she burst into yet another of her rages, arms flailing, legs kicking like a mule, bucking, thrusting, trying to bite me, fingers stabbing to gouge out my eye, the fitful sobbing of dry tears, before sitting tight-closed in a ball, shut away, White Poppy.

And so the pattern repeated itself, day after day; eating nothing, her mouth dry, her lips cracked, sipping only the occasional drop of water, sweat running from her skin. She screamed out loud, shouted out in Cantonese: 'I can't stand this any more, take me... take my life. Take me far away from here!' so the Interpreter again translated for me, as White Poppy hit out me in terror with her claws and I believed that everything was lost for ever!

5

When the China dragon opens his eyes it is day and when he shuts them it is night. Kiao: the mystic Dragon, the great and ever-existent Beginning and the End. At night I lay awake staring into the sticky darkness, listening to the wind that stirred memories of old ghosts. The mysterious passions that lead us to break the rules, what are they, where are they from?

I pictured her, the pretty prostitute, using her cosmetics, hair piled high, sitting forward on the high-backed dark-wood chair, polishing her face, applying the smooth white powder, tinting the mask with carmine.

While White Poppy slept she was peaceful: regular sighing punctuated only by the rapid breathing of her dreams, moments of restless twitching, thrashing around the mat, twisting out of the simple Chinese gown, revealing her gorgeous, gentle body; exposing her full, perspiration soaked breasts, caramel-coloured oval nipples, the roundness of her bottom, her tempting naked thighs, feet quite broad and soft, the toes long and straight.

I heard her crying many nights, sobbing uncontrollably into her rags, wanting to comfort her, yet not wanting to risk her claws. The terrors of childhood, black clouds, thunder, waves. Despite that rank and disgusting, dishevelled, dirty mess, I wanted to kiss her, to kiss her all over, wanted to hold her tight in my arms. Attempting to cuddle her as she slept, moving my mouth to cover hers, she woke suddenly, hitting out at me, tearing sharp fingernails into my skin, screaming out the loudest abuse, wailing, howling.

Lying on her side, chin set firm she watched me, her bold eyes following me around the room, frightened, small. Rushing out to her toilet, she brushed past me, and I smelled the sharp odour of her skin, the rank oiliness of her hair, a particular female smell that excited and repulsed.

I heard the sound of horses' hooves, signalled her to keep quiet, pushed my hand across her mouth, felt hot breath escaping through my fingers. It was a sound that made my heart freeze, the sound of men returning to reclaim their prize. She bit me hard, drew blood. The horses passed. She screamed, and she screamed.

6

Twilight dawned on shuttered doors: the blinds, still lightly frosted, were rolled up with the break of day. I felt the need to keep looking over my shoulder, that there was something moving in the shadows of the walls, but White Poppy was fast asleep. I heard it sighing in the trees, branches agitated by the wind. I heard it in the gale outside, restless spirits agitating in the eaves. I heard it in the rasping sighing of her sleeping breath. And amongst those last vestiges of life, I thought it must be Death.

Sitting upright, still, on the rush-mat, White Poppy smiled, almond-eyes striking fire, twinkling back at me, opening out the soft features of her new-flowering beauty. As if wakened from a long sleep she looked around the room, seeing it for the first time, shading her eyes from the bright light that streamed in through the shutters. We shared no common language, had never been introduced, and yet there was language aplenty in her eyes, in her cheeks, on her lips, her whole body spoke to me in its sexual silence.

I watched her sitting outside alone in the sunlight, close by the dwarf plum trees at the entrance to the inner paved court beyond the Interpreter's house. I watched her playing with her thick long black hair, letting it run through her slender fingers like sand, listened to her singing softly to herself, unaware that I was watching her from within, drinking in the details.

In the sunlight her face glowed with power, a golden radiance shining bright about her, wisps of hair blowing about her moist lips as she fanned herself briskly with the sandalwood and silk fan. Leaning forwards, legs tucked up beside her on the split-cane seat, knees together, maternal, she made small movements with her hands, adjusting the folds of her pink silk gown, the beautiful Chinese doll, Yin Hsueh-yen.

Coming in from the Chinese garden, White Poppy hesitated – only a brief moment, but a hesitation nevertheless. Mouth open, cherry lips apart, she stopped and looked across at me: red lips unmoving, still, strand of saliva between their glistening moistness, dew-hinged corners of that most erotic mouth.

And for that isolated moment it seemed that she would kiss me, that she would walk across and press her own hot lips on mine in gratitude for what I had done for her; would press me with her perfect parted lips.

Everything about her seemed to slow as she lay back down on the floor, her body moving in slow motion as she lowered herself on to the mat: her body separate, excluded, out of time totally with all the movement that went on around her. Lying on her back, looking up at the flaking ceiling, she talked all the while, muttered on in Cantonese, then, suddenly, she smiled at me, a wide-mouthed, white-toothed smile that flooded her face with power.

She stood before me, the little Chinese whore, secretive, internal, shrouded within coarse linen, head forward, down-dropping like a poppy, black hair forward, parted slightly at the crown. She stood hands clasped forward in front of her, a ship with sails unfurled, falling in graceful folds, filled and trimmed, looking down at the floor, silent, still.

Head bowed, her hair everything, her shining coal-black hair, tinted, ebon-hued, shining, glowing carbon tinged with the molten copper of the sun, touched with colour from within the room itself – light reflected, washed with blue, tinted purple, iridescent, violet, cobalt, wine. Her head moving, lifting, oriental face revealed, as though some curtains had opened from across a stage, sliding back to reveal the bright properties within. Next act beginning, there, standing before me in her stillness, was a girl I had not seen before, a vision of White Poppy I had not rehearsed. It was like seeing something for the first time, the grasp of certain essential details, the learning of the new: an introduction to that which was foreign in all but her innermost self.

And as her eyes came up over the horizon, opened, blinked, I knew that this was it, that here was the other half who would make my life whole.

'Who are you,' I asked her. But there was no reply, nothing more than a self-satisfied smile, closing her dark eyes before me.

In my mind I kissed her on the mouth, touched my lips against her own, sealed her mouth with mine, held it there until she couldn't breathe, began to choke. I only knew what I had seen about her, what I had heard from her in

Cantonese. I wanted to hear it all first hand from her lips, I wanted to make her struggle, for me, but her secret remained deep within.

The silence was unbearable, the waiting tense. Later, I watched her in the yard doing energetic cartwheels within the confined space, jumping down on her hands, flicking her legs over and over. Finally, she sat with her covered legs, splayed open wide, pressed her head to her knees, each knee in turn. Acrobatic agility, tucking her arms around her knees. There was a bright new sparkle in her almond eyes, and I could see she was on the mend, but only for herself – not for me!

7

Early in December 1838, panic spread through the *han-chien* – those Chinese who kept 'in' with the foreign opium merchants: two thousand brokers, 'pushers' and addicts were arrested. At the hour of the Horse (11.00am) on 12 December, a Chinese official walked into the exercise yard outside The Factories where his men put up an execution cross under the tall American flagpole, to which Ho Lao-chin was to be tied and strangled, condemned to death for running an opium den. A crowd of foreign merchants watched as he arrived, iron chain heavy round his neck, the mandarin's servant giving him one last cynical pipe of opium.

His arms outstretched ready for the cross, a crowd of seamen on the shore leave from the *Orwell* smashed it up, hitting out at the Chinese close by who started throwing stones, the sailors smashing bottles under their naked feet.

The merchants retreated to the Factory buildings and were held there under siege – there was little chance of escape. On 28 March three of the four streets down which we British might escape were walled up by the Chinese. Great gongs sounded all night making sleep impossible, the waterfront crowded with Chinese troops. Out across the Pearl, three concentric lines of boats held an armed guard of 300 Chinese.

Twilight dawned on shuttered doors; the blinds, still lightly frosted, were rolled up with the break of day. White Poppy was sickly, had succumbed to a bad cough. There was the tatty photograph I carried with me. A simple view taken of Dover Harbour, showing tall-masted sailing ships with a party of English women in front, officer's wives, walking forwards. Eliza ran her bright eyes over it, looking at each girlish face in turn; their happy faces, their expensive clothes, making her smile – the upturn of her lips, the swelling of her cheeks, the slight twist of the twin scars above the right. I pointed to the ship and the group of women, and then pointed to Eliza herself, extending my hand to her. She hesitated, looked away, looked back at the photograph. Grabbing it from me she tore it in half.

Picking up both pieces, I stuck them together with a band of gummed paper at the back, and handed the photo to her once more. She hesitated, looked away, looked back at the photograph, back at me, before taking it quickly, holding it tight. She held it close to her face, hand trembling, shaking, looking carefully, closely at the women, the sisterhood, as though remembering something, some fond detail from her past. Her eyes filled suddenly filled with tears, and she handed it back to me, the tears rolling down her cheeks, warm tears, salt tears, a girl's greatest weapon.

There are those who go back on their word; those who make promises they will not keep. The sands of time trickled away, the last grains slipping slowly through life's timer. Throwing some mulberry twigs on the fire, the Interpreter's wife watched the rice pan boiling, the steam lifting the cover, sending out the most delicious seafood-smell, making my mouth water, my stomach grumble in readiness.

8

A knock at the door. My throat went tight. White Poppy looked back at me in panic. The Interpreter's wife entered slowly, put down the refreshing tea, leaving the room as quietly as she had entered. I opened the door, surprised to see a face I recognised, the cold blue eyes, walrus-face, a name I did not know – the opium-merchant from The Factories. He now sported a fashionable thick moustache. He came in, took off his tall hat, stood before me, hands on the table and smiled.

'Good Morning, dear chap, and how are we this morning?'

The perfect speech of the perfect English Gentleman. He extended his right hand and I shook it as a matter of course. It was hot and sticky.

'Fine', I replied, 'Everything is fine.' I looked away from him out of the shuttered window. There was no-one else outside. Apart from the Interpreter's wife, myself and White Poppy there was no-one else inside the house. I prayed that Eliza would not come out of the back room. He of course would know her at once, had been involved in the negotiation for me to see her at the deserted pagoda.

He said 'We have been worried about you, dear chap. Heard you got into a bit of bother with the authorities?' He smiled, I replied.

'Yes, many months in prison, the total loss of my personal freedom, and deportation to Macao. You could say that!' I laughed. Macao, *had* he known about Macao?

He looked deep into my eyes.

'I heard you were no longer around these parts, and I was sorry to hear about the girl.'

He looked around the room, pressing his fingers on the table once more, and began to pace around picking up this and that, his eyes on the door that led into White Poppy's room.

The 'girl', White Poppy: when we had last met she had been the opium addict, the whore. There was no sign of the Interpreter's wife, but I heard her coughing as she prepared the food. The merchant walked towards the door of White Poppy's room.

'Shall we go outside,' he said, suddenly, 'it is far too hot in here?' He moved to open it.

'No', I said, calmly, 'the yard is this way.'

'Of course it is. I am forgetting myself!'

My heart missed a beat he had quite obviously been to the house before, he knew as well as I did the way into the courtyard, but he was curious to see in the room where he thought the boat-girl was.

He changed his mind, opened the door in front of him with a quick and sudden movement. The room was empty; there was neither sight nor sound of its precious occupant. He must have been tipped off about White Poppy's presence there, had he come to take her away? I looked out through the shutter into the street – it was empty.

'Where is the good lady of the house?' he asked, his eyes searching the room, too obvious to go right inside, poking around, looking over the small chest at the end where I knew White Poppy must be hiding, no other way in or out of the room apart from the small shuttered window that led out into the market.

He walked back across the room, and passing out into the yard said a few words in Chinese to the Interpreter's wife. She looked at him, then quickly back at me and got on with her preparation of the vegetables. I knew something was wrong. Of course she smiled at me as we passed but looked even more pleased than usual as we walked by her into the cold but sunny yard, the pale winter sun poking through a layer of thin cloud.

They had found out, they would be coming for her. I would now have to go through the pretence in the hope that White Poppy would not stir from her cramped hiding place until the merchant left the house. She was doomed, we were both doomed before even we had begun.

He had heard: he knew the ship on which I was planning to leave. Did he know also that the whore would be coming with me? I saw the bees swarming towards the honey-pot: the Brotherhood hot on her trail, the fierce land-pirates eager for revenge.

9

The Indian Basket Feat: A large oblong basket was brought in and placed on a low stand so as to be clear of the platform. The magician entered, holding a drawn sword in one hand, dragging in a young lady by the other.

He said.

'She has offended me and must be punished.'

He proceeded to blindfold her. She ran off the stage in terror, and the attendants brought her back and forced her to climb into the basket. The lid was closed upon her. The magician was angry now, had worked himself up into a fury. Suddenly he started to thrust his sword again and again into the basket. The girl's screams were at first hideously loud, but at length dwindled away to a dying groan. The magician raised his sword in triumph; it was dripping in blood.

There was a long and silent pause, and hushed silence filled the hall; the only sound to be heard was swallowing in dry mouths, and the hissing of the lit gas in the jets around the walls. The magician wiped his sword and addressed the spectators.

'Ladies and gentlemen, I fear you imagine that I have hurt the young lady. Pray disabuse your minds of the idea. She had disobeyed me,' he paused 'therefore I determined to punish her by giving her a fright.' He raised his voice. 'The fact is she was not in the basket when I thrust my sword into it. You don't believe me? I will show you.'

He turned the basket over to face us, and we could see that it was now quite empty.

'Should you want further proof, here is the young lady herself to reassure you.'

And the girl came tripping in from the rear of the hall, pulling off the blindfold and smiling.

The merchant stayed and stayed and we chatted over tea, and I thought of White Poppy suffocating in the box, the pain in her contorted limbs. Was it he who had watched over me, was it one of his men who had checked my every move in Canton, who had trailed me since first stepping on Chinese soil? At last he picked up his hat, extended his hand once more.

'Well, good luck, dear chap! Hope all goes well for your journey back to England.'

Saying goodbye to him at the door, shaking his clammy hand, I felt physically sick. How much time was there left? It would be dark in less than an hour and I had to get

White Poppy away from the house, from Canton – there would never be another chance like this.

She was unconscious in the chest, her limbs contorted in blue pain. I hauled her out, placed her down on the mat, gently massaged her back to life. Coming round she was shaking, frightened and hurt. She kept her eyes away from mine, looked everywhere but straight at me. It was already getting dark outside. I pointed to her belongings. We would have to leave soon, before the Interpreter returned. He would know, he would understand. I assumed it was his wife that had given us away, the sailor and the whore!

I created a diversion in the kitchen, set fire to some oil; acrid smoke filling the air we made our escape.

10

The Chinese basket had been packed with lotus leaves above the horrible surprise inside – the hacked-up torso, butchered body of the common whore, complete with tattoo, sent back by the boat from Hong-Kong. With the substitute 'White Poppy dead, the real White Poppy should have been free. I watched her turning her eyes skywards, rolling her dark eyes as she ran, viewing the dark heavens which contain the very source and secret of life, eyes like two bright stars.

The spider shifts once in the gathering darkness, one last movement in the corner of its web, agitating the threads; orange sun setting in the West, it waits with infinite patience.

I had thought about it carefully, showed Eliza the drawing, gestured her to what she was to do. The Chinese beauty was to shave her head at the front, knotting a male plait at the back. She would be Hua Mulan, heroine of the Five Dynasties (420-588): her praises sung in the Song of

Mulan. So much did the princess love her father that, when called to battle against the Tartars (and finding himself unable to go), she went in his place for twelve years disguised as a man.

She moved her head slowly, eyes full of contempt, glared at me through her slit eyes, coughing all the time. She shook her head in defiance. No, she would not do it! When I was not looking, White Poppy hacked off her hair.

11

Letter to Queen Victoria, March 1839

The Way of Heaven is fairness to all; it does not suffer us to harm others in benefit to ourselves. Men are alike in this all the world over: that they cherish life and hate what endangers life. Your country lies twenty thousand leagues away; but for all that the Way of Heaven holds good for you as for us, and your instincts are not different from ours; for nowhere are there men so blind as not to distinguish between what brings life and what brings death, between what brings profit and what does harm.

Our Heavenly Court treats all within the Four Seas as one great family; the goodness of our great Emperor is like Heaven that covers all things. There is no region so wild or so remote that he does not cherish and tend it. Ever since the port of Canton was first opened, trade has flourished. For some hundred and twenty or thirty years the natives of the place have enjoyed peaceful and profitable relations with the ships that come from abroad. Rhubarb, tea, silk are all valuable products of ours

But there is a class of evil foreigner that makes opium and brings it for sale, tempting fools to destroy themselves merely in order to reap profit. Formerly the number of opium smokers was small; but now the vice has spread far and wide and the poison penetrated deeper and deeper. If there are some foolish people who yield to this craving to their own detriment, it is they who have brought upon themselves their own ruin, and in a country so populous and flourishing, we can well do without them.

But our great, unified Manchu Empire regards itself as responsible for the habits and morals of its subjects and cannot rest content to see any of them become victims to a deadly poison. For this reason we have decided to inflict very severe penalties on opium dealers and opium smokers, in order to put a stop for ever to the propagation of this vice.

Your Majesty has not before been thus officially notified, and you may plead ignorance of the severity of our laws. But I now give my assurance that we mean to cut off this harmful drug for ever.

A plump man of medium height with heavy black moustache and thin beard, Lin the Clear Sky (Lin Tse-hsü) reached the walled city of Canton on 10 March 1839. Two weeks later, Captain Elliot, the British Superintendent of Trade, sailed up to the waterfront below The Factories, having avoided the blockade of the Pearl. Elliot hoisted the Union Flag, and another siege of The Factories began, the Chinese servants scurrying away like cockroaches from a fire. How close we had been to escape!

BOOK IV THE VALLEY SPIRIT NEVER DIES

Canton, China
1839

1

Sight does not depend on open eyes, rather on the courage to see. Blindness is the absence of light; stupidity is the inability to see. When the hare and its companion race across the dale, who can say, 'The female's this, and that one is the male?' Chinese folk song.

The bright moon pearl is concealed in the oyster, the dragon is there. The Chinese believe that the dragon's skin has five colours. He moves like a spirit; he wishes to be small and he becomes like a silkworm; great, and he fills all below heaven; he desires to rise, and he reaches the ether; he desires to sink, and he enters the deep fountains. The times of his changing are not fixed, his rising and descending are undetermined; he is called a god (or spirit).

All China within is navigated, and run through with rivers which intersect and water it all, such that you may sail and navigate boats to the far ends of the land. Almost all cities are built along the banks of rivers that flow every way to the sea: there is nothing more natural than to travel by boat, and certainly (as a seaman) nothing more natural to me.

We had to leave Canton, and much was arranged with the Interpreter's help, for which I paid much silver. As a European there would be no way I would be allowed to leave Canton, but unless I escaped across China for Shanghai then my cause would be lost. For every hundred leagues more that I might manage to put between us and Canton, represented a dilution of the chance that I would be known for who I really was: intelligence carries only so far (and of what interest could I be to those Chinese in distant provinces). Anyway I hatched my plan, and it all depended on the White Poppy – without her absolutely none of it could work. First I had to keep myself covered totally, hunched up in pilgrim disguise, while White Poppy spun some story about my awful disfigurement, the fear of disease from my pus-running eyes. I could only just see out of my good eye, through the rags bandaged about my head, and White Poppy led me along slowly, as I followed dutifully behind. We would travel much by dark, within the darkness of our souls.

2

A good runner leaves no track. January, the coldest month, the weather chilly but fine. We had on heavily padded jackets, layers of warm clothing underneath. I bought us a boat trip. Sailing slowly down the Pearl, making the journey I had not thought possible, the crew poling the small craft to compensate for the lack of wind, we passed the last of the houseboats. The decorative wind-vane, a red sword and mirror, unmoving at the masthead, the mat-sail furled.

Night falling, the moon shining bright on the grey water sprinkled with stars, lights winking, the orange fires of simple homesteads, the blazing flares of the Grand Junk were now distant. Supper was freshly caught fish from lines let down into the water. Accommodation was basic, the after cabin of the captain, our bunks in the centre, and a communal room forward. Heat was from a stove, but the coal was damp, smoke lying heavily around us. White Poppy began to cough.

Dressed as a young man, feminine form beneath loose robes, felt cap and gown, men's shoes, breasts bound flat with bands of coarse linen, hair cropped at the front, head shaven, long plait hanging at the back; twin scars above her right cheek, she passed as a youth, although she smelled female to me, the boat-girl underneath.

Later the wind blew up around the floating boat, howling through paper-filled cracks, freezing us in our separate bunks, curled up beneath scant covers in the dangerous darkness. I listened to the chattering of her teeth, woken frequently by her coughs, male gruffness to her voice. There was a sense of inevitability about what was coming, but I believe nothing is really predetermined after all – that there is always a choice to be made, even if it is the other person who makes that choice.

3

Passing the last of the flat fields, entering the territory of the secluded valleys, mist-veiled peaks distant, we continued on foot, making good progress along narrow pathways, simple mountain tracks. Canton now far behind, Shanghai even further ahead! I watched her as we walked: the threat of the unsaid. I wonder about her inner feelings now, her continued suffering, her pain? What lay ahead for us then – escape from China, glorious freedom, or Punishment – Torture – Death? I caught sight of White Poppy's black eyes; she was watching me, looking me up and down as I walked before her. Staring at her, she looked away, looked back down at the ground in front of her shuffling feet. And I knew why she was worth it, why she made me smile inside.

Looking out at the stars, thinking of her tear-wet eyes, I knew that White Poppy had nothing but contempt for me. It began to snow. The snow continued unceasing, dark hour upon hour, pressing down under its weight, covering the way we had come; snowflakes dancing past the trees, burying the trail before us with its dense white thickness. She coughed all the while, crying out in pain.

'Shanghai': I drew the Kanji with a stick in the snow. She nodded, blotted out the Chinese characters with her rough-bound feet. Walking slowly across the frost-bittern wilderness, watched over by the naked, skeleton trees, pointing snow-clad branches white against the evening sky, crossing the mirror-lake, we approached the glowing orange lights.

For my part, a soul had been saved. Yet for her part, White Poppy would not want to leave behind the wider family, the fatherland of their souls. She looked distant, lost: were her thoughts back with the houseboats, forest lanes of gaudy red and green, did she hear still (as I did) the noisy clutter of sampans and junks crossing the harbour, agitating the dark waters of the Pearl? Where the water is shallow the fish will not stay; where the wood has few trees, the birds will not sing. Few monks lived in the ancient sheltered temple, its rooms with the remnants of dried grass that grew every summer on the floors; few travellers crossed the ruined bridge then rimed with frost, a stretch of silver, watered, ice against a backdrop of frozen willows, their burdened branches moaning through the wind.

There was a creeping inner passion, a tingling excitement spreading up from my loins. Here was my soul mate. Here in this heathen land was the treasure that would transform my past. Here was the woman who would give me fine sons. In her eyes there was such mystery, such depth, such honesty. I could never love another more. But she was Chinese. And, yet, why should she want me? Why should she give up China, her home, to be with me? I wasn't sure, yet I knew that being with her was the right thing to do: the salvation of her soul, the Christian conversion of one sweet soul. I saw it in her eyes – she would be free. She would be mine, God said so, and I believed Him.

For a split second I saw it in the boat-girl's eyes, and I believed what it was I saw. We sat alone, the first time we had been alone, and I caught sight of her eyes: what we can know about a person because of their eyes. And her mouth, and the fragrance of her skin, and the very different fragrance of her sex. We sat alone, and she shone – her hair glistened, her skin shone like polished alabaster, and her eyes sparkled with new light, catching its brightness like the dewdrops glistening on a spider's web against the rising morning sun. Her mouth, that pink softness, wet Chinese lips that mirrored that which remained covered below. But she didn't smile, did nothing to elicit any response. She just *was* - the most perfect creation - who would herself one day create.

When away from people, she walked ahead of me, head down, reverent, gave me a lengthy stare, a gaze that went right through me, that touched me at the core. I saw only her eyes that peeped out from her own pilgrim hood, but that was enough to show the danger, the wolf in the wood. Then she smiled, and her dark eyes filled with new warmth, and the wolf was gone back into the trees, her slit eyes brimming with new fire.

The Chinese girl was my only interest now – that and taking her safely out of China. I had never had anything of my own before, no one that I could call my own.

4

Two strangers travelling blind. Chinese spring begins some time between mid-January and mid-February depending on the actions of the moon: the wind lessening the frost, chrysanthemums sprout, willows bud, and the plum, apricot and mountain-peach blossom. The Second Month (March) there were already some rainy days, the water pouring in through dilapidated ornamented roofs. Eliza's cough had not improved.

The coastal Bhuddist sanctuary was far from comfortable, but safe. One of the many temples, Bhuddist, Taoist (Dowist) – Tao, the Supreme Spirit - that are little more than dingy haunts of bats and spiders; assorted gilded figures seated in rows along the walls within the faded buildings, pictures of the Bhuddist hells, the beating, the burning, the splashing with hot oil for those that succumb to the pleasures of the senses: incense-burning, closely-shaven monks dressed in coarse grey, walking chanting to the beat of a drum, the ringing of a triangle and bells.

It poured hard every day, soaking us, chilling us inside the scant buildings in the sodden land. Yü yün: rain and cloud, the intercourse between the heavy marching skies and the wet-running, fertile earth. Rain dripping from moss on deserted steps, far thunder beyond willows trailing in the lake, drops drumming down on every floating lily pad (flowers closed tight waiting for the sun) until the savage rain was done.

We breakfasted on rice noodles boiled with sliced cucumber of sorts and beaten eggs. The waiting was boring, and Eliza was increasingly restless, given herb tea for her persistent cough, a pungent concoction of rhubarb, liquorice and ginseng. God must be getting tired of my prayers! We sat cross-legged, watching a silent monk on his knees before an altar, shaking a bundle of bamboo sticks in a round container until one fell out; watched him check the number on it against the temple's printed texts, to see what the number said would occur – a chance event. When they had finished calling to the Bhuddas the monks supplied water to wash our faces, served up deep-fried coiled noodle cakes, 'hairy ear' pastries, cooked red dates, and soft dates, four dishes of fruit and nuts to go with our tea, and as much pancake, bean-curd soup, and rice-pudding as we wished.

The kiss impulse is strong, and White Poppy's full lips became the focus of my attention, the moist opening stretched taut each time she crouched down. We spent hours in prayer, played finger-games and dice, walked round the rain-soaked gardens between heavy showers, where we stood together by a bubbling fountain of green jade, hidden by wild persimmon trees, in which I thought I saw her kiss my reflection.

I wished I couldn't smell her, but when she moved close to me I breathed in her femininity, sniffed the air when she passed me, when she left her salty jasmine fragrance suspended in the breeze. Each day I waited for the moment when I should smell the trickle of fresh sweat, the fragrant odours of her herb-sweetened breath, natural oiliness of her hair, the animal smells that aroused animal passions.

The twisting of her scarred face, the pouting of her sleeping lips, the boat-girl: White Poppy cried out, sobbing in her sleep, weeping for something lost to her. But now I had found her could I keep her? The taming of the dragon? That battle had only just begun.

5

Forbidden – everything we had done together was forbidden. And yet it wasn't working: we irritated each other. She did nothing to help me, nothing to help *us*. She showed nothing but contempt for me – the look in her eyes, the heavy set of her mouth, the way she turned her back on me, the way she would not look at me as we ate. Her coughing caused great irritation, too, and we lost hours of sleep on our separate wadded mats.

Dressed as a young man, she sat shrouded in her loose Chinese robes. She stood out in the garden, surrounded by the blossom, and I could not forget that she was female underneath, that all of her thoughts were those of a woman.

My main concern now was getting through China with the minimum of inconvenience, of taking White Poppy by ship from China to India and from there back to Europe, Dover and then London. I had great plans for us both. However, the whore's main concern seemed to be to sit around deep in thought, staring still at the fire in front of her, watching the burning and final smouldering of the logs. I didn't really know what she had left behind: I had many clues as to what her life had been in Canton, but because she spoke almost nothing but the most basic English the rest was just a guess.

So many times it seemed that we'd be discovered because of the Poppy Whore, who seemed to be working against me. If I went and sat in one corner of the room (near to her), she would sit in the other; walking across the garden to sit with her by the pool, she would walk slowly away from me to the shaded trees where she sat on her own away from the sun. Her response to everything was mechanical: she marched on like a soldier.

White Poppy, Yin Shooeh-yen: prostitute used to that male-controlled perversion; she who as a woman in China was powerless. Dressed as she was, like a male, I reasoned she had the potential for more power now than ever before, would receive more male respect than she ever had as a woman. And yet I didn't know – I couldn't ask her, because she spoke no useful English, and I knew little Cantonese. I showed her kindness and affection, yet she shunned me, wouldn't look at me. It seemed that she was punishing me, that I was having to pay for something I had done that I didn't know about.

There was no love lost between us, no real friendship, but we each depended on the other for our escape, and despite our differences I supposed we looked out for each other: she was my talisman, saved me from harm, and I did the same for her! It was an unspoken code. But if we were stopped, if ever we should be caught together, then the end would be final and death would be our joint reward. Everything that had happened between us, everything that had been for the two of us together, was forbidden, taboo!

Was that a glint of pleasure I saw in her Chinese eyes, a sparkle of humour shining out from beneath her covering hood? White Poppy's hypnotic gaze – her 'tricks' to captivate potential captors: did she class me as one of those? *Do you see?* Her eyes said from deep within her pilgrim hood: wicked, mysterious, magical, and in a weird way, free.

A bright April morning, perspiring in the shade, mosquitoes whining in the humid air, crickets chirping, frogs croaking in the sunlit sparkling weeping-willow edged pools, we did the last of our chores, settled-up in silver and left.

Travel by sea would be quickest. We looked for a sea-going junk, walked by a floating theatre, large junk moored to the river bank, intrigued by the grotesquely-painted faces, the gold gods, the sacred red, the evil white, colour of death. The morality play, conflict between good and evil for the human soul. We watched the traditional classic Chinese dance, horizontal rotations, curves around the circle; long sleeves, red clothes, coloured fans emphasising the movement of the arms and skill of the waist, running around the stage, wind and fire wheel, spinning round, stressing opposites of circulation - withdrawing before advancing, bending before rising, dropping low before rotating high.

I watched the pleasure in her eyes that peeped out from beneath her hood; saw the movements on her lips – the boat-girl. I wished she could talk to me, that we shared a common language, but the only linking bond was that we were, in truth, both escaping refugees.

A dispute resolved, the trading junk's owners having been divided as to whether or not we should sail with them (a decision made easier by the giving of silver), we left the South China coast on a large triple-masted Hainan trader, heading up the coast for Swatow with a cargo of salt fish. Peaked mainsail kept flat to the wind, stiffened by six battens of bamboo, we pulled into the sheltered bay of the Devil's Claw.

Half asleep in my bunk I heard footsteps outside, running and shouting, put my hand on my knife. Grabbing White Poppy by the shoulder, a hand across her mouth, I shook her awake. In darkness, we bundled our few bits together. Beyond the oiled paper screen I saw shapes moving in the shadows, a distant line of fire-brands snaking their way to the boat. The crew had been drinking, had given us away. We were not alone. We saw boats moving out towards us, torches ablaze, heard more shouting in Chinese as they realised our escape. White Poppy swam ahead of me, slowly, quietly, the ripples of cold water flowing gently behind her.

Gliding against sharp rocks, we slipped in amongst them where we could. In the pale moonlight, her lips were cool blue, her face silver-white. Her hands were cold, but she pulled away from me, once-broken fingers sliding through mine. She looked right through me, her eyes unfocused, sad. A blinding light, the most tremendous bang; gunpowder exploding, massive report echoing round the rocks – a pirate schooner having made its way to the trader – saw the sinking of the first boats that headed out from the coast, lights dying suddenly in the sea. The Brotherhood? The other boat rowed its way back to the shore, bits of body floating all around.

6

White Poppy was sick, coughed violently from the seawater in her lungs; put her head down between her knees. In the dead silence that followed, the water lapping the rocks, it sounded like gunshot across the sea. I held my breath, strained to hear any other sound: the lights moving away from the shore dwindled and died, we were quite safe. Eliza vomited once more on the rocks, and I stroked the back of her head, a mere child.

The boatmen had been 'talking' in signs: the secret sign, pointing in turn to the sky, earth and heart. In the Kwangsi Mountains, the foothill jungle, the Heaven and Earth Society (the Triad) kept alive a sentiment of nostalgia for the Ming Dynasty. Bound together by secret oath to overthrow the Manchus, the Hakka people were new spirits in the slowly rising tide of the Christian God worship. These roving bands of blacksmiths, stonemasons, miners, former salt and opium smugglers, Miao tribesmen among who opium was now forbidden. The Hakka women do not bind their feet.

An altar with tapering candles, no cross, three cups of tea, three bowls of rice, incense with hymns and prayers, fire crackers exploding, beginning to 'worship' the one God, the Chinese Protestant God, *Shang Ti*, Emperor Above, in a long black robe, with golden beard. White Poppy, too, had been talking in signs.

7

Canton lords it over a delta plain, rice-fields stretching as far as the eye can see, criss-crossed by innumerable creeks and canals, with the distant sails of hidden ships (canals enclosed by embankments in summer to prevent high-water flooding), above which the Si kiang and its tributaries flow through narrow valleys and twisting gorges, flowing around obstructing shallows, dropping sharply in white rapids, water lowest from early December to mid-March.

White Poppy had to let me walk next to her, but made sure that there was always some little distance between us as she led the way. She did not want to notice me, seemed deep inside some inner thoughts. She kept muttering to herself, the same words over and over in Cantonese – head down, wandering ever onward.

Drifting into sleep, resting lightly beneath the trees, I imagined her, as she would be. Lying still, watching the hidden China whore, her eyes were like tiger's eyes, cat's eyes adapted for night vision – big with large pupils – glowing from the flames. The makeshift fire crackled heartily. Clasping her fingers between her knees, I caught sight of the missing little fingertip of her left hand. In the distant darkness, her face shone from the flames, the redness of her lips, the blackness of her eyebrows, her gorgeous, glistening, half-closed eyes. No smile. Unholy light. Snake eyes heavy, ruby-dribbled lips. Wet lips, whore's lips, where had they been?

We passed canal after canal, crossed dyke after dyke, river after river, listening to the sad slop of sodden cloth on stone, well-covered women beating out their washing, beating out their sorrows, at the water's edge on massive washing-polished stones; watching fisherman cast threaded nets to draw in struggling silver fish.

We criss-crossed the Canton delta at a snail's pace, floating past paddies still cracked and dry where there would be wet rice growing in great sweeps before the purple distant mountains, stepped terraces climbing cultivated hill-sides to the aquamarine sky. We travelled great distances, but that journey never went as far as the journey in my mind when successive 'doors' were shut despite the opened 'blinds'. Freedom and space, it was a wondrous experience, but for how long?

I caught sight of White Poppy's black eyes; she was watching me, looking me up and down as I walked before her. Staring at her, she looked away, looked back down at the ground in front of her shuffling feet. And I knew why she was worth it, why inside she made me smile.

Leaving behind the last of the flat fields, entering the territory of the secluded valleys, mist-veiled peaks distant, we continued on foot, making good progress along narrow pathways, simple mountain tracks. Canton now far behind, Shanghai even further ahead.

8

Spring is the time for kites, the best season for flying. At the time of the Pure Brightness Festival (the beginning of April), it is customary to pay respects to one's ancestors, people begin their spring outings, fly their kites.

South of the Yangtze (Yandtze) River, the climate rainy and humid, the wind is mild, and soft-winged kites float upwards through the air – insects, birds, waterfowl – tissue wings that flap as the kites rise: red-throated swallows, several hundred strung together spread out high above bridges, where children compete in sending off their own.

Look at us! If she was caught – what would they do to her – what would happen to me – how would they torture her – kill her? How would they dispose of me?

In life many roads are little more than tracks that wind through places previously unseen, that rise higher than the clouds, that drop lower than the sea: some lead to great cities, others terminate abruptly at rivers or streams. I have done my best to explore those roads left unregarded by the rest, roads that seemed to me worth following, roads that ran as deep into my own mind.

We had a choice: there were always choices – to go this way or that, to continue or to turn back? Oh how the blind lead the blind! I chose a narrow path that led upwards out of the valley, would soon reach the highest point to see where we were headed, cool wind tugging at our clothes, hills running away from us in every direction, bobbled land flowing distant, sun shining brilliantly, clothing the far hill sides in deep shadow, in awe of the China that raced ahead.

White Poppy pushed back her shoulders, set her proud chin forwards, strutted like the man. She passed her time singing softly to herself, head low, staring down at her feet, mail plait swinging sorrowfully behind. She never showed signs of complaint. Rock-grazed, sore, we made our way through the dangerous mountains, and each day I noticed more of the woman growing from the girl within. Were we being followed? From the way she kept glancing about her, I assumed we might be.

Much of our travel was by boat along the China rivers. I had been warned by the Interpreter many years before about the taboos of pilgrims sailing: how it made the boatmen really angry if pilgrims sat on the gangplank, or sat with their arms wrapped around their legs (that would bring stormy weather), and, 'finishing eating,' he said, 'do not put your chopsticks across the rice bowl' (that would cause further delay).

We had left Canton up the Pei kiang or North River towards Samshui (Three Rivers), travelled slowly by boat to Shiuchow: travelled hundreds of miles on to Chenchow, 'oldest' city in China, through the forested mountains of Hunan province, along the Lui ho to Henhchowfu and the Sian kiang to the capital Changsha, City of Iron Gates, the river running wide into Tung t'ing Lake: saw the awesome Yolu Shan, celebrated ancient university hill – narrow, twisting streets paved with rutted granite.

We walked in amongst the street-traders, travelling fruit-sellers; walked through them slowly, carefully, in the search for food; drawn into them by the spiced aroma from cauldrons of soup, sweet odours seeping from the food-market under the covered way; strong-smelling black roots and pepper-like powdered spices, dried yellow fungi, sacks of medicinal bark, piles of snakes dried rigid like sticks, powdered horn, bags overflowing with seahorses. In shallow bins before fish-stalls, yellow-headed tortoises climbed over each other's backs, beyond racks of leathered birds. We passed groups of men talking, crouching in that characteristic Chinese pose.

Breakfast, like every meal, was basic – wild fruits, herbs, berries, nuts; drinking from freshly-cracked raw birds' eggs (sometimes cooked over a fire), small fish caught on a simple line with a hook of bent wire – fish skewered on bark-stripped wood and then baked. We stole crops and fruit, helped ourselves to vegetables and salads, begged rice-cake, hot tea. If we were lucky we were given salt fish, dried meat, a lump of hard-pressed cheese, bowls of cooked rice, milk.

We walked through loose pine needles that stuck into us, pricked our skin, found there way into our clothes; through scattered chestnuts, leaf-covered forest floors, bitten severely from mosquitoes, covered our exposed faces and hands with mud (which also kept out the sun). Water: spiritual cleansing and rebirth.

White Poppy woke early, stretched, yawned – stretching out her arms above her head, forcing out her legs; rubbing her eyes with the back of her hands. She urinated behind trees, or squatted in long grass. She bathed her face with cold water on waking, showered beneath running stream water, under waterfalls when she could, washed her plaited black hair, bathed naked in shaded copse pools, swimming across the deepest water with strength – when I looked away, pretended that I did not see her wetted loveliness; water running in rivulets, dripping from her sallow body, running down her arms and her legs; water dripping from her Chinese fingers; water drops sparkling on her firm buttocks and around the dark nipples and her breasts; drying herself quickly, tucking away her freshly-scrubbed female skin. She rubbed her teeth with betel nuts, massaged her gums with small pieces of soft wood. Her fingernails broke naturally, were kept short by rough terrain, although she removed the rough edges with a granite-like stone. Like a cicada escaping from its chrysalis.

I watched the spider spinning her web, weaving her way up and down the tender-leafed twigs, letting herself down on a thread, pulling herself back up, across, down, joining her fragile sticky net across guide threads exuded from her body already. Withdrawing to her dark space, crouched together in a ball, she waited for the fatal pull.

9

Up and then down again, up and then down. In the valley below us isolated buildings lay huddled at the edge of the great grey plain that stretched back towards a familiar narrow band of distant, fertile fields merging into the rippling mid-day haze. A dusty goat track winding back down to the valley bottom, the hillside descended steeply, stepped terraces abandoned, clambering down to where the naked hillsides began, slopes covered with sharp rocks. I intended that we walk up the mountain path ahead of us, knocked her arm, guided her towards the gravel track with a gentle movement of my hand.

White Poppy stopped, turned and glared at me. She stood before me, little Chinese whore, secretive, internal, shrouded within. I felt impulsive, aroused.

'Yin Shooeh-yen,' I said, quickly, 'I want you.'

She knew what I was saying; I knew she understood enough to know what I meant. She stared back at me blankly. She hit out at me, pushed me away with full force: the response was sudden, angry, fierce, and she shouted at me, her eyes no more than angry slits, her mouth contorted in pain.

So we fought, so we argued, as we made our way into the hills – we disagreed about which way to go, what to eat, when to eat, and yet we needed each other – needed my religion to survive. I began to regret such a retreat – I should have left Macao without her, should have returned home, then, to England.

But how peaceful White Poppy looked when asleep: what softness found its way to her dirty face, when she twitched, when she smiled within. I thanked god for her. It was my intention to seduce her, but to give something timeless back to her in return. I put her first always, let her have food and water when there was only enough for one, let her sleep when one of us had to stay awake: yet at the same time she was tricking me, eating more food when she thought I was asleep, drinking more water when she thought I wasn't aware. She became moody, withdrawn, gave me every reason to hate her, gave me nothing but trouble. Many days I thought what the hell, let her suffer, let her wither and die, leave her to the wolves.

However, no element is superior to others – water, wood, fire, earth, metal – a balance is maintained in nature: although water can put out fire, fire can make water boil! The whore was the one, who could speak Cantonese, and enough Mandarin, who knew China from within. And so we continued, each talking the language of our own: neither understanding anything of the other. Lips tight, she smiled at me in contempt, her black-bronzed eyes shining with perverse delight. Her eyes, her damned penetrating Chinese eyes that upset me, burning right through. Hell fires.

10

The wind blew behind us, wafted strong scents down the mountain paths, fragrant mountain blooms carried high on the air, intermingled with something else, perspiring female flesh. I walked on, not saying a word, just chanting, singing, repeating my Christian prayers. I wished she would walk in front again, would change her pace, but she wandered slowly behind with the rhythm of the skies, ribbon clouds threaded high and moving only slowly with the breeze that agitated the sheltered places, caused the edges of her hood to flap against her single-plaited hair. I tried to walk faster: she had set up the pace like a donkey treading its sure-foot weary way up the mountain path that leads to the end of its life, ever mindful of falling boulders, feet careful between areas of loose stone and rocks. And we kept up that pace till nightfall, and did so every single day.

White Poppy, whose heart was an unfailing fountain of courage, I watched her pilgrim lips. When the sun was highest, the ground at its driest, I wanted her lips. I watched them moving as she walked. I wanted to drink from them, to sip from those lips with mine. I watched them in the shadows, shrouded by her male hood. And on occasion it would allow entrance to the sun, and her lips glistened, inviting, moist, soon dried by the searing heat. I watched the movements of her tongue as she sang to herself, as her nostrils flared, her eyes sparkling with liquid light, but that dried too in the glare of the sun. And she blinked, and she turned further inwards, took herself away as she frequently did, and her eyes glazed over, and she walked in a trance, foot following foot following foot. And I wondered what she could be thinking as outwardly we walked travelling pilgrim man and 'boy' close together but inwardly such a distance apart?

11

It was unmistakeably a tiger that I saw – bold, barred, dark-striped patterning extending down the sides of its body, ochre coat colour, underparts almost white. The

South China tiger is a large and solitary cat, highly prized in Chinese medicine. In the more inaccessible mountains they live well away from human habitation. Tigers are considered to be the most dangerous of animals.

I saw the tiger again distant, watched it striding to the trees where it blended into the undergrowth beneath; watched the last parting of the giant grass, which reformed after it, and it was silent, gone. Yet, turning the corner, the tiger stood facing us, sharp teeth, roaring – an elderly female, blocking our path.

White Poppy did something strange. She stopped still, eyed it, psyched it; fought it with her mind. Punching, with tiger's eyes, she stood legs apart, bending her knees, fists clenched, palms up to her waist, held her breath before expelling it with force. Head moving slowly, she followed her prey, watched as the tiger thought about running towards her: her slant eyes intense, very black. The tiger walked away. One quick glance back at us and it was gone.

How much pleasure can be wrung from pain? Was that a glint of pleasure I saw in her eyes, a sparkle of humour shining out from beneath the covering of her hood? As the sail unfolds and captures the spirit of the wind, was I at last beginning to see the woman that lay beneath the mask, the woman that had stolen my heart?

12

In the hill country fascinating Buddhist monasteries occupy the most beautiful and sheltered spots, grow sharply from the land. The hills are dragons. The Chinese do not build on their tails. The Buddhist temple with its three shrines built at different stages up the mountainside, where we climbed the winding path and steps to the upper shrine beside a roaring waterfall, where we walked along the last of the village ridges beside the many grave plots shaded with sweet gum and camphor trees, the early-morning air heavy with the wood-smoke fanning out across the valley.

As night guests, intruders in secret, we gave the monks money for new building; they asked us no questions, accepted us for what we were. Leaving White Poppy at prayer in the shaded rural temple, like a lighthouse across its stretch of silver sand, I walked away through the herb garden that clung to the edge of the beached whale of a hill, sat down on a sandstone seat in a crescent of red and yellow flowering shrubs, beside massive stalked rhubarb-like stems, canopied leaves shading me from the sun.

White Poppy sat out on the steps, my *Bible* open on her knees. I watched the intensity of her youth, the slow movement of her hand across the page: she would not understand one word, and yet she recognised that this was from the culture towards which she was being drawn. She placed there one of the muted golden-yellow flowers that grew nearby on the sun-baked rocks, shut the Holy Book around it, saw me watching – tucked it behind her.

I said sorry to God but the temptation had been too great, and I had been very patient. I said a prayer: that I believed it was the way it was meant to be. There was a purpose in everything, and every purpose was a part of the overall plan. I looked deep into Eliza's eyes and 'said' sorry, but no word left my lips, not an expression crossed my face. I stared into her eyes, and she stared back, before looking away, before turning her eyes back down towards the ground.

Eliza walked on ahead, White Poppy, not looking at me at all. We had been sleeping in broken-coal-barked trees to avoid detection at night: sleeping near but apart. Striding up slowly through the naked landscape, sun-bleached trees, we pilgrims both, entered the sanctuary of another towered Buddhist monastery; pinkish-red buildings, bright gold-fringed pagoda, snuggled against a hillside festooned with garlands of pink peonies, crimson azaleas.

Passing through the outer boundary wall, walking along gravel beside a trickling stream, beneath trees of blooming cassia, we entered an ornate carved gateway, knocked the smooth polished stone at the hole in the wall.

Gate creaking open, a young monk emerged, took us into the inner court, main temple buildings on all sides, fragrant, formal garden stretching before us with tranquil pavilions, lotus pools of liquid sunlight, cicadas singing. Given fresh fruit, rice-cakes and white wine, linen covers for our beds, he left us alone in the guest-room with its moon window that looked out over a great statue of the Bhudda. That night the wind roared, after which it rained solidly for weeks. I was bored, wanted to get away, to sail again across the China Sea.

13

The first Opium War started in 1839 when the Chinese government confiscated opium warehouses in Canton. June 3 1839, the destruction of the opium began near the coastal village of Chen k'ou where three large trenches were dug, lined with flagstones and timber, surrounded by a fence of bamboo. The cakes and balls of opium, broken open, thrown into these trenches, covered in 2 feet of water, salt and lime tipped in; the stinking, decomposing sludge stirred and drained into the creek running down to the sea. Though opium was secreted away, stored, buried underground, hidden in chests disguised as coffins, laid in false tombs.

The murder at K(G)owloon on 7 July (1839) changed the lives of the rich British merchants and their families: Chinese servants leaving them, they were forced to flee their luxurious homes along the Macao ridge, in a flotilla of small craft, to live crowded on-board ship in the harbour of Hong Kong. The British traders were incensed – driven also from The Factories at Canton, their Opium confiscated without compensation.

'War will follow,' was the word on the street. 'With the British, there will be war.'

No matter what we search for in our endeavours, the true treasure lies hidden within. My own religion brought me danger, the sign of the Cross, yet I stuck firm by my decision, for God was the only way. If we were being watched, if we were to be caught, we would not be returned, but would be tortured and put to death for our sins. Potential terror at every turn, we could never truly rest. It seemed that we had been left alone, though I was beginning to feel more uneasy with every passing day, that something was about to jump out and surprise us at every hidden turn.

The Six Month (July), day was again giving way to night, the mountain forests were stark and still, not a wisp of cloud in the sky, when there appeared a white cloud of extremely fine texture, like blossoming white cotton fluff.

White Poppy, fragrant whore, rose amongst thorns. My patience had gone – I felt caged even as I walked, prisoner to my thoughts that ranged restlessly inside my head, and looking out now at her, it was like looking through prison bars. Festering uncertainty – like a running pustule next to the prettiest, most perfect mouth; however, I knew then that what I felt for this precious whore was love.

And so we continued long day after day, the pilgrimage into the soul, and White Poppy aroused in me the most passionate desire. I pushed aside all thoughts of everything but the day ahead and our survival for another day. The boat people were now far behind us – was it too much to dare think that we were at last on our own? White Poppy stumbled on with tiny steps, her eyes downcast and heavy: the 'boy' leading the master, who stepped in *his* steps, following *his* footprints exactly in the wet grass, across the sticky mud, wet sand. That way there would only be one set of prints, only one person having walked that way, to the casual observer following next behind.

Looking into her black eyes I knew I had failed. I remembered my mother looking at me like that, the cold stare. I felt a shudder down my back from my neck. I had loved my mother as a young child; I had trusted her. I had thought she was the most special person in the entire world, and yet she did that to me – shunned me, cast me aside, and showed no difference as to whether I lived or I died. Compulsion, desire – she had rejected me, punishing me for something of which I was not aware. She had stared at me, distant, glared at me for daring to 'share' my feelings with her.

White Poppy: when I looked at her lips, she looked at my eye patch; when I looked at her eyes, she looked at my mouth. When her eyes caught mine, she looked away quickly, picking at her fingers. In her Chinese eyes, I saw something smouldering, burning, something that head been dormant, coming alive. Yet she withdrew herself, shut herself away inside, closed her eyes to me. The door that had been slightly open now tight closed.

14

Sun setting, shades of night closing in all around, the final shafts of sunlight extinguished in the trees, we settled down each night to the new light of our fire. Watching White Poppy eat, watching the rapid movements of her mouth, watching the action of each finger as she licked it in turn, I knew I would rather kill her than let her be touched now by another man; would rather see her hooded face destroyed than let another have that closest contact with her scarred and hidden beauty. Watching her, looking at the contempt in her whole body, I knew I had been foolish – what 'love' could there be between a British sailor and a Chinese whore; what lasting feeling between *us*? We were as different as the sun and the moon, yet both part of that same system of forces that could never be explained. One would not survive China without the other!

When she was not aware, when her eyes focused on some distant scene, I stared into them, moving past the lashes that flickered with their own beat, past the soft flesh, through the shining wetness into the deep brown, drawn into the curved black, deep ocean of her eyes, vast liquid sea stretching inwards, where sailed the brightest of her thoughts, where I saw tall-masted ships heading for the furthest shore. Her eyes reflected the sky, made black that which was blue, convex mirror of the clouds. I tried looking at her lips, to see inside their moist creases, to watch the saliva, the slow movement of her teeth washed over by her tongue, but I was drawn back by her almond eyes that turned suddenly and looked straight at me, focussing all that sea on to the spy, flooding it into my own, her eyes burned right through me.

I caught her looking at the photograph, the pieces stuck together on paper, which she carried with her, folded, in her pocket. Dover harbour, tall-masted sailing ships, a party of English women in front, officer's wives, walking forwards. She ran her bright eyes over it, looking at the girlish European faces, happy faces, their expensive clothes. Catching my eye, she burst into tears. Sobbing, she walked away.

I began to see White Poppy as I had not seen her before, the little details, the reality behind the facade. When she ate a particular food I knew why she ate it, what it meant to her; when she watched a particular place, I knew why she looked there, what she saw. I discovered the ranges of her smiles, the different positions of her hands, the set of her feet. I grew to sense what she was feeling, saw her thoughts working while she walked. I knew when she would laugh, when a smile hid tears. I knew when she was tired, when she wanted to sleep, could tell when she was bored, when she needed a treat. I began to see China through the eyes of this one Chinese. I also knew that there was still much simmering internal hate for me.

As I created our togetherness, White Poppy destroyed it, as I built up the blocks, she knocked them back down. She knew I knew little things about her – enjoying a peach she would throw it away, glancing quickly at me to register my 'pain'; kicked it distant. Catching her laughing she would stop, catching her smiling, she would frown, poke out her tongue; pout out at me. Yet I noticed her watching me sometimes when she thought I wasn't aware, glimpsed a shared smile when she forgot herself; felt thrilled when impulsively she went to touch my hand and then, thinking, drew back.

And my passion grew for her inside, until the time she might surrender to me when it would be perfection itself – the emotional map I prepared through her, the guide to her innermost soul, and each day she filled in more details, provided more clues. There was nothing I would not sacrifice for White Poppy, nothing I wouldn't do for her to make her life happy, and yet I knew nothing about what got her to where she was then, no details of her childhood, her life as a whore. Of course I had clues, had seen the evidence of that life, saw the signs she carried with her – the tattoo, the scars, her crooked fingers, tip-less little finger, the pain in her eyes; saw that she was more sensitive than she made out, that she had created a false person about herself. But the surround was beginning to crumble, the real Yin Hsueh-yen beginning to fall out. I would find out about her, would get to the mystery of her heart.

Approaching small villages we met many Chinese, huddled groups going about their own private little business, pleasure drawn inwards as we passed. Who knew where the secret societies were: who knew who had prior knowledge of our coming? I wanted to ask her; I wanted to ask her so many things, and yet we shared no common language except in that which we shared through the close presence of our very separate bodies; through facial expressions and gestures, through our various exclamations, grunts and moans, through our body scents and sounds.

I looked at her – the girl, the woman within the girl (within the 'man') – remembered that she too had once been the virgin. The much-prized Chinese virgin: all necessary bonds and agreements made for marriage, a girl was taken to the baths where the 'sisters' first examined her purity with a pigeon's egg, inserted a finger wrapped in white linen to break the virginal vein, to get evidence of that first dark blood. For me, she was still the 'virgin', and would be until the time that we should lie together, when I would take her soul.

Drifting in and out of sleep, I watched the glowing embers of the fire – cinders shifting, ashes falling, orange becoming grey, settling, cold – last flame eaten by the creeping indigo dark. Lying still, watching Eliza, I thought how her eyes were tiger's eyes: cats' eyes are adapted for night vision – big with large pupils, they glow from reflected light, as hers seemed to shine from the flames.

15

Some 280 miles long, runs the valley of the Pei kiang, main route through from South China to the Yangtze valley: beyond Samshui some 90 miles to Yingtak, above which the river has steep gradients, narrowing considerably where it flows through great gorges, sandbanks and more rapids, and the current is swift.

We continued by a succession of small craft towards the Tsientang kiang, travelled on towards Yuanchow ki in Kiangsi Province (more rice in the flatlands, and hills becoming steep mountains), passing through Linkiang, struggling on to the provincial capital Nanchang ('Southern Prosperity') on the Kan river. Nanchang has fine walls, some 22 miles around; the centre for decorated porcelain and pottery.

Summer over, granaries full, the sky a cloudless blue, it was a time to relax. The mid-autumn festival is a mountain one – the Chinese climb the mountains, fly their kites, picnic on the chrysanthemum-blooming slopes. Autumn altars are built outside, support the long-eared moon-hare, candles and incense, a dish of thirteen moon-cakes – one for every Chinese month – filled with sugar, spices, nuts, and plates of pomegranate, melon, apple and peach.

We walked beyond the small village shrine against the backdrop of a travelling fair, left behind the shadow-players, shrill piping music, the agitating beat of a drum, moved through the people gathered round for a chat with friends. Lying still, my eyes closed, and trailing in the water, I pictured a ship, her sails blowing full, catching the sun, purest virgin white; drifting as a seagull above the tropical blue sea, sweeping, swooping, soaring, diving into the brilliant pool, from which the White Poppy lifted her face, water running from her black hair, droplets sparkling in the sunlight, her cinnabar lips.

We crossed the high-peaked stone bridge, crumbling arch over bubbling waters, made our way along the river towards the juniper trees, smoke rising into the still air, watched strings of coloured-paper lantern-kites, cylinders of bamboo, a candle lit in each: lanterns fitted with rollers, heating, rising with the wind; sliding along the cords, weaving, diving, soaring high into the sky; in the dark, the dead of night, a moving trail of stars exploding crimson fire.

Box kite flying low – it draws the children – flat faces pressed up towards the sky in anticipation, awe – children who run out to watch as the adults play.

Seventh Night of the Seventh Moon. Far behind us, in Canton, women would be getting ready incense and candles, preparing melons and fruits to worship the Grandson of Heaven.

At midnight the wind blew away the clouds and the moon appeared full and bright, dragging silver chains of light across the river water reflected with the pinpricks of a million stars. The Herdsman (the star, Aquila) and the Girl Weaver (the star, Vega, daughter of the Jade Emperor) took their places in the Heavens.

I sat there with her, looking at the moon, at the sprinkle of stars. I knew the story – the Interpreter had told me. I wondered what he was doing now. The Jade Emperor was angry when his daughter, Vega, became too lively, forsaking her weaving on the loom for her new husband, Aquila – banished him to the other side of the River of Stars, the Silver Stream of Heaven (the Milky Way). He told them they should meet once only every year, on the Seventh Night of the Seventh Moon, crossing over the flood of stars by a bridge of magpies (unless a single drop of rain should cause the overfull river to flood, washing away the bridge of birds).

Coming in from the Chinese garden, White Poppy had hesitated – only a brief moment, but a hesitation nevertheless. Mouth open, cherry lips apart, she had stopped and looked across at me: red lips unmoving, still, strand of saliva between their glistening moistness, dew-hinged corners of that most erotic mouth. And for that isolated moment it had seemed that she would kiss me, that she would walk across and press her own hot lips on mine in gratitude for what I had done for her; would press me with her perfect parted lips.

'I want you,' I had said quietly, the memory was fierce. 'I desire your sweet flesh.'

She stood there before me, the little Chinese whore: as she had stood there before me in the Interpreter's house.

16

Walking along the banks of a willow-lined river, the leaves now turning yellow, we were greeted by the mother of a boating family, one of a pair of houseboats moored close by. Hearing a noise behind me I turned; found myself looking into the disfigured, pock-marked face of a young girl, an eruption of pox close to her dead eyes: a thin leafless tree in the shadow of a wall. Soon joined by a smiling girl, her disfigured twin, eyes sparkling right in the cruel sunlight. Both girls would die of the disease.

There were other boats further along the river, where we saw the procession of a small bundle wrapped in white linen, the corpse of a young baby. White is the colour of mourning: white is the colour of semen, and thus of life. Semen is the Chinese spirit of Life: on death it is this spirit that leaves. White is the colour of the opium poppy.

Crouching low before the Chinese family altar, the gilded shrine enclosed by candle burning to the dead, White Poppy wept, clutching her hands against her chest, fat tears rolling down her cheeks, her black eyes heavy, unfocussed, sad, amidst the wailing and beating of drums, the blowing of shrill pipes; incense burning, the baby's corpse, linen-wrapped in the white of death, was buried in a shaded copse overlooking the river, sent off with the howling and wailing of the women dressed in sackcloth.

Others sacrifice to the Queen-Mother of the West at the foot of the mountain, bury their offerings in the soil: rather than at the summit where the Sky God is worshipped with an offering that is burned. What was she thinking: as she stood there? What thoughts tore round inside her mind? Although her eyes were now dry, did the whore shed great tears of sadness inside? Who was she really? What was she doing on this journey, what was her purpose in dragging along with me? What did she really mean to me? Why did I bother? Did I really need her to escape? Yes, I suppose I did. I was a navigator of the sea; White Poppy was more comfortable navigating across the land.

She spoke enough Mandarin Chinese, to check our way. I watched her hand gestures, and those given to her in reply. Yes I needed her. I had to guess always what she was thinking, what thoughts were behind the unfamiliar words on her young lips. I never really knew, just followed when she went ahead; just moved to this side or that when she beckoned to me to do so, signalled to me with now familiar movements of her fingers and her hands. I had been told in Canton of subversive language, female writing, which women used to communicate with each other in the home – expressing their anxieties about being married and intimate life, heretical ideas about arranged marriages and family oppression.

The Interpreter had told me a little about the secret communication with sworn sisters; had mentioned their signs – secret script. But everything between us was secret then.

17

Babies die at birth; many more die before birth, aborted by their frightened mothers, those too poor to keep any more, instantly borne away down stream. Called to my mother's bedroom one Easter morning I saw my new-born sister lying doll-like, dead, inflamed eyes, congested lungs: her withered form across the pillow, later tucked inside the paper-lined box for burial, wearing the grave clothes my mother kept in the chest of drawers by her bed.

She climbed out of bed, washed herself, dried between her legs with a bit of tattered rag, and got on with the day, prisoner of her own life, soon back out with the women in the Dockland park. Women rightly fear pregnancy, childbirth; fear the tearing, ulceration, vaginal infection and disease: there is little birth without God-given pain. I still smell the burning of the rags, the stench of the flesh and bones cremated within, unborn body – sad soul assigned to dockside heaven.

The boat-girl, White Poppy, Yin Shooeh-yen: she had flourished just as grapes grow best in the poorest, driest soil. Her eyes reflecting the glimmer of a dying taper, she looked right through me, her slant-eyes swollen, red, unfocussed, sad. I wanted to kiss her, wanted her in every way, wanted more than anything to close my mouth over hers, to get rid of my sadness, to relieve my inner pain. All I could think of was the boat family's shelf on which stood the small tablets representing their ancestors – their own bloodline stretching back in time: each new-born child registered in that record, given a place for his lifetime and for all future time – his name and his fate.

The souls of those who die with no-one left on earth to look after them are remembered on the Yu Lan P'ên Hui (early autumn Festival of the Hungry Ghosts), which begins on the 15th day of the Seventh Moon and lasts until the 30th, with gifts of food to appease the evil they may bring to the living. The spirits of the dead are allowed out of Hell to wander the earth, seek what comfort they can find – those with no family, family-line died out: ill-intentioned, dissatisfied and vengeful spirits.

We passed smoking joss sticks at the crossroads, alongside the road, by temples, large bonfires at night, when dead bodies get up and walk, trouble the living; bad spirits cause accidents and misfortunes that kill, hanging around the dead, waiting for them to let go the human soul. What God was with us now? At Ichang and other ports on the Yangtze, folk float candle-lit red paper lanterns (the Bhuddist lotus); light the spirit-way for the return of drowned and disconsolate souls, and lanterns are hung everywhere from arches and in the trees, as they are on Lantern Festival Day. For several miles downstream, floats the silent tide of twinkling water lilies, luminous sea of light, drifting, sinking one by one.

Walking alongside the fragile boats moored by the bank of yet another small river, I watched White Poppy as she strode ahead of me, whistling. Did she miss her men, her family, her boat? Did she miss anything of her life in Canton? What was it that had gone wrong? I wanted to ask her so much, wanted to tell her so much more. She had lived her own complex life there bound up in the lives of so many lifeless men, her own ordered existence; had given her body as often as it was there to be given, something beautiful to be used, abused: a life with little hope – to be bought, battered, buggered, bruised. And yet I knew nothing about *her*. What did she feel for me? With me she would have so much more should we make it to Shanghai. Was there anything more than companionship as we travelled further from Canton? I needed a sign from her, the tiniest indication of regard.

Watching her, looking at the contempt in her whole body, I realised I had been foolish – what love could there be between a sailor and a whore? I had misunderstood the Chinese culture: we were as different as black and white. And, yet, in another way we were inseparable – refugees, outcasts both from a system that was set to kill us both.

As the days passed I resigned myself to the fact that we might not make it to Shanghai *together*, and that should we make it across China, we would then part, would each go our separate way through life: each different in every way as we made our way to our final destined day!

18

White Poppy was crying, sitting crouched forward, her head in her hands, sobbing. I touched her arm gently, pressed my fingertips into her shoulder. But she pulled away, shrugged me off, pulled herself closer into a sorrowful, ragged ball. Wiping her eyes on the back of her sleeve, wiping her running nose, she was up and off again, no sound having left those sweet lips: that Eve, that shocking image of seduction.

I followed behind in silence; pleased by the oily odour of her hair wafting behind her on the breeze, glad when the sun came back out from behind the mountain, cheered by the warmth of its new light. We walked slowly, through the steep-sided narrow limestone gorge, rock cathedral, jagged rocks piercing the cornflower-blue sky. I watched her. Near Gigow, Jekiang (Kikow, Chekiang), the Yoong giang (Yung kiang) flows in a narrow river-valley flanked with low-wooded hills, small settlements along the gravel banks, sharply-ragged scarps that run down to the southern basin of the Yangtze.

White Poppy forgot herself, became the girl – openly flirtatious as we tramped along. Her face impish, coy, she sang to herself as we walked, skipping seductively, her eyes manic, her lips full. The moving gravel clattered beneath her leather-soled feet, rubbed hard against her sinking ankles. She opened her slant eyes wide at me, daring me to look at her, pupils dilated, nostrils flared, teased me with her movements, darted around me, smiling, showing white teeth, the tip of her tongue. ***All in my dreams she did, and only in my dreams.*** I watched her. I wanted to hold her; to kiss her in such a way that would not stop once it had begun.

Before us stretched the China mountains: mighty summits piercing the clouds, points of access to Chinese heaven and the immortal gods; like on the brush-painted scrolls - needle peaks and pine trees, mountain-top temples, incense burning summits. The great mountains produce clouds and send down rain. The Chinese fear too much rain in summer, fear the autumn drought, fear heavy rainfall down the mountains as tea stalls collapse and paths wash away. Evil drained away by flowing water, rivers flowing out from the centre. Summit crags – white clouds as thick as loose cotton we could hear pilgrims but could not see them.

Looking back at me, firm toss of her plaited hair, she (the boy) 'smiled', the last moisture of her tears glistening before it dried, and her eyes sparkled with an ancient vigour, like the oceans deep at sea. She had cried within her hood, I heard her weeping as we walked. And I wanted to stop her, to hold her, to hug her tight, like a mother hugs her small child when she has had a fright. The way ahead turned around and then upwards, promised refuge beyond the precipice rising dizzily sheer above us to massive overhanging fortress walls. Opaque towers of secluded hope soaring skywards, pulling us onwards, luring us to the highest point from where the precipice dropped terrible, ragged below us: another step and we were over the edge, falling broken through the mountain air.

Having spent so much time in the China mountains, I rather fancied a grave in a green churchyard amongst ancient, solitary hills, surrounded by rough-stone walls with flowering shrubs, so chosen as to unfold a succession of blooms through the seasons – May roses, ending with white jasmine. White Poppy: I felt her – just by watching her I 'felt' her, just by listening to every sound she made I 'felt' her, breathing in her fragrance when I could. And I had touched her hot flesh when she was asleep, left the perspiration drying on my hand, and I had touched it to my tongue, tasted her. And I had let my lips brush by her lips when she was asleep, but I never let them touch, satisfied to feel the warmth of her sweet breath blowing against my face.

But there was a deep rending dread inside of me. I did not understand these people; I did not understand their land that would forever remain alien to me.

Who are you, I thought; even then I was not sure, but I saw new facets to her personality every day. There was something deep that she kept hidden though, something that was just for her not me. Eliza, the 'youth', head new-shaved at the front, male plait knotted at the back. Her breasts bound flat with bands of linen, which she only undid at night, out of sight, in the dark. Twin scars above her right cheek.

19

At the rustic inn, first rank pilgrims each had a table to themselves, laid with candles, cakes, mixed fruits, meats, nuts and seeds, were entertained with the spectacle of Chinese theatre, cups of wine and women. Cold night warmed before an open fire. The pilgrim associations, Sheng-hui, society members on their pilgrimage: some women-only groups, tingling uncontrollably inside: that indefinable sense of firsthand wonder. These sparks of heaven fanned into a flame, the flame into a fire, the fire into a star and the star into a sun. We watched them, and mingled with them, thousands of pilgrims crowding so tightly that there was not room even for a strip of paper between them, as they pushed past canopied stalls selling drinks and fried food, men coming rushing out to offer the food freshly-done in pure sesame oil, fragrant and crisp. Such was the excitement, clamour, noise, the rush for the gates, as they made forward for their great ascent that we had to hold on to each other to avoid being torn asunder by our ruthless fellow travellers, as we were compressed through the narrow door.

The mountain sedan-chairs had curved poles and a square compartment for the passengers to sit in, poles tied to the carriers' shoulders with leather strips. When they climbed up the steps the sedan chair moved sideways like a crab. White Poppy laughed to see it tip. Her eyes lit up, shone inside her hood; her mouth split apart in the widest smile. But she saw me looking, stopped, shut away that emotion from me – the great whore, licked her flaking lips and looked away. As dusk gathered, the mountains grew purple; sun going down, the blues deepened, the reds retreating, the white of the moon appearing in the East, a glow of fresh and pure light in the cloudless sky. Between the first and second Gates of Heaven, strange peaks became visible, distant ranges like a lotus of a thousand petals. The midnight watch. Wayside beggars, fortune-tellers, providers of travelling lamps had lanterns burning, so that all along the way it was as bright as day. Opening the north window of the great hall, we saw a bolt of white silk stretching from the foot of the mountain to the summit. The pilgrims formed a stream of lights visible across the valleys that bobbed in the dark like a moving dragon. A mass of fireflies flickering light from a thousand boxes – the train of pilgrims making their way up the mountain to the shrine. We heard the distant chant of their prayers carried back to us on the wind.

White Poppy stood still, mouth open, lips apart, eyes fixed on heaven. I moved as close to her as I could, felt the touch of her male plait against my hand, listened to the drawing in of her hot breath. The kiss impulse is strong; her full lips remained the focus of my attention, tinged as they were with unspoken terror and fear. There could be no future pain that we could not endure together: there could be nothing left that China could do with us that we could not shrug off – we were powerful, painless, free! I laughed to myself: what did they know about opium here? What did they know about the Canton whores – a different life altogether? I laughed to myself for amongst them was 'royalty' the great prostitute, 'queen' – White Poppy.

20

A light drizzling of rain followed by warm sunshine. It was near the end of autumn, the countryside bare, the mountain tops obscured by dense cloud. The days were now shorter, the weather setting in cold and wintry. Several wet days later, we reached the remote hamlet at the foot of the highest mountain of all, stayed the night at the only inn, slept uncomfortably in a whitewashed room with a charcoal brazier, beds with coverlets embroidered with sesame flowers. Rising early, we made our pilgrimage up the mountain to the ivy-clad temple that clung to its side, long ascents of rock-cut steps towards a massive studded gate: a well-made door fits so tightly, makes no use of bolts, and yet it cannot be opened from outside.

We walked unhurriedly through the squalor, the grounds neglected, overgrown with weeds, breathing in the haze of joss sticks, the oily smoke from a handful of red tallow candles. The grey-robed monk gestured to us to follow him up a flight of stone steps; taken to the very edge, to a final rising wall of sheer rock with shallow steps cut into it, a slack iron chain at the side for support. We stood together at the top, on a rock-cut platform no wider than six people, teetering on the edge of that most wonderful panorama below, its dizzy impressiveness exploding into a chasm of awful depth, sheer rock dropping quickly away out of sight: God's view of the earth, mountain upon mountain rising on every side in rugged grandeur, isolated outcrops, rocky towers pointing skywards to the Creator, solemn silent stillness above the clouds: that image again of the teenage boat-girl standing tall above me; sad mystery of her sparkling eyes, cruel penetration of her gaze, erotic fullness of her crimson lips.

White Poppy would not look at me. In the presence of the monk, she stared carefully, fixedly away. The teeth of the mountains yawned at the grey sky. I saw yellow-skinned giants striding along the valleys placing the mountains as they wished. She sighed within her hood, sighing long and loud as she looked out across her homeland, something in her eyes – something different, mysterious – focused on another place in a different time.

The monk gestured to us to go back down, leading the way carefully, holding onto the chain. I pulled her towards me, took hold of both her hands, held them tightly as though she might fall. She looked at me carefully, slowly scanning my face, but there was no love in her Chinese eyes, only the hatred for what I had done to her, the pain I had injected into her soul by taking her away from Canton. The monk called to us from below, beckoned to us to come down, and a fierce gust of wind blew the hood from my 'boy's' proud head, the plait swinging defiantly in the wind. I am female it declared, this whole body is female:

look at me, don't you see. Her lips looked thin, her face pale, her almond eyes downcast, forlorn.

Her hood slipped back off her head, her hair had been growing, although she shaved her head frequently – surely they had seen that she was a woman, a girl? What had the huddled groups been thinking as we passed them? Was she as precious to the Chinese as I sometimes believed she was? Were there those who would pay dearly to have her back? How good was what I had considered to be such a good disguise?

There are none that travel so high as they who know not where they are going are, guided by the sun and the moon, the positions of the constellations and the stars. We were lost – in terms of 'love', I knew that we were lost!

The Demon from the North fears the Demon from the South, the Demon from the East fears the Demon from the West, and all dread one another. Temples built on the summit of high mountains are free from their visitations – no demon would risk meeting a rival there. Night falling, there was hot food, aromatic tea on the table. The monk offered it first to my 'boy', holding the edge of the cup between his thumb and forefinger, his middle finger touching the bottom of the cup. I felt uncomfortable inside, realised the danger we were in: Triad members when far from home received favours and protection via secret signs and a language of their own despite not sharing a common dialect.

In her disguise, White Poppy took the cup as expected, and the monk continued in silence. Handing me my tea, his fingers curled around the whole cup, he said, 'Yam sing.' ('Drink to victory!'). Hope, the Anchor of the Soul. The hands clasped in brotherly accord.

Standing out in the monks' garden, looking up at the chilly night sky, at the smoky moon and the rings of stars, I found it hard to believe that they were the same stars that sparkled high above my head, and closing my eyes I listened to the non-existent sea, remembering Macao, the distant waves breaking over algae-covered rocks, running free, swooshing, sweeping slowly in.

Dreaming, the soul goes wandering, encounters adventures as real as real, remembered as dreams when we wake, when the soul returns to the body. But when the soul wanders it is very dangerous. Then the body is open to possession by spirits that could take over the body entirely, making it impossible for the soul to return.

21

The night passed without incident and I woke to the chatter of sparrows outside. It was a beautiful autumn morning and I lay awake listening to the monks chanting, the air fragrant with the smells of incense and hot food, drifting in through the single shuttered window to the rear of the monastery. Looking out of the window, something caught my eye in the shadows, a slight movement, the glint of reflected steel. My heart raced and my mouth went dry. Armed guards were coming for us.

I heard the commotion outside in the Hall, the fierce shouting in Chinese. I shouted to White Poppy who sat straight up on her mattress, her eyes bulging, frightened, like a fox caught in the iron jaws of a trap. I ran to the door and threw down the wooden bar that would keep them outside. The shouting increased; there was loud banging on the door. She pulled on her clothes while I created a diversion, kicked over the burning coals, the burning bedding by the door now beginning to fill the room with dense smoke, orange flames licking their way up the tinder-dry eaves. As their guest-hall went up in flames, we made our escape.

We ran and ran into a forested area. They sent dogs after us, and we watched them sniffing around, coming so close to us but totally unaware of our presence. We hardly dared breathe, watching and waiting in hiding, having covered ourselves with river mud, walking along the rocky stream-bed to throw them off our scent. The dogs ran round and round sending their masters on a merry dance, until they were called off and the small group made its way back to the monastery. We kept on that night, travelling by the broken light of the cloud-obscured moon, arriving at an isolated rural farmstead.

The next morning we made ourselves known to the farmer. After a hard day's work for both of us, a meagre supper, he sent us to sleep on the straw in a ram-shackle barn. In my sleep I returned to earth as a ghost, moved silently into the room where I saw her lying naked on rich silks, and yet I had no hands to caress her, no arms to clasp her, no lips to press against her own.

A muffled scream, a familiar choking voice: the disguised whore was no longer by my side. Rushing outside the barn I saw, my 'boy', fighting; saw White Poppy punching and kicking her stocky male attacker; the she-tiger, striped cat, snarling, vicious, her mouth open wide, teeth savage, claws tearing, she knocked him to the ground.

22

White Poppy had spotted the thief in the distance, noted his tracks along the forest floor. She listened, watched, her eyes narrowing, cat-like, fierce. Her breathing altered, she took deep breaths, nostrils flared, head erect, eyes opened wide, chin set firm. I saw the muscles moving in her arms, the muscles tightening in her legs, as she moved forwards, tiger-like, gripping the branches with her bare feet, naked toes curved inwards, long nails like claws that helped her climb to the highest point over the gully.

Head moving slowly at first, she followed her prey, watched as he came towards her, as he moved into her range, ready to spring on him, knock him to the ground from behind; making her way carefully along the larger branches, body low, limbs extended long, pushing herself forwards with ease, crouching lower as she got nearer the edge of the thick canopy of leaves, ready to spring, ready to devour him.

She was aggressive, showed her anger, her frustration, snapped at me when I tried to talk to her, turned away muttering to herself in Cantonese. The butterfly showed herself to be a scorpion within. As we walked my arm brushed against hers accidentally. She glared at me, pulling herself away in an exaggerated gesture of displeasure. She fought against me with her mind, would not look me directly in the eye, would not smile, but set her eyes forward on the track ahead, and stumbled on, placing one foot before the other long hour after hour, stopping only for a drink, for a bite of food, and this went on day after day until I could stand it no more. I tried singing to her, smiled at her in passing, but nothing, no response. Sometimes I watched from the side, and her eyes glowed angrily as though she was fighting another battle within. And so she kept her distance, walked faster when I tried to catch up with her, when my shadow moved over hers.

For her part, White Poppy was wilting; communication had broken down between us. Although we shared little common language, her face had spoken a thousand words; her eyes had contained a thousand lies. Now there was nothing: dressed as a young man, feminine form beneath loose robes, breasts bound flat with bands of linen, hair cropped at the front, head shaven, long plait hanging at the back – there was nothing.

I had been there before. Many times I had stood at the city wall, outside its very gates, but there was no way in. Every now and then a part of the gate would open, an inner door, and some male Chinese would hurry out as though there were others there waiting to get in. But I never saw them, the Canton ghosts.

It was the same with White Poppy; I stood there ready to breach her defences. Every now and then her eyes would move, her dry lips would open, but only for a moment, only to breathe when she was climbing, out of breath. And now and then a Cantonese 'word' would fall out, an exclamation, sigh; fall out to be lost in the silence.

I went on ahead to see what lay before us, treading carefully, quietly so as to let no creature know I was there. Pushing aside the branches, peering through cool leaves, I saw the small group moving towards us, tiny bodies making their way along the rough mule track we had disturbed with our own feet some short time before.

Mid-morning, the cool sun mid-height in the clouded blue sky, walking tired into the majestic approach of the mountains that spread ahead of us in grandeur, I saw the black shapes moving closer, the little group travelling down the mountain path towards us, in the direction we were headed, recognised the style of the officials as they approached. They would pass where we were, making their way along the main exit from the grey-brown mountains.

Grabbing White Poppy's hand I pulled her roughly into the scratchy bushes that ran alongside the rocky pathway, pressing her down into the dry gully beyond. From within her dishevelled male disguise, she looked at me in slit-eyed panic, surprise. I signalled to her to keep quiet, to keep her head down. We lay still, pressing ourselves flat against the warm flat earth, fragrant with bruised ferns: in the rainy season the gully would be a flowing torrent. Our eyes met and held. This was it; this was the moment of truth.

In our closeness, I breathed in her unwashed fragrance, the Chinese odours of her fond body, and looking at the little of her face that showed from her covered head, caught the beauty of her almond eyes, the magnetism of her smile, raised skin of her scars. In the bright sunlight I saw every individual pore, the fine hairs, the crease of her salt-dried lips, slightly apart, erotic in their fullness. After eating she had wiped her mouth on the back of her hand, wet saliva dried on her skin. I wanted to smell it, to breathe in her oral smell, tried to find an excuse to get her hand near my face. Holding her close down in the ditch, her hands extended upwards above her, palms down, no distance from my nose, I edged a tiny bit closer, breathed deeper to smell that which seemed so attractive; edged my head a little nearer, as I caught the waft of the drying saliva, the saline-musk smell on her skin, watched a sulphur-yellow butterfly perform a mad floral dance. Brushing my lips against her hand I kissed it briefly, tasting salt, the greasiness of our last meal, felt exploding fire below. The sun burst forth from behind the clouds, lighting up the mountain with the most intense bright light, where the horizon rose into elevated summits, the vast pyramidal peaks of the river-rushing mountains.

We waited, silent, still, listening for the sound of the mules; the trample of feet as the mountain sedan chair was carried by with its imperial messenger. I wanted to peer up, to see the red and gold crest of the conveyance, but I dared not look and closed my eyes instead against Eliza's sweat-soaked body, remembering the confines of Canton. I held my breath, listening, waiting for the passage of these angels of death. Can enemies ever become true friends?

She started to cough, would give us away. I closed my mouth over hers to stem all sound, kissed her full on the lips, tasting her warm femininity, metallic sweetness of her tongue: swallowed her cough – took it deep down. She started to struggle. I thought she was going to stand up and give us away. She wriggled down in the dry gully below the scratchy bushes. Pulling away from me, silently, she would turn and look at me, would wipe her mouth with the back of her hand, would spit into the dust. But for that moment, we were one: joined by our mouths we were one complete whole. That 'kiss' that made everything before it all right! This taste of China, the fragrance on her lips – erotic, exotic, raw: *the vision of my tongue down the throat of the little China whore.*

It came suddenly, noisily, trampling dust and small stones over us, wafting the strong smell of the mules, of spices, becoming quieter, the smell dissipating slowly in the still air, and again there was silence broken only by the buzzing of grasshoppers, the singing of birds. Her lips, her throat, the sensation was intense, the culmination of taste, touch, sight, sound and smell: the taste of her flesh (lips), the cool softness, resistance, pressure; the sight of her scarred cheek, her eyes startled, unblinking, wild; the sound of her breathing, the air through her nose, salivation in her throat, swallowing; the smell of her skin. The first time I tasted her, swallowed from that wet mouth, greedy for more, White Poppy.

23

I remember when you left me. Alone I grieve, ever keen my sorrow. I imagine I see your face, feelings tangle, bruise my heart. I remember you, ever keen my sorrow, night after night unable to sleep. Ts'ao P'ei (D'ao B'ei). *Empress Chen* (Jen), *Jade Terrace*, p.65.

The early-morning air cold, ground covered in dew, spiders' webs were transformed into wet-jewelled trophies in the bushes below the cliff. The sun rising, warming our backs, the village soon disappeared below us as we climbed, but the climb was difficult, tiring, left our fingers bleeding, raw. We had our first major row, a true fight borne of tiredness and despair. Nostrils flared, teeth exposed from her upper lip, her breath coming fast, White Poppy threw herself at me, lashing out with her fingers, kicking with her legs, tried pushing me with her feet, this fighting female fiend hidden within her 'male' persona.

There was bitter disappointment in her lack-lustre eyes, the look of despair. Tears running down her mud-streaked cheeks she Poppy ran away from me, not looking back, fighting her way through rank bushes and into the trees. I felt so angry, foolish, about to lose everything. I heard her sobbing, saw a last quick glimpse of her covered head, and she was gone.

The magnificent Lushan Mountains (reaching up to 4,000 feet), rocks covered with many Buddhist temples, stretch to the port of Kiukang (City of Nine Rivers), sitting on the Yangtsze river at the outpouring of Poyang Lake, some 450 miles from our destination, Shanghai. The Monastery of benevolence has a gilded, life-size Buddha, and in the temple is a bell which is toiled without ceasing:

every stroke sending a flash of light into the Buddhist Hell. From Kiukang we had travelled slowly by Yangtsze river boat to Anking (355 miles from Shanghai), from which we saw the sharp peaks of the sacred Nine Lotus Flower Mountain. Anking, walled capital of Anhui province, sits high above the river, like a boat, with water on three sides: the Great Pagoda, outside the Eastern Gate, is its mast. Each tier of the seven storey pagoda is hung with a million golden bells, which tinkle in the wind like broken ice jangling at the edges of a frozen lake. And there she left me.

I listened to the sad tolling of the monastery bell, heard the chanting of Catholic priests, saw the procession of Christ, the Cross, the sanctuary light burning in my thoughts. I sat down on the mountain path for White Poppy's return, kept a look out across the valley beyond the trees – high terrace among passing clouds, where the road was far – impossible to make out. Nothing. With the dying of the day, the orange setting of the sun, the White Poppy was nowhere to be seen. The silence was disturbing; there had always been the sound of her breathing, the rustle of her clothes, the movement of her lips, the blinking of her slant-eyes. The lonely mountains creaked their disapproval as I lay down by my fire to sleep.

I looked around for her, thought I saw her trailing behind me in the shadows, but that was all they were, shadows around the rocks. I saw her black eyes, her vermilion lips, felt the warm touch of her fingers, smelled the unwashed odour of her hair, her body. I missed her, missed her more than anything I had ever missed before. But she would be back; she'd be there in the morning. But she wasn't there and the days passed in sad silence; a string of mornings came and went, drifting into deepest oblivion.

Sitting in the cloistered shade, fingers of scented mist disappearing with the sun, I sat alone with my thoughts: we had never said 'goodbye'.

Compulsion, desire: desire so strong, desire so blind. Movement on her crimson lips, in her black-bronzed Chinese eyes. It hit me suddenly, she was no longer a whore, had not been one since leaving Canton. Thinking of the White Poppy I could hear the sweet young sound of another Chinese voice, Yu Ji, heard her laughter, felt the soft touch of her lips. She had been the one for comparison: Yu Ji had been the standard against which I had given White Poppy points for looks, for the way she made up her face, for the way she walked, the way she stood, the way she laughed, the way she talked. It was ten out of ten for everything. Yu Ji was more of a six or a seven, but Yu Ji had given me the taste for Chinese women.

The spider, waiting patiently for her fly. Yu Ji, had she had any part in this? No, what could she have known about it? The threaded net of corruption and intrigue. I was the *Joss-pidgin-man*; White Poppy was my *Larn-pidgin.* I smiled. Having travelled hundreds of miles, Eliza had done something few other Chinese women could ever have done: women who lived their whole lives enclosed, in isolation with their own sex. The White Poppy had travelled free across her own land! I wanted to tell her, I wanted to make her realise the enormity of what she had achieved. But I did not speak the same language, and she was no longer there.

'Every man,' the Interpreter had said, 'has his own taste in women.'

Yu Ji, cherry lips, scarlet silk, dressed in red – red kite distant, floating, free – laughter and light on her lucid

Chinese lips; blood red lips (pushed forwards already by protruding teeth), female fount of life. *How many heroes are stretched dying upon their pillows?*

Taste that which makes a woman. Yu Ji had been taken away (the Interpreter had informed me). She had stripped quickly at the gatehouse, ripped off her clothes in fierce frenzy, had made her breasts bare, but it was too late! They who do not catch those they wish to catch (those in power), take out their wrath in those they find amongst those poor souls that remain behind. Coming towards me, she had hesitated, Yu Ji – only a brief moment, but a hesitation nevertheless, and on her neck had been bruises, as there were on her arms, and bruises on her legs. Yu Ji died in pain (the Interpreter had said, quietly), she who had told on me? Taboo!

24

The spider shifts once in the gathering darkness, one last movement in the corner of its web, waits with infinite patience. I watched peasant women washing clothes down on the rocks: women who displayed a coarse vulgarity and carelessness in their movements, their armpits damp with sweat; women with their hair all over the place, garments tattered and torn, stained skirts over their thick peasant legs. White Poppy was a lady; the whore was of a different class.

At first I had not been looking for love, had not ever really known love with my own family, although there was kinship, affection for my sisters (though one by one squalid London life took each of them away from me). I had the deepest respect for Father Patrick, but never love. With the women I met as I travelled the world I had sex, but never love, not until the White Poppy did I feel the pull of what turned out to be love (and intense guilt for what it was I had done)?

Do you know what it is like to have found one special stone on the beach, one special girl amongst millions? It feels impossible – no hope at all when that one stone is dropped again, but there is no natural law that says only possible things come true – as Father Patrick told me so often, 'life gives us equal chances for failure or success!'

I continued alone, and more hours became more days, and more days became more weeks. I travelled ever more slowly as homesteads came and passed, walking the flowering, fertile fields. Without White Poppy, my travelling companion – 'boy, my spiritual journey had come to an end; without her there with me the China trek was a pointless one, I felt depressed. What is life unless there is someone special to share it with? Escape from China was not the point, it mattered not where I lived; alone, I would return to sea, would resume the life that had become second-nature to me. I continued on, headed for the coast.

I had been interested in the particular, in White Poppy; nothing else about China bothered me all that much: I saw a thousand different details every day, a vision of something significant beyond ordinary significance. With the Whore there was atmosphere, drama, an overabundance of pleasuring a perpetual state of arousal, the most intense sexual excitement.

Then it was all gone. I could not bear to think of life without her. Once you have felt something you can never 'unfeel' it, once you have seen something you can never 'unsee' it: the blind are saved so much pain. It is only when we have pain that we realise how glorious it is not to have pain: we only know the light because of the dark that comes before and after it.

I had heard her crying many nights, sobbing uncontrollably into her rags, wanting to comfort her, yet not wanting to risk her claws. The terrors of childhood, black cloud, thunder, lightning, precipitous waves. I heard the familiar singing in the skylight above me – cheerful warbling song from the eternal lemon-yellow canary in its cylindrical bamboo cage: how happy he did sing from his heavenward, swinging prison. I saw the half-closed slanted eyes, those silent vermilion lips; saw the distance of a thousand years, the China mountains – silent peaks, silent rocks, silent trees, bathed only by the tears of the rain, silence broken only by the strange sounds mountains make at night, creaking, shifting movement of the rocks, night cooling of the sun-heated stone.

The days she withdrew from the poppy drug: lying still on the rush mat, I saw her, mouth open, staring up at the ceiling, shaking, arms stiff, legs knotted together, knees up, writhing, pushing backwards with her heels – Yin Shoeh-yen. Lying on her side she had watched me, bold eyes following me around the room, frightened, small. Love is based on thought. *We create love* – we create the fond circumstances for its growth. We surrender to its creation – make another love, by our love.

25

Rice is the principal crop of the Province of Chekiang, and much of the land is intersected with natural streams and artificial waterways used for its irrigation. There are forests of mulberry trees for the thriving silk industry: it seemed impossible not to lose my way. The North Mountains of Hangchow (capital of Chekiang province) contain monasteries and wonderful caves – the Cave of the Purple Cloud, the Cave of the Yellow Dragon, the Gem Spring of the Dancing Fish, and on the West Lake, the Island of Three Pools of the Moon's Reflection and the Pavilion of the Lake's Heart. And yet what did they matter to me then? While she was away from me I imagined every horror possible. Had she been caught? Had they seen through her disguise? Had she given me away? Had she gone and told them who I was? I doubted her in my despair, and I despaired further because of my doubt. Oh where was that hatred now?

'Yin Hsueh (Shooeh)-yen, I hate you!' I shouted it out to the silent mountains, the last miles of high ground. 'I hate you, I hate you, and I hate you.' I made up my mind to forget her, cursed her to Hell. She was a bitch, a bitch from Hades. Without her I was nothing, the journey was a pointless one, and I drifted along, broken ship on a cruel sea. Time changes our perception of things, reveals more of the small details, and separates the individual parts. But in some ways the more we experience, the more we see, the less we know. Without White Poppy there was nothing. I heard the music of a two-stringed lute, saw the shadows moving behind the paper screens, felt nothing more than a shadow puppet myself.

Had they followed us, had they taken her away from me? I imagined her imprisonment, saw her death. It was the only image that brought tears to my eye that made me cry: I could not imagine what it would be like to never see her again. Despite everything that had happened between us, I felt we had grown very close. Damn China, damn the whole country! Just let me get away, just let me reach Shanghai and sail away for ever, and leave it to the healing nature of time, and the passing of the years when I would forget her, would forget everything about the damned land, and all my China years would eclipse to nothing more than a handful of memories, nothing more than the dust in my shoes.

Sitting by the roadside at the Peach-Leaf Ferry, watching the formations of the alabaster clouds, I knew how much I was in love, and that my life would now be nothing without her, White Poppy.

26

Sitting by the roadside at the Peach-Leaf ferry, watching the formation of the alabaster clouds, the touch on my shoulder startled me. With a rustle of dry leaves Eliza stood before me, looked into my face – the familiar black eyes opened wide – grinning, warm tears in her soft eyes as she ran back to me, plait bobbing, stretching up, brushing her lips against mine, throwing her arms around my back, hugging me close. My tears washed away the dirt on her cheeks, ran down her scars, dropped to her lips, mingled with her own: no matter how much we have someone, we never really appreciate what we have until it's gone.

Walking amongst the late autumn flowers, golden landscape, natural altar to the afternoon sun, head held high, was that a glint of pleasure I saw in her eyes, as she looked ahead, watching the boats drifting slowly down the stream? The multitude of vessels, some going and other coming, some under sail and others with oars was they tears of pleasure that White Poppy cried? '*I want you.*'

Having made our way slowly through the pass between two mountains, we climbed upwards to get an idea of where we were headed, scrambling precariously, fingers bleeding, a fresh breeze cooling us: on one side a perpendicular cliff down to a swift flowing stream, and above us a decaying fortress, a series of imposing ramparts and towers lining the sky. A neighbouring hill had a little temple on the top, its glazed green tiles shining brilliantly in the sun, overhung by the dull green of a solitary pine: quiet, still, abandoned with no sign of life apart from white birds circling slowly overhead. I pulled her along by the hand, felt the female intimacy of her long fingers, *despite being to all outward appearance the 'boy'*; the erotic pain of that first contact, until we reached the top and I let go of her fingers and headed straight towards the outer gateway of the temple precincts, wooden gates standing open wide, great hinges long rusted. Passing through a second gateway, the gate itself having rotted away, I walked into the deserted temple, face to face with the heathen gods – weather-beaten, heads crowned with bird droppings, sitting calmly in their dilapidated shrine exposed to the afternoon sky, alone, but there were newly charred stumps of incense-sticks lying on fresh ashes in a bronze bowl.

White Poppy remained outside the inner gate, vulnerable, exposed; refused to enter further, tears in her seductive almond eyes. I had been there before. Many times I had stood at the Canton city wall, outside its very gates, but there was no way in. Every now and then a part of the gate would open, an inner door, and some male Chinese would hurry out as though there were others there waiting to get in: the invisible Canton ghosts. It was the same with White Poppy; many times I had stood there ready to breach her defences. Every now and then her eyes would move, her lips would open, but only for a moment, only to breathe when she was climbing, out of breath. And now and then a Cantonese word would fall out, an exclamation, sigh; fall out to be lost in the silence.

27

The day almost gone, standing on the outer plinth towards the rear of the temple, I looked out and over the breath-taking view, the hillside dropping sheer below me, teetering on the edge of nothing, empty space stretching to the barrier of rippling mountains opposite; naked, scarred, purple lights and shadows in the sunset, glowing golden, red; quiet, apart from the moaning of the wind that stirred her loose clothes, the rustling of the long-bladed grass. She refused to enter further. I grabbed hold of her hand, pulled her roughly towards me. She began to wail and then scream hysterically, throwing herself against me, pounding closed fists against my chest, pushing to get past to leave the small precincts and to escape down the hill. I shouted at her to stop, to shut up. But she didn't, and I hit her hard across her face, a fierce slap across her Chinese lips, knocking her to the ground. And she stopped, staring at me with incredulity, pain, such hate in her gorgeous slant eyes, her mouth dry but bleeding, her lips full in anger, and as I bent down to her she tore out at me with her claws, threw herself against me, weeping with tired frustration, and she lay there whimpering, hands over her head, trembling – the citadel taken, the battle lost. Little girl lost in an adult body, she had pushed the male plait away from her face, looking across quickly at the temple, where the outer gates were then shut, before lying still.

As if wakened from a long sleep she smiled, parting her swollen lips, opening out the soft features of her new-flowering beauty. I felt her scars, even more aware of her crooked fingers, the missing tip of the little finger on her left hand. The lips are the entrance through which we get inside those we love, through which we taste the very essence of the life that lies within. Each girl a bud to grow, to blossom, to flower, to produce more of her kind, and yet so unhappy, so very, very sad: *the opportunity for things to go wrong is intense.*

Everything slows down, the concentrated gaze, the focus on the sacrificial body before you, mind drifting free in some other far off place, yet totally aware of every potential touch, each little feeling of two bodies poised for contact. Focussed on the 'black eyes', the lips, moving back to the eyes, flickering, staring still, watching them expand, brown irises moving, polished pupils spreading, shining black growing large. Head still, forward, ready, mouth set, lips apart, swelling, glowing, face flushed, hot – sweating. Parting her proud red lips, she pressed her dirty mouth against mine. Throwing her arms around my neck, digging fingertip deep, she closed her silk-cool lips over my lips, searching roughly, pressing against me, pushed her tongue inside my mouth, choking me. And I tasted her; feeling the back of her male-plaited hair, matted dirty; smelling the unwashed odours of her body, eager to get inside her, to rip off her rags; searching, frantic, as I unbound and exposed her full breasts, feeling their returning firm roundness, perspiration wet, cool nipples rising to my fingers.

I kissed her Chinese face now wet with saliva, running my lips across her shining cheeks, the tip of my tongue along her scars, searching for the return of the fragrant mouth, her swollen lips. The taste was everything, the touch of her lips, the forceful pressure of her hot mouth: taste it, feel it, taste it tingling across the tongue. OOOOOhhhhh... feel it dripping, running, flowing. Smell her skin, the salt-musk-pungent smell around her lips; taste her flesh, taste that which has been desired so long; let her lie against me, feel her breasts firm, hard against my chest, pressing, lying, tightening. Pushing up her rags, opening White Poppy with my fingers, taking our fate into my own hands, I pushed inside her naked thighs, took hold of her boyish hair, pressing into her, forcing her into the dry earth below the temple.

28

Floating, lifting, rising, soaring through the air. The frost was bitter. As winter approached, the temperature becoming colder with each passing day, I began to worry about White Poppy and her ability to keep going. The north wind blew violently for several days, black clouds gathering for miles around. It was very cloudy, bitterly cold, the hard ground covered in burning frost.

As the first new snow began to fall, flake by flake, softly, slowly, snowflakes dancing in the grey sky, soon filling the sky with a swirling whiteness, I felt a mixture of exhilaration and defeat, of joy and deepest sadness. White mist swirling, filling our lungs with its freezing coldness, we ran together to keep warm; ran along laughing, skipping like children, kicking up the snow, our breath vaporising in the cold still air that rose over the frozen lake. The mist thinning, the sun peeped out over the top of the peak, the sharp frostiness of the early-morning air penetrated slowly by the glowing rays of the rising sun that shot up behind the snow-crest of the distant, silent mountain, beyond the vast ocean of white snow. For us, China would soon be history.

On New Year's Eve – the last day of the old lunar year – it snowed once more, a flake and then another flake, the weather becoming more severe by the day. The Chinese New Year is a splendid affair, fifteen days of holiday until the Lantern Festival on the fifteenth, the first full moon of the year, villagers making paper lanterns, kites to be flown; we passed by strips of red paper painted with lucky sayings, proverbs, pasted over doorways, door-god pictures and versed hangings posted on gateways for good fortune: the air heavy with the smells of roast pork, baked carp, hot rolls deep-fried in goose fat, steamed buns stuffed with minced pork, washed down with cups of hot rice wine. On this festival everyone eats rice dumplings, shaped like the full moon, made of kneaded rice and flour, stuffed with sweet things and boiled.

Fire crackers lit to frighten evil spirits away, rounds of gun-powder going off like gun-fire, green branches burned to mark the passing of the Old Year, it is a time when old scores are settled and prisoners cleared out by mass execution. In Canton, the prisoners would be kneeling down in rows, the executioner passing from one to the next, dealing death with a single blow to the neck from a long and heavy sword; *terror and fear*. Pulling up her skirts, White Poppy relieved herself by the wall, made water that rushed steaming between her feet.

The Lantern Festival on the 15th day of January, nightfall, it would soon be New Year. A myriad paper lanterns hanging in the trees, hanging from arches across the streets within the city walls, wind blowing them lightly to and fro, illuminating the fairy-garden whole: red and green dragons flying over mountains, storks gazing skywards, lanterns of golden lotus, towers of jewelled jade. I watched White Poppy watching them, the wonder in her tear-burned eyes. We'd stood transfixed before the kitchen window. A deep metal plate strewn with celery stalks and herbs, upon which lay a whole carp, split open. The cook basted it with oil, sprinkled it with ground Sichuan pepper and cumin, trickled over a dark chilli sauce, and cooked it.

The fish sizzled as they plucked its flesh from its bones with chopsticks. Later the guests left, fulfilled.

From high on the hill we watched them, crouching together, hungry in our dangerous darkness, shivering, freezing, moon risen high in the star-sprinkled sky, surrounded by the noise of the fair, its fire-eaters and jugglers; a gyrating New Year lion, decorated paper head, bells jangling on tassels of coloured silk, dancing to the beat of a drum, chasing a somersaulting monkey, and a clown on stilts; watched the procession of bright lights making its way forward, marching to flutes and drums, streaming incense as it went. And we slipped away as the fireworks were set off outside the gate – lotuses showering golden rain, golden-threaded chrysanthemums of fire, orchid sprays some ten feet high, crackers exploding with thunder, rockets ripping light-trails in the velvet sky.

We spent the night in an outhouse stable that smelled sour and earthy warm. It snowed fast, blowing in hard from the sea – flakes flurrying, wind-blown blossom dropping from a whitewashed sky. Wind rising, we huddled close together, stamped our feet to keep them warm.

Yes, she was witnessing the manifestations of her ghost world in more ways than one. Pink cheeks amongst pink blossoms. The blind is drawn aside for the briefest moment, yet we catch the vision of a million years.

Through the window of a country house, I watched a group of women eating sweet rice-dumplings, New Year's cake. Finished eating, they washed their hands rinsed out their mouths. White Poppy shivered, her teeth chattering, her body shaking convulsively. Then it stopped, then it went quiet and she sank down, still, in her rags, a crumpled package against the low wall, below the buildings covered in the white of death: the shivering chill of hell, a gnawing ache in every bone, in the darkness, silence broken only by the falling of the snow, the swoosh of water on the beach, the blackness of the rushing sea, a dog barking distant. We were almost there. Shanghai could not be far, but White Poppy was dying – her lips were blue, her face was blue, her skin seemed somehow tighter.

There were few people about on the frozen lake and by the frozen river. Bundled up in long heavy coats they went about their meagre work, blistered scales of frostbite on their wind-chapped ears and lips. Peasants from the surrounding countryside who had come into town to sell their produce, and bedded down with their potatoes and cabbages in open carts at night. At intervals there was the warmth of a charcoal fire. We nibbled discarded winter roots. I had not felt so cold, had never felt such extreme pain in my fingers and my toes. Prison had been hell, but those Canton winters now seemed nowhere as severe as that winter in the North. The winter was harsh; the China winds were fierce from across the coast. Our clothes, our ragged clothes, were covered in chilling frost. I knew we must get padded jackets to survive, but how? The bright whiteness hurt our eyes, the sun-sparkled snow shining all around: it was beautiful, one of the most beautiful views I have ever seen snowfields sweeping away vast into the distance, beyond outcrops of snow-covered trees – it was magical but without any magic.

It got cloudy in the afternoon, and the sun went out. This was it, this was the end for us both, and we would die frozen in each other's arms: White Poppy would die in her frozen white, beautiful bride of death.

As new snow fell deeply on top of that which had fallen over the weeks, snow compressed deep, compacted ice, we were too cold to run together to keep warm; were too cold to appreciate the true danger as we ascended the heights, keeping away from the hidden edges, making our way towards the smoking orange glow of an unexpected hamlet ahead.

We got padded jackets, certainly not new, exchanged the last of my silver for the jackets and some hot food – there was no other way of staying alive. It was very cold and the ground was frozen hard, all water frozen solid. Our padded jackets saved us from the worst of the bitter frost and we made our way down out of the mountains for Shanghai.

Waking to the vision of a pale winter sun, of snow melting beyond a window, a vision of a wooden cabin and the heart of a roaring log fire, we saw the religious hermit, he who had discovered us covered in snow, who took us in: he who hauled us one after the other into his isolated mountain home; he who gave us hot vegetable and rice broth to warm us back to life. But life for what – where was there left for us to go?

BOOK V RIDING THE BACK OF THE TIGER

Shanghai, China
1840

1

On the Third day of the Third Month, acrobats perform Sparrow on a bamboo Tip in Taoist temples. A tall bamboo pole is erected in the courtyard. They climb to its top and dance there, slide up and down its swaying length, strike many daring poses while with every change in the wind, the audience sweats below. We had been right to trust God.

Before the dyked canals of the Shanghai delta, the sharply lined, treeless hills and rich lowland valleys of the rugged islands of the Chusan Archipelago, stretch 35 miles north-eastwards from Luhwang shan. The sea, with its deep channels and anchorages, is heavily impregnated with mud from the tidal Yangtze, where ships to freedom anchor near Woosung, threading into the crowded Whangpoo harbour.

The Yangtze would break its dykes several times in the early 1840s, inundating vast lowland areas, killing millions in the floods, freeing thousands more to prostitution in the coastal cities. We were in a dilemma, '*Ge seung foo booi*', as White Poppy put it (we now had to 'ride on the tiger's back').

Shanghai itself is a sprawling, festering place: squalid waterfront, walls hung with the heads of China pirates. The place was a mess - narrow, poorly paved streets; dirtier and smellier than I remembered those at Canton were, beggars everywhere, nothing very grand. Barbers plaiting pig-tails, street entertainers, fire-spinning jugglers, the only light in that hellish, soaking darkness, before the dark brown stain pressing out into the blue sea at the end of Perfumed Melon Street.

Sitting together on the quayside, the sailor and the whore, watching the early morning sun coming up over the horizon, watching the fishermen packing their nets, cleaning their boats, scrubbing the wood clean, White Poppy slipped away to pee, hauling up her clothes, squatting in the way that women do, the amber liquid flowing from her, steaming in the cool air.

But she was seen, was watched by two men beyond the stacked bales of cotton: who saw that what she had between her legs was not that which they expected for a youth, that despite her shaven head, her long pigtail, everything else about her said 'girl'. Pulling back her clothes she ran like fury, chased by the two Chinese who ran after her shouting furiously.

I watched in horror as both men rounded on her, driving her towards a corner like a frightened rabbit. I picked up a bale of cotton and hurled it at the first of them knocking him out of the way, but the other turned with a vengeance, and I thought I would have to use my knife. Grabbing White Poppy by the hand, I pulled her away from them, picked her up and ran with her to the safety of the open where we could see who was coming to attack us, sea wind scraping in my lungs, tearing at my throat.

I put her down, and we ran as fast as we could, dodging in and out of the waterfront buildings, feet pounding painfully on the stone flags; to be caught now would mean the sudden end to all that we had striven for, China would be our home for ever. Slipping into the back alleyways, we hid amongst the loads on the waterfront, pulling ourselves in tightly, hardly daring to breathe as we watched both men searching, walking up and down the rows of cargo, prodding with their long sticks, until they were called back to work, laughing, hands gesturing down below.

2

'I don't like to put a master mariner in the fo'c'sle,' the captain of the *Georgina* said, 'but I'm willing to sign you on as a quartermaster.' His cold blue eyes sparkled bright. 'We have four quartermasters – two in each watch, one at the wheel and one standing by – there are no other duties than steering – and they live in the half-deck with the apprentices at the break of the poop. That's the best I can offer you.'

With a strong shake of his hand, I agreed. The East India merchantman weighed anchor and set sail from Shanghai, painted wooden figurehead, golden tresses of 'Georgina', facing into the stiff breeze. She was a 'flier' but would still take some five to six months on the passage of twelve thousand miles from the China Seas to London, through Suns Strait and round South Africa, with refreshment stops at Mauritius, Cape Town and Saint Helena.

Myself and a standby quartermaster we replaced each other hourly at the wheel (which operated the rudder by a manual chain-gear), on the stroke of the ship's bell, so that each of us had two tricks of one hour at the wheel in each four-hour watch. In heavy weather, helmsmen together we handled the wheel skilfully. In the Northeast Trade Winds, the ship made frequent tacks. It was a delight to steer her, sails swelling as the yards were hauled around at each tack, her officers in their smart uniforms alert so that she never missed stays.

I had slipped White Poppy on to the *Georgina*, under cover of darkness, having previously arranged with the

British captain for *my* passage to India; stowing her away below decks, slipping her food when I could, mugs of cold tea, emptying the jar in which she pissed and shitted. I started each morning with exhilaration, the sun shining high and bright, the sky a cloudless blue on every side; a fresh, dry, breeze blowing in the sails. Listening to the rush of the sea, hiss of the water above the bows, Chinese whispers of the sea around jagged passing islands rising from the typhoon sea, I saw ribbons of terracotta fish-spawn trailed across the water.

Pink-eyed, restless, the rat-catcher's ferret twists its long thin body in its even longer, thinner prison box. Huddled in her rags, clutching her little bundle tight by her side, riding the sea in perpetual darkness, shut away down there in the suffocating heat, the whore was starving, her eyes having lost their brilliant sparkle, a tremble in her twisted hands.

The sea plays strange tricks on the mind when one is far from land, there is a totality of nothingness, when al around is sky and sea, when all that breaks the monotony is the ship herself; she who whispers mysteriously as she makes her way forward, wind filling her proud sails, billowing canvas taut, above the wrecks that litter the bottom of the jealous sea. A few days out from Sumatra, listening to the murmur of the sea, the balmy evening quiet and still, I watched it getting dark, the rising of the moon, observed her climbing sharply to the zenith, ship's masts scraping the clammy tropical sky. Towards midnight, the wind was abeam, blowing off the land, driving us at some speed, sea smooth – not a single cloud in the star-peppered sky.

Some little time later it was gusting, large clouds forming London-grey ahead. We were going home to freedom, and I felt that first thrill of being free, excited by the coming storm.

3

We shortened sail, topmost yards sent down on deck, the wind howling, blowing a gale, filling the sails; blowing them clean away over as heads as we battled to lower them, soaked to the skin, no stars shining now, no moon to light the way of a lone ship suffocated by the blackened screaming heavens. Ship's hatches under water, deck boats torn away, smashed to pieces by the roaring, screaming wind as the sea boiled, a mass of seething foam. The rain fell in solid spirals, fierce columns of water bouncing upwards from the deck. The wind blowing hard in the squalls, a terrible chilling howl, the ship pushed over flat on her side, cross-trees skimming the smother to leeward, knocked back each time we attempted to bring her to, sailing blind.

White Poppy lay still below decks in the hold, frail body hurled from side to side, helpless in the suffocating darkness, tossed around in the smashing, bruising black. Ship tossed on the heaving sea, God's toy now, pushed around like the driftwood boat of a young boy. He kicks at the boat, turns it on its side. Twin ships forge on, bows cutting through the mounting waves, steering clear of ripping rocks by the jagged gale-blown land. The memories are still strong. First ship strikes, splintering, back broken, sprawled out across the rocks, lying like a dying whore: womb slashed, bloody guts spilling out all around. Second ship turned on beam, capsized, agonising long in the cruel sea, sails blown out in tatters: beached ship broken, smashed bow crushed into the unwelcome land.

During the storm White Poppy hung on, wrapping herself in discarded canvas to protect her body. But she was badly bruised, her face swollen, eyes cut. She was repeatedly sick. She needed medicine, fresh air; needed proper food, proper care and attention, to stop her dying.

4

In the calm that followed, I carried White Poppy up on deck, the wind and rain having ceased as suddenly as they had begun, the ship standing up again, rocking gently from side to side on the mirror sea. Not a breath of wind stirred the air as she lay floating underneath the dense misty cloud that hung all around us, vast canopy, still, in the centre of the cyclone, that had unfinished business still.

I had little time, the storm would return, would come in again with a deafening roar, striking her sideways, with a force that would match the wrath of the captain when his eyes met those dark almonds of the Chinese whore. There was blood caked on her lips, dried vomit at the corners of her mouth, her face puffy and bruised. The elderly grey-haired master opened his mouth to speak. His cold blue eyes took in the details of the rat before him. His fast mind calculated the risks, the reality of what he saw before him – a pathetic Chinese girl on her knees, breasts exposed through the rips in her stinking, salt-soaked rags. This was a violent storm indeed! His eyes moved over the dirty face, searching for clues as he stood there tall before her, unblinking, thinking, before looking long and hard at me. What did he make of the oddity of her hair obviously once shaven at the front, at the rat-tail of the plait that hung limply behind; at the scars above her right cheek, at the tattoo of the snake just visible on her upper arm. What clues were these? She wore the rough clothes of a Chinese youth, and yet beneath the mire there sparkled the most intense female beauty: I saw that the captain saw it too.

'God help you,' he said suddenly, forcefully. 'You poor wee thing, God help you!'

He extended his hand briefly, touching her lightly on the head.

'Take her away,' he shouted to the First Mate, 'take her away and get her some food, get her cleaned up.'

He stood before me, God judging the sinner, looking up into my good eye. I felt the full force of the storm on his lips, the full chill of the focussed blue.

'You, Sir,' he said coldly, 'You Sir have let me down badly.'

I returned his gaze, and at that moment felt something pass between us, a sort if understanding, a warm glow of something deep inside: the common humanity that binds men together.

'Take him away. Lock him below! One week, no food, no water!'

Back in came the wind: howling, boiling typhoon sea... The journey back to England was a long and tiring one, many different ships, and many different stages, until finally we made that last voyage to London up the Thames, sailing into the metropolis of urban filth and decay, the docks crowded with unsavoury characters of every sort. White Poppy was repeatedly sick, and for the first I kept her hidden away.

BOOK VI SPARKS OF HEAVEN BURST INTO FLAME

London, England
October 1840

1

Back in England, this would be White Poppy's future home. Making our way across the chill grey dockyard, we walked towards the soot-blackened brick, massive walls, darkness; movements in the shadows, decay and disease. We walked shrouded, by the red brick offices and outhouses, beside the yards kept shipshape by unskilled labourers, now drawn up in a line, the strongest-looking selected to work for the day. I acknowledged the parish prig, the Chaplain, on his way to *Tuck Up Fair*, as the Gallows were so fondly called, beyond the *Floating Academy* – the Hulks, the prison ship down in the Docks.

London in winter, floating in the quiet fog, veiled wonders along the great River Thames over which hung bridges with coronets of lit gas, where smoking chimney buildings sailed like tall ships; rank, land and property, riches, shining, sparkling in amongst the destitution and decay. My phantoms were there in the stinking Thames swirling fiercely by. I had business to attend to in the City and then we'd leave by coach for Kent.

Six o'clock that Friday morning, donkey-barrows laden with fresh fish stretched from the Monument to Billingsgate, and the last of the London whores dragged home. Long rows of carts and donkey-barrows gathered in the early-morning streets around Covent Garden: a carthorse munched the apples on a neighbour's cart. In the dark shops under the Piazza, gas lights hissed burning bright like stars, shadowy shapes moving briskly in the cold dawn air, welcome relief found by the glowing charcoal braziers. From within her enclosing hood White Poppy watched them; Eliza in her English clothes – understanding not one word; black wool coat over a dark blue silk dress trimmed with pale blue, and black laced boots, her scarred Chinese face hidden. It would take time for her hair to grow, for her body to take on the soft shape of a woman once more, having travelled so long as 'male'. Understanding Cantonese, she was oblivious to the harsh voices, the ramblings about her.

Like a stirring hive of bees, low murmuring hum building with the sound of a distant sea, the dock-side market grew anew beneath the pink-red sky, vast square unfolding, bursting into life as the new-risen sun painted in the details, the multicolour of vegetables and fruit, where a girl lay dying; the spectre of the hungry working girl outside the gin palace, tightly shut up, revealing nothing but sleep and silence. But go in at night and be dazzled by gaslight. On the first floor, an immense *salon* with a row of tables separated by wooden partitions on one side; on both sides of each table were benches made up of sofas, and a stage where the prostitutes, all dressed up, displayed themselves; enticed the men with their glances and remarks, drinking their tea. *Prostitution – that most hideous vice.* I feared we'd miss the moment of sunrise, but the entire expanse lit up in an intense burst of incandescent orange; one of those transcendent moments that burns into the memory and lingers for a lifetime in one's soul.

White Poppy walked a little distance from me but by my side. She was like a child to me, vulnerable, trusting, free. She looked at me with her large and child-like black Chinese eyes, my precious China pearl. She moved her left arm with its wrist-bangle of green-dragon jade, celestial semen turned to stone, and stared at me with the look that said: *I will go with you but don't you dare try to touch me.*

2

Nightfall, we stepped from the carriage and made our way into the City, past a splendid public house: plate-glass and gilding, stone balustrades, rosewood fittings, light and brilliancy, at the intersection of two impossible streets. Under a hissing gas light, a shaggy-bearded trickster invited bystanders to bet on which of three thimbles covered a large dried pea. *Crikey mate, and you a gent you can't help but win.* He was a buttoner – one who enticed another to play a game which cheating ruled – card-s*harping* under the arches, assisted by a *nobbler* – in this case a ragged girl, his confederate in the practice of thimble rigging, encouraging up the person marked for plunder – the *plant.* No matter which thimble was chosen, the pea had mysteriously moved to a different place – sleight of hand, with the promise of making easy money many fools would lose their hard-earned money there. They might spend time on the shin scraper – the ever-revolving treadmill, if ever they were caught. Nearby was Holywell Street, monument to every sort of filth and foulness, with its bookshops dealing in indecent prints and volumes; the display of vile disgusting obscenities in the windows of the old lofty gabled houses with their overhanging fronts, and nearby, available *ladies*, on the fringes of the Minories. Sailors went there, bought printed items loathsome to the eye, indecent plaster medallions also: *offensive to the morals of any well-regulated mind.*

White Poppy, wrapped Chinese jewel, followed me in under an ornamented parapet, illuminated clock, plate-glass windows surrounded by stucco rosettes, profusion of gaslights in richly lit burners. Through double doors of etched glass into the tobacco-smoke filled room, a bar of French-polished mahogany, elegantly carved; two aisles of great casks, painted green and gold enclosed within a light brass rail - *Old Tom*, *Blue Ruin* – an unpolished wooden floor, the exotic flash of silvered mirrors: multiple reflections of every debasing act. In the yard three players rehearsed a skit on this woman *on the shallow*, going about half-naked, undressed, to excite compassion. She had been a *fine* wirer, a long-fingered thief emptying the pockets of fine ladies. The second had been *flyin' the blue pidg'n* (stealing lead from roofs); the third was a *bit*-faker (coiner of money). The players recited a verse, a moral tale:

'Like *bug* hunters, they went, those midnight prowlers who robbed drunken men, moving on to *much* worse, the *dead lurk* – entering a dwelling while the family were at church.'

The skit ended with all three thrown in the *Salt Box*, the condemned cell, after being told the error of their ways (and being given God's forgiveness), by the prison chaplain, *Lady Green,* to rot until they *croaked.*

After a night in separate rooms in a well-appointed coaching inn, we made the coach trip down to Kent, pulled by two chestnut horses. As we left, by other carriages passing by, I heard: 'Chuck down your mouldy coppers': the tiresome chant from the ragged Thames urchins, searching for the few spare coins thrown down from those on the coach, into the mud; acrobatic children, running alongside, making cartwheels – turning head over heels on their hands. 'Give us your brass!'

3

Imposing villa in mottled yellow brick, not six years old, unfussy brick tower to the east, chimney stacks rising tall above a pewter-slate roof; bushes straddling the path, central porch standing forwards in greeting; cheerful, plain brickwork with horizontal flint banding; simple bays, gables sharp, bargeboards broad and uncarved; smooth lines heightened by the shadows of the late afternoon sun. Grand house, alone, above the sea at Birchington; not far from Margate, in Kent; bought with drug-won silver, it was our new home.

She followed me in through the lobby, across the exquisite terracotta and black hard stone tiled floor. The house was silent, smelling of lavender polish and new wood. Planned round a large hall rising the building's full height, the stairs climbing up to the gallery landing, florets of circular stained-glass flooding red-blue-yellow-green light, edged bands of bright purple; above crisp stonework, red brickwork bonding exposed timber within, unadorned panelling in all the main rooms, mosaic tiling, decorated alabaster and gold.

White Poppy ran up there, looking back with a wicked flourish of her skirts – disappearing into the unknown, feet tapping distant on the polished wooden floor. Luscious crimson, open mouth, entrance of the most erotic lips, red lips, wisps of raven hair blowing about their silent moistness, a sad smile hiding tears. Gorgeous, glistening, black-bronzed almond eyes, blinking slowly, sadly, reflecting all around, long lashes flicking, eyelids closing over those beautiful polished stones. Those eyes, those beautiful staring brown eyes, penetrating, deep, the first time in the house; the first time and her eager to explore all the rooms. The Boat-Girl was not used to houses still, but marvelled at the size of everything around her – muttering all the time in Cantonese. But she soon showed her cold indifference to him.

White Poppy, Eliza, sweetly pretty, who scarred your face, broke your fingers, cut off the tip from your little finger? Who put the shadow of fear into your eyes, trimmed the edges from your smile? Like her outermost Chinese clothes, her innermost secrets would be shed.

She stood watching on the floor tiles tessellated white, terracotta and blue; walked across to the kitchen window, looked out into the garden, brushing back her growing hair, searching for something, scanning the fallen leaves for a glimpse of something past, remembered, seen. She watched the occasional solitary sailing ship, only sign of life breezing along the grey horizon, leaden East Coast sea, the house standing defiant, naked, raw, standing proud above the sea-fields. I felt the need to keep looking over my shoulder, that there *was* something in the shadows beneath the yellow brick wall. But we were safe here! I heard it sighing in the leaves of the tree branches agitated by the wind; I heard it in the wind that blew around the eaves; I heard it in the rolling waves breaking distant on the shore. There was something there that I could not yet see, something lurking in the shadows that White Poppy would no doubt one day reveal to me.

4
Ninsun went into her room, she put on a dress becoming to her body, she put on jewels to make her breast beautiful, she placed a tiara on her head and her skirts swept the ground. Then she went up to the Altar of the Sun, standing upon the roof of the palace; she burnt incense and lifted her arms to Shamash as the smoke ascended... The Epic of Gilgamesh, p72).

Birchington in Kent, is a close-knit neighbourhood of coarse-yellow-brick cottages and cottage-like dwellings; children in coarse clothes, ragged boots, heads covered from the biting cold in their unheated rooms, faces framed in coarse linen, woven bonnets covering heads with faces shining red from the chill that hangs beneath their low ceilings, box furniture, bare floors, cracked walls; children get ready for the festival of Christ. Ragged youths fight and quarrel on the streets, boxing with bare fists, running, keeping warm. It was unusual to see a Chinese person anywhere in Kent. White Poppy walked everywhere with her head enclosed, her face covered by a hood, which itself attracted attention. I felt protective of her, because of what they might think of her. But one day they would marvel at her unusualness, the novelty of this stunning Chinese. How they would stare at her when finally she was 'exposed'.

Outside it was foggy, thick grey mist swirling in from the sea, and the expensive village girls went out to their carriage, footman with a lantern held up high above his head, coat buttoned up to his nose, walking slowly in front of the horses. These girls were not whores – each girl destined to be a trusting wife. The village hall was bright, glowing softly from lanterns hanging at the windows, thrusting light into the foggy night. Village girls stood smiling in their white frocks trimmed with blue sashes, washed hair brushed neatly, pale white faces scrubbed a rosy red; standing together ready in the hall, shivering from the cold, from the excitement building in their veins.

The girls stood together, ran together, danced holding hands, skipping round together in a ring, singing verses of *The Village Blacksmith*, high-pitched voices rising to the roof. Hair parted down the middle, ringlets hanging down,

Eliza acted dumb in that new company, hid the sharp beauty of her olive oriental face, kept it covered, smiled sweetly when talked to, nodding, lips compressed tight, legs pressed together, close beneath her voluminous multi laced dress.

To love, honour and obey and amuse her lord and master, to manage the household and bring up his children. To seduce, but to give something back in return. Shrouded in her crumpled white muslin dress, Eliza was sad, White Poppy cried, shed tears daily for something deep within her past, withdrew away from me, shut herself away, alone in her bedroom. From our first day in Birchington she had wept. I watched her through the opened door. Were we ever not at war – with each other, with ourselves inside?

Drawing-room with dark patterned wallpaper stretching from the brown painted wainscot to the picture rail; the furniture massive, chiefly walnut and rosewood; the Japanese Oak dining table - long, extending, richly polished and dark with age, White Poppy sat still with her hand over her eyes: who knew what she thought about so far away from her Canton home? Crystal clusters and mineral ores glittering in the heavy-curtain filtered light; sunlight kept out by the heavy brass ringed brocade curtains hung on great poles, Nottingham lace curtains, heavy plush burgundy velvet side-curtains. The walls encrusted with oil paintings, watercolours, engravings, embroideries and silhouettes, and now occasional photos also of her Birchington life. Before the smallest window, on a small oval yew table, the single cream-coloured and chocolate-brown orchid, flowering once more, sweet scent spreading with the hours. I watched her distant, sitting still by the window listening to the cliff top quiet, penetrated only by the insistent ticking of the clock that chime regularly, mechanical reality of this clockwork life.

5

When it rains, Eliza, drips wet tears down your wet thighs. When it rains, Eliza; runs the black kohl around your mud-brown eyes, water pouring down your semi-naked body, in rivulets at your feet, that patter through the puddles that lie weeping across the street, that ends in a high brick wall against whose running surface you wetly fall. When it rains, Eliza, your dry mouth calls out in pain, your eyes turn your inner sunshine from brightness into rain. The words left my lips slowly, eaten by the silence.

'You are the most beautiful creature!'

She stared at me blankly, eyes ever moving, quivering, flicking here and there; assessing the situation. She played with her long crooked fingers, looking down at them in her lap, looking back up at me, her eyes full of mystery, of wonder, of repressed fear, the mystery and the mist of tears in her teasing almond eyes. So what was different then? Could intense hatred turn into love?

What she was inside, who she really was, only time would tell: only the passing days together here in England would let me into the deepest secrets of her soul. What did *she* really remember – what did *she* think? How I longed to know the tortured thoughts that flickered through her mind.

'Who are you,' I asked.

She stared back at me, was always staring, distant; glared at me for daring to 'share' my feelings with her. I was sure she knew more than she said, and when she opened her mouth, it was only to speak in Cantonese. When I looked at her lips, she looked at my eye patch then my one good eye; when I looked into her eyes, she looked away at my mouth. When her eyes caught mine, she looked away quickly, picking at her fingers, as though she had something unpleasant there, like grains of sand itching under her skin. In her Chinese eyes I saw something smouldering, burning; something dormant then coming alive. Yet she withdrew herself, shut herself away inside, closed her eyes to me. The door once slightly open, now shut tight closed. Red lips that move, a spider's thread of saliva hanging between them. Guy Fawkes' night the starlit sky was clear and the ground sparkled with frost, the wind blowing strands of Eliza's hair across the corners of her mouth.

Reflected in her eyes, the bonfire roared high with tongues of orange fire, toasting her bright cheeks; scattered fireworks exploding all around, Catherine wheels whizzing. Beacon out to sea. Holding her hands, feeling the crooked little fingers where broken bones never grew together straight. Remembering summer shadows deepening, remembering, the brightly-coloured one-girl boats that skimmed the water-trafficked surface of the Pearl, lazy insects shrilling to the descending cloak of darkness; Christmas tree of paper lanterns around the lolling flower-boats, red-paper lanterns of the public brothels dotting the suburbs where the sky burned crimson. Remembering, the main streets lit with oil lamps, night watchman making his rounds, beating his gong, calling time; fire-crackers popping, snapping, rockets shooting high into the velvet sky, orange sparks showering, falling down. Remembering, a blinding light, the most tremendous bang; gunpowder exploding, boat sinking, bits of body floating all around; monastery fire burning, orange flames licking their way up the tinder-dry eaves, guest hall erupting into fire.

6

Three times a week I accompanied White Poppy to Broadstairs, through the magnificent gold-scrolled wrought iron gates and railings of the Chinese Doctor's manor house above the sea. It was a classical house set nakedly in a vast smooth sea of lawn, with a nearby lake with an island, and a swift stream snaking its way down into the woodland; a park with a belt of trees surrounding the pastoral whole. Asymmetrical, irregular in outline, a tall pointed spire on the east wing tower, pitched roofs with ornamented ridge tiles dwarf the crenellated parapet at the centre, twisted brick chimneys rising above the battlemented pitched roof, set above a heavy, protruding, buttressed porch enriched with fine carving and magnificent copper moss-grown domes.

The Great Hall there was embellished with armorial bearings and at the far end a flight of steps climbing through a high Gothic arch to a salon below the tower. The Tudor Room, lavish with dark woodcarving and bright colours, a blue ceiling above studded with golden stars, darkness, solemnity and doom, led into the study; the Tudor Room where I sat waiting while Eliza had her earliest lessons. She was learning English from the great Reverend Ambrose Jeptha Johns, Doctor of Divinity: would supplement the little English she had learned in Canton – the educated Chinese whore, and then I would know, then she'd tell me the secrets of her China past.

There was an Icehouse of cup and dome construction with the cup below ground level with a walled roof of mortared brick. Ice cut from the rivers and ponds in winter, and packed in straw, lasted through until the autumn. In the summer it kept butter, lard, eggs, milk and other perishable foodstuffs fresh. Rock-works planted with alpines had interspersed fragments of white marble in imitation of snow, and spar and quartz in imitation of ice. There was also a massive glasshouse with pine pits for producing pineapples, a vinery for grapes, and separate smaller houses for early strawberries and other fruit, and a showy coal-heated conservatory with exotic tropical plants and trees. Eliza went there frequently to study. It was the most wonderful house – if I'd then had children of my own, I would have asked the Chinese Doctor for his permission to take them there.

White Poppy also received lessons of a different sort from the good doctor's wife Mahulda Katherine. She took it upon herself to teach the battered Chinese Poppy how to be an English lady, and with this little bird under her wing she transformed her charge into something fit and wholesome, who would not stand amiss in English society. Her orientalism was a novelty indeed, but she was In England now. Boned corsets usually arrived with adolescence, but White Poppy was gradually introduced to the prevailing mode of dress. Mrs Mahulda Katherine Ambrose Jeptha Johns introduced her charge to the wearing of these stiff stays, showed her how to skewer her hat through her hair with long bonnet pins, encased her arms in long tight gloves and her ankles in high buttoned boots, all paid for by myself. White Poppy became accustomed to the knee-length short-sleeved chemise; over this a back-laced, boned corset, then a camisole of white cotton shaped to the waist over it, and numerous petticoats. Corsets ensured English women controlled their physical appetites and reminded them constantly to control their moral ones too. It was this change in dress that necessitated the employment of another lady in our house, to take care of White Poppy's lacing and unlacing, and to attend to the very different laundry necessities and her other personal and moral needs.

From my first week back in England I was reminded of the application of God's law: emotion in women was a negative feature, and women were subservient to their masters who were men. That was outside the house but inside the world inside our little seaside villa, Eliza lived in a very different world indeed: neither British nor Chinese, but an amalgamation of the two very different cultures and our own interpretation of everything in between. The moral law: synonymous with religious law. It enshrined the duty of obedience to God. As head of the family a man derived his authority from God; his wife derived hers from him, and so on. Any disobedience was subversive. Daughters were expected to be obedient with no reason given.

7

The moon was bright through the bedroom window and I could not sleep, listening to Eliza breathing, in this 'glass cage', the rasping sighing of her tormented sleeping breath, but she would not run away from me (this time). I wanted to know her secrets, to get inside her tortured soul, and one day she would know enough English to convey that information to me.

Again, I picture the disastrous brothel-junks that form the jewelled necklace around Canton's throat; the long and slender flower boats and the Christmas tree of paper lanterns, beyond which red paper lanterns of the public brothels dotted the suburbs where the sky burned crimson with the blood of brothels; female blood flowing from the generations – old wounds of daughters, mothers, grandmothers, great-grandmothers and before: blood burned black with fire. Sleeping soundly, breathing softly through her mouth, White Poppy snored when she turned and lay flat on her back, dribbled from the corner of her mouth. I listened frequently to the changing rhythms of her breathing, waiting for the moment when it stopped, when it panted, when she wrestled with her dreams, breathless, alive.

I saw the burning tear-drops glide. The twisting of her scarred face, the pouting of her sleeping lips, the boat-girl: Eliza cried out, sobbing in her sleep, weeping for something lost to her (but she couldn't yet tell me what it was); lay wilted along the massive four-post bed (imported from Paris), clothed in green silk, woodbine scrolled figured metalwork, brass foliage entwined, ivy leaves climbing, above cushions of jade and copper-coloured chintz.

She woke melancholic, faded eyes tearful; shut herself away from me in the bedroom where she went quiet for days, silent, brooding, unwashed hair a-mess; going without food, sitting on her own in the great birch chair by the fire, legs crossed beneath her, wilting in its great heat. **The beautiful Chinese doll, Yin Hsueh-yen.**

Dressed in green watered-silk, hair loose, she walked across to the bedroom window, sat down on its wide ledge gazing out over the sea: ear-rings bobbing, watching the rush of the white-capped waves beneath the pewter sky, wind whipping up the foam, agitating the land, plucking at the tender chalk cliff. For a moment, she was silent; silence shattered by the squeal of the gulls that swooped and dipped near the afternoon shore. She spent much of each day watching the sea, the few ships passing: stands up, looking out through the opened window, silhouetted against the bright light shining in, through the shadows, a radiance all around her, blurring the definition of the details in the bedroom: this forest in springtime, wall-papered with cascades of Chinese willow catkins and flowers, that match the long three-panelled carpets on the polished wood floor; cane seated, stained maple chairs surrounding the birch dresser with its multiple mirrors (relief-patterned, behind) – scattered with opaline ornaments, glass engraved through silver stain. The mahogany washstand had towel rails on each side, tiled at the back against splashing: the basin, enamelled ewer, the shell-shaped soap-dish, and a similar one for the sponge, her wooden toothbrush, nailbrush, a water bottle and a glass. The large polished copper hip bath in the bedroom, filled with large metal copper cans in which hot water was carried up from the kitchen.

Our household being quite small at first, we employed a general maid-of-all-work: Ettie, 12 years, working-class girl from the village, a shock of crisp blonde hair, and sharp Forget-Me-Not blue eyes. It was her first position in domestic service. Initially on two days a week the house was cleaned, the laundry washed and aired, but otherwise White Poppy preferred to do it all herself, kept everything in its place as she had got used to, living in the cramped confines of a Canton houseboat. However, Ettie, quite knowing despite her rural roots, soon took on the household chores - scrubbing, cleaning, sweeping, dusting, attending to the fires, and she helped with the cooking, though White Poppy retained control of the kitchen. Ettie, started work at 6.30 and finished around 11 at night. She had arrived not knowing the names of even simple kitchen items. But there was nothing wanting in her, she certainly wasn't stupid; had just never used these items in her simple orphanage life. She hadn't then a clue of handling our expensive and delicate china pieces, and no idea of balancing a tray for tea.

Ettie was polite: when spoken to, she stood still, as she had been told, keeping her hands quiet, and looking at the person speaking; she talked only when necessary to deliver a message, and then quickly and quietly; she responded with a brief curtsey when she received an order, and never forgot the proper form of address – Sir, Ma'am, Miss or Mrs. She graciously gave room to all of us in the house and on the stairs, making herself as invisible as possible, averting her eyes and turning herself to the wall. As was usual, no male friends allowed. I noticed White Poppy talking to her in Cantonese, and Ettie graciously listened, a patient dream. Since the early 1800s, servants slept in the kitchen or in cupboards under the stairs, were given limited furnishings: a simple, wooden bed; a wooden ladder-back chair; a simple dresser; and a basic washstand and candles; gas lighting was reserved for use *Upstairs*. But White Poppy treated Ettie well, gave of her time to educate this pretty little miss who soon found her place in the tiny spare room of her own. We kept a large open fire in what became the Servant's area. Ettie took great pride in her work. Eliza afforded her simple pleasures, the sunny sitting room for reading, and a piano in the Servants' hall; and there were walks around the sea-top garden.

8

Don't look at me that way; take your hands from your hips. I had found it difficult to go out, to leave White Poppy on her own. But she would wander through the large hedged garden in which she could lose herself and roam. She sat out there at night, in the circle of trees, watched the rise of the full moon, and she knelt, and she prayed, petted and caressed by the sea breeze, head forced down, touching the earth. *I will find out about you, will get to know you well; will peel away the Chinese layers that are bound to your soul.* She stood by the drawing-room window, beyond which torrents of rain and gusts of wind agitated the sea-top garden. Standing behind her, looking-glass reflection, still, I viewed her with pleasure, watched the movement of the back of her shining black hair, soft contours of her neck, soft curve of her naked shoulders, gentle arching of her back in the closet, at her toilet. Her hair longer then, reaching down almost to her shoulders, tied loosely in scarlet velvet ribbon that trailed to her dimpled bottom.

She's a whore, a worthless whore.

I heard my Mother's words: at least the words that had come from her mouth; that I'd heard in prison, when I had seen her in my dream. No, my Mother was the whore: White Poppy had been part of something far more horrific, inhuman, bestial and obscene. Turning round suddenly, she shocked me, looked vulnerable, sad – the face leaving the looking glass, the 'twin', White Poppies becoming one: breasts full, thighs tapering down to the indentations of her knees. She looked at me with tiredness, like a forest clothed in mist. She stared at me, eyes opened wide – black almond orbs filled with terror: her perfect heart-shaped face, chin like a pointed lemon. And then she started to cry like I had never seen her cry. Her dearest servant Ettie was dead, just a few weeks after her 13th birthday. She had been with us less than a year, before she died of some wasting disease that left her thin and gaunt; the physician said she had bad blood. After that, White Poppy shut herself in her room again, and I heard her crying; I heard her prayer.

Our servant-girl Ettie's replacement was the Housekeeper, Phoebe, 22 years, with red hair and green eyes, another local girl: referred to always as Mrs Phoebe, she looked after all domestic affairs, kept the account book, the expenses of the house. Very different to our gracious little Ettie she was in her own way conscientious, caring and kind, performing all of her duties with good grace. But White Poppy generally looked after things herself in the house, and in her own way. She had been house proud on her Canton houseboat, and now transferred that domestic pride to dry land.

9

White Poppy's family altar, small shrine, shaped like a tiny house, hung upon the spare room wall, a selection of homemade Chinese gods, daily offerings of burning incense, dishes of dried fruit, rice, candles kept burning there. The Kitchen God, his lips smeared with honey on the eve of the Chinese New Year: on that night he goes to heaven and makes report on the family – the honey to sweeten what he may say about everyone. The goddess, Guan Yin (Bhuddist); the god, Guan Gong (Confucius); the sea goddess, Tin Hau Taoist); the *Da Wang* (Great Kings); the *Tu Di* (Earth Gods) – worn clay figures; the Household Gods – Kitchen, Door and Earth. Altar pictures, tapers, smoke. I see the boat family's altar-shrine: past – present – future. The Chinese professor, who is teaching her English has had a hand in this, has helped her purchase every one in London. Eliza lights the candles one by one, room glowing bright, light penetrating the shadows, like a miniature rock-cut shrine. She has her own special places where she talks quietly in Cantonese, wet sparkle in her eyes, where she read texts written in both English and Chinese as she learns to speak English.

Taoist (Dowist) symbols written in red on thin strips of yellow paper, burned and the ashes mixed with water to be swallowed: paper possessions on the Taoist altar, Taoist deities and sages; large joss sticks burning, fresh oranges before the gods; strips of paper, prayer indications, charms of protection against sickness, danger and bad luck. White Poppy enters a trance, crying out, screaming with fear, showing signs of possession, violent shaking, takes up the paper cut-outs of those she may have harmed – chanting in a loud voice, banging blocks of wood. Holding a three-sided dagger, two bells on the brass handle, she stabs all the evil-wishers, beheads the two paper tigers, asking them to release her. Then everything paper is burned in one big blaze in the kitchen stove and she shakes violently, falls to her knees.

I believe in the one God, who is maker of heaven and earth. One God, the Loving Father. I believe in the Christian secret of inner peace. I believe in Jesus Christ the Saviour.

10

Sixteen years a Maiden, One twelve Months a wife, One half hour a Mother And then I lost my life. Death in childbirth was common – an epitaph from Folkestone – James Stevens Curl, *The Victorian Celebration of Death,* 1972, p21.

Bloodied sacrifice of her monthly bleed: naked, eyes closed, legs stretched out straight before her White Poppy placed her extended fingers at the parting of her legs, drawing up her knees; bathing them in the wetness of her own weeping, touching her self without pleasure, taboo. Withdrawing her fingers, extending her arms, opening her eyes suddenly, she looked into mine, holding me still with her gaze. With revulsion (and yet a strange sense of pleasure), I felt the touch of that bloodied flesh on my lips, tasted the copper-salt coldness on the tip of my tongue. And I felt the horror of all that had passed in and around us in China, and thanked God for his deliverance of our tortured souls.

With her middle left finger dipped repeatedly into her own menstrual blood, she traced a small circle on a piece of white cloth. Yellowish-red smear drying, she held it still over the flame; dropped it as it caught fire, flames climbing, orange-red energy consuming the whole. The black ashes she mixed with gum, rubbed into smooth paste, which she smeared over the hearth.

11

Baptism for Eliza – renewal, redemption for all that had gone before, in order to be saved, *in the name of the Father, Son, and Holy Spirit* (Matthew 28:19). The White Poppy was Christian now – since when she 'took the cross' in China, and her dark eyes made the vow to me, as she touched that metal first to her lips and then to mine, to follow that new way. She stared out to sea, often alone down by the shore: brilliant sunshine, sharp frost – just like being in Canton, at home.

Early Sunday morning sunlight streaming in through the stained-glass window, patchwork of light stretching up to the Lord's Table overlaid in white linen, set plain for Lent; the February air cold, chill around the shining Silver Cross where sunlight sparkled in the Kentish Ragstone Chancel, side chapels hung with cloth; wooden reredos painted with the Ten Commandments and sentences – the Creed, the Lord's Prayer, some Words of Scripture. We sat side by side in the Perpendicular nave of Birchington's ancient flint church.

Drawn bonnet of shot black silk, hair flowing smooth to the shoulders of a black ribbon-edged cloak; viridian velvet dress, bodice trimmed at the neck, tapering down to a deep-pointed waist; hands eager in black gloves, agitating a netted purse, burgundy silk lined with green; above black laced, long and narrow half-boots just over her ankles: Eliza.

'Our Father which art in Heaven, Hallowed be thy Name. Thy kingdom come. Thy will be done, in earth as it is in heaven...'

Eliza seemed away from me, distant, shuffling quietly as we knelt in prayers, her hair hanging loose around her oriental face, falling down from her black bonnet.

'... Forgive us our trespasses. As we forgive them that trespass against us...'

The eyes are the windows into the Soul through which we SEE inside those we love, the very essence of the life that lies within: those eyes closed we are excluded. Each poppy has its one dark 'eye' at the centre, through which its nodding head examines the world about it – the blue skies above, the dark earth below, examines the faces of those who bend down to pick it up. Each girl, a bud to grow, to blossom, to flower, to produce more of her kind: victims decked out for the offering. Wet lips, whore's lips, where have they been?

Good eye closed. I see the Chinese hill with the little temple on top, its glazed green tiles shining brilliantly in the sun; remember the erotic pain, the excitement, of that first fond contact, the tears in her Chinese eyes. But then how eager she had been, how wanton, open, free. How hard she had kissed me; legs opened wide for the sacrifice, for the penetrated wound, female juices, flowing, free. Her tears when we parted. Whistling kite singing in the wind, breeze rippling, blowing through your tail. Float off, float high, Dragon Kite sweeping down, soft plumed feather tail, head to the ground, turning, soaring, lifting, sweeping, singing heavenwards, free, completing the closed circle, the unison of the snake.

The whisper of Chinese lips, salivation as she swallowed, the shrinking of the dark oak all about us creaking to the whitewashed mediaeval walls. Before the Reformation it would have been more colourful, brightly-lit with candles, lights and tapers, walls painted, windows with brilliant stained glass, and lights and images above the roof outside. She looked around the church in wonder, eyes moving across the treasures that surrounded her; following the line of the wooden roof where the new day sun shone through the gable window; gazing down its saffron-yellow shaft along the terracotta tiled floor, cutting across the dark box pews.

'And lead us not into temptation; but deliver us from evil...'

Surrounded by a sea of people she was alone, still; shrouded in her winter mantle, face covered against the cold, skirts tucked in behind her, she shone out like a beacon, radiating a welcome pagan light, a holy brightness glowing from her cheeks, whispering the words, head held low, hands pressed tightly together.

'Almighty God, unto whom all hearts be open, all desires known, and from whom no secrets are hid; Cleanse the thoughts of our hearts by the inspiration of thy Holy Spirit, that we may perfectly love thee, and worthily magnify thy holy Name; through Christ our Lord. Amen.'

The ringing of the tower bell, the broken-bread burned the palms of my hands.

'The Body of our Lord Jesus Christ, which was given for thee, preserve thy body and soul unto everlasting life.'

The ruby wine stained her lips.

'The Blood of our Lord Jesus Christ, which was shed for thee, preserve thy body and soul unto everlasting life. Drink this in remembrance that Christ's Blood was shed for thee, and be thankful.'

In the summer sun White Poppy's hair smells warm; its black heat burning my mouth. Tide out low, the beach sparkles; sand shingle beach, jade water running out through the flat chalk rocks. White Poppy takes off her boots, steps carefully across the miniature ragged islands, barnacle-encrusted chalk, paddles in rock pools warmed by the sun, squishing warm sand between her toes. Above ripening yellow cornfields, bloodied with swathes of common red poppies that run down by the water, cotton-fluff clouds leave the land; start their journey out to sea. In the summer, in the long grass beyond Birchington Bay, grasshoppers fly and whirr. Sailing ships anchored deep, heads facing into the freshening wind, calm after the storm, masts pierce the cloudless garter-blue sky over the beautiful green-glass sea.

Back home, she rubbed herself with scented oils, massaging them into her skin, sat brushing her long black hair in her bedroom – one hundred times always until it shone brilliantly, softly running the bristle brush from her crown down over her shoulders, brushing with her left hand, smoothing it down gently behind it with her right.

March 2, 1841: Major-General Sir Hugh Gough arrived off Canton from Madras to assume command of all land forces. Lin's actions had brought war nearer still, demanding surrender of 20,000 chests of British-owned opium, surrounding the foreign merchants' warehouses and quarters at Canton, ordering Chinese servants to leave their masters. After the siege of the Thirteen Factories (Hongs) the opium was handed over and destroyed. No more did merchants and their families live on Portuguese Macao. Since the Kowloon incident on July 7, 1839, there was still no surrender to Chinese justice. To safeguard the British, Captain Elliot moved the men, women and children in a number of small vessels to anchorage at Hong Kong. Driven from Macao and their Factories at Canton, the British traders were incensed: their opium confiscated without compensation and all other trade at a standstill. Most of the Thirteen Factories had been destroyed, burned down to the ground, the Chinese mob taking away all that they could. Lord Palmerston sent a formal ultimatum to the Imperial Government demanding restoration of the confiscated goods and security for our future trade. Chinese officials were to open fresh trade negotiations at Canton.

Eliza did cartwheels, somersaults across the floor, startling me with her acrobatic agility; could bend over backwards, forwards, pressing her stomach to her tongue. She bent forward energetically, whipping a glittering wooden top shaped like a solid copper bell, whipped string wound around it firmly, set on the ground: whipped it up with speed, until spinning swiftly, silently, it looked as if it was standing still, like its shadow on the ground.

May 24, 1841: More troops arrived, a total of some 2,400. Captain Elliot decided to begin the sea attack on Canton, which was no easy place to reach. Though long and armed, the paddle steamer Nemesis needed little more than 4 feet of water and could go almost anywhere they wished. Large warships had approached Canton and bombarded its guarding forts. The 26th Regiment under Major Pratt landed at the Canton Factories without incident, strengthening the post. General Gough's task was a formidable one, Canton being a well-defended city with high walls. Yet, in little more than half an hour, *the heights overlooking the North wall were gained and the British flag waved in triumph upon each of the forts commanding it. On the night of May 21, a great fight was fought. By the burning of houses and the disabling of the guns, the Chinese artillery was rendered ineffectual and compelled to retire within the city walls. 10 o'clock the next morning, a white flag appeared on the Canton city walls, and the air promised peace.*

12

A new bride represents wealth in a quite basic way; it is through her that the family line continues the hands that create! *Sunny Saturday morning, June:* made-up, White Poppy looked beautiful, cinnabar lips, her face shining with a delicate radiance, elegant in the pelisse robe of white muslin embroidered in white with a floral design, mounted over matching satin. The dress had voluminous sleeves set low at the shoulder, and she had on garters of white silk trimmed with blond lace, and pure white shoes. She stood beside me, reflected in the full-length glass, her glossy black hair pinned high beneath a wedding bonnet of tulle trimmed with orange blossom and orchids from our own hothouse, a decorative bouquet; and me in my black dress coat and trousers, white silk waistcoat, white necktie, white gloves. She stepped forward along the aisle; *her* bride-wealth was everything inside. The wedding ring of pure gold, noble and durable, circular without end for two persons to be united as one. I spoke.

'Sweet maid, in this ring behold the symbol of my love for thee, in that it hath no ending.' I put the ring on each of her left-hand fingers in turn, saying at the first, 'In the name of the Father'; at the second, 'In the name of the Son'; at the third, 'In the name of the Holy Ghost'; and at the fourth, 'Amen'. Eliza replied.

'Good Sir, in this ring also behold the symbol of my love for thee, inasmuch as it hath no beginning and no end.'

13

Inspire your husband, whatever his temper, with confidence, and, above all, with esteem and affection, and you will exercise over him the most powerful influence of all. In a family, which constitutes a little state, a chief is equally requisite. That chief is husband and all the members of the family owe him respect, submission, devotion. Whenever your husband returns home, receive him with a pleasant smile. Accost him with warm and open cheerfulness; let your countenance express the delight you feel at seeing him again; let a day's absence appear, for you, as if it were a separation of a quarter of a century, contrive cleverly to chase any dark clouds from his mind. Better a hundred times to sacrifice every acquaintance, every friend, than to sacrifice one's own dear husband. Weep with love, but never with jealousy. Cold rains do not produce beautiful flowers.

Pink-bruised sky, purple shot with orange. The weather is bitter cold, ice sheets across the window inside, ice forming at the edges of the silver-crackled sea beneath the star-spattered sky. Standing out in the garden, staring up at the chill, at the bright moon and the ring of stars, listening to the sea beyond the cliffs, remembering Macao – distant waves breaking across the rocks, running free, splashing gently, swooshing, sweeping slowly in, I wanted her in a way that I had never been sure she really wanted me! I 'watched' White Poppy carefully just by feeling her, listening to her gentle sighing breathing, buried in her mass of hair that flowed down wild across her shoulders: it was difficult not to cry – for such beautiful perfection, it was difficult not to cry wet tears.

Christmas Eve was bitterly cold, cloudy, moon now gone from view, it snowed fast: snow-flakes flurrying, wind-blown blossom dropping from the white-washed sky; covering the naked bending trees, blanketing the coastal cottages with sparkled frosted ice, snowflakes sweeping low across the garden, blowing in hard, building high against the windows, suffocating all sound.

14

The Chinese Saviour Zas enters the world at midnight on the 24th day of the 12th month. On this occasion the golden cock atop the Tree of Life does not wait until dawn to wake the sun. For the Chinese the sun is represented by a cock in a circle, the Bird of Dawn flapping his golden wings as the Sun rises behind him. In honour of the advent of the spiritual sun it crows all night long, and all the cocks in the world are stirred up and begin to crow, dispelling the evil spirits of the night which abhor the truth of the sun's light and shrink back into the darkness of Hell.

White Poppy forgets herself, becomes the wild girl. She sits with her mouth open, her lips apart: I can see the tip of her tongue. She sits still, watching me, knees up to her chin, long purple skirts flowing about her; white petticoats around her like the petals of a flower. She sits the way wild girls sit; the way certain women sit, when they forget themselves and go back to being the girl. She giggles softly, a quiet laugh in her throat, throwing back her hair, staring hard at me, waiting for me to smile, to laugh.

The doors are all locked and we are alone. Dining-room dark, green velvet curtains drawn closed on long brass poles, shadows of six tall, turned-back chairs, flickering from the firelight, standing sentry against the gold flock-papered walls, steaming apple wood hissing in the glowing orange grate. Japanned goods and papier-mâché are arrayed along the sideboard that climb the wall, tall back, with a looking glass heavily framed, and an assortment of shelves scrambling up the sides. It has large recess cupboards and elaborately carved doors: amber, stuffed birds, a snake, wax fruit under a glass dome, paperweights spill across its surface, with tall beeswax candles and two goose-necked gas wall brackets on the wall.

I experience the exquisite sensation, my body rising to her pleasure, feeling the heat of her hot flesh, pure wetness running down her skin. Moving my fingers slowly down the contours of her scars, feeling the twin outlines bitten deep into her cheeks, letting my fingers trace their path over to her mouth, running them along her lips, she kisses them gently: walking across rippled sand to the edge of the sea, salt water lapping, calm. Let my fingers float away.

Link hands, feel the heat, hot perspiration as her palms press close on mine; hot pressure of her knotted fingers, closing tightly, firmly. Flames, heat, her face lit with her own internal pleasure, skin glowing from her inner light, her chin set firm accentuating the fullness of her mouth, lips apart, dry, hot, burning from the Port Wine. Leaning forwards, breasts hanging loose inside her dress, her drunken eyes are soft, liquid light, lustful, free; moaning in her throat.

With fingers shaking she removes the silver tinsel, takes out the bright baubles from her hair, letting it cascade down free across her shoulders, never taking her eyes away from me, eyes sparkling star-like in the soft glow of the ormolu candlesticks grown from the long sideboard inlaid with apple and pear. The Poppy nods her gentle head, taking off her dresses, underclothes, laughing, spreading herself to her best advantage, boat-girl laughing coarsely, loud, mouth wide, white teeth cutting through the gash.

Snake-eyes heavy, bulging black across the dark oval oak table, silvered with pickles and preserves, sparkling by the candlelight that eats continually into the shadow where her soft face melts in the flickering glow, rivulets of wax flowing before the apple-log fire.

Hot lips curved upwards, crimson, cruel; ruby-dribbled lips parted carelessly, wet-honey tongue, soft hairs shining below her scar-mapped, goose-greased cheek. Head forced back, lips pressed open wide, wet mouth on wet mouth, knees up, legs apart, spread-eagled above me on the padded chair, she comes forward clumsily, silk-tearing, ripped love-soaked lace, breasts open, bare, dark line of hairs down to where she is pungent, purple; moist and wet. Before the spitting apple-log fire, dressed in shimmering green, sliding down, she sits cross-legged on the floor, shimmering fabric tucked over her dripping knees. She squats low and opens her eager legs for me. Holding her hair, wrapping it around my fingers, taking her chin in my hand, pressing her cheeks with the other, squeezing them together across her hanging mouth, pushing her engorged lips forwards: her lips ice-cold; cool, like Chinese cucumber. The taste of her is sudden, intense: viscid wet residue on my fingers. Her almond eyes contain everything and nothing: she opens them wide at me and smiles: *OK*, they say, *all this...all of this is all yours.*

Pressing her tongue in behind my left knee, licking her way up towards my groin, I feel it explode: capsule 'bleeding', white milk flowing. *The lick of death, taboo.*

15

The expectant mother now, White Poppy prepared her own baby clothes. The corset was now no longer necessary to be worn throughout the pregnancy. She had expandable laces over her bosom, and steel stays instead of whalebone. A chemise, flannel petticoat and bed gown were expected in the later stages of labour. She would not engage a monthly nurse, preferring to keep the bedroom clean, wash the baby's clothes; care for her baby herself throughout the night. That was her plan. The nursery – the room next to her bedroom was whitewashed, it was given safety bars over the windows, a high fireguard in front of the grate, a central table covered in wipeable oilcloth; chairs, highchairs; a toy cupboard; nursery china cupboard; small carpet. Her growing baby would be fed there and educated there, would blossom and grow. What could stop her happiness now?

BOOK VII SISTERS DIVIDED

Birchington, Kent
July 1849

1

When the red flower shows its beauty, and exhales its heady perfume.
Chang Hêng Ch'i-pien: Tannahill, *Sex in History*, 1980.

White Poppy transformed herself, and her English now much improved, she told me the story of her one-woman struggle to become her self. She lived the first part of her life as a boat-girl, whore – the next as the high class prostitute, Sister of the Snake; and now for the later part of her life she was determined to be the loving mother and devoted wife. She was surrounded by much love in a bitter, cruel world. She moved from a kind of private life to a more public one In England, and then retreated into the private life again, when the external life threatened to overwhelm her. Despite her infamous past and the struggle for her beauty to hang on, she had the talent for survival against all odds, seemingly living in within her own charmed circle.

Early afternoon we sat out in the summer garden drinking small cups of China tea, tiny birds singing in the red-tipped, yellow-flowering bushes next to the white-painted summerhouse overlooking the cliff, above the wide-open sea. White Poppy talked quietly, wide sun-hat shading her face, long black velvet dress flowing down over her embroidered black slipper feet: the perfect illusion of bridal innocence and allure. So many years had passed and her spoken English was much improved.

'I sat on the bed,' she said, 'watched the other girls in the small room. I thought how pretty they were, how pretty I might be. I listened to their singing, the sounds of the Canton harbour all around.'

Chinese lips forward, she took a sip from her steaming tea, put down the white bone china cup on its saucer.

'Just ten, Sir, my hair dressed up in multiple knots, face powdered white, painted lips, eyebrows painted black, I struggled to play a lute. Within the group, the Sisterhood, I was shown the love manual,' she said it with disgust, 'the different positions.'

White Poppy adjusted her black skirts, bright sunlight absorbed into the black velvet, pushed back her raven hair, provocative, sexuality simmering within, taking another sip of her steaming tea. I watched the concentration, the moving forwards of her full lips; enjoy the widening of her shining almond eyes.

'Each girl, all of us spent our early years keeping the older girls happy, keeping their rooms in order, helping them with their make-up, their clothes. We were dressed up when taken to the flower-boats to serve tea, materials for smoking. I had beautiful sunset-yellow clothes, lime-green shoes.'

The brightest of the boat-girls, like White Poppy herself, were taught writing, arithmetic and painting. From birth to six years they were raised with care, fresh flower buds nurtured for their rude teenage plucking.

'For some rich man to buy our virginity, unlock our thighs. True virgins were rare. At thirteen years men *tried the flower*, at fourteen years they *cultivated the flower* and at fifteen years they *plucked* it.' She laughed coarsely, forgetting herself, pushed her hands between her knees. 'Enriched with crystal green wine they fucked us at fifteen. That was what SHE told our clients, but some girls were used from ten. My parents sold me for much silver to a woman-dealer from the provinces, to make me agreeable to men. Like many other drought starved families in Canton they could not afford to keep a daughter. My *death* was their life. I knew nothing else, didn't know what I had been sold for; thought I was going somewhere nice.'

She shouted out the bitter words towards the sea beyond the cliff top at the end of our garden. Turning slowly, she shrugged her shoulders, sighing deeply (always sighing deeply). She went quiet, muttering to herself as she played with her hair, black eyes to the ground. Then she spoke quietly.

'Deep garden sound floating on the moon, the glimmer of flower-scented paths, ascending the Azure Tower tears wet the sleeves of my spring dress.'

And she went suddenly quiet, and that was all she said to me. She then spoke suddenly, quickly, changing tack altogether.

'Good Chinese women should sit with their knees together or their legs crossed,' she said solemnly another time, when we were alone together on the beach, 'that's why the Chinese character for woman has two lines crossed over each other.' Almond eyes scanning my face, she produced a little smile. 'It means that a woman sits still and stays at home.'

'And what is the Chinese character for man?'

She drew it for me, traced its outline in the sand.

'Man,' she said with force, 'that means field and strong.'

Later that same afternoon, White Poppy walked me over to the sectionalised dial garden planted with flowers that in summer sunshine open or close at regular and successive hours. She sat me down on the beech garden seat there, rested her head against my left shoulder. She talked quietly.

'We sat together in the baths. I listened to the sound of flesh slap flesh. We sat side by side in silence and I knew some ritual was about to take place. When you are new you do not know these things.'

Shrubby Hawkweed and Spotted Cat's Ear open at six o'clock in the morning, followed by African Marigold (seven o'clock), Scarlet Pimpernel (eight o'clock), Field Marigold (nine o'clock), Red Sandwort (ten o'clock) and Star of Bethlehem (eleven o'clock) until noon, which is the Ice Plant hour.

'My garment was lifted and pulled over my head, leaving me naked. Silently, she pulled me on to her knees across her outspread thighs. She was much older than me.'

Common Purslane opens at one o'clock in the afternoon, sun high in the sky, and from two o'clock until four, Purple Sandwort, Dandelion and White Spiderwort close in succession round the circle. Jalop opens at five o'clock, and at six o'clock in the evening opens Dark Crane's Bill.

'She stretched open my legs, moved her cold hands down my thighs, began to explore my breasts also, nipples erect. Her fingers entered my slit, moved there rhythmically. She kissed me hard on my lips closed in all sound.'

There were tears in her eyes, tears that spilled out silently, wetting my shirt, White Poppy.

'You know I didn't love you, Charles, not at first, just saw you as a means of freedom and escape.'

So, had she betrayed him after all?

2

Tide coming in fast now, approaching the topmost beach, waves trickle in over the sand, sucking it in like a sponge, agitating the rough carpet of broken mussel shells, ragged silver-blue, bubbling at the edges. Child-dug trench falling to the incoming tide, castle, ditch and islands falling to the speeding sea; seaweeds floating, red-brown swirling – feathered ferns, floppy fronds, wet sheets spiralling red and green.

Just as the sun was setting, top edge about to disappear from view below the sea, an emerald light shot up above it for a moment on the horizon, and White Poppy giggled, and smiled, watching this briefest vision of the sun's green ray. She flashed her eyes at me, tugging at my hand.

'Did you see the green?'

I nodded; we kissed.

There is a male lust for the virgin, for the letting of first blood, essential essence of human life. White Poppy lay back across the padded sofa, body blending into the dark woven silk damask. The morning sun had not yet penetrated the room, her room. She spoke from her distance.

'At first life on the Junk was sweet.'

The words flowed slowly, soft movements of her shining crimson lips, her face framed by the burnished black hair falling down over the shoulders of her flowing purple velvet pelisse robe figured in blue. But they were the *only* words, and she closed her mouth firmly, as if to say that's enough, that will do.

Minutes later she started speaking.

'As a new possession I was treated with care. I enjoyed my time with the other women, had my body massaged and perfumed with scented oils. But that pleasure soon turned to pain.'

Beyond the huddle of houseboats the Grand Junk had stood, before the gaudy red and green, where the fragrance of smoking jasmine and opium cut through the stink of the brackish, steaming river, salt-sour like rank seaweed.

Grand Junk – burnished gold blazing deep-water bright, its flag flying high, I can see it now: rich symbol of a vermilion and blue serpent swallowing its own tail: protected by three war-junks, each with its own protective general, and magistrates' ships nearby – very high lodgings, well made houses within, gilded, sumptuous, rich – great golden windows shrouded with nets woven of fine silk.

Where a mirror flashed its message, winking eye from one giant of the twin pagodas of the Sea Pearl Temple that stood erect mid-river, vast defended citadel with gun-ports against coastal pirates. And the Grand Junk had flashed back its reply.

'The Junk was lined with mirrors of great size and beauty that reflected all around us, multiple reflections of all of our base deeds.'

She moved her left arm with its bangle of green-dragon jade; celestial semen turned to stone. She turned over wriggled her bottom, exposed her pale legs, pale pink stockings, cotton tops well below her knees.

'Puberty at fifteen, what a horrible, limiting state of things!'

Her black eyes blinked, breaking the flow of sexual energy, closing in the force that had driven me since the start: her face softening at the edges, her mouth with new mobility, her bottom lip dropping slightly, revealing white teeth.

'My sisters in sex, givers of pleasure and punishment both. We were treated carefully like precious treasure, given delectable delights to stop us from being bored, the inferior female sex!' She laughed out loud. 'For the first time I wished I was a boy, all that blood and mess, wearing a linen cloth for protection, given hot ginger tea, a little opium, for the cramps that came monthly to me.'

Letting her head fall backwards over the sofa, perfumed hair hanging loose over the fat, padded arm, dropping down to the floor, cascading pool of jet-black, she looked at me, nostrils flared, eyes bulging, upside down. Who could hurt such beauty, so pretty, perfect, pure? What sadistic soul had committed such disgusting violation against her sex? I saw the imagined faces behind the Junk's great golden windows shrouded with nets woven of fine silk. The Grand Junk, there they lived and there they stayed, sex toys for the rich, sexual food for the sharks who prey on young girls, eager to taste new blood, to try new fish with their teeth. She had told me of professional virgins, girls repaired, given new blood for convincing *first* bleeding for those prepared to pay highly in silver for such pleasure.

From the Grand Junk, she, the river Pearl, was taken at night into the walled city – walls 25 feet high, 20 feet wide, 83 bulwarks and seven gates with breast-works, entries sumptuous and high, battlements above like steps - passed below the red paper lanterns of suburban brothels where the sky burned crimson, into the bloodied velvet darkness, world-ceiling dotted with a myriad sparkling stars. Where the red flowers show their beauty: closely anchored flower-boats, packed like fish-scales along the illuminated waterfront. A train of girls clambering ashore from a small boat that had wound its way slowly into the floating village, seven girls on their way to some secret hideaway in the walled city.

'As a snake girl other demands were made on me. I learned to pretend, to say yes to gain further favour, the freedom of space, some time on my own. Imagine having anything you want,' she whispered by my ear, 'imagine having the power to change into something else.' She opened her eyes wide, looked straight ahead at me. 'I wish I had been born male. Stripped naked I was paraded before the whores, I listened to their sneers. They made me bend for them, inspected me like an animal, checked inside me, stroked me, touched me all over, slapped me for fun, hit me harder for their pleasure most perverse. I hated them.'

Her black eyes glistened with pain, her mouth tight, tongue pressed firmly against her teeth.

'They were worse than the men, took me away from everything I knew. They had whips of bamboo, cleft in the middle: ten stripes drew blood on the buttocks or thighs, twenty or thirty spoil the flesh altogether: one hundred were incurable.' She wiped a tear from her eyes, sniffed, blew her nose. 'I felt defeated, life no longer worth living. I refused to tell them what I knew about you, the *British Imperialist*.' She spat out the words forgotten in hate, fingering the tattoo. 'I suffered because of that. But you gave me freedom I had never had before. For you I felt respect, shared the choice as we made our escape.'

She grabbed hold of me, pressed her face against mine.

'You were my only true friend, the only one I could trust.' She smiled sweetly, brushed her lips on my own. 'An outsider, free from the bonds of brotherhood, of sisterhood, of family, you were free. And I longed for part of that freedom for me.'

She had been imprisoned, too.

Distant, out across the water beyond the twin towers of St Mary's Church at Reculver, the Isle of Sheppey hovers at the boundary between land and sea; clouds building there before us. Pulling up her skirts, White Poppy relieved herself on the chalk: made water that rushed between her feet and down to the beach.

'The rain brings new life,' she laughed, 'fresh grass where there is desert.' Her eyes were large, bright, manic, mad; she talked quickly, agitated like the sea. 'I was not allowed to think for myself, not allowed to make my own decisions. In China that is forbidden for women. I could only make my choice from what I was told, could accept or not accept.'

She scanned my face for response, walking her little distance in front of me, turning back frequently, waiting for me. Then she stopped still, turned suddenly and touched my hand.

'We were like caged songbirds that turn December into April with their sweet singing. But for us it was always winter. As children we were taught not to show emotion, to hide what we felt.' Her smile withdrew inwards, she moved back away from me, alone and enclosed. 'Try catching a shadow! My world was a man's world in which I was the male receptacle, sexual toy, humiliated, hurt. Enjoyed then destroyed!'

Distant rumble of thunder, grey clouds piling high above us: clouds towering, pillar-like, tall, wind coming in squalls, strong and then less strong, one moment movement, the next everything still; whirlwind scouring, spiralling round, lifting dried seaweed, hot sand; sea boiling, and then calm. Lightning flashing distant, crack of thunder echoing; rain pouring, bursting suddenly over the sea, solid sheeted water splashing back to the sky: how many coastal sea-days have we watched like that?

White Poppy flowed elegantly into the drawing-room: brocaded purple silk bodice trimmed at the neck, flat folds of material, draped with a point at the centre, a la Sevigné, curving down at the shoulder into tightening blue sleeves, repeated at the waist, above the spreading curves of the flounced double skirt also in blue, over dress boots of white silk.

In the darkness she lit paper lanterns, silence broken only by the ticking of the clock, the sound of the rain beating at the windows, not unlike seawater swooshing on the beach.

'Skirts are spreading wider every year,' she said, turning, flowing, skirts merging into patterned elegance as she finally sat down. She had been talking and talking, was very unhappy, had a lot to tell me, continued in competition with the storm.

'Dressed in laced white cotton, I sat for the mandarin, still. He talked to me about Peach Blossom, my friend, said: 'She follows me like a sunflower follows the sun.' Her bright face ever forwards, eyes eager to please. Yes, her face followed him. But that was my friend, so different to me.'

She laughed: laughed coarsely, throwing her hands in the air, flicking her hair to the wind.

'She had a very fuckable face, if you know what I mean, lips like a vulva, and yet HE chose me. Legs forced opened wide as he buried his face in me like a flower given to a bee. I was given amber wine and then beaten and misused.' She looked away from me, watching the rain falling down in grey ribbons from the black sky over an agitated sea. 'A door led to an inner room with a small bed and a bright fire. The first man, he pushed me down on the bed, thrust his penis in my mouth. I choked. *(Lightning flash)*. The second man, he wanted me like a dog, forced me down on my hands and knees, fucked me from behind.' *(Thunder)*.

The Mandarin, 'Ou Ch'i' (Oo Ji) with his cold, apathetic indifference, the veiled contempt of the polished Confucianist gentleman, head shaved at the front, braided in a single plait behind, with his Aladdin hat and silk robes, his fancy brocade footwear – the oh-so-proud magistrate or mandarin. She said the name, 'Ou Ch'i.'

Sending the boy out of the large room, he had gestured to me to sit down and talked to me quickly through his Interpreter. I remember watching the water clock to his side, water rising by the second. He was the one.

It had taken less than three minutes, and his final remark was 'No', nothing could be done for the girl. He closed his file – 'Joi gin.' ('Goodbye.') – Stood up and left the room. I had been left on my own with the memory of the snake swallowing its own tail that I had seen engraved on his thick gold ring, the outline that matched exactly the flag flying high on the junk, rich vermilion and blue: like the tattoo of the bungalow whore, and that of the boat-girl, before. White Poppy continued.

'From his pocket the Mandarin took four grains of incense. *(Lightning flash).* He put one grain on each breast, the third above my navel and the fourth above the hood of my clitoris. He lit them, watched in fascination as they burned down to my skin.' *(Thunder).* 'He locked the door behind us, held me close, bending my arm behind me, dragging me round like a feather. Pulling back my hair, forcing his mouth over my mouth, he drew a long-bladed knife from his cloak: "Move an inch," he said, "and you shall feel ten more!" He banged the knife on the table, warning me to keep still. Ripping off my silk gown, he drew its point across my breasts, watching in wonder as it cut me, as the blood seeped from the flesh. Holding my hair in one hand, wrapping it around his wrist, he stripped me of my clothes with the other, made me kneel, threw me down to the ground. He kicked over the table, dishes and cups crashing to the ground. *(Distant thunder).* And then he fucked me, on the broken china he presses himself on to me. Oh how he fucked me and would not stop. Turning me over, waving the knife in front of my face he cut me again, slashed twice above my left cheek. Pulling his great weight off me, he wiped himself on my thighs. Then he beat me, hit me until I bled from my nose and my mouth, kicking me in the ribs and stamping on my arms, until I fainted from the pain, unconscious.'

She looked at me, mouth open.

'My crime? I offended a man who was mad.'

3

Bedroom dawn-moon bright, White Poppy sat still, watching me, knees up to her chin, long purple skirts flowing about her; white petticoats around her like large petals. She sat the way girls sit; she sat in the way women sit, when they forget themselves and go back to being the girl. She spoke at last, though the words did not come easy.

'I have felt so angry until now, Charles, could not speak of this most bitter pain.' She stopped talking, went silent, started talking suddenly again. 'My father looked sad, there were tears in his eyes, but his words to me were quite simple. It was "because I was so beautiful", he said, that he had to do what he was going to do to me.' She sighed and blinked repeatedly, closed her almond eyes. 'May the gods forgive him, 'she blinked back her tears, 'may God forgive him for his ignorance? But "he had to combine with such beauty", he said, it was what he had dreamed about, was what his dreams had told him to do.' She went silent, opened her eyes wide and looked back at me. 'So he did,' she whispered, her voice low to her chest, 'and afterwards he smiled, Charles, he kissed me and smiled and said that I had saved his soul. I didn't believe him then, and I do not believe him, still.'

'I was raped by my Father.' She was crying now, nibbled her bottom lip. 'He took me into the back room,' she sobbed, 'after we had been looking up at the stars. He sat me on his knee, put his hand between my legs, finger-fucked me like a whore.'

White Poppy looked away from me, touched her hands protectively to her chest, feeling the skin below her throat.

'I was just nine-years-old.'

She stopped talking, looked down at her knees, ran her trembling hands over her stomach.

'One evening, after drinking rice wine, he climbed on top of me as I slept and raped me. He was the first man that had me that way; it was the evening before they sent me away.' Hatred in her eyes then, she had bitterness still for what passed between them that night. Something that should never have been – something that shocked me in the extreme. She touched my chin. 'I never forgave him, and I never will!'

She had told me of the City of the Dead that lies under the earth, a bridge as thin as a hair across a deep gorge: where it is always dark and winter, always about to rain. Within its 18 hells are foul tortures like the tree of Flaming Swords, the burning Iron Wheel: does her father continue still along the cycle of birth and rebirth, unending? White Poppy, asleep I smelled her cheeks, ran my nose around her mouth, licked down her thighs, tasted the inside of her salty knees, closed my mouth over hers, let her air enter mine.

4

Now you're married we wish you joy, first a girl and then a boy. Seven years after son and daughter, pray and couples come kiss together. Kiss her once, kiss her twice, kiss her three times over.

Wakened from her long afternoon sleep, the White Poppy stretched, smiled, parting her swollen lips, opened out the soft features of her new-flowering beauty.

The lips are the entrance through which we get inside those, taste the very essence of the life that lies within.

When I am with her, watch her standing there in front of me, I feel so happy, so eager to hold on to her, to hug her tight, to kiss her once more – could never tire of kissing her, of holding her chin, of pressing her lips and closing my mouth over hers.

Running my fingers over her lips she nibbled them, took them inside her mouth, lubricating them with her tongue. Her breathing was gentle, relaxed, and out of the corner of my good eye I watched the rise and fall of her breasts spread downwards out across her chest as she lay there naked on her back.

'You are beautiful my Eliza. You are more beautiful than the prettiest of the Dragon Jade Princesses: your hair is softer than the softest fur, your eyes are brighter than the most brilliant of the stars, your lips are sweetest...'

She put her left hand over my mouth, pressed inwards with her middle finger extended in front. Withdrawing my own fingers slowly, turning over so that my face was level with hers, I smelled the wonderful natural fragrance of her hair, kissed her neck, kissed her cheeks, the corners of her mouth, probed that which moved, laughing. Moving my mouth slowly, I kissed her on the lips, softly at first, feeling them swell, feeling the new warmth that ran through them as they filled with her blood, pressing my mouth against hers – gently, hardly touching, letting my mouth rest against hers, the lips smooth like silk, kissing harder, kissing hardest as our lips joined together, creased corners pressed flat.

'I love you,' she said, pulling apart from me.

Leaving the deserted China temple, glazed green tiles by a solitary pine, White Poppy had been submissive, sweet, had interlocked her crooked fingers in mine. As if to make sure, she had come back over to me before leaving, kissed me full on the lips, opening my mouth wide with her own; forcing it apart. Closing her almond eyes she had kissed and kissed me, not wanting to let go, holding me, finger-pressing my back, sucking the life out of me with her bleeding, perfect lips. And in that final moment something intimate passed between us, an interchange of life, a fusion of our souls, a joining together of something deep inside – a link that would never be broken: I love you, she had said with her body, her heart, her soul. *I love you!* She had broken the wooden hairpin in two; gave one half to me as a parting present, as a special reminder of our 'pact'. It was then that I had believed that everything would be all right, provided that Chinese Nature let us through.

A walk before breakfast at ten o'clock, Eliza spoke quietly, softly.

'Sparks of heaven fanned into a flame, the flame into a fire, the fire into a star, and the star into a sun'.

She lay there still beside me, eyes opened wide, eyelashes flicking, watching the dust particles floating in the sunlight that streamed into the room: Yin Hsueh-yen, staring at the patterned ceiling above our heads. She lay stretched out, naked, warm, chin pointed upwards, Chinese nose to the air, mouth opened, lips wet, fertile, wide; saying nothing more, nothing to break the silence of the room. We made love like we had never made love before: made love by just lying there, luxuriating in the stillness, the silence all around. My head pressed close against her chest, I listened to the beating of her heart, the pumping of her blood, felt the gentle movement of each tiny muscle twitch against her body folded: not relaxed, but knees up, breathing warm against my arm which was somewhere up and over and around her neck.

5

Name or person, which is closer? Person or possession, which is more? Winning or losing: which is worse? Lao Tzu, *Tao Te Ching*, 44. *All men within the four seas are brothers.* Confucius, *Analects.*

Traditional, conventional Chinese society is ordered by set rules; by relations fixed for eternity. Like the Five Relationships, of emperor-subject, of father-children, of husband-wife, of elder brother-younger brother, and of friend-friend. They are bonds of relationship; they are bonds not to be broken. We drove out in the two-horse carriage, sped by Kentish cottage gardens: wild tangles of roses, hollyhocks, pinks, sweet Williams, lavender, crown-imperial, honeysuckle and heartsease, scented geraniums, fuchsias, sweet-scented violet, both white and purple, beneath the flowering hedgerows. White Poppy talked.

'The male child returns to the women's side, and is kept away from men for seven years, after which he then gives the obedience, the respect, due to the father.'

She told me of the boat people. She spoke slowly, carefully. It upset her talking about it, brought tears to her eyes.

'They set up a paper tent. The new members pass through the gate of two crossed swords. Through the curtains, I saw them kneeling down, instructed in the mystic language of the society by the Master in white. Each one pricks the tip of his finger with a needle till blood is drawn, takes a sip from the bowl in which this blood is mixed with water. I was only five years, Charles. I wondered what they were doing.'

The Triad Lodge was the City of Willows, she told me, Paradise. The Triad, also known as San Ho Hui, Society of the Three Elements in One (Heaven, Earth, and Man). The Triad Lodge was like a traditional Chinese town, rectangular in plan with four gates. The Altar was towards the West gate, the journey having started through the East. Beyond the first entrance (before which traitors were executed), and the second and third entrances, was the Heaven & Earth Circle before the Fiery Pit, towards the Stepping-Stones and the Two Planked Bridge. They were flanked on each side by an inward facing diagonal of officials, and behind them, on both sides, memorial tablets. At the end was the Altar, with the Incense Master to the left, and the Leader to the right.

'They brought in a man with his hands tied with cord,' she continued. 'He was put in front of the Principal and ordered to prostrate himself. He remained standing. A man came and gave him 20 blows with a bamboo cane. He was asked if he would join the society; he remained silent. The question was repeated three times more.' She opened her brown eyes wide. 'Still no answer, the Principal made a sign to those who were armed with drawn swords; they advanced and made a motion as if to cut off his head. The Principal ordered them to stop, and asked again if he would become a member of the society; still he refused.' She gave a tiny sigh. 'The Principal orders him to be stretched on the ground, and two men come and beat him on the back with bamboo.' There is an added gruffness to her voice now: 'Tomorrow morning let him be put to death. They kept him confined for the night, and the next morning he was killed.'

'It was soon after seven o'clock when they all arrived. They started to eat and drink rice wine with much noise. At eight o'clock the drums sounded and they arranged themselves in order, sitting opposite the Datu idol. Their faces were red from drunkenness.' She pressed her hands in her lap, made her self more comfortable in the high-backed chair. 'The Principal sat down on the tallest chair with two men at his right and two men at his left. After them came eight men, with drawn swords, four to the right, and four to the left. One man burned paper in front of the idol. After him came eight men with drawn swords, who guarded a man with unkempt hair, his chest naked.' She lowered her head slightly. 'He bowed down in front of the Principal till his head touched the ground. The armed men now advanced, shouting, and laid their swords on his neck. They remained silently in this position until a man came forward to the candidate's side. The Principal spoke.'

She made her voice even lower; looked fierce: 'Who are you and from whence do you come? Who are your father and your mother? Are they still alive?'

She raised her voice, now sounding timid in reply. 'I am … of … and my mother and father are both dead…'

Gruff once more: 'What have you come here for?'

Timid, and very respectful: 'I wish to join the Heaven and Earth Society (*T'ien Ti Hui*).'

Gruff in reply: 'You are deceiving; your thoughts are not as your speech.'

Nervous: 'I will swear that I am good in faith.'

'Then swear.'

The candidate took paper, burned it. 'I swear that I am good in faith, he replied.'

She smiled briefly, the tension disappearing from her face.

Almighty God, unto whom all hearts be open, all desires known, and from whom no secrets are hid; Cleanse the thoughts of our hearts by the inspiration of thy Holy Spirit, that we may perfectly love thee, and worthily magnify thy holy name; through Christ our Lord. Amen.

'Are you familiar with the rules of the society?'

'Yes, I understand that I am to take an oath by drinking blood. I promise not to tell the secrets of this society to anyone, under penalty of death.'

'Truly?'

'Truly.'

Her eyes were then opened wide, and she pursed her lips. 'A vessel containing rice wine and a few drops of blood from each member of the society was placed in front of the idol, together with a knife. The candidate took up the knife, made a small cut in his finger; let several drops of blood fall into the cup.'

The Blood of our Lord Jesus Christ, which was shed for thee, preserve thy body and soul unto everlasting life. Drink this in remembrance that Christ's Blood was shed for thee, and be thankful…

'The Principal said, Drink in presence of Datong pekong. The candidate drank a small cupful, and the Principal and all the members drank a little, each in his turn.' Her voice was gruff again, but this time it held conviction of a different kind. 'Tomorrow go to our secretary, and ask him for a book in which you will find all our rules and secret signs.'

6

Outside, rolling waves, booming Thunder Dragon roar – rain, down dropping, dreary. The Chinese mother-to-be smoothed her hands over her baby-swelling stomach, softly, slowly, feeling the roundness. There were a few purplish stretch marks, but over the years these had faded to faint silvery lines. Her mouth was dry, her breasts felt heavy and swollen. She could feel her nipples pressing against her bodice. She splashed some cold water in her mouth.

Charles walked round naked, penis swinging gently. His body heat was powerfully erotic, and she writhed as he moulded and pressed her buttocks with his hands. His face inches from hers he filled all of her senses – the scent of him, the taste of his lips. He kissed her again and again, moving around the inside of her mouth with his tongue, drinking in the sweetness from her, holding her at the back of her head so she wouldn't move. She felt the shivering first touch of his fingers on her exposed skin, the tickle of his fingers across her stomach, and she opened her legs gently, and his fingers slipped in.

His thick black hair, tanned, olive skin; a strong, square chin. She felt his hands smoothing down her back, moulding her hip-bones with his palms. His bare chest covered in dark hair that whorled whorls around the flat brown discs of his nipples, down to the dark indented navel. The broad width of his back, tanned, well-muscled, define. She breathed in the particular scent of him, moving both hands up and over his shoulders and down the length of his arms, feeling the thrill of his muscles and the texture of his skin. She stroked his back, walking her fingers down his strong spine, as he pressed his hands over her pubic hair, running his thumbs along her sticky groove. She drew her fingernails lightly over his skin, scratching him with gentle pinching, feeling him twitch and rise below.

Moving closer still she pressed the cushion of her lips over his skin, felt the shiver of pleasure running through him, tasted him, moving her hands purposefully up and down his strong thighs, twirling her fingers through the dark hairs, making small circles round his balls, could feel his heat, enclosed his penis in her hands. Opening her mouth wide she enclosed him there, feeling also the hot, wet warmth of his mouth as he sucked on each breast, and she felt that female pull, deep above her sex; heavy moistness between. He licked between her thighs, and she let her self go towards oblivion, swirling colours pulsating behind her closed eyes, the contractions shuddering tighter and tighter. He probed the bud above with the tip of his tongue, lapped the viscid Poppy Milk as she exploded within.

7

'The length of one's life is fixed at birth,' White Poppy said, 'what is written down in the register of death cannot be changed. I went into the room, put on the dress as he commanded, the Canton Factor, bowed down low before his feet. I put on the jewels to make my breast beautiful, placed the tiara on my head. My skirts sweeping the ground as I walked before him.' She sighed, twiddled her fingers in her lap. Her polished fingernails had grown long now. 'He put down the translucent river pearl, put it down on the table in front of me. He had a small tan dog with him. It sniffed my hands, watched my every move. He told me to take the pearl from the table, that he was to give me my reward.' She screwed up her eyes, looking away. 'Uncurling my fingers, I put out my hand, watching him, watching the tan dog, all of the time: the flickering cruelty in the Canton Factor's eyes, sour smile on his lips.'

She stopped talking. Her long nails were like claws, tiger's claws. It was unmistakably a tiger that I saw out of the corner of my good eye – bold, barred, dark stripes, underparts almost white, and yet it vanished when I looked more closely, its features becoming hers, both creatures of the night.

'I put out my hand and touched the pearl,' she said. 'As quick as quick he cut me, drew a sharp blade from his robe and cut down at my hand, which I pulled away in fear. But too slow, as the heavy cold blade bit deep into the tip of my little finger, severing it through the bone; the dog didn't move.' She flicked her pretty eyelashes at me, remembering long-forgotten pain. 'My reward as he had promised!' She laughed, went quiet, pressing her hands closer to her body. 'It bled and bled. He rubbed gunpowder on it to stop the blood.'

Customs, rituals and routines: a face began to take shape in my thoughts, and I heard words to match those slowly moving lips remembered, and my answer: *'If you don't like it,' I told him, 'you can go and hang!'* He had turned slowly, looked at me with contempt, black moustache hanging long each side of his down turned mouth. I had grabbed the document back from him, stuffed the folded paper in my pocket. He had given me the address, the right of entry. I remember how glad I had felt then, how much I believed I was in control. 'Charles,' he'd replied, slant eyes staring, still. 'Charles Sansovino, you drive a hard bargain.'

So, *he* was the Canton Factor, the one who had caused White Poppy so much pain. I had not won with him after all. Justice – had any justice been done? Well, I had stolen

Canton's greatest whore, had taken her through the last 'closed' door. White Poppy spoke:

'The little finger tip he fed to his dog.' She paused, and her eyes took on a different look altogether. 'A sister must not take the side of her own sister against her other sisters, must not give away the secrets of the sisterhood. These things are secret, Charles, are to be kept secret for all time.'

'Yes,' I laughed, 'if a sister breaks the law, may she be eaten by a tiger, be drowned in the Great Sea, have her eyes bitten out by a snake.'

'Stop it, Charles, stop it, don't make fun!'

I kissed her on the mouth, sealed her lips with mine.

White poppy, Eliza, Yin-Shueh yen, shining light, was part of a great sisterhood, the *hui t'ang* or secret society of the 'She-Tigers' of Canton; that strong-minded sisterhood, with its own female leadership of power. She-tigers were the fighters amongst the prostitutes, made money to the benefit of all sisters. The top person, however, was a man. It was not possible to survive without a headman to negotiate with the official Chinese.

The high-class whorehouse, the impressive bungalow harem with the two stone lions in front, was run for erotic profit by the She-Tigers of Canton, not the Brotherhood as I had supposed. It seemed that the fraternity had really only become involved because of my last visit to the Mandarin: he with the thick gold ring engraved with the tail-swallowing snake – after which I was thrown into gaol. The Interpreter must have been as unaware of this as I had been myself. The Manchurian Hoppo was the She-Tiger's agent: embroidered crane on his purple robes – standing before the Goddess, the mirrored shrine, their top man who negotiated their rights with the Canton-controlling Brotherhood. I could keep quiet no longer.

'I thought the Brotherhood was after me because of you, Eliza, because of your importance to them.'

She smiled back at me, my sweetheart, eyes glowing warmly in anticipation of my words. I continued.

'Really, it was because of the evil opium, because of the threat the devils thought I posed to their supply, because of my nosy interference. They weren't interested in you at all!'

'No, Charles. They were interested in me. Prostitutes were only a part of the drug ring that was so very important to them: common women who supplied common pleasure, and the Prostitutes of the Snake, animals who serviced the needs of the highborn Chinese. I was despised because of my *supposed* foreign contamination with you: I who was raised to remain pure Chinese.' She smiled a shallow smile, held me by both hands. 'I wanted you, Charles, wanted to be with you. But there was always that voice inside my head,' she hesitated, 'the voice that argued with itself, that said: talk and you might as well be dead! But while I believed in the future, kept on moving forward, let go of the past, I knew it would be all right.' Half closing her eyes, gazing into the distance, she played with the ends of her hair. 'Because of my horoscope, the right stars, I had been chosen to be the Mother of the new Leader of the Brotherhood, Hung Obedience Hall of the Golden Orchid: my son, my own little warrior to be, fathered by one high-born Chinese, destined to be the next leader of the bloodline. Destined,' she laughed quietly, 'but it was not meant to be.' She sneered. 'Of course it had nothing to do with love!'

Eliza walked a little distance away from me, and started tugging at her hair.

'I stood by the magnolia tree in the courtyard, my hair matted and muddy, my face scratched from my escape. *She* twisted my arms behind my back, shoving me forwards, then let go of me, pushing me viciously against the wall, where I fell down. They hauled me up and between them pushed me backwards and forwards, spinning me round and round like a top, banging my head against the prison walls, until I became dizzy, toppling, falling down the flight of steps before me. They came to inspect me later. The guard pushed me down, and turning me over tore off my underclothes. Holding my breasts tightly, pressing me against the cold slabbed floor he fucked me from behind with a wooden club.'

She squeezed my hand firmly, sobbing then, pressing herself against me, and I smelled the arousing fragrance of her hair, watched the pretty movement of her lips, the tears drying in her eyes.

'I was burned, whipped, slapped along the side of my face. I was told I would be made to look so ugly that no man would ever look at me. My little fingers were compressed, broken; my hands were scraped against the rough-stone walls until they bled. The She-Tigers threatened to burn my womb, to sew up my queynt. These were not ordinary women who made me kneel before them, breasts hanging naked, who hit me across the chest with a stick until my nipples ached with pain.' She stopped talking, looked at me, her eyes still wet, but there were no more tears. 'One seized me, held me tight. Another took off my clothes. They laughed at me as I struggled to get free.' She looked over her shoulder (as if imaging someone there). 'A third slapped my face to stop me struggling, ignoring my tears, as I was dropped to the floor where I lay in the dust sobbing, heart pounding fit to burst.' She looked back at me, screwed up her mouth. 'No, Charles, no ordinary women, these.' She flashed her eyes at me. 'They kept on at me, hour after hour, until I was so tired I could hardly stand. The one in charge, the one who shouted out the orders, struck me with her whip, lashed out at me with the leather, stinging my bare arms. The pain was unbearable, but I was used to it by then: I bit my lip, trying not to cry the tears that would satisfy her, the skin rising up in bright weals. 'She raised the whip again, and this time I closed my eyes. She cracked it savagely against the ground to show what she could do with it if she wanted to. Was I supposed to be grateful, Charles? I searched her eyes for a clue. But there was nothing that I recognised as woman; her eyes remained closed off to the ordinary Chinese womanhood. She was a fighter, a rebel, a She-Tiger of Canton. Her face remained blank.'

White Poppy continued later.

'I watched an old woman being pulled along by a coarse rope tied around her neck, hit viciously with a stick when she collapsed on the ground from exhaustion, when she refused to get up. Her crime? She had talked too much, had said things that should never have been said. Eyes closed; face bleeding, strands of her sparse grey hair stuck to her skin, cries dying weakly in her throat. And she, the aged Whore-Mother, lay completely still, free of all pain, dead.' She blinked. 'Her lips silent for all time.' A single tear dropped from her eyes which now focused distant, remembering much suffering from the past. 'I lay still, didn't interfere; then at the last moment leapt forward as she passed, the murderer, catching her by the leg. I was so angry, Charles: I was so angry that she could kill the person who had reared her, who had looked after her as she grew, who provided her with the means to eat and to sleep and to grow.' She stopped, blinking slowly, black eyes large. 'She toppled, falling heavily, knocking me over. We struggled together, but she gained the upper hand, kicked out at me, caught me in the stomach with her foot.' She opened her mouth to speak and then stopped, the words drying in her throat before reaching her dry lips. 'I hated them,' she spat out. 'I hated them more than words can ever tell you.' She hissed through clenched teeth. 'I vowed to heaven that I would destroy them, that they would never be allowed to forget what they had done to me. And then they fed me the opium, made me eat more of it every day!'

'I told them nothing about you, Charles. I knew nothing. I didn't know what they wanted. They kept on about the British leader, the one with the covered eye.' She smiled at me – such a brilliant, eye-sparkling smile. 'You worried them, you gave them something that confused them, but they tortured me for the information.'

I knew then that it was the English merchant who had been the go-between, the real British spy. Narrowing her eyes, looking at me with the deepest affection, White Poppy laughed. 'Had I known anything I would not have told them: always, death would have been sweeter than betrayal. You see I had heard about you, and later, I read your eyes. I was in love with you.' She nibbled her lip. 'Yes, Charles, by then I was so much in love with you, but I thought you had abandoned me. 'She looked away from me. 'That you had gone forever, that my water had quenched your fire.' She went quiet and then kept muttering to herself, the same words over and over: 'The enemy within, the enemy within.'

However, nothing is lost until it's lost. Before the stellate mirrors, she had stood, her multiple reflected loveliness in purple, silver and gold, white smoke floating away around her, giggling like a child, drifting slowly with the vapours; sitting there with her pretty legs wide apart, laughing like a child, crying hidden tears that she only felt within. Opium drugged to a point between happiness and despair, her body had supplied sexual release for the influential Canton rich: proud, pretty, Prostitute of the Snake, one of the 'chosen' few.

Not all were so lucky. Ji-ou Yoon had been taken to the prison courtyard where she was stripped by two men. I see her half-closed, slanted eyes, those silent vermilion lips. Made to kneel down in anger, face slapped hard across each side, beaten with bamboo rods on the mouth. I see the distance of a thousand years, the china Mountains – the silent peaks, the silent rocks, the silent trees. Head pushed down between her knees I can hear the cracking of her bones. Each girl a bud to grow, to blossom, to flower, to produce more of her kind: Canton victims decked out for the offerings. I see them all before me now, each and every one, and I have a yearning to go back to them, to say 'I'm sorry', for I truly was.

8

The weather was bitter, snow lying in shallow drifts upon the ground. The fires burning well inside, we rested aimlessly in the twilight. Taking her dark nipple in my mouth, feeling the bumpy areola with my lips, sucking, swallowing deeply, smelling her milk-soured flesh, drawing in the firm flesh, filling my mouth with its choking softness; thin dribble of new-mother's milk flowing, baby-nourishing sugar-water trickling down my throat. That earliest sensation of physical pleasure, gorged on the mother's breasts. *Liquid life* in that which has its roots in the beginnings of time itself – woman with her aching hardness, swollen, sweet. She was THE woman, female, mother, fertile, moist: contained the very essence of life – that perfect once-virgin self made whole. Now I understood the perfect Chinese balance: nothing else mattered but that life. And the divine child, untainted yet with adult sin; childhood is so divinely ideal.

The birth of our first child (in 1842), then another, combined Sicilian-English blood and Chinese. There was no joy to exceed it, nothing more splendid than to see those who are the miniatures of your true love, in their petticoats and frocks.

Charlotte Louisa Sansovino, new-born (the first), infant, toddler, child –watched her grasping, pulling to sit, hands opening, reaching by rolling, sitting to stand, standing holding on, walking holding on, walking without support; at two years watched her running and kicking a ball; at four years watched her as she hopped, buttoned up clothes, smiling wickedly with her twinkling, brown, almond-shaped eyes. Her Chinese name is Huan-yue (hwahn yoo eh); happiness, joyful.

Abigail Amelia (Angelina), new-born (the second), with her cool blue eyes, her mother's self-assurance – the process started again. She suffered from bronchial attacks for most of her life, as did many of her friends and family. She was also plagued by dizziness and fainting spells, which she (and her doctors), later attributed to overexertion. The secret of eternal youth – there would always be children. Her Chinese name is Xiùlán (Sheeyou Ian); Elegant Orchid.

They lay back across the padded sofa, innocent young bodies blending into the dark woven silk damask, each watching the other; each with her slightly large head; blousy buttoned white nightgowns, and the sleepy inward curl of their straight toes. Soft hair hanging loose, brown eyes, blue eyes, peering sleepily through the closing evening shadows, moonbeams falling like shining silk, their skin soft as it brushed against me, as they kissed their 'goodnights', their lips cold, their whole faces cold, pretty features smiling up at me.

They go everywhere with God: religious education was important, and the girls attended Sunday services, were encouraged to read the Bible every day and took part in daily family prayers. They also had their romantic poetry and drama – amateur dramatics in the parlour.

Unrest and violence followed the China wars, and by 1848 the crisis had come. In February revolutions burst out on the continent. In March there were riots in London, Glasgow and other large towns. In April the government filled London with Wellington's troops, who barricaded the bridges and Downing Street, and garrisoned the Bank. In June the Houses of Parliament were provisioned for a siege.

Time changes our perception of things, distorts the small details, blends together the separate parts. At first we don't see the holes, the cracks; do not appreciate what each one is. And yet we soon grow fond of where the sun shines in, where the full moon lights the floor, where the wind shakes the windows and rattles the doors. The details become important, more important than the whole. And where White Poppy walked it was like that, too, where the house surrounded her, breathed into her with its own life, a life given vigour by the nearby sea.

White Poppy employed her Lady's Maid, Hannah, a sweet mousey-haired French girl, 23 years, from Toulouse: neat in appearance, with very good English, she could read and write well in both English and French. Handling her mistress' clothing, jewels and personal effects, she helped White Poppy dress and undress, maintaining her wardrobe, and laundering her most delicate clothes. She prepared the beauty lotions for White Poppy's ageing skin, and brushed and styled her grey-streaked hair. As each of our girls was born, she helped with them too. She called them her dearest ones. Using her dressmaking skills she made new articles of clothing for all and every occasion. She played with the children after washing and dressing them, brushing and braiding their hair.

Eventually, as the children had grown older, White Poppy allowed us to have a Cook, too: Nellie, 37 years, a careful brunette with deep brown eyes and a quiet sad face; tearful at times, and again quite stern. She met with White Poppy in the morning to review and approve the week's menus with her, and was then off to market to buying fresh fish. Her last duty at night was to turn off the gas and secure all doors and windows. The House was often filled with gay laughter then.

The gale roared fiercely, threatened to de-slate the roof, smoke blowing back out from the chimneys and out and into the rooms. Night black, no moon, no stars; children in bed we gathered our coats about us, fighting our way breathless down the Epple Bay Gap to the winter sea: suck and roar of the smooth flint pebbles, swooshing shingle raked violently, white water clawing, booming against the chalk cliffs. Eliza's hair damp in the sea-salt air, her cold lips brush my own, salt-rimed, raw: hair twisted into a tight knot at the crown, ringlets dropping to her shoulders, down over her Chinese ears.

9

Fingering the engraved silver compact in which she kept her cosmetics, her silver instruments of oral hygiene, White poppy got ready for bed. Going across to the dresser she fumbled beneath her clothes, taking out a crumpled red paper packet, opening it carefully with trembling fingers, Chinese eyes sparkling with sad pleasure.

'Look, Charles, I have this!'

She held it out for me to see, gestured to me to take it. Inside, a tuft of fluffy black hair, the cut-off strands of one new-born. Tied with five-coloured silk, it was her hair exactly. Taking it from me quickly, she carefully refolded the paper, closed the packet with a kiss.

'My son,' she said proudly, 'my son! He was so beautiful... ebony hair, bright eyes... he died of sickness!'

Each birth is a new child, part of a family, a greater brotherhood and sisterhood that stretches back in time: a child of the children that have gone before: each part of the whole, and the whole part of the each. He had come with us secretly across China (she then told me), tucked somewhere safe inside her underclothes (as she travelled as a young man).

Tears rolling down her cheeks, she could stop blowing her nose. The red silk handkerchief was soon soaked. *We stand in our own shadow, yet we wonder why it's dark*. Square tower rising above the surrounding roofs, iron railing and a narrow walkway around the top: I see it now as I write these words here in my Journal. The pawn-shop owner Lo Da Gang, hard-faced, grey-bearded old man who spoke some little English: I see him, the slow movements of his mouth. The chubby woman Ah Zi, who appeared carrying a baby, her black hair cut with a fringe, slit eyes as big as saucers. I see the soft movements of her hands. Crying, the baby pushed itself against her breasts, a handsome black-eyed boy, not more than three months old: opening her clothing she had offered a full nipple to his lips. ***Eliza? The crumpled red packet? Inside a tuft of fluffy black hair, the cut-off strands of one new-born.***

Then she told me, and I actually saw *him*, her beautiful, dead boy! I see him now; see White Poppy's face in his.

'What sickness did he die of, your son?'

'Poison.' She looked away. 'The she-Tigers poisoned him.' She sobbed. 'They stuffed his little mouth with opium, bitter juice of the White Poppy. The Sisters were interested only should I have had a first-born daughter, she who would have had the same pure blood; she who would be their warrior, their female leader.' Reaching across, she held my hand. 'So, my first child was a boy; as far as they were concerned he would have to die.' She pressed my fingers tightly (her eyes dull). 'I couldn't bear that, would never let them do that to him. I thought he should go to the Brotherhood, that they should have their male leader instead.'

She stopped talking, fidgeting with her hair. Common prostitutes had abortions, used other means and methods of penetration to prevent pregnancy, denying entrance to their womb, but White Poppy's baby had been anticipated, expected, welcomed to be high-born of the Brotherhood, born of the Prostitute of the Snake, *the* She-Tiger of Canton. She talked again.

'In return, you were to be released from prison, Charles.' Her voice dried in her throat, her lips dry. 'But it was not to be, the Brotherhood's claim to my child was ignored, the Mandarin would not have his child [he with the thick gold ring engraved with the snake swallowing its own tail – how that memory burned into me, the words as they formed on her lips.] The Sisters threatened to poison him, to kill him in any way they could; to kill me if necessary.' She sighed long and loud, clasped her hands between her knees. 'After my son's death, I felt like a ghost: I had lost everything. Although the birth was painful, I had felt no pain like it before, what joy I felt that day, how happy I was inside, and yet he never really was mine.'

The tribadic princess, the enclosed inner circle, the Jade fairy Maids. Legs open, she leaned forwards letting her hands hang down between them, looking at her toes, pressing her feet close together. 'Because of me all was destroyed for all time.' Her eyes glistened with her pain. 'I was despised for going against their code. I was to pay for their destruction. That was why I had to escape from Canton. You know, Charles, I only received that freedom because there were those who preferred the greater profits to be had from opium, than the profits from having me captured and killed. But you, you little darling,' she smiled, opening her eyes wide, 'you pretended to have me killed, sent back that corpse with the tattoo, and I was free. Now do you see how much you helped me, the only non-Chinese?' She looked embarrassed, ran her long fingers through her hair, smiled. 'I saw you as a means of escape, thought I could use you to save myself. That was all it was at first, a matter of convenience, for once I found out, I would have been as good as dead.' She looked away from me. 'An Englishman, a foreigner, I was encouraged to betray you for my freedom, but I couldn't, could not throw everything away for the only man in China who understood me, who loved me for *who* I was.'

Through a tiled entry *he* had taken her (so Eliza told me), into a court with solaces of small trees and bowers, with a little fountain. The teahouse was of several storeys, furnished with polished black wood furniture inset with grained Ta-li marble, displayed its seasonal 'flowers' on the uppermost floor. He had kept her there: he who preferred the tea of mountain leaves plucked fresh after the first fall of winter snow: Cloud-Ball tea – green, sweet and fragrant: tea infused in lidded bowls (*chung*) poured into small porcelain cups.

Looking at her then, sitting there before me, chin resting on her knees, black hair flowing down over her legs, White Poppy, I desired her more than ever, could not stop myself from shouting out at 'my possession' of China's greatest treasure. 'You are mine, my lady. I won you, you are mine!'

With an air of supreme boredom White Poppy leaned back over the arm of the chintz covered chair; shaking her head to and fro, she loosened the pins from her dark and glossy hair which tumbled about her shoulders in wild disarray. With a fierce change of heart, she grasped the whole, coiling it carelessly upon her head, stabbing back into it with the pins. In her Chinese face was the look of the petulant, scolded child.

10

Punching with tiger's eyes White poppy stood legs apart, bent her knees, fists clenched, palms up at her waist. Glaring eyes followed the movement: she punched out to the right, punched out to the left, breathing out, breathing in, her Chinese eyes bright like stars, the mother! She looked back at me, looked at me straight.

'Your powerful blue eye; your body tall and broad.'

She took off my leather eye-patch, saw me truly naked.

'I wanted to hate you, Charles, another *man*. I wanted you to mean nothing to me.' She kissed me firmly on the lips, pushed me hard between the legs, giggled when she felt movement there. How it is possible to hate and love someone at the same time! 'But I was intrigued by you, you were a novelty, so unlike any other man I had been with, so wonderfully un-Chinese, taboo!' She squealed out loud, threw herself against me. 'Yes, I *knew* you were in love with me, and fell in love with you, the man who started my life.'

The train of girls coming ashore from the small boat: White Poppy had made her way to the walled city with its gates, shut in, enclosed in the ascending narrow streets. And I had expected that she would remain there, would disappear into the rabbit warren that was Canton. But no, several days after that sighting the Grand Junk sailed and the White Poppy went with it on a voyage along the coast towards Amoy. And it was eight months later that she was taken back to give birth, leaving her son at the pawn-shop under the Triad protection of Lo Ta Kang.

Whilst I was in the Canton bungalow, the palace of a Thousand Dreams (access to which had been through the Factor), White Poppy had been giving birth at the teahouse. Several days later, as a sign of his 'respect' for her, the Factor had cut off her finger tip. Later, the She – Tigers cut off her boy! But she had been successful, had severed the very threads that held her to the web: the She-Tigers, she had destroyed them. In running away with me she had left them helpless, angry, exposed: the message had got back to the Brotherhood through the oily mouth of the Interpreter's wife, and those vengeful males soon made their attack. I watched the corona of the moon, small band of bluish light expanding into rings of white and reddish brown. I didn't want it ever to stop.

11

If it be then Thy will that I should die in Childbirth my last prayer is that Thou shouldst grant me in death the blessing I have so earnestly desired in life and enlighten...

The house was filled with beautiful photo portraits of our glowing girls – truly exceptional in every detail. Nothing brings back those long ago days like the thought of those little photos, and the family feelings they aroused. The photos – some in soft focus – revealing the intimate and spiritual intensity of these immaculate blooming flowers. That childhood innocence, so different from the world of adults: childhood divinely ideal! Those photographs revealed that invisible umbilical cord, stretched to snapping point, as she, the mother, gazed on the children she knew would eventually leave her. White Poppy loved them all in the way that only a mother can – her precious brood of pulsating female flesh; eternally beautiful – those beautiful English flowers crafted in the natural spirit, fresh from God's hands: no shadow yet of sin fallen on any single one of them. The soft realism of their pale flesh, radiantly luminous, their sparkling eyes, the details almost of the individual hairs on their heads; the girls wearing the shorter geometric patterned dresses, bodices boned with whalebone, scalloped, ruffled, beribboned and pleated; long fingers below starched white cuffs; the wisps of their curls, and the Chinese knot of a bow. And me, I am sitting in the armchair, upright, still: the photo portrait showing well the blending of my dark clothes and similar dark background of the familiar room; leather patch over one eye – the only difference from an earlier, painted portrait, was the white hair.

Wet collodion photography – announced publicly in Paris in 1839 – involved glass plates, slow exposures and various chemical solutions and procedures; the plates had to be developed quickly, and the small positive contact prints were made in sunlight, but the technique allowed a minute, and intimate, degree of detail, even-gradation from light to dark. There were holes in the wood panelled kitchen wall. Each the reminder of something that had been nailed there before - some precious picture, ornament, mirror; each an item special to its female owner and placed there at her will. And the holes formed a random pattern like the stars, like those random pinpricks in the fabric of God's sky. There was a crack in the wall by the black door, where the air blew through, where a feather held against it rose a little upwards before falling to the ground. Where Eliza walked it was like that, too, her rustling skirts agitating the air around her as she went; where the house surrounded her, breathed into her with its own life, a life given vigour by the nearby sea.

I told them bedtime stories: they loved to hear such tales – the stories of the haunted ships. *On the Kent coast there are certain water elves and sea fairies that keep festival and summer months in old haunted hulks. They need young female flesh to keep on living, plot how they might accomplish to take a man's wife. The water elves watch the fisherman as he goes down to the bay, to where the water is shallow between the two haunted hulks. He places his half-net and awaits the coming of the tide, falls asleep in the sunshine. He wakes up late, it is dark and the night air cold. He listens to the singing of the increasing waters among the pebbles and the broken shells, and then he hears a sound that made his blood run cold, the sound as of a hatchet employed in squaring timber echoed far and wide, and lights begin to glance and twinkle from every hole and seam on board both haunted ships. He freezes inside, knows they are making someone a "wife". Swiftly emptying the catch from his net he returns home fast and his wife cooks the fish for their supper.*

Eliza had given each daughter a gold posy ring, symbol of her affection and to protect each from harm: Rock Crystal for simplicity and purity, Sapphire for hope, Amethyst for humility, Emerald for tranquil peace, Onyx for sincerity (victory over one's enemies) and Diamond for invulnerable constancy. Inscribed inside each the same inscription: '*United hearts death only parts*'.

'We have our children,' she told me. 'We can share their lives with them; let them tell us how they see the world. Children make everything right, give order where there is chaos, make the complex simple. With children we are allowed to be children once more.'

Feeling contented, full, his wife goes to bed early, and he stays downstairs mending his nets. The firewood burns, hissing and crackling, sparks bursting out loud. The fisherman hears knocking outside but he won't open the door. He sits up all night, but dozes in the early hours and wakes by the light of the rising sun. It is quiet, there is no sound outside. He peers through the window – there is no sign of anyone there. He goes to the door and opens it wide. He finds standing there, a piece of black ship oak, rudely fashioned into something like human form. Had he opened the door, had he admitted his visitants, it would have been clothed with seeming flesh and blood, and palmed upon him by elfin adroitness for his wife; the water elves stealing the real woman for themselves. If they succeeded in carrying their female prey to the waves never might she return, her final gasping sound drowned out beneath the sea.

How the girls loved that final line, tucked themselves in close against me. They loved it even more when their

Mother was in the room. Angelina, watched the words formed by her expressive lips; tears drying in her large blue eyes (the colour of mine), as she sat by Eliza: *her dearest darling daughter, Precious Angel here on Earth.*

'My Mother, you never look sad, you're always smiling.'

The sweet innocence of the young.

'But I do get sad,' her Mother replied, 'some things make me very sad inside.'

Angelina grabbed her hand, held it close.

'But you're silly to get sad Mamma, when you have me!'

12

For ten days of its life the cut seed capsule of the White Poppy exudes its milky juice. White Poppy stripped herself quickly, ripped off her clothes in fierce frenzy, made her breasts bare. She danced in front of the looking-glass, stood up high on her toes, turning slowly with sweeping movements of her arms, turning, twisting like a naked ballerina. She watched herself carefully in the glass, lovingly, letting her hands, her fingers trail slowly down her pigmented breasts, across her baby-swollen stomach, resting lightly on her thighs. She spun round slowly; making herself dizzy, black hair following the spiralling movement of her head. She tripped across the floor with natural elegance and ran towards the bed, falling over her feet, crashing on to it, hair settling down across her sparkling face. She lay there on her back, her Chinese eyes flickering, watching the patterned ceiling above her, as the room spun round and round; holding on tightly, digging her fingertips deep into the bedclothes.

And then she started laughing, giggling, tears of joy streaming from her eyes, pressing her knees together, hands held tightly at the parting of her thighs. I had rarely seen her so happy. All day she had been so full of energy, her eyes so full of sunshine, such laughter on her lips. She had pulled me round the garden; had held my hand tightly and taken me round after her, stopping to let me kiss her, to close my mouth over hers. But only for so long, and then she was off. She pulled me out of the house and along the garden, pulled me towards the cliff, and taking my head in her hands she made me look out to sea, pressed my lips close with her fingers, kissed me sweetly on my mouth, her eyes manic, mad. *Do you see*, said her eyes? *Do you see this free beauty that is all ours, the world that is ours in all its glory?* And taking both of my hands in hers, she kissed me – softly, gently, lovingly, exquisitely, letting her lips linger over mine, cool as silk, pressing them gently closer, following with urgent movements of her tongue, and she closed her eyes.

Looking beyond Eliza, past the wisps of her fragrant hair, I watched the movements of the waters, the slate-grey English sea, tried to see the world through her eyes: beautiful simplicity, the balance between opposing forces, in a sky where the sun was bright but where there was also the faint orb of the moon; saw the beauty of all we had together. Taste her lips; smell her female smell; feel the heat of her hot flesh. Gorgeous, glistening, half-closed eyes, filled with the distance of the thousands of years; luscious open, crimson mouth, faint crease of a smile at the entrance of the most erotic lips – red lips opened wide, wisps of black hair blowing about their silent moistness, a smile that so frequently hides tears. White Poppy's pretty Chinese face disfigured by twin scars above her right cheek: I closed my mouth over her mouth, the girl; the woman within the girl. *I have taken her soul.*

Watch her playing with her long black hair, head forward, hair parted slightly at the crown. She stops singing to herself, raises her head slowly, large almond eyes, peering up at me. She opens her mouth, lips forming words that do not come; her mouth widening with luscious sensuality. Closing her cold lips over mine once more, she took control. How could I ever forget the beauty of each special moment with her? She pushed me backwards, sat facing me across my chest. Leaning forwards, hair cascading softly over my face, she lowered her lips on to my lips, pressing down with new force, with all the heat of her Chinese passion. I felt her hot breath; tasted all the passion within her mouth, as she forced her heavy breasts down on me, forced her pelvis over my own, pressed down with the full power of her now-wet thighs. And then she was moving again, wriggled herself up me, pressing into me with her chubby knees, pushes away from my legs with her feet, moving her bottom towards my chest. Her mouth now above my head, gasping above me, she pushed herself higher, thrusting her knees around my shoulders, pushing forwards, pushing down, pressing herself on to me. Legs opened wider, pressing herself to my face, moving that sticky wetness over my mouth, she sealed herself fiercely against my lips, and with no further restraint, she came.

13

Eyes wide open, moist orbs reflecting the bedroom in their blackness, White Poppy lay next to me on the bed, told me an afternoon story.

'In Canton there was a poor man who lived in a deserted kiln, who earned his living by collecting firewood from the hills and manure for fuel on the streets. He lived alone and was usually very hungry, having very little money to buy food. When he did earn spare coppers he saved them.' She closed her eyes, playing with the ends of her long hair, pulling it around her face. 'On the last day of the Old Year, the poor man went shopping with the two hundred coppers he had saved. Walking through the market he saw nothing worth buying except for a picture of a beautiful, green-eyed girl. Enchanted, he couldn't take his eyes away from her.' She paused, adjusted her position on the bed, snuggling herself against me, lay back with her hands behind her head. 'Next morning, when the city-folk congratulated their neighbours as is the New Year custom, he hung the picture on the wall of his kiln, put a bowl of cabbage under it in offering, and kneeling down, paid reverence to the green-eyed beauty.'

My mind was drifting elsewhere. The Painted Lady fluttered out in jewelled elegance from the stern, alit along the wall. Young Chinese eyes bright like shining polished stones; sleek, shoulder-length black hair cut across in a thick fringe combed down to her brows; high-collared lemon silk gown with a soft pink sash around an hourglass waist. She clasped her small hands around her marble neck, pressed her elbows to her breasts, pursed her blood-red lips (pushed forwards already by protruding top teeth); petite teenage face powdered and rouged; embroidered slippers on her naked feet, Yu Ji. How the memories flooded back lying there, still beside White Poppy. She looked up to me and smiled, as though she was about to tell me some great secret.

'One day, returning home tired and hungry from his work, the poor kiln-dweller opened the door to the smell of food. Opening the cooking pot after making reverence to the picture of the green-eyed girl, he saw it was full of bubbling food.' She opened her eyes wide at me. 'He was frightened, did not dare start eating, put some of the food beneath the picture as he always did, and after bowing down before her, ate until he could eat no more. He could never remember having been so full.' She looked at me in eager anticipation, raised her eyebrows. 'The next morning he only pretended to go out to collect manure and hid behind the kiln to see who entered his home. Nobody came, so he crept to the door and looked inside. He saw a beautiful girl at the hearth, starting to light the fire. On the wall the picture was nothing more than a blank piece of paper. Astonished and overjoyed he was not sure what to do, in no way wanting to break the magic spell. So he went back out and entered again with noisy footsteps and a warning cough.' She paused, licked her dry lips, grabbing my hands tighter, holding them close to her naked chest. 'Looking round the door the girl's picture was hanging on the wall as before, the fire burning in the hearth, cooking-pot full of hot food.'

She stood up from the bed, went quiet, walked over to the bedroom window, looking briefly out to sea, which was loud then, the tide high up the beach. She turned at the window, stared into my good eye: the story near completion? 'In the afternoon the poor man went out once more and waited behind the kiln until he heard familiar gentle steps, the noise of pots and pans, the sound of water being poured into cups, the rattle of the bellows, the clatter of fire-stones and tongs.' She breathed faster, pressing her bottom against the window ledge, holding her right hand against her chest, her eyes open wide. 'Holding his breath he took hold of the door, opened it quickly, and running inside he rolled up the blank picture and hid it. Looking around, he saw the beautiful green-eyed girl in a corner of his kiln, and knelt down in front of her to declare his love.' White Poppy yawned, stretching her legs: sighed with pleasure. 'She drew him towards her, saying, As things are as they are, let us live together so that you are no longer alone. The man did not believe what he was hearing, thinking: can this possibly be happening to me? Time passed and the girl got pregnant and gave the poor man a son.'

Skin glowing by the warmth of the coal fire, the White Poppy came back across to the bed, reached across, held my left hand in hers, squeezing my fingers, pressing it to her womb. She stared at me in silence. I wanted to hear the end of her tale, wanted to know what happened to the man and the girl. I stroked her hair gently below me, as she purposefully made me wait.

'One day she asked him, do you still have the roll of white paper? He nodded, and she continued, not once taking her beautiful eyes away from his. "I would like to see it, please." The man thought we have lived together three years and we have a son; why should I be afraid?'

White Poppy glanced at my eye, at my hands in her lap, again at my eye, her face more serious now.

'So he went and took out the scroll from its secret hiding place and showed it to her, saying, look, this is... But suddenly she was gone from before him, and the beautiful girl reappeared on the paper. He threw himself to the ground, distraught, weeping, the baby crying beside him, but the picture remained lifeless, still.'

Eliza rolled over towards me; lay flat on her back, eyes open wide. She stared up at the white ceiling. I wonder what was the point of this, why had she told me that story? Looking beyond me, eyes focussed on another place, another time, her voice low, she continued. 'Even the most beautiful girl knows that she must grow up,' she whispered through closed lips, 'that her young body, her beauty, will not last for ever.'

We search for love, we find it; we lose it by trying too hard to keep it. I found it unbearable, this baring of the soul. I found it painful, but I was curious, wanted her to go on, wanted her to reveal her deepest secrets to me; the answers to the deepest questions still, peeling away the layers until we got to the innermost core.

My mind is filled with yet more memories of a past that seems so very fresh, and yet so very distant. Throwing some mulberry twigs on the fire, the Interpreter's wife had watched the rice pan boiling, sending out the most delicious sea-food smell. They had found out; they would be coming for her. White Poppy was then unconscious in the chest. Was it the wife who had given us away, the sailor and the whore? I created that diversion in the kitchen, set fire to some oil; acrid smoke filling the air, and we'd made our escape.

14

We walked together, hand-in-hand, along the shore: sea-breeze chill, bright winter sunshine warming our backs, fingers intertwined, gold rings pressed close together. She, so very pretty. I told her:

'The things you fight about when you are young, you don't fight about when you're old.'

'The desires are the same,' she replied, with a flick of her hair. 'It's just that you no longer have the energy to do anything about them.' She smiled, looked away, pushed at a dead seagull with her boot. She talked to me as we walked, wrestling with the 'truth', and I watched her as always, glancing at her animated features, quick movements of her mouth, the four seasons of her eyes.

Eliza, she had attitude – obvious outrage still. She squeezed my fingers tightly. 'I love you, Charles. I love you so very much.' Love and intense inner passion: the power of the truth that had made her so happy, so in love with life: I could see it in her eyes. She continued: 'My body belongs to me now. I'm not afraid of anything.' She stopped, stood still, looked up at me with large eyes. 'But I remember how I felt about myself, disappointed, disadvantaged, distant. I never really felt in touch with *me*, kept the real me distant, tucked away safely for the happy future that I prayed would one day be there for me.' She blinked, touched her tongue tip to her upper lip. 'Well, these are the happy times, Charles, and I feel strong inside, powerful.'

Closing my mouth over hers, feeling the contact of her lips, tasting the essence of what makes her woman, I felt like crying: crying from the pain of happiness, so deep, so complete, for my White Poppy who conquered daily the innermost passions of my body and my soul: she who set me afire with her body: she who quenched me with her soul. She in whose love I was drowning!

Expanse of rippled sand illuminated by the rising silver moon, thin clouds scudding fast across her face, the air was warm, calm, blowing Eliza's hair about her. There were tears in her eyes.

'Can one grasp the wind?' she asked, slowly shaking her head, 'and hold on to it? I don't want ever to lose you.'

BOOK VIII THE CLEAR BRIGHTNESS

Birchington, Kent
Autumn 1854

1

In the evening
Lighted red paper
Lanterns trail long after
Tails of
Night soaring, paper kites:
Floating
Upwards, flying high,
Lifting,
Rising to
The star-lit sky,
Wind strengthening
Blowing free,
Breeze-rippled spiral paper tails:
Twin dragon kites rising,
Soaring, flying.
Twin dragon kites falling, sweeping, lying,
Heads touching,
Diving
To the ground.
Turning,
Rising,
Lifting, dipping;
Cords breaking,
Sweeping,
Soaring.
Heavenwards,
Free.

Early morning, old women collect the star-lit dew of angels into a bottle and use it to wash the faces of children. In each dewdrop everything is reflected from the rising sun. How quaint we say? We look at old people, we watch them, listen as they tell us how they feel, looking round their familiar rooms filled with memories of a soon speeded-by past. I want to be that old person, to know how it feels, to encompass the deepest darkest sadness, yet illuminated with moments of the most absolute joy, then I hope I can say to my children's children: I lived here, I did that, that was me. *This Journal is my collected thoughts and feelings, and the essence of my memories – so that should be quite possible for me.*

Now in the 1850s the competition between Britain and America was fierce in the tea trade from China, since high premiums were charged for the first shipment of tea to reach London, Liverpool, or New York. By winning such tea races, merchants and ship owners, make their fortunes, which in turn lead to a boom in the production of those greyhounds of the sea by shipyards on the river Thames.

From the mound at the end of the garden I watched my girls flying their huge silk box kite sailing red through the agitated Sunday afternoon air, their shrill voices travelling back on the wind that moaned over the chalk cliff at the end of our garden: Charlotte Louisa, 'Charlie', 13 years, and Angelina, 11 years; Sophronia, Sophia – Sophes, 5 years, was inside with their mother, Eliza. Children, angels, no affectations, no conceits – *the connecting link joining us with the inhabitants of a better world!* Excited, standing feet apart, laughing, black hair tugging in the breeze. Pearl bangles clasping white wrists, they did not realise I was there. How different they were – free in their play and pleasure – when out of sight of us, their parents.

Charlotte Louisa lifting her head slightly, coyly, neck slender, tilting her shining face away from the sun, hat rising, revealing oriental features of great beauty, glistening hair strained back behind; another Eliza, brown eyes, the most Chinese. I watched the white sails of a barque beyond her, making her way along the coast behind them, far out at sea, wind blowing fresh in her sails, sails catching the late-summer sun. Charlotte Louisa held the reel tightly, powerfully, paying out the cord, massive kit soaring high, climbing higher, reel whirring, jerking, stops – the whole cord now run out, red kite straining to make its getaway. Laughter on her lips she urged Angelina to cut it, to let it go, to watch the red box drift away.

'I haven't the heart to let it go Charlie. It's such a beautiful kite, the best we've ever had.'

'Our Mother will make us another one, my Angel, she does so every year!' Charlotte tugged her arm. 'Do let it go... pleeeease!'

Kite flying was just for fun I had told the girls when they were much younger. The Chinese call it sending off bad luck, as Eliza told me: cutting the cord, sending off a few of their best kites every year.

Angelina cut the cord with delicate silver scissors from her sewing purse that she had touched already to her lips. The red kite drew away, swept out over the sea: they watched it until it was gone: Angelina, fascinating, lovely, innocent – fascinated - full of gaiety and playfulness, blue eyes resting for a moment on everything beautiful, sublime, and her beautiful elder sister, Charlie. *A tear for the new-born lamb; sad for the beggar but afraid to go near, her heart like softened wax, and the impressions then made on it remaining for ever.* Looking at both daughters, the love in their pretty eyes, I could not forget the young Chinese whores working slit-eyed with their ravished bodies, until age left them unattractive, dull.

Charlotte Louisa, Charlie, another Eliza, the same brown eyes, was the most Chinese. Clasping her long straight fingers between her covered knees, she talked to me softly, sat brushing her long black hair – 100 times until it shone brilliantly, softly running the bristle brush from the crown down over her shoulders, brushing with her left hand, smoothing it down afterwards with the right, as her Mother had shown her as a young child. When Charlie sat before me on the edge of the bed, and I watch here, watched the shining in her hair, the shining in her eyes, the movement of her lips; watched her as she talked, head turned away from me; watched the slender curving of her neck, the falling down of her young shoulders, the narrowing of her back to her waist: watched the pressing of her immature thighs, the flexing of her childlike knees, the positioning of her ankles as she touched her feet to the floor. I wanted to cry. I had seen it all before, in her Mother, White Poppy; my wife. And I felt such intense longing, such strong desire to go back, to run back in time to when it was the White Poppy, Yin Hsueh-Yen, boat-girl, there before me, for that very first time.

Hair swept up off her face Charlie came towards me in the moonlit darkness, preceded by the most exquisite scent. I heard her breathing; listened to the salivation of her lips, the paper rustle of her clothes; that flash of colour in all that is dark, my daughter, my dearest darling daughter. Charlie, she had become the new grown woman, future mother, fertile, moist: contained the very essence of life. She flung back her hair, brought it quickly forwards, her hair flying softly around her beaming face, and it felt so right to be there close with her: so right to hold her in my arms, to press my face against her hair. It was so right, my dearest darling Charlie, because *here was a man who would never hurt her.* And then, of course, there was my pretty Sophia, five years, blue eyes, black hair.

My girls, our girls, part of a great sisterhood, going all the way back to Eve. Educated at home: dancing, playing the piano, learning Johnson's *Dictionary* by heart, sitting down with English books, reading the plays of Shakespeare, translations of the classics, making their own clothes: a governess and nurses teaching them needlepoint and poetry, English grammar and mathematics. Unlike other fathers I do not believe that study is bad for a girl. Indeed, I think it is the very making of her. They spoke Cantonese as well as they spoke English, my three girls: each one a bud to swell, to grow, to blossom, to flower, to produce more of her kind.

We had a Butler then: in his late 40s, a distinguished figure with an imposing presence. He arranged the dining-table, announced dinner, and waited at table. After carving the joint of meat, and removing the covers from other dishes, he served the wine and set out each additional course. While we enjoyed dessert he made sure that the drawing room was in order, for the family's retreat for coffee or tea. He made sure the lamps were alight, and that the fire was glowing warmly. Summer 1857: Seated in the drawing-room, the sisters clustered together, their heads forming that fond female frieze, before the vases and the candelabra on the vast mantelpiece behind; in contrast to the floral-patterned wallpaper, long nets by the panelled doors – their long and flowing polka dot design dresses, laced cuffs, making them look as though grown physically from the floor. Purple orchids starting to bud: Angel, Charlie. Both girls dressed in long burgundy velvet dresses, black hair tied back with burgundy ribbons, stood waiting, looking out through our bedroom window, beneath the heat banded panes of magenta and mustard-yellow glass, young bodies silhouetted against the bright morning sunlight shining into the room.

'Charlotte Louisa, come and say goodbye to your Father!'

She ran over to me, Eliza in miniature, stretching up tall, pressing her soft lips on mine.

'Goodbye my Father, do have a good day.' She smiled prettily, half-closing her oriental, almond-eyes, rubbing her somewhat Chinese nose, withdrew back to her bedroom and her books.

Angelina ran forward, laughter bursting in her eyes – blue in a cloud-swept sky – her voice, vibrant, velvety, low; gave me her own special hug and a kiss.

'Bye My Father, bring back some treats for me, please?' She flicked back her raven hair, walking slowly to the window, turning round, watching me go. 'Take care, Papa! Take care!'

The words fell from her drying lips, slanted eyes turned upwards to her Mother, pearl bangles clasping her pale wrists: intermingled essence of England and China, our daughters, the mixing of two great seas. And each of them then had their Mother-given emblem, the tattoo of the snake.

2

Into the wood – the dark, dark wood – Forth went the happy Child And in its stillest solitude Talked to herself and smiled; And closer drew the scarlet Hood About her ringlets wild. Annotated poem to a photo of Agnes Weld, Croft Rectory, Yorkshire: Lewis Carroll, 18 August 1857.

Tiny envelopes scratched by fountain pen ink and sealed with wax, labelled with that neat handwriting and bundled into little packets with string. White Poppy was getting older, there were wrinkles now, and white hair, but always with that same deep twinkle in her dark almond eyes. Between the private bonds of family and the public world, and the household servants she got to grips with that paradox; push and pull between the internal essence and the eternal reality.

On the occasion of Phoebe's birthday she gave her an ornament symbolising faith, hope, and charity, and a book, *The Story Without an End*, about divine love and providence. Phoebe: grown-up apparition in a flowing red velvet dress, hair pinned high, unchanged she remained generous, unconventional, loyal servant through and through.

White Poppy stood at her family altar, small shrine, shaped like a tiny house and hung upon the spare room wall, a selection of homemade Chinese gods, daily offerings of burning incense, dishes of dried fruit, rice, candles kept burning there. Clean hands and a pure heart, she lit additional candles one by one, room glowing bright, light penetrating the shadows where she didn't always like to look. White Poppy back with her own Chinese prayers – her link with China, with the distant Chinese past, her ancestors and her gods; her own special place where she talked quietly in Cantonese, though of late her voice had become more agitated, and her words of prayer were quite loud. What was it, I wondered, that still remained hidden in the darkness; what phantoms haunted her there still?

3

Expanse of rippled sand illuminated by the rising silver moon, thin clouds scudding fast across her face, the air was warm, blowing White Poppy's hair about her. There were tears in her eyes.

'Can one grasp the wind?' she asked, slowly shaking her head. 'I don't want to lose you.'

15th day of the 8th Chinese month (towards the end of our September), it is the time of the mid-autumn festival: a full-moon festival for women, celebrated through the night.

'The moon is cool like jade; it is cool and moist even on the hottest of nights,' she said, fingering the bangle on her left wrist – serpentine green jade. 'And jade is the symbol of chastity, of purity, of the good woman.'

Amongst large white arum lilies, bushes of blood-red roses, our girls, Angel and Charlie, stood together in the garden; stood facing each other in their long white gowns, black hair tied back with red velvet ribbons; heads bent forwards, chins down, concentrating on the placing of some expanded paper lanterns, threaded paper cocoons hung from forked branches.

Night fallen, bright moonlight filled the garden, silver light across an altar built outdoors; dish of 13 'moon cakes' (the number of months in the Chinese year), pastries filled to bursting with spices, sugar and nuts, beside the long-eared Moon-Hare amongst the candles and sticks of smoking incense. I left both girls alone together until they finish their head-together talking, and came in. They lay back across the padded sofa, young bodies blending into the dark woven silk damask, each watching the other, multiple reflections of the central female theme. Soft hair hanging loose, brown eyes, blue eyes, peering sleepily through the closing evening shadows, moonbeams falling like shining silk, the girls at one with the world, their skin soft as it brushed against me, as they kissed their 'Good nights', their lips cold, their whole faces cold, pretty features smiling up at me. With a flick of their skirts they were off again, pushing, giggling up the stairs, Charlotte in front reading words remembered from her poetry book: 'Night mist wearing thin the shaken blossoms fall.'

The moon was bright through the bedroom window and I couldn't sleep, heard the female voices distant, lying still, thinking about the Old man in the Moon: he who arranges all marriages from his heavenly seat: he who writes in his book the names of all new born: he who knows who all future partners will be. Yin Hsueh-yen, each of her girls, a part of her and the Moon home.

That Christmas promised to be the most special of all. In the sitting room the immense tree was covered with bonbons and coloured wax lights. There were smaller trees on the tables, some of which the girls had made to look as if partially covered with snow. Each of us would give one present to each other: perfect, absolutely perfect!

4

Time passed and winter was upon us once more. P'i-lan feng (the Varambhaka wind): the cosmic gale that Buddhists believe will blow at the end of the kalpa or cosmic eon: the wind at the world's end. There were restless spirits out there, agitating the windows, shaking the trees, testing the doors, the locks, pressing in hard under the eaves of our house above the raging sea. Eliza woke in the night; the wind was strong, blowing a gale. She was trembling, pressed herself close to me. Great sea without restraint, the storm had awakened something excited in her, something sexual, something raw: howling gale, wrecking waves battering the cliff, thundering with their own internal booming roar. Hips pressed tight against me she pushed forward with her pelvis. Her kiss was hard, jabbing tongue brutal against my own. She clutched at me with fumbling fingers, forced her cold mouth over mine, teeth pressed into my lips, sucking the life out of me.

Later, she walked me out to the beach. Air icy, sky clear with a sprinkle of stars, winter-strength winds smash, waves lashed against the sparkled shore, ripped branches from trees, taking plants to where plants do not grow. Speeding whitecap waves mounting, spreading, rushing in across the pebbled sand; new waves growing, reaching high, steepening, overbalancing into shattered, spin-drift foam. Booming like thunder, rumbling hooves of Neptune's white horses, white waters scoured the anxious beach, surging back out to sea.

As we approached Christmas, the weather growing colder by the day, I felt nostalgic, thinking of China when we last left her in winter, the biting cold; the vast snowfields, the clear brightness before the approach to Shanghai - 14 years before, and yet it seemed like only yesterday. And I remembered when Eliza first told me that it was at Shanghai that she felt the first glimmering of a love for me. It was a bitter cold night, ground covered in hoarfrost that stuck out high like wool from a new coat. The moon was full, high, and the stars sparkled with renewed brilliance. I remembered bitter Christmases in London as a child. In 1813, England had arctic conditions; the snow fell heavily and there was a Frost Fair on the frozen Thames – I can still smell the spit-roasted pork. And I remember being frozen: the air was so gold, and the frozen ground hurt my feet. In 1815, Tambora spewed out volcanic ash in Indonesia, which obscured the sun: Northern Europe had severe frost and snow through June and July 1816. There had never been a winter since as cold as that!

The atmosphere of the cold, frosty Christmas Eve was alive in Birchington village. I hurried home with eager anticipation as the shopkeepers closed up their shutters, as the snow began to fall once more, flurries blowing all about me in the wind that blew in strong from the sea. *When we live in joy we mourn the speed of the night.* Standing in the hall, taking off my cape, I heard Angelina speaking harshly to her younger sister. There was an Advent wreath there hung from the middle of the ceiling: interwoven ring of evergreen holly and ivy with four red candles.

'Do you believe, Sophia? If you don't believe in Lord Christmas you won't get any presents.'

'But I do believe, Angelina. I do believe in the spirit of Lord Christmas. I've seen paintings of him dressed in green. And here's a small figure of him for the tree.'

The girls had made the Kissing-bunch of interwoven hoops, garlanded with holly and ivy, red ribbons and paper roses, which they had hung up before the front door in the hall. Three small dolls hanging from strings within it – Jesus our Saviour, Mary the Mother of Jesus, and Joseph, surrounded by rosy-cheeked Kentish apples and China oranges also tied to strings, and various brightly-coloured ornaments. A large spray of mistletoe had been carefully tied below: twin leaves and translucent, pearl-like berries, symbolic of the celestial semen, dew, or sap of the Supreme Spirit. It is the custom to pluck a mistletoe berry for every kiss taken for Atonement, reconciliation and goodwill.

The chatter ceased abruptly as I entered the room, and we listened to the moaning wind, snowflakes falling, blowing in flurries, building up against the multi-panelled window. Belief? *How I wish I could believe that which is seen by innocent eyes.* Christmas – excitement: it had got deeper, further inside, but the feeling was still there – no longer a fluttering in my heart or the palpitations in my stomach I felt as that docklands child. The house was warm from the roaring fires, and they were decorating the Christmas tree, putting up sprigs of magical mistletoe, holly and ivy with their immortal winter berries. The red male berry would protect the household; and the female ivy, with its leaves that remained green throughout the winter, was a symbol of immortality.

As darkness closed in the heavy curtains were closed at the windows to shut out the cold. The house was filled with laughter and mirth, the excited chatter of the girls. Later there would be carol-singing by lamplight, groups going door to door singing; wassailers also, more usually the poor, offering a drink from their wooden bowls for a donation of food, drink or money in return. I listened to the chatter among the younger members of the local village carol singers who then bothered our girls with their questions, as they gathered near the garden fire – beacon burning bright; would be seen far away off shore.

'Is your mother a Chinese princess? She is very, very beautiful? Her scars? Did she get them fighting a China dragon?'

'Yes, she did.'

5

Christmas Day we celebrated at the Mass, heralded by the peal of Church bells calling us to church for carol-singing and readings of the Scriptures. Christmas dinner was a sumptuous affair. Goose took pride of place on the Christmas table, with apple sauce, mashed potatoes, and an assortment of winter vegetables followed by Christmas pudding made from beef, raisins and prunes. The pudding had been made on Stir-up Sunday; each of us stirred it ceremoniously, adding another silver coin for luck. Boiled for several hours and then left to mature until Christmas Day. The Cook proudly carried in the steaming pudding fresh out of the copper. The kitchen air had the smell of washing-day from the steaming cloth, mixed with the combined smells of an eating-house and of a pastry cook. The pudding, like a speckled cannon-ball, hard and firm, blazed with ignited brandy, and a sprig of the red-berry holly stuck into the top. Christmas dinner ended with gift-giving and pulling of Christmas Crackers.

Later, we settled around the hearth, enjoying hot cup and chestnuts roasted on the fire. The girls had helped me drag in the massive Yule log from the garden, trimmed with greenery and ribbons we would burn it in honour of pagan gods, to encourage the winter sun to shine more brightly. There were glasses of *Purl* (heated beer, flavoured with gin, sugar and ginger) and *Bishop* (a Punch made with heated red wine, flavoured with oranges, sugar and spices). Mince Pies - made with mincemeat and spices - were also eaten for the 12 days of Christmas, ensuring good luck for the next 12 months. The day ended with music, carol-singing and parlour games of Forfeits and Blind Man's Buff.

I watched White Poppy making her way from the house, wrapped up in several layers of coats, walking quickly across the weather-crisped lawn, her skirts dragging a trail through the frost. She made her way to the brick house at the end of the garden, where she walked up the few stone steps to stand on the redbrick wall, looking out to sea. Lamps out, candles extinguished and curtains open wide I pressed my face up against the chill glass, holding my breath so that it did not fog, and I watch her, the clouds of hot breath as she breathed out into the cold night air. She had wanted to be alone; it was important to leave her alone, for her to be with those thoughts with which she most wanted to be. She would see the sea, would listen to its echo below the chalk cliffs on the beach; she would see the lights of ships as they made their way towards Margate and the North Foreland. She would not see the lights of Sheppey from where she was standing, but she would see the ships that came thence: the Poppy Princess.

Before New Year's Eve the gods must be placated. Eliza told me. 'At the end of the last month they report to the Jade Emperor, Yu Hang-ti.' Only the tiny hearth god had spent the whole year in the family: in his dust-covered niche he kept watch over the fire. 'Since,' as she had once told me, 'he keeps the register of the family; he may take away the days of one who disappoints him.'

On the 24th day of the 12th Month I give him his farewell dinner: sweet cakes, candied fruits, sweet rice – cover his mouth with honey. I feed him these sacrifices that are to be given only by a man. The god must go now: seated on a chair of bamboo, drawn by a horse made of paper, he is taken into the garden. We set him alight, throw on straw and dry tea, watch orange sparks, glowing threads rising to heaven, smoke whirling around our heads; small pagan beacon burning bright above the sea. Before the fire is out I take glowing embers into the house, start the new fire burning in the kitchen hearth. White Poppy has lit long tapering candles, has made ready the bed and perfumed it. In the candlelight she lets fall her silken robe, drops on to the bed naked, sits upright, legs cross, breasts full down her chest, still. 'Sān lihn faailohk!' ['Happy New Year!']

New Year's Eve the Chinese clean up their houses and their yards, put up a new portrait to the Door God and a portrait of the ghost-catcher-spirit Zhong Kui, paste red paper scrolls with rhymes written on them on to their doors, nail up an inscribed peach wood plaque, as we are doing now. She looked across at me, her eyes following the flames in the fireplace behind, and I could see her, as she was when she first told me in English about the Chinese New Year.

In love there can be no holding back, no reserve, no secret places. 'In the evening, they prepare incense sticks, fresh flowers and offerings to welcome the gods. They pray for a peaceful year.' She walked across to me, black eyes sparkling, touched her fingers to my lips. 'They offer sacrifices to their ancestors, banquets are prepared in every house. All of the family, young and old, sit around the table, sit with candles lit, eating fruit and cakes and playing games, wish each other well for the coming year.' She brushed her mouth against mine, teasing it gently with the soft contact of her lips. 'People stay awake late: the elders sit around the fireplace as the children play their games for the New Year's Eve Vigil.' She kissed me hard, poked her tongue in against my own – closer now that we shared that special knowledge? 'Tangerines and lychees are put beside the children's pillows; they eat the fruits before going to bed, for good luck.' She paused. 'Before we enter the New Year,' she looked at me in earnest, 'everything must be clean, there must be no bad thoughts in our hearts, with our neighbours we should be friends.'

6

'Sâangyaht Faailohk! Happy Birthday to you, Happy Birthday to you, Happy Birthday dear Eliza, Happy Birthday to you!'

Luscious crimson lips puckered and blew, 40 birthday candles flickered, glowed and died as she blew them out, smoke floating in expanding wild spirals that shot across the room. She clapped her hands together in delight, banged her crooked fingers, the little finger without a tip, cut the rich-fruit cake, pressed it between my lips, before feeding each of her three children.

The February sun shone egg-yolk pale behind the white curd clouds, the moist air heavy with rain. The beech-woods at Blean near Canterbury smelled of damp fungi, of decay, as we trampled in a line through centuries of compressed leaves: Sophia, Emily, Charlie, Eliza, me, the soft-prickled shells of the beech-nuts strewn around, enclosed in the timeless silence of the chill woods. And there was the smell of wood smoke fragrant, strong – blue smoke wafting through the trees – a sharp smell that made me falter, remembering, the Chinese hill country with its Buddhist monasteries, the many grave plots shaded with camphor trees and sweet gum, early morning air heavy with the wood smoke fanning out across the valley. And the memories of the opium valleys in India!

White Poppy poked out her tongue, laughed to see it steaming in the cold air, came up to me, lips opened, thrusting it hard into my own lips sealed tight, locked in the close embrace: mouth to mouth, breath to breath – the children pretended not to notice, walked faster ahead, looked away. A woman is sexually stronger than a man is; her reproductive organs bear the strain of producing children, of giving birth and nurturing them. At breakfast she had said she had something to tell me, that there was a surprise.

'I'm pregnant,' she'd said, almond eyes glowing, 'we are going to have another baby. This time,' she had squeezed my left hand tightly, 'I am sure it's a boy.'

7

The ceiling of that bedroom was painted dark blue with twinkling stars. Other rooms had walls painted in clear, bold purple or green. Unlike the prevailing style that more usually consisted of fussy ornamentation, gaudy chintz, and vegetation representations on the walls. The girls lay on the beds in their loose bright robes, tied with a gold cord at the waist and covered with Chinese shawls. They wore bangles of oriental gold and silver bracelets that jangled with the animated gestures of their hands, as they talked. All with their Chinese-dark hair, skin, and eyes. Though ... had more auburn colouring and she and ... were taller and more slender as well.

The conjuror showed the audience the magic box containing the "living head of an ancient Sphinx". 'Sphinx awake!' Slowly the head opened its eyes and surveyed the audience as if gaining consciousness. He closed the box then opened it again. Gone was the head and in its place was a little pile of dust.

White Poppy stood alone in the small shrine room, dressed in a long Chinese robe – serious, absorbed – fat joss sticks burning – glaring Ching primary red and gold in all-too-vivid splendour; a small altar with offerings of fruit, cakes and wine, and above it some spirit idol. She knelt before it, praying and presenting the offerings, calling upon the spirit to reply to her questions. She walked across to the small table standing in the corner, its surface, covered with sand. She wrote there with a 'pencil' made of peach tree wood shaped like a T; the horizontal piece being the handle, the end of the upright hooked. She rested the pencil tip carefully upon the sanded table. The stick started to move in a rapid wavelike rhythm – her fingers hooked around it to keep it from flying off – apparently of its own accord, writing characters in a the mystic Chinese script, that required her expert knowledge to interpret what the spirit has stated in reply to her questions and prayers.

8

Summer 1858: our three girls sat on the sofa; sleeve ruffles, their linked hands and skirt hems forming a line of intricate detail along the curved edge of the sofa's patterned upholstery; vertical striped and dotted dress fabric, layered with ruched sleeves, and distinctive beaded bracelets.

My young daughter wakened suddenly from her long sleep: long arms and shins bare, heavy-lidded gaze, wrapped in luxurious Chinese fabrics – Oriental harem girl. Angelina (then 14 years, Emily as she preferred to be called), watered plants in the July garden, hair in soft ringlets, head-dress of Honiton lace and white flowers; stooping down before the roses; her shining face expressionless, blinded as she was by some secret unseen pleasure, dazzled by an idea that absorbed her most completely, laughter bursts in her cool blue eyes as she spotted me watching her through the opened kitchen window. I remembered her words from the evening before; saw the pout on her face: 'Oh, I can't be bothered with hair-pins, they are such a trial.' She strutted forward, chin up, head held high. 'I don't think I look at all more elegant with my hair bundled up behind!'

She was there before me once more, her face beaming, bright.

'Look my Father; are these not just the most perfect roses? Can't you just smell them fragrant on the breeze?'

Her voice was vibrant, velvety, low. She sat down quickly on the heavy cast iron seat, brushed flowing raven hair from her face; more laughter on her pale pink lips. She was self-assured, had her Mother's confidence.

'Papa, answer me, please!'

Becoming a young lady, she was beginning to stop being careless or silly, wearing her skirts a little longer, but not as long as the ankle length dresses of her sister Charlotte Louisa, then 16 years, who wore her waist-length hair up high; whose narrow, fragile shoulders overshadowed her discrete breasts, robust hips, strong thighs, with sinuous arms, wrists, delicate, deft.

Charlotte Louisa, first born: she was very pretty (all three were), with her Mother's chin, a slightly Chinese nose, the same oriental, almond eyes. She, too, would break men's hearts. My dear darling 'Charlie', aggressive, threatening, distracted in stroking the face of her youngest sister, Sophia Justina, talking, hissing from her throat, voice rising sharply.

'Come on Sophes; let me push you on the swing. Hold tight now!'

Sophia, then 8 years, same blue eyes as Angelina, black hair short; white peaked cap, navy-blue velvet dress with a large sailor's collar, white cuffs, waistband, white pinafore down below her knees, neat black leather boots. She jumped on the swing, little legs dangling down.

'Wheeeeh! No, don't push me fast. No, Charlie, stop it, stop it now!'

Sophia Justina, a bit of us both – innocent, inquisitive, magical, free – mental power (and the pain), laughter.

The silvery sound of their voices - soft laughter like feathers in the wind, my daughters! We left the sheltered cliff-top garden and went down and walked together along the windy beach, across chalk rocks between the strands of sand, stepping stones through the rock pools, over a driftwood bridge, and with a jolt I remembered the opium whores in Canton, who themselves were once girls, and I felt ashamed to be a man. Three proper pretty girls, but a boy would be just perfect. Their mother presently joined us, walked elegantly along the beach, long black dresses flowing behind her. She called out to us, smiled; that smile that still tears me apart inside.

9

Woman, the unconscious whore, witch; she who gets pregnant, who descends inside herself through the blood, to hear and taste and smell that new life that grows within, that later rips out from her inside.

The girls ran up to their mother, three faces shining bright, hair tugged by the wind. Eliza listened to them, because she was interested in what they say. It was so exciting for her - everything was so exciting for her then. She listened to them, thinking of her growing boy inside. When each Pearl was new born we cut off a lock of her hair, tucked each precious gift away in its own silver case. I keep them in the Library where I have my books about sailing and the sea. I have them tucked away in a small drawer in the massive oak desk, with my black leather-bound Holy Bible, and these writings in my Journal, written here for eternity.

My daughters, I know you will read these thoughts when I am gone, and it gives me comfort to know that you will know how much I love you and your Mother, from whose belly you were born, and you will understand the great distance we went before we were together. The details are here, my sweet ones, no matter how awful, how cruel, for it is important that you know. This is it, this was me and your Mother – this was us.

My dearest darling daughters you have each given me more happiness than a man can expect here on earth, and each of you will go on, will fall in love, will give birth. And there will forever be a part of China here in England. Promise me one thing, that after you have read this, you will look after this Journal with your collective life. It contains the details, the other side to what you saw, what we kept from you because we could not bear to see you hurt, or sad. It broke our hearts each time you cried. Do not cry for me, for your Mother, when we are gone but rejoice for that time when we shall be together again in Heaven, be it English or Chinese.

Distant, out across the water beyond the twin towers of St Mary's Church at Reculver, the Isle of Sheppey hovers at the boundary between land and sea. In the summer heat, the quivering air, I see the masts of the massive gilded junk, the black-and-white chequered sides of graceful double-decked East Indiamen, sky-scraping masts puncturing the China sky. And in the sunset clouds, multilayered orange interlaced with blood, I see the luscious crimson mouth, faint crease of a smile at the entrance of her erotic lips, sad mystery of her sparkling almond eyes, White Poppy.

10

The Clear Brightness Festival 1857: on a day in the Third Month of the Moon Year (early April) the Chinese sweep their ancestral tombs. They take with them baskets of food and wine. They bow down and pour libations, so White Poppy had told me; they weed and add new soil. 'Although we go out sad,' she had said, 'we return happy, wearing green willow in our hair.' They start catching crickets in the burial places, for cricket fighting starts in the Seventh Month and everyone grows them on in bamboo containers, clay pots, bamboo cylinders and jars. They all gather together at cricket pits and field their trained crickets as sport. At the time of the Clear Brightness women celebrate at the shrines of ancestors where they are exposed to the evil influences of the spirits of the dead.

'Women contact this evil power,' Eliza told me, 'take it upon themselves and exorcise it.'

At the shrines the punitive power of the ancestors is passed on through the women. In the temples and cemeteries it is different – ancestors form a collective ancestry there, where women have no place: the only way they enter is as names inscribed on tablets. The right to give orders falls to the father, because he belongs to the lineage of ancestors. His son reveres him because he sees in him a potential ancestor. Each father does as he chooses bathed in the unsettling heat of the China sun; emphasising the importance of a *son*.

The wife is employed to run the house, nomadic, homeless, she lives as a stranger in her adopted family until her first male child is born and reaches maturity, then she can rest: she who had submitted to the authority of her own Mother and father, the Mother and Father of her husband, her husband herself, and, finally, her son. For Chinese Eliza there was not yet a living son. She had spent the evening inside with the girls, tucked away in the kitchen, baking. Silent sea, lamplight flicker, gorgeous aromatic smells, I imagined them at their spells: Eliza, as the mother, instructing the girls, the mature woman passing down the mystery and the magic, the essential living life. I heard them, but they did not tell, not even when we broke the hot bread together in the kitchen, tasting the heavenly taste that resulted from the yeast.

Gathering together the folded red paper lotus flowers, we walked to the far edge of the sea, the tide having long since gone out, the water calm, spilling across the beach. One by one I lit the paper lanterns, vegetable-oil-soaked wicks, let them float away, watched them scattering in the breeze, the swift current carrying them bobbing out to sea.

11

Arzier, Switzerland, 1857: the holiday season upon us, Eliza decided on a trip to Europe. The rain ceasing for a few minutes the mists rolled off as the clouds lifted to reveal distant Lake Geneva, luxuriating in the clear warmth of the hot August sun. Some two to three hours distant from Arzier, above the Lake in the Jura, we made our way upward through grass glades between forest tracts of fragrant pine. We were there the previous spring, amidst the lilies of the mountain, and the lilies of the valley, beds of moonwort, and the earliest vanilla orchis.

We followed our Swiss guide to the edge of a deep natural pit, at the base of which, through a brief chasm, was a low dark cave, the subterranean glacière with its flooring of ice. It was instantly cold. We lit up the cave with our candles, sat crouched on the ice drinking our wine, finding water, which iced and diluted the wine, in small basins in the ice; the water falling pure from the roof of the cave, drops of water, which fell now and then, sometimes hitting the most sensitive spot at the back of the neck. Eliza giggled like a girl. Beyond us was a long wall covered thickly with sheets of white ice, a solid floor of darker-coloured ice, and a high pyramid of snow reaching up towards an uncovered hole. The air was then very dry. Beyond that was the ice palace, the chill ice spread out like a fan, the water having been frozen pouring from its base. A lofty dome opened up into the roof, beneath which clustered columns had formed from the clear porcelain-like ice, delicately fretted and festooned, and glittering icicles hanging like curtains from the roof, prismatic colours reflected when our flaming torches flashed suddenly upon them. Everything was slippery ice and we glided through the mysterious halls of spells, making our way deeper into the mountain, to the final four principal columns of ice, two columns of which poured out of fissures in the rock, once streaming cascades frozen in time. There, amidst a central cluster of icicles, crystal forests and frozen dreams, we wended our way slowly in amongst the ice pillars, listening with horror to the shivered shattering, the breaking of falling ice.

In the autumn ice was carried from the cave on men's backs as far as the rough mountain road, and then packed on one-bullock chars and taken to the nearest railway station. They used gunpowder for the flooring of ice, and expected the eighth part of a pound to blow out one cubic metre. That Night of Fires the flames flickered and the pyre began to crackle, and fiery tongues leapt forward, and up the sides they climbed, soon licking the dying plants stacked there, so that their stalks shivered and bent, the sparks a whirling dance of sparkling stars. Mothers lifted up their sleeping babies, and with outstretched arms held them in the night air before the sacred flame now belching forth thick smoke, lit by the quick flashing of the flames. On the summit fire reigned triumphant. Fanned by the wind the pyre roared into flame, red crest bristling over the circle of the surrounding mountains, sinking deeper into shadow, as the light of the fire grew ever more intense. The smoke-filled sky hung like a high, motionless sea, with islands of cloud islands dyed purple from the reflection of the flames. And all the heights around were crowned by these giant beacon fires.

12

Taken before the Canton Goddess, the mirrored shrine, incense burning, my head forced down low in supplication, hooded figures turned inwards to the centre of the crescent moon, faceless, silent, still. There sat the girl, the boat-girl, ornate before the stellate mirrors, multiple reflected loveliness in purple, silver and gold; a garment covered in little bells and chains of gold, shimmering, shining, melting at the edges where the flaming air burned crimson above her fertile throne, decorated with the withered vine for thousands of years. Eliza spoke.

'When I was a little girl,' she whispered softly, 'I used to sit with my Mother and look up at the stars. She told me that each of them was the lantern of a little fairy.' She smiled at me sweetly, her teeth shining white in a little-girl smile. 'And when I saw fireflies dancing over the boat, she told me they were the fairies come down to earth, their power weakened from their journey; said that their lanterns would glow orange, and then die.'

She looked at me carefully, Chinese eyes scanning every movement of my face. 'As the fairies sacrificed their brilliant silver for a brief dance on earth.' She twiddled her hair, not taking her glistening eyes from me, sad. Her Mother? I realised she had stopped talking about her Mother. I asked her again, waited for her reply.

'She abandoned me. From the moment I was born she abandoned me.' She looked away from me. 'That is all there is to say.'

We got ready for bed but White Poppy was silent, moody, walked across in front of the looking-glass before the bed. She brushed furiously at her hair, angry with her mortality.

'I didn't ask to be born,' she cried, suddenly. 'I didn't have any choice in it; none of us do.' She turned quickly, flashed her dark eyes at me. 'You can say, therefore, that I owe my parents nothing.' Her mouth was an angry gash of oily red, her eyes like fiery coals. 'My parents? Huh! This is what I would say to them, both of them.' She took a breath. 'I did not ask to be born. I don't owe you a thing.' She breathed in deeply, exhaled with a gasp. 'It was their choice. It was because of the course of nature. It is the way things are.' She frowned. 'I had no part in it at all.'

Pushing my right leg into the coolest part of the bed, Eliza's soft eyes scanning my face, her lips open, still, I felt the warmth of her mouth on my face, her gentle breathing, and closed my mouth over hers, tasted once more that which tastes sweeter than anything I know, heard the blood rushing in my ears, pressure of her hot mouth on mine, pressed close, lips opened wide; felt her heart beating fast, breasts pressed close against my chest; felt the pulsating wetness on the upturned fingers of my right hand. She whispered in my ear.

'I love you.'

13

July 1857, Eliza was seven months pregnant. Wind stirring crested waves, water surface moving, gentle sea rising, trickling in over the shore, we watched the big sailing ship coming over the horizon, bow forwards, sails growing white in the rippling summer haze, tall masts reflected, distorted in the blue sky above.

A Painted Lady butterfly, proboscis probing honey sweet spikelets of white Buddleia, the pretty butterfly set her wings, fluttered carefully around, rising high above the summer fragrant garden. Everything quiet, still, just the loud ticking of the clock, mechanical heart of the bedroom as it beat away time. Tick-TOCK. Tick-TOCK. Tick-TOCK. The girls were away in Broadstairs; we had the weekend to ourselves.

Blue smoke, burning, ashes rising in the wind; smell it through the opened bedroom window. Eliza's breathing was gentle, relaxed: out of the corner of my good eye I watched the rise and fall of her breasts spread loose across her naked chest: milk-swollen hills above the stunning pregnant mound of her stomach. I saw Canton in the shadows, focused in through the scattered offshore islands, glimpsed the lemon trees before the twin pagodas of the Sea pearl Temple, the Thirteen Factories, the city wall, the dotted graves white, like abandoned bones, before the distant hills. This time I willed it to be a boy.

Holding the sea-sponge in both hands, soaping it well, Eliza covered my back with foaming lather; fairy fingers massaging my tired shoulders, soothed the aching muscles while awakening new desire, stepped into the bath tub with me, pressing herself on me, rinsing off the soap, massaging me with the soft and natural brush of her own. I notice the first fine threads of silver in her raven hair.

Towards nightfall, sun setting, darkness rising in the east, the last gleam of sunset flashed green from the horizon, I held White Poppy close to me.

'See it, Eliza? Whoever glimpses that living light will never be deceived in love.'

Pitch black, the sea glowed luminous, an eerie phosphorescence tingeing the tips of the waves trickling into the shore. We touched it with our fingertips, brushed them against each other's lips, tasted the salt from the oceans that stretch all the way to China. It was just poppy perfect, the way it always was with her!

Marriage: that double tending of body and soul; preparation of two souls for Heaven - the inextricable connection between joy and pain.

'You must be vigilant,' she had told her daughter, Charlie, 'in rooting out all evils but also quick to confess and forgive weaknesses.'

'Take this celebration cup of joy, today, as you would oft take the Sacramental Cup careful hand so as not to waste or spill the sacred Good.'

In children such springing hope was natural, she mused; except for those who had seen the shadow of the valley, for whom the sunshine was no more. Yet hitherto Death had not seized too many of her most beloved ones, at least not until that day, when her heart was held in bondage.

14

As Confucius says: We do not know life, how then can we know death? Dressed in purple satin, heavily pregnant, White Poppy sat cross-legged, her hair down across her face hanging into her lap. She threw the split oyster shell halves before her – looked serious, then smiled, framing the question in her thoughts: crackled backs up, it would be 'Yin' ('No'); smooth insides up it would be 'Yang' ('Yes'). One back up and one inside up would be propitious. Three throws: overall prognosis? She smiled, lifting her facial scars. But what was the question? She wouldn't tell me, just turned her thoughts inwards and concentrated on the shells, jangled them in her left hand, threw them once – she smiled; twice, she smiled again; three times, she looked concerned, her eyes black, momentarily blind to all but those shells - her startled Chinese eyes, nimble fingers, soft lips moving. She held my hand, squeezed it tight, leant across and kissed me on the lips. 'I do love you,' she said, and cried suddenly, holding my hand tight. I loved her deeply. I loved her more than I could ever have imagined I would love another person. I could not bear the thought of life without her.

Coming in from the Chinese garden all those years back in Canton, she had hesitated – only a brief moment, but a hesitating nevertheless. Mouth open, cherry lips apart, she had stopped and looked across at me: red lips unmoving, still, strand of saliva between their glistening moistness, dew-hinged corners of that most erotic mouth. I will never forget that look or the feeling that went with it: there is never a time quite like the first. I kissed her on the lips, pressed my mouth over her little girl smile, sealed in that which must never be lost.

Life, this thing of shreds and patches, patchwork combination of life: what was the inner meaning of the whole? The potential of a full mouth, red lips touching, moving apart: mouth touched, red lips tasted, perception from within. Waves trickling in at the furthest edge of the sand, gulls skimming, fishing. Playing with her driftwood boat in the rock pool, Eliza tried to sink it with stones.

'I want to go back, Charles.' She tossed back her hair, flicking it behind her ears, laughed at my puzzled look. 'I want to go back to being a child. I don't like being grown up. I don't want to know about adult life.' Little girl lost in an adult body, she kicked at the boat with her foot, angry wave turning it on its side. 'I want to see the world through child's eyes again, but happy eyes this time. I want everything to be wonderful, special, new. I want to see only the blue sky, want to watch fairy-castle clouds rushing over the land, want to watch it all just for me.' She looked as though she would cry, chin quivering below sad lips. 'I want to see it as I used to see it when I was just a little girl, when I didn't know there was anything else, just me and my family, and our boat and the boats around it, and Canton; end of my own world, when I didn't know the word evil.'

'It's a pleasant dream.'

'No, I don't want a dream. I want it to be real!'

'But it can't be, Eliza, it can't be!'

'Our children,' she said, and smiled the biggest smile. 'Children make everything all right, give order where there is chaos, make the complex simple. They are the key to our future happiness.' She laughed. 'With children we are allowed to be children once more.'

White Poppy, Yin-Hsueh Yen, I had never known her use a word that would hurt another's feelings; had always put herself second for the sake of the whole.

15

Sunday, one sunny afternoon, 1857, White Poppy dropped the apple pie on the floor in the kitchen and I snapped at her: hurled abuse at her as though it was her fault, as though she had some control over the pie that could no longer defy gravity. I felt unusually angry inside, looking for an excuse to shout back at her, as the pie slipped from its enamelled dish, as the steaming apple burst out from its crumbling crust. I let fly with angry words. *Don't ever hate me*: I imagined the words forming, saw the pain in her pretty Chinese eyes; black eyes, unmoving, strong; crimson-edged like the glowing embers of a traveller's fire reborn, wind-blown ash sparking, colour spreading as new flames dance on that flame-determined grey. She picked up the white china jug filled with yellow vanilla custard. *Don't ever hate me for what I have or haven't done.* She blinked; her eyes then moist with tears, her cheeks taut in humiliation that accentuated her scars, in contrast to the obvious dryness of her mouth. Tipping the jug forward, holding it at arm's length over the shattered pie, she let the custard flow like yellow lava. *There*, said her eyes, *the tragedy is complete*!

The poppy season is a short one. On rough roadside mounds at the edge of the grain fields turning gold, I see the nodding heads of the solitary red: watch them in their black-centred, bloody splendour – Cantonese boat-girls, standing naked, bending, raw. I watch them nodding heavy in the warm July breeze, waiting to see the first red petal drop. Silken clothes shed to reveal soft flesh, falling, floating to the ground. The first quiver, first movement of any petal, signals the doomed future of the rest. Until, last petal dropped the seed capsule stands aloft, naked, bare.

From the natural sweep of the main bay from the jutting point at Nayland Rock to the main town beyond the distant harbour and sea wall, Margate has been a flourishing sea-bathing resort since 1736, with its pier and promenades, and bathing machines along its level shore covered with the finest sand. By land it is 72 miles from London, takes 13 or 14 hours in a coach with up to six inside and others riding outside. But there are steamboats now, and before that yachts and hoys sailed down the Thames from London: just as the winds and tides happen to be for or against them, pleasant and agreeable or puking up their insides. The South-Eastern Railway, having been extended from Ashford to Thanet, was opened on 1 December 1846.

Eliza strode slightly ahead of me, making her way along the esplanade to the Margate sands. *Don't ever let me become the hated woman*: she looked across at the Sunday afternoon couples in the park as they put up with each other in the misery of their old age; looked at the undisguised hate in their eyes, the angry blame on their tortured faces, unspoken abuse on their lips where there had once been love, passion, protest at the limits imposed on each by their sex. She watched them listening to the blare of brass that assaulted them from the bandstand, the shrill and boom of music that put new rhythm into their twisted fingers, new movement into their toes, which they resisted, held out against – the joy that might remind them of what they once had.

Taking my fingers in her own, she touched them to her lips; her mouth open slightly, her pink lips apart. No, she would never hate me, would never shout at, rebuke or blame me – like fire that has spread through corn sheaves barren black, harsh words once heard can not be taken back. *The poppy petals drop*, as always they must drop.

At Canton the white Factories have gone now – removed by the war. Gone too are the waterfront brothels, red paper lanterns ripped to shreds long ago, the sky no longer burns crimson, smells of charred remains, not jasmine or opium; no more white petals in springtime like scattered snow. Moored at Whampoa Island some 13 miles south of Canton (and limit for the largest sailing ships), bobbed the black-and-white chequered sides of graceful double-decked East Indiamen; opium factories, gun-ships, surrounded by sampans like greedy piglets around a sow, in which the poppy-drug was taken to isolated bays along the ragged typhoon coast. Even at those ships there were crimson-lipped whores: there, too, the women – Sisters of the Snake – had their own ship, their own female piglets, their own link in the Canton drugs ring: the 'She-Tigers' of Canton, anything but common women who supplied anything but common pleasure.

Their ship blown up, destroyed by British gun–ships during the war. So, White Poppy had been held there: Yin Hsueh-yen had been kept there prisoner, until she squealed, but the conquered had become the conqueror.

Evening falling, dusk, Eliza knelt in the last shaft of weak orange sunlight streaming in across the soft, polished wooden floor, the top of her head forward, whorled crown of black that shone in the lamplight battling with the deepening darkness. Everything quiet, not a murmur of a sound, even the sea was in retreat, the tide then out low, only the voices of the girls, distant, and the ticking of a clock.

The pain White Poppy suffered from her pregnancy was intense: she said it was as though rats were gnawing at her stomach. Indian opium was her only relief from that pain – half-a-dozen drops of laudanum banishing a measure of that misery in five or so minutes. She muttered more about the White Tiger. 'Do you see her, Charles? Do you see the White Tiger?' *Yes, I see her; have been seeing her more and more.*

White Poppy's brow was no longer smooth white; her hair was now dark brown burnished richly with silver. Her skin was still very fine in places, enamelled and Chinese dark. Her bright almond eyes were liquid, soft, beneath their sweeping fringe of dark lashes, dark eyebrows, and her Chinese nose. Her mouth was still exquisite, soft.

16

Set me as a seal upon thy heart, as a seal upon thine arm. The Song of Solomon, viii, 6. Each time we woke up together, each time I saw those black eyes, took my mouth from her mouth, and closed it tight against the lips between her thighs; White Poppy was a total part of me, a part of everything that I did. And she wriggled and she giggled and she squirmed as I worked there with my tongue. That was it, the fulfilment of my dream, I who ate daily from the Tree of Life, from the Fountain of Everlasting Youth, who had been shown so often what for others must remain unseen.

Early morning dew, moisture on Eliza's lips, we watched the joyful awe of sunrise – moment of division between night and day – stars and moon retreating on one side, the light of dawn rising on the other. I held her close in my arms, felt the stomach-bursting flesh of what would be England's latest birth, tried not to notice the mother's continued tears of pain. 'All I want,' she said quietly, 'is somewhere peaceful, where I can be at one with my dreams, where no one can hurt me any more, where I am quite alone.'

BOOK IX

THE DEAFENING SILENCE
1857

1

Name or person which is closer? Person or possession which is more? Winning or losing: which is worse? Lao Tzu, *Tao Te Ching*, 44.

'She's a whore, a worthless whore.' I heard my Mother's words: at least the words that had come from her mouth, in prison, when I saw her in my dream. No, my Mother was the whore: White Poppy had been part of something far more horrific, inhuman, bestial and obscene. Night falling, standing back through the door of the drawing-room, I watched the flicker of her eyelids, clumsy re-positioning of her soft mouth as Eliza, the White Poppy, read aloud.

'Space,' she talked slowly, pulling her fingers through her shining black hair, 'the way the body touches the other, the angles of touching, filling of space.'

Dressed in purple, a combination of the red of Love and the blue of Truth, she withdrew her fingers, ran them under her nose.

'Time is the way one body moves on the other body, the speed, or slowness, of its moving.'

Her long hair groomed to perfection, shining white now, like the foam of the China Sea; she smiled at me, almond eyes opened wide. She laughed as best she could laugh. There is a male lust for the virgin, for the letting of the first blood, essential essence of all human life. And from that lust there may grow love.

Each the image of the rest, our daughters talked to their swollen, pregnant Mother in her bed, pagan Goddess, lying there prone, wrapped up in her white woollen shawl. They came and sat with her, as a group and sometimes alone, where clear sea-winds stirred the curtains: stared at her outline in the candlelit room: spent time with her, read to her, showed her what they had been doing with their lives – Angelina's pressed flowers, Charlotte's needlepoint, Sophia's Chess.

Through heavy waking eyes she watched them – her Poppies: Charlotte Louisa, 16 years, head poised, elegant, pretty, smiling, half-closing her oriental brown eyes, wrinkling her pretty Chinese nose; courageous, free, the image of her Mother.

Angelina (Emily), 14 years, laughter bursting in her cool blue eyes, her voice vibrant, velvety and low, strutting forwards, chin up, head held high; self-assured, free, she is the image of me.

Sophia Justina, eight years, same laughing blue eyes, running her fingers gently along the scars of her mother's cheek, touching her fingers to her Mother's dry lips; inquisitive, innocent, in looks somewhere between her Chinese Mother and me.

The girls did not really know about Canton; did not know much about their Mother's past. Sophia believed her to be a Chinese princess, daughter of the Dragon Jade King. All three believed what they want to believe. Apart from Eliza's damaged body (from a fight with a dragon, Sophia decided, there was no evidence of the Canton years: everything that had happened kept safe within our thoughts, deepest secrets of our China past.

Holding them close, in turn, she covered her daughters with her love, kissed them on their cheeks, stroking their faces, feeling their black hair, letting it run slowly through her crooked fingers as she drifted into sleep, listening to the falling rain, sheeted water beating hard against the windows, running fractured down the patterned glass. Then again, she greeted them in the sun that filtered into the bedroom above the sea.

2

Poppy petals fallen now, blown away, the seedpods are ripe, seeds shaken out of them, blown hard by the wind. Sophia stroked her mother's stomach.

'Life is so unfair my Mother.'

'Who ever said it should be fair, Sophia?'

'But you're the best Mother in the world, Mama. You deserve so much more.'

'Stop it, Sophia! Life is not fair, it never was and it never will be.' White Poppy smiled, aware that she was angry, a pleasant softness returning to her mouth. 'Accept it, please, my dearest Sophia. Accept it.' She stroked her daughter's silky hair, looking carefully into her bright blue eyes. 'I cannot leave my bed, but as long as you are here to come and tell me of all the beautiful things outside, then I will continue to be happy.' She coughed, adjusted herself, settled down further into her bed. 'You make my life just perfect, all three of you, as will the new baby. You bring me happiness every day. I could not wish for more.'

'But we miss you, Mama; miss your laughter in the garden.'

'I will soon be better, I'm just tired from my confinement, let me rest.' She yawned, touches her fingers to Sophia's mouth. 'Let me rest.'

3

Seen from high above, the broad walk of Christ's Cathedral Church had looked serenely solemn; traceried tree branches caressing the manicured walk. Eyes closed, the Cathedral rising up vertical from the grass, making its way up the buttressed walls, the Perpendicular Gothic towers, to the gargoyles grotesque, slanted roof moving from the demonic to the celestial, sharp pointed spires, stone needles, piercing the winter sky. They had walked together up the steps – she saw them now, through the splendour of that Gothic church, into the lofty mediaeval cosmos held captive within the magic stone and glass: Paradise, end of the pilgrim journey. They had walked hand-in-hand – she felt that now, through the lofty pointed ribbed vault nave, underneath the sternum, rib cage of the gigantic mother; made their way through the candle-lit shadows towards the memory of her own crucified son within her darkened vault-like womb. White Poppy saw them – the Sailor and the Whore!

Her daughter, Sophia, seated on her knee, intimate circle, hands held together close. She moved her left arm up and back around her Mother's neck, her tiny fingers pressing into the maternal flesh. The geometry of her chequered dress: cursive, charming; and the white dress, puffed sleeves, white ankle socks and flat ankle, soft black leather shoes, holding her close; pressing her cheek against her Mother's forehead. Like many gifted people, she had the capability of believing one thing sincerely and completely while doing something entirely different. She looked up at the large, gold-leaf framed portrait in the grand drawing room overlooking the sea: muted colours, faithful replica of her Mother's beauty. The other pictures Father had taken down: in its gold-framed magnificence, it was ever the only one. White Poppy, Eliza, sitting stiffly still on the high-backed stool, her small but full figure beneath the pink gown embroidered with red and rose-coloured chrysanthemums, proudly erect, serene; looking straight ahead, chin inclined upwards, almond eyes twinkling with pleasure, sparkling with the touch of Chinese white; cheeks, twin scars above the right, red lips repressing the most bewitching smile.

4

At night, White Poppy lay on top of me, and I didn't want it to stop. She then pressed my head against her stomach, where there kicked new life, where I could hear the beating of his tiny heart, new life – my son? Blue smoke burning, ashes rising, floating, flying heavenwards, free: valley bottom rippling through the wood smoke haze above the gentle wooded slopes of the Assam Indian hills, snow melting high on the ridge, water dripping from the hanging mountains.

I see the green-tiled temple, frost-bitten wilderness, distant, silent mountains – so often I feel the presence of these silent peaks, silent rocks, silent trees, silence broken only by the strange sounds which mountains make at night. Leaving the deserted temple, glazed green tiles by a solitary pine, she had been submissive, sweet, had interlocked her crooked fingers in mine, and in that final moment something intimate and unforgiving had passed between us, an interchange of life, an exchange of soul-fluids, a linking together of something deep inside: I love you, I love you, I love you. AND I ALWAYS WILL.

And then she had broken that hairpin in two, gave one half to me as we parted, special reminder of our pact eternal. Made of Chinese peach-tree wood, I have it still (as White Poppy still has hers). [For the Chinese: the very wonderful *persica* or *peach-tree* situated in the Happy islands of the Eastern ocean, is said to coil up its leaves to a height of 3,000 miles, a golden cock sitting upon it when the sunlight dawns.]

'There are two rules,' the boat-girl had said: *Chinese women are sold into perversion by those who love them most. Chinese women have no power against the men who have the right to rule over them.*

5

The coal-fire crackled in the cast-iron grate, great chunks of shining, gold-seamed coal, glowing orange over ashen grey.

'I have something to tell you,' White Poppy had said, breathlessly, 'something I can no longer hide.'

Her dull eyes held renewed sadness, fear. She twiddled her fingers, pressing her knees together, pushing up her lower lip.

'I betrayed you Charles,' she paused, dabbed at the corner of her eye, 'for the sake of my son, I betrayed you.' She had stopped talking, dried her eyes. 'Charles look at me! Charles... please? Don't look like that, don't look hurt. Let me explain.'

I sat down in the chair opposite her, preferred not to talk.

'Although I could not admit it, I preferred it for you to be dead, with you out of the way there would be no conflict.' She cried again, tears streaming down her cheeks. 'My son was to be released, but they went back on their word, killed him, put you in gaol anyway! I told them I had seen you down at the waterfront; your eye-patch gave you away, told them you were after their opium. But I made amends; you were released because of me, also, because of what I let them do to me. How they made my mouth so very sore, they hurt me so much.' She fiddled with her hair, looped it tightly over her fingers. 'I waited, but you never came for me, Charles.'

She could see I look puzzled, didn't know what she meant.

'You never came for me down at the waterfront, left me waiting there in my pain.'

'I'm sorry Eliza; I don't know what you mean? When should I have come for you?'

'You mean you really don't know?' She sighed. 'Oh Charles, what have I done to you? I had been taken to the deserted pagoda, was tied up for days before they took me away from there.'

'Who? Before *who* took you away from there?' (I remember the firm pressure on my shoulder, the bespectacled face; hear the voice... my voice: 'You have a message for me?' The reply: 'She is all right. She is being looked after.')

'Were you not given the message, Charles – did he not tell you that I was waiting there for you, that through the Factors the opium deal would be done?'

The opium deal, the route to salvation! (Oh my poor darling, what had they done to us, *what had they done*?)

'I took the opium to the pawn-shop as arranged, Eliza, took the package in exchange for the address, believed I would soon be seeing you.'

She stared at me so intently, so little and lost, rubbing her hands together in her pain.

'I was not told that you had handed over the opium and that I would be given to you, but the opium should have gone on from the pawn-shop. It should have gone to the Brotherhood direct, through the Factor, unless he kept it for himself, sold it on at a profit, left me to the Brotherhood, and you to them, too.'

'Betrayed by my own countryman, what a fool I was, what a complete idiot to have trusted myself to his care!'

Eliza continued, talking fast.

'I had received a message from the Interpreter that you were keen to see me; that you wanted to spend time with me, that you had pure Indian opium.'

'So that was why I was misled, that was why I was attracted to the bungalow, the 'Palace of a Thousand Dreams'! It was a trap, to take me off your trail?'

'No, Charles, you really were to meet me there: it was to be arranged that I would have sex with you and kill you. Yet I was elsewhere giving birth. With you out of the way, the Brotherhood would be off my tail, the Sisters arranged it, and, unknown to them, my son would be free to live in exile, the Brotherhood were willing to arrange that for me in exchange for information leading to your death. I saw you from the Grand Junk, I watched you rowing by.' She laughed, moving closer to me, touched my hand with hers. 'But they got to me first, substituted another whore, planned on letting you think you still had some freedom, when all the time they were tracking you, watching what you did, where you went to. They knew where you were all the time, Charles, the Interpreter's wife made sure of it.'

There was that one last question for White Poppy: one last answer that I just had to find out.

'Why did you run away from me?'

'Yam sing!'

I didn't understand, didn't connect with what she was saying as she stood shameful in front of me, wistful, eyes opened wide.

'Yam sing,' she said again, 'Drink to Victory!'

The image remained there in my thoughts: hot food, aromatic tea, the ivy-clad temple: the monk offered a cup first to White Poppy, held the edge between his forefinger and thumb, *middle finger touching the bottom* – the Triad sign, or right hand outstretched with all five fingers apart; touching of the middle finger of the right hand with the thumb; sign language for when the brothers did not share a human dialect.

'The monk, he knew us for who we were. He took me aside, talked to me afterwards, Charles, as you got ready for bed.' Her eyes flickered – so beautiful, vulnerable, and soft - her lips magenta-mauve. 'He told me to stay away from you, that he would otherwise kill you.'

She looked down at her fingers, restless.

'I had to let you go, was made to run away from you, to leave you to make your way through China on your own.' She sighed long and loud. 'The next morning they came to capture you: he had said nothing about that. You started the guest-hall fire that saved both our lives.' She held my hands so tightly, squeezing my fingers until they were white.

'I knew that I was bad for you, that as long as we were together your life would be in danger, so I decided to let you go, to rid you of your death doll. I loved you so much that I thought it better for you to be free without me, than for you to be dead in my arms. I did it for you.'

Her gorgeous almond eyes filled with tears and she looked away from me.

'Going against the deepest feelings in my heart, Charles, pushing aside every thought of love, I ran away from you.' She paused. 'I wanted to go back, wanted to run back and stay with you, but I kept my distance. I had to be sure – that you really were the one for me. I was never actually all that far from you.' She dried her eyes on the soft white cloth of her dress. She took hold of my hand. 'I kept a watch on you; would have come to your defence if you'd been challenged in any way.'

Sitting by the roadside at the Peach-leaf Ferry she had come back into my life, startled me as I sat watching the alabaster clouds.

'I loved you, Charles. I always loved you, right from the first time I opened my eyes and really saw you in the Interpreter's house.'

The Interpreter's house: the market sounds, sound of horses' hooves that made me freeze every time I heard them.

'I saw you watching me in the garden. Coming in from the garden I saw you, watched you watching me, saw the desire in your blue eye. For the first time I had found a man that *wanted* to kiss me, to make love to me, because of who I actually was!'

She hit me playfully, banging her fists on my chest. Her eyes afire, tiger's eyes, burning bright like the candles in evening lanterns, as night displaces dusk.

'I wanted to let you want me, but I couldn't, not until we were well away from Canton. You were male and considerate to me, put me first. You were a language that I did not understand. And yet all the other men in my life had used me, abused me, let me down.'

She stopped talking, the room silent, and I felt the fierce pumping of her heart, heard the swallowing in her throat. 'Love shows in your eyes if you let it grow. Love would have shown in my eyes, Charles. I could not have risked that!'

6

Genesis 3:16 for Eve's sin, in sorrow thou shalt bring forth children. Anything to keep White Poppy awake. Above the summer garden, our girls playing distant by the sea, the sea in full retreat, tide now out low, the bedroom was like some great glasshouse, alive with potted plants, cut flowers all around her on the foliaged brass bed. Her pregnant stomach massive, rounded, swollen like some great blue-veined gourd, her breasts purple-streaked, heavy; coloured with the sunlight filtering in through the neat banded panes of magenta and mustard, giving her body an unusual mottled hue. Window open, the girls' voices hung distant on the still, warm air, no movement, no breeze to stir the curtains, heavy, still; early afternoon clouds, transparent cirrus, ice-threaded, high.

She held me close, my hands pressed in hers, looking hard and long into my eyes; red-faced, hot, sweat running from her skin, soaking the bedclothes which had to be changed every few hours. Wiping away tears of pain, she could not sleep, had cramps in her stomach, writhing around the bed in agony, waiting for the waters to burst, too agitated to talk: later, flooded by the river of the water of life.

Late afternoon sunlight disappearing from the land; orange afterglow withdrawn before the creeping indigo dark, White Poppy's eyes have a new sparkling sharpness, staring right through me. Bed creaking, breath coming fast, breathing slow, coming faster, slow, slower; panting, sighing: a baby cries, the mother has not cried out with pain, the nurse taking the knotted rag from her bleeding mouth, mother tearing, bleeding below.

'It's a girl!'

7

I am the dark girl from the ninth heaven. Because I committed a crime my punishment is to live here for a few years on earth.

Tears drying on her cheeks, White Poppy tried to smile.

'I do so love you, my dear Darling Charles,' she said, pulling apart from me, making us all the more close in that separation. Opening her long dark lashes, her slant-eyes met mine, and I felt again the bond that had grown there all those years.

'I'm sorry, Charles. I'm sorry I've let you down!'

She gripped both my hands firmly, squeezing them tight against her chest. 'I'm very sorry my dearest husband, please forgive me, but I must leave you.' She blinked back large tears that spilled anyway from her almond eyes. 'I know it's time to go.'

Holding her hand I felt all the love that she had to give us, felt the power within her that stretched back through the years to the beginning of time; the life, the love that would be projected forward into the next century and beyond; the power she had within her, the great evil that she had tamed.

Yawning, her Chinese eyes filled with tears like dark stars, strands of saliva at the corners of her dry mouth, and she swallowed although there was nothing there to swallow. I loved her; loved her more than ever she could know.

'Kiss me, Charles, hold me; hold me tight. Don't ever let me go!'

I kissed her on the lips; sealed close that precious Chinese mouth. Her eyes closed, I squeezed her hands gently to make her open them again, White Poppy. I kissed her and *felt* her, like that very first time I kissed her, tasted her, swallowed from her wet mouth, greedy for more. Taking out the broken hairpin half that she had given me, made of Chinese peach-tree wood – exact match to her own – I pressed it against her half that she had hanging round her neck.

I love you.

8

Once more I feel the erotic pain, feel that distant slap of my hand against her pathetic little face, the blood on her lips in Canton; see her as she throws herself at me, weeping with tired frustration, lies there whimpering, hands over her head, trembling: lips apart, swelling, glowing. And again I feel my own tears that once washed away the dirt on her cheeks, ran down her scars, dropping to her lips; shining black hair loose against my face, turning slowly towards me, taking its soft strands across my lips, falling free as her mouth comes into view, smiling, cheeky, lips taut for a kiss. Eyes closed tight, I hear the sound of her voice, her laughter: see the twinkle in her eyes, feel the soft touch of her mouth, taste that which drips from those other lips, forbidden, free. Within those Chinese eyes, within that head, deep within that perfect Chinese body, are the secrets of the universe, the secrets of all time, access to that which would last eternal: the mother, White Poppy, Yin Shooeh-yen.

She opened her exhausted Chinese eyes and smiled. Almond eyes burning bright, the September sky was split in two. White Poppy grimacing in pain, coughing purple blood. Mother, giving birth: tearing, bleeding, thighs bathed in the wetness of her own weeping blood. She moved her lips but there was no sound apart from the rattle in her chest, the scraping of her inner flesh. Late tears leaving her almond eyes, made their way down her shining cheeks, down her scars, leaving their wet salt trail, as she had started to bleed and bleed and bleed. The

Doctor prescribed *opium* to ease her passing – for her puerperal fever there was no cure.

Outside, thunder, rolling Thunder Dragon roar – rain, down dropping, dreary: those dark almond eyes closing, watching the sun go down, the disappearance of the moon, the stars popping inwards, light disappearing into the gloom... where the poppies nodded like solemn widows. I see her still, standing there amongst the closely-anchored flower-boats at Canton, walking along the deck with low railings, red lanterns all around. Half asleep, my good eye just open, I see the White Tiger stalking our bedroom, hear the soft pad of her paws across the floor.

Her lips quivered at the corners and she smiled the most brilliant smile as the storm made its way out to sea. I lay still behind her, listening to the vibrating grumble of the softly-beaten kettle-drum of the heavens, dying heartbeat of God's orchestra. In that moment, sudden, terrifying, long, White Poppy was gone.

9

The silence was deafening, rush of blood in my ears, fast pumping of my heart: I couldn't breathe, I couldn't cry, her fingers tight in mine. Everything stopped, still, for my White Poppy who I first fell in love with some 23 years before. In the silence that followed the last shifting of her body, I could hear the squeak of the planets turning in the heavens, the roaring of the stars, the tinkle of the moon as she made her way across the sky, the rustling of the clouds as they parted to let her through, as the world stood still, planets grinding to a halt, and the sun went out. Holding her cool hand, running my fingers along her peaceful lips, her almond eyes stared still at me, unseeing, their brightness fading by the second, and I closed her eyelids with practised care. In death, I kissed her one long last time, tasted the drying salt-sweetness of her mouth, breathing in her warm breath, stealing the last thing she had left to be stolen: fairy come down from heaven, she who sacrificed her brightest silver for that briefest dance on earth – 40 years only. I stole her soul. [I was 51.]

The tears came suddenly, furious fast. My Eliza was dead, White Poppy, Yin Hsueh-yen. The void shattered by a howling wail: crying, fretful, distant, tense. *Where is my Mother*, it asked, *where is my milk?* Picking up Beatrice, our precious Suyün, wrapped in her woollen shawl, I placed her against the cooling nipple, watched her last sucking of that milk-swollen breast, heard the last milk flowing into her mouth. Another with White Poppy's Chinese eyes.

10

Six black horses with black ostrich feather plumes pulled the black hearse elaborate with silver and gold decoration. Etched glass protected the sumptuous polished coffin within, on its bed of brilliant flowers under a canopy of more black ostrich feathers, posy of purple violets and daisies. The grand hearse proceeded at walking pace before the procession of coaches, blinds drawn – black, symbolic of night; mourners in secret: the gentlemen wearing full mourning dress and crepe bands round their top hats, the ladies dressed in black, with black veils, black-edged handkerchiefs and black gloves. Our daughters had mourning fans of black ostrich feathers and black silk, mourning-jewellery, brooches and rings containing miniatures of their Mother painted on ivory; seed pearls set in as symbols of her tears; lockets enclosing photos of the White Poppy, and a lock of her once-raven hair, all in Whitby Jet set in silver. Charlotte carried baby Suyün: these daughters, perfect illusion of bridal innocence and allure, pale white life supporting black-edged death. Passing down the dark avenue of yews, the grand procession turned in through the huge orange-brick gateway flanked by its pair of ivy-clad lodges, and stopped in the cemetery. The mutes with their black silk dresses, the assistants with black silk gloves and hatbands, descended from their seats on the carriages, and the procession moved forward slowly at walking pace past tall trees, amongst which were the black marble obelisks, mausolea, and stone urns, along the avenue leading to the chapel in the centre.

The Jade Fairy Maid White Poppy was buried with her first-born son's lock of black hair *from China* in its crumpled red packet, together with the yellow flower from the monastery pressed inside the black, leather-covered Bible; also with that auspicious tatty photograph, simple view of Dover Harbour, showing tall-masted sailing ships with a party of English women in front, officer's wives, walking forwards. Both pieces stuck together with a band of gummed paper at the back. I have planted Kentish poppy seeds on her grave: they will grow, will bud, will flower – blood red like lips, and the bobbing pods will spread their persistent bloodied red. I left her clothes on the bed, her prized possessions all around her. In anger, in love, I cut off her hair, felt its long, cool softness run through my fingers, placed it carefully in a polished black ebony box. I feel her presence all about me, a quivering in my body as I sit watching the room, *sit reading this my Journal.*

11

Boat alive with music on the river running green... Butterflies in pairs flutter powdered wings... Deep garden sounds float on the marble moon... Twilight dims on shuttered doors... Far thunder beyond water trailing willows... Drops drum down on every floating lily... Cold of night begins to pierce my filmy gown No sound... except... The spring tide to lap the abandoned town.

Sometimes as I fall asleep it seems we are back together once more: *teenage boat-girl standing out above me, conical straw hat, wide-brimmed around her shaded Chinese face* ; and I hear the sound of her voice, her laughter, see the twinkle in her eyes, feel the soft touch of her lips against mine. But most of all, I see her eyes, her *gorgeous, glistening, black-bronzed almond eyes, blinking slowly, sadly, polished ebony reflecting all around; long lashes flicking, eyelids closing over beautiful polished stones.* I see her before me in the mountains, watch her as she walks, as she clambers slowly ahead of me, the gentle bob of her black-plaited head, making her way up to the temple, glazed green tiles shining brilliantly in the sun, white birds circling slowly above the solitary pine. And it is from her *luscious, crimson, open mouth, entrance of the most erotic lips, wisps of raven hair blowing about their silent moistness, a sad smile hiding tears,* that I feel White Poppy's warm breath blowing away fine strands of hair lying across my cheek, smell the fragrance of her skin, taste the sugar-and-spice of her Kentish poppy lips, and I hear her whisper on the wind. *'I love you.'*

EPILOGUE

'Father?' Sophia's voice is pleading, intense. 'Father are you ready, can we go now?'

It is already getting dark, the sky clear with the first sprinkle of stars: the answer has to be 'yes', we are ready, although I do not want to be. The girls have spent the morning folding squares of red paper soaked in pine oil to make them waterproof, made the water-lily lamps according to my instructions (as White Poppy had once told me), popped in the twisted parchment wicks. Gathering together the folded red paper lotus flowers, we walk across the rippled sand to the far edge of the sea, the tide having long since gone out, the water calm, spilling out across the beach: like standing beside a great China river. One by one I light the paper lanterns, the vegetable-oil-soaked wicks, let them float away, watch them scattering in the breeze, Suyün on my knee, the swift current carrying them bobbing out to sea. The lights glow softly in my tears, a miniature streaming fairy sea, until the last winks out and is gone. 'I love you.'

I watched the white sails of a barque beyond her, making her way along the coast behind them, far out at sea, wind blowing fresh in her sails, sails catching the late-summer sun. Lifting her head slightly, tilting her shining face away from the sun, hat rising slowly, the poppy flowered. The sun was hot, very hot, but although the sun was bright, the brightest light, darkness was hidden behind. The white water lily floating beautiful above the leaf-muddied pool: within those eyes, within that head, deep within that perfect Chinese body, were the secrets of the universe, the secrets of all time, access to that which would last eternal.

A flower and not a flower; of mist yet not of mist; at midnight she was there; she was as daylight shone. She came and for a little while was like a dream of spring, and then, as morning clouds that vanish traceless, she was gone. P'u-Hua Fei Hua, Po Chü [772-846], Shenshi Province [*Collection*, No. 4].

THE END

Printed in Great Britain
by Amazon

50150447R00180